DRIVING UNDER · THE · CARDBOARD PINES

AND OTHER STORIES

BOOKS BY COLLEEN McELROY

Poetry

Music From Home: Selected Poems
Winters Without Snow
Lie and Say You Love Me
Queen of the Ebony Isles
Bone Flames
What Madness Brought Me Here: New and Selected Poems

Fiction

Jesus and Fat Tuesday
Driving Under the Cardboard Pines

Non-fiction

Speech and Language Development of the Pre-School Child

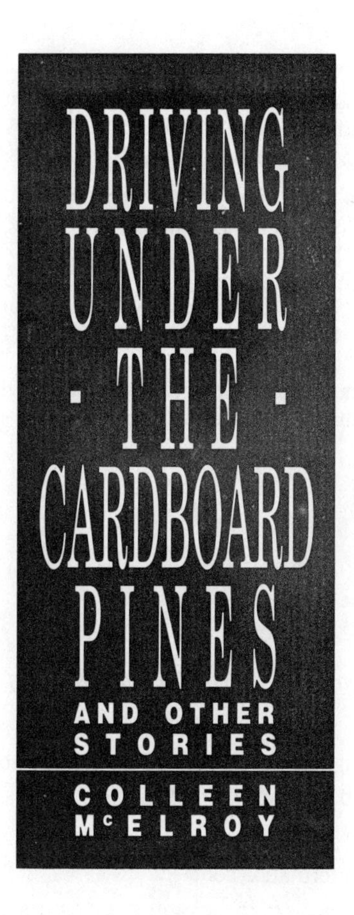

Creative Arts
Book Company

Berkeley
1990

Acknowledgments: The following stories have appeared in somewhat different versions in these publications: "The Way Station," in PENDRAGON (Spring, 1982), and "The Blooming of Asphodels," in SEATTLE REVIEW (Autumn, 1982).

Lines from Anne Spencer's poem, "Lady, Lady," were taken from *TIME'S UNFADING GARDEN: Anne Spencer's Life and Poetry*, J. Lee Green (Baton Rouge: Louisiana State University Press, 1977), and quoted by permission of J. Lee Green. Lines from "How Death Came to Man" were taken from *GUIDE TO THE GODS*, Richard Carlyon (New York: Quill, 1982). Lines from "Aztec Definitions" were taken from *TECHNICIANS OF THE SACRED: A RANGE OF POETRIES FROM AFRICA, AMERICA ASIA & OCEANIA*, Jerome Rothenberg (New York: Anchor Books, 1969). Lines from *MOODY'S MOOD FOR LOVE*. were used by permission of James Moody.

For information contact:

CREATIVE ARTS BOOK COMPANY
833 Bancroft Way
Berkeley, California 94710

Typography: Cragmont Publications, Oakland

Cover Design: Charles Fuhrman Design

LIBRARY OF CONGRESS CATALOGING-IN-PUBLICATION DATA

McElroy, Colleen J.
Driving under the cardboard pines and other stories.
I. Title.
PS3563 .A2925D75 1989 813'.54 89-17450
ISBN 0-88739-073-0

Printed in the United States of America

A very special thanks to
Kate Gray and Frances McCue for their generous assistance.

Contents

Sweet Anna

"I'M GONE TELL YOU SOMETHING," the old woman said. She lifted one eyebrow and looked at the girl. "There was a time when colored folks couldn't get no job cept out in the fields. That's where I was when I was way younger than you. Out in them fields. Then long comes the war and I got me a job in that de-fense plant cause my mama didn't want me working them cotton fields no more. Most of my kinfolk worked them fields. I worked them till Hadley was killed overseas in the war. Hadley was my husband. Only one I had, but Maw-maw was fixing to get me married to some old man over near Jackson when I come upon this poster what said, UNCLE SAM WANTS YOU. Showed some women working the de-fense plant. Colored women. That's when I told Maw-maw I best try my luck up North. Said wasn't no reason for me to be staying in Mississippi. That's what she told folks round where we lived. I member her words to this day—'This here's the last one of my chillun to go out in them fields,' Maw-maw said. 'Had eight of 'em out there fore they was half-growed. Done put enuf of my sweat in them fields. Time for this chile to move on.' And that's exactly what I did. Went up North and got me a job in the de-fense plant."

Jessie waited until Annalea had regained her breath before she offered her another bowlful of black-eyed peas. Annalea worked the peas, gumming them with the good side of her mouth while the dead side allowed a dribble of food to leak onto her chin. Jessie glanced at the photo album lying on the bed, a page open to a picture of five women—six women really, if Jessie counted the white woman standing off to the side smirking at the five colored women who were facing the camera.

Jessie didn't know who that white woman was and she didn't care. Her attention was on the other women, skin tones ranging from light to deep as if someone had taken the brown end of a palette and added subtle shades of sunlight and midnight.

"That ain't the best picture we had," Annalea said. "Somewhere round here, I got some pictures taken at the USO dances. That there picture ain't nothing but one of them things they was always trying to get us to buy down there at the plant. Every week or so some fool come up the road with a camera and catch us right at the top of the hill fore we go in the plant. Mostly, we was dressed to beat the band. Slick as they come. Lipstick too. You know, chile, in them days, wearing lipstick was a sign you membered when there wasn't no war. Still we could do a man's job and do it better than some men even. So we'd just strut down that road and let 'em take our pictures. Not that I look so good in that one," Annalea laughed.

Jessie laughed along with her, but to Jessie, it didn't matter how good or bad the photograph was. An only child, she'd spent most of her life inside photos, and having one of black folks that didn't involve rape, riot, or slavery was enough to warrant her full attention. In this one, the women were dressed in patchwork fashion, a 1940s imitation of Marlene Dietrich, Billie Holiday, and Lena Horne: baggy pants, thick-soled heels, their hair turbaned in scarves, or half-covered to show sausage-roll bangs or buns coiled around wire rats pulled tight to the scalp. They wore cloth coats, and one, a tall, skinny hickory switch of a woman who stood above the others like a giant, sported a fancy fur-collared coat that made the group look as if they were posing for a snapshot before heading toward a round of dining and dancing. Jessie didn't know who that tall woman was, but Sara Flynn and Annalea were easy to find. Sara Flynn was the pale brown one wearing glasses, and Annalea was the shortest one in the photo. The fact that she was standing next to the tall woman in the fur collar made her seem even smaller. Jessie could have studied those faces for hours: her cousin Annalea's look of surprise, her Aunt Sara Flynn's distracted squint, the tall woman whose fur collar did nothing to gentle her face. And on the end, a fragile, moon-faced woman, and another one who was laughing as if someone had just told a joke.

"That one there is Plum," Annalea said and pointed to a light-skin woman who was laughing. "Yeah, that be Plum alright. And the one look like a wood sparrow, that's Sissy, with Big Myrtle standing tween me and her. I tell you, tween Plum and Big Myrtle, why me and Sara Flynn had the best crew on that 'ssembly line. Even Patty O'Halloran had to own up to it. She the white woman in back looking all evil. Big-boned woman. One of them red-headed, pink-skin Irish. Straw boss.

Gave everybody a fit. Had this thing bout picking on them what come from the South. Thought she could get to me cause I wasn't no bigger than nothing back in them days, and she had it in her head I oughta be a big woman, coming from the South and all. See, they grows them big in Mississippi. Ask your Antie Sara. Yeah, ask Sara Flynn."

Jessie nodded, but instead of questioning Sara Flynn, she talked to her cousin, Mavis. When she telephoned that evening, she caught Mavis just before she left the house. Jessie's mama had warned her not to call home too often, but Jessie figured she was the one stuck with Annalea and she could spell "often" any way she liked. At first, she called home every other night, but after Annalea started telling her war stories, Jessie alternated the calls between her mother's house and Sara Flynn's. Calling Sara Flynn's meant she'd run the risk of talking to Mavis. If Jessie hadn't drawn short straws, Mavis would have been sent to take care of Annalea. But Jessie had lost, and she was the one stuck in Annalea's clapboard house the whole summer of her sixteenth year, while Mavis was back home, running the street and partying from one end of town to the other. And Mavis was in no mood to be distracted whenever Jessie called to report on Annalea's condition, or for that matter, recount Annalea's stories.

"Mississippi! How come I ain't never heard bout her being from Mississippi?" Mavis yelled into the phone. "How come she telling you bout Mississippi? I bet you just trying to get Mama to make me come stay with you. Well, Jessie Crawford, you just got yourself another think coming. I ain't going nowhere near Annalea. I don't care what she been telling you. She must be telling you bout some other woman anyhow. She been sitting up in that house so long, she don't know who she talking bout."

When Jessie told her what Mavis had said, Annalea just laughed.

"Pret-near the truth, chile. I sho come to be somebody altogether different since I left from home. It's like I done shucked off all that life. You know, like the snakes do. Just thow off the skin and keep on going. I musta lost me a whole lot of skin over the years. Specially the time I was working in that de-fense plant. It was hotter than six shades of Hades in that place. Even with them windows opened, you couldn't get the smell of metal from outta your nose. Left your sweat smelling funny and your mouth tasting sour like when you been to some old dentist. Different kinda odor too. Sometimes the air was so bad, your nose bled and your skin would get to itching like it was ready to leave the room without you. Yeah, like one of them old cottonmouth snakes we useta find out in the fields. Maw-maw always made fun of me when I tripped cross one of them snake skins, but I tell you, it always made me feel so sad, I'd cry.

Maw-maw would say: 'I cain't figgah you. Cain't stand snakes, now you crying like you done lost some chile.' But that old mottledy snake skin put me in mind of a lost soul. Like a piece of something peeled off and left there for somebody to step on. Something to tack on a wall or thow in the garbage. Didn't seem right, losing a piece of yourself, so careless like that. But I done lost pieces of myself from here to Mississippi, so long the way, guess I done turned into somebody else sho-nuff."

Jessie wondered what Anna had been before she changed into a woman who spent most of her time rocking away the heat of the afternoon, her head resting against the back of the chair, her oversized hands hanging loosely from her thickly veined wrists. In the days that followed, Jessie watched her and tried to imagine how she might have looked when she was young. The Annalea she saw looked like the kind of woman who never had done more than retire after a lifetime of cooking food in the grade school cafeteria all winter, and closing herself up in the corner of the sun porch all summer.

In the winter, Annalea had been just another part of the school kitchen, something screaming kids could use as a reason for not eating their lunch. There had not been much love lost between Annalea and the children, but when she was sitting in her rocking chair, she resembled a petulant child seated in a corner for punishment. In that chair, facing the backyard garden, she could pretend the world behind her did not exist, and too often, sitting in that chair allowed her neighbors to forget she existed. When her neighbors did pay a visit, they talked only to Jessie, and if Jessie didn't warn them, sometimes they'd start to comment on how Annalea's life had taken a turn for the worse before they realized a set of ears had turned their way. That's what Annalea was—all ears, and like a lot of old women, she had little skimpy hair, thin in patches and not very long where it still clung to her scalp. But it was Annalea's complexion everyone remembered: a splotchy kind of Mercurochrome brown with patches the color of dried school paste, like a reverse pattern of liver spots dotting her skin until it resembled the worn fur of a teddy bear that had been around too long. And now, in her old age, she covered herself with Coty face powder which caused her to look more like a withered oak leaf dusted by the season's first snow.

"Annalea's older than dirt," Mavis had argued. "And I sure as hell ain't gone be stuck in that house all summer with her sitting there looking like some old voodoo doll. She look like one of them things that got all ratty and the stuffing so loose, it just drags the ground, butt-ugly and washed out, so it ain't brown. It ain't orange. It ain't red. It's just old. I don't care if her skin did turn that way from working around them welding torches. She still look like some piece of left-over something."

And that was the Annalea Jessie had seen the day she'd arrived to take care of her—an old woman left in the corner of a cluttered house like a sock missing from a family's wash, or a favorite glove lost in the rush to end a visit. Jessie had not visited Annalea for nearly six years. Before that summer, Sara Flynn had designated Mavis to take care of Annalea, and Mavis had always hated going. Even though she got to ride the train all the way from Kansas City to Detroit, Mavis would poke out her fat lips and pout for days before she left, then have little hissy fits and act evil for days after she returned. Not that she was any nicer to Jessie when she didn't have to visit Annalea, but Mavis had gone out of her way to put Jessie in Annalea's little sweatbox of a house for the summer, and somehow, some way, Jessie intended to make her pay.

"Short straws. And I fell for it," Jessie thought. Then, without ever seeing the word 'revenge' in her mind, she set about the business of doing something, for once, that Mavis had never tried to do. That something became snooping around Annalea's house.

Actually, Annalea lived in only one room of the house. The other rooms were nesting places for boxes and bags of collected paraphernalia, some of which Annalea, herself, could not remember. Except for the kitchen, the sitting room that held Jessie's bed, and Annalea's bedroom—a sweet little room with embroidered curtains, hook rugs, and dozens of odd-shaped picture frames—the other rooms smelled of times far older than Jessie was. Where Annalea's bedroom had little side-tables full of knickknacks and walls full of pictures, the walls of the other rooms were hidden behind cardboard containers, and the windows were clouded with stale air that had not passed through a living body. On holidays, when the family gathered in Kansas City, discussions of what to do with Annalea could fill most of an afternoon. Many families have relatives like Annalea, stubborn old remnants of another age who are likely to be as difficult in their later years as they were in their youth. These are the relatives who have been left alone a few years past the time when they should have been offered company. When the family realizes what they have bred, they shake their heads and walk away, puzzling over who will finally be the one to talk some sense into Granny Dear, or Uncle So-and-so, or Cousin What's-her-name.

"You kinda remind me of somebody, chile. I don't mean your mama. You favor your mama alright. All of you girls kinda favor each other, if the truth be told. But your ways sorta put me in mind of somebody." Annalea slowly lifted the lid of her milky eye and stared at Jessie. Behind the sticky film of her lens, she saw the girl as a dim figure crouched on the edge of the footstool, like the expectant pose street beggars had assumed during those years when everyone was hungry, when blacks and whites both had stood in ration lines. That was after she'd left the defense plant, long after most of the women she'd known had slipped out of her life. Annalea sighed.

"For a while, there was just four of us. Chile, I tell you: We thought we was bad. Leastways, Big Myrtle and Plum did. I don't quite know what I thought about myself in them days. But the gover'ment had hired us. Hired me straight out the fields, and hired Big Myrtle after she lost most of her teeth while she was dancing out there on the Chit'lin Circuit. You know the one I'm talking bout?" Annalea asked. Jessie shook her head. "Well chile, the Chit'lin Circuit's where colored folks toured when they was entertaining down South. Big Myrtle come from the Circuit bout the same time I come from the fields. We got on at Plant #4 where they was making bombs big enough to fill up the back of a pickup truck. Welding, that's what we did. Me and Big Myrtle and Sara Flynn and Plum. Lord, I member Plum. UM-um. Plum was a pistol. Sassy. Wouldn't give a cripple man a crutch if she could get away with it. Some folks be like that. You know what I mean?"

Jessie knew. For years, Mavis had plagued Jessie, teasing her about being too fat and later, when she lost the weight, about being too thin. Mavis made fun of Jessie's glasses, the sack dresses and thick-heeled oxfords her mother brought for her, and the books she read. "That chile's got a tongue like a knife and a mouth like a doorknob," Mae Willie Crawford had said. "But don't you be letting Mavis get to you, Jessie. You just keep God in your heart. Everybody's got they problems and Mavis got some long with the rest of us." None of it consoled Jessie. She distinctly remembered how Mavis had behaved just last spring when Jessie had finally convinced her mother to consider a pair of sling pumps to match her Easter outfit. In the end, Mae Willie Crawford had put Jessie into sensible shoes with bulky heels that made so much noise, Mavis had rushed from the house that Sunday morning. "Oh, I thought I heard the milkman coming," Mavis had said, although both of them knew the milkman had not used a horse-drawn cart for years. "I wouldn't let my mama put me in them shoes," she'd said. "I fixed it so I could get some pink satin shoes with pointy toes," she'd said, and switched her butt off to the Easter dance with Harold Quentin, leaving Jessie to walk home with her mother and Aunt Sara Flynn. To Jessie, that was just one more time Mavis had gotten the better of her.

"I sho Lord hope it's my turn," Jessie thought.

She had planned to work her way from room to room, box by box, but when she'd finished with that first carton full of photo albums and bric-a-brac, most of which Annalea did not recognize, the old woman would not let her return to that room. In fact, it was several days before

Annalea allowed Jessie to enter any of the inner sanctum rooms, as Mavis called them. "Who knows what evil lurks in Annie's inner sanctum," Mavis would laugh.

"I'm gonna know," Jessie thought, and pressed her search. But she found it was hard to sidestep an old lady bent on staying in her way. Annalea fussed over her food and set Jessie's teeth on edge with her complaints of too much salt or too little liquid. "I gotta have me some pot likker," she'd say. "Old folks need something to get they sweat moving. In that de-fense plant, them torches got so hot, the sweat be boiling right there on your body. I spect I ain't got rid of all that poison from that de-fense plant. So you take this here stuff right back to the kitchen. Make it so's I can eat it, else my stomach gone make me take a whole mess of that Sal Hepatica."

"She just want to keep you in the kitchen," Mavis said. "Why you think I didn't want to be stuck with her? Running her mouth all the time bout nothing. She just think all that talking gone keep you cooking. And even if you do, she ain't satisfied. She was on my case all the time bout this ain't right and that ain't right. Now if Annalea kept me hopping, she must got you jumping cause I know you can't cook a lick," Mavis laughed.

Jessie slammed down the phone and didn't call Mavis until the beginning of the next week. But that phone call made her move from Campbell's canned chicken soup to bowls of homemade chicken and dumplings, plates of mixed greens, helpings of black-eyed peas, and slices of warm gingerbread with thick cream frosting made from Pet Milk.

"After all them years of cooking at the school, it's bout time somebody's chillun brought me food steada the other way round," Annalea said. "Who done learnt you cooking, chile?"

Jessie tested her options before she answered. "You like what I fix?" she asked Annalea. And when the old woman nodded, Jessie smiled and said, "My mama taught me cooking."

"Mine did too," Annalea said. "Course I had to unlearn most of what Maw-maw learnt me. Had to when I first moved up North. Maw-maw wouldn'ta understood much bout living up North. Now Plum, she claimed to understand some of everything. Specially the way we was treated at the plant. They made us all dress the same, you know. On the lines, we was identical. Nonymous. We wore them coveralls, blousy things. Had our heads covered up with some helmets. And everything was gray. On the line, we was all gray. Black or white, young or old. Even them that was crusty mean. Like Sara Flynn. Yeah chile, your Antie Sara was one mean sister. All the women was mean. Had to be. And that's what was in that plant mostly. Women. Enuf women for an army I spect.

Women was doing some of everything during that war. Some took jobs with the railroad working them track crews. Out in the weather all day. But that was too much like the Delta for me. Got me a job in the de-fense plant long with the rest of them women. Oh, there was some men at the plant. The head honchos what had been there long before the war. Some since the last war. And some younger ones that wasn't fit for nobody's war. They was what was called 'essential personnel.' But the workers, they was women. Let me tell you, there was some of every kind of woman there. It was one of the first times a colored woman could get a decent paying job. Negroes we called ourselves back then. Negroes in good jobs. We was right up there with the rest. All of us nonymous under them gray-ass uniforms."

Having said that, Annalea closed her eyes and fell asleep.

Jessie was always caught off guard whenever Annalea moved from awake to asleep between one breath and the next. It was a while before Jessie discovered Annalea's secret was her hearing aid. She merely turned off the sound to her one good ear and let in the rush of noise that took the place of deafness. With practice, she had been able to make folks believe she really was sleeping behind her closed lids, but if anything disturbed her, one twist of the dial tuned in sounds again. Jessie had discovered this the hard way. During one of Annalea's sleeping bouts, Jessie had ventured into an inner sanctum room. She had opened a box and released a few items from their dusty tomb when the door flew open as if someone had kicked it. Jessie didn't need to turn around. She knew Annalea had slammed her walker against the door, and she knew Annalea was standing there, waiting for her to speak.

Jessie held up the broken fork for a salad serving set. "Is this here real silver, cousin Annie?"

"You gone poke round in all my b'longings, you best ask me first," Annalea said.

Jessie waited. Then she heard Annalea moving away from her, the legs of the walker hitting the floor like jackhammers. From that point on, Jessie made sure Annalea really was sound asleep before she ventured into any of the storage rooms.

Mavis grumbled, "Never let me near them boxes. Ain't no telling what she got in there, crazy as she is. Mama said, half the time, Annie don't even remember getting up in the morning, but I'm gonna tell you, girl, when that bony old woman's up and moving, she can run your butt off if you let her," Mavis laughed. "She look slow, but like Mama say, still water do run deep."

For once, Jessie had to agree. Annalea appeared to move slowly, limping onto her arthritic hip. That limp combined with her hearing aid and cataract eye made her appear old and infirm, but when she wanted attention, she summoned speed from somewhere. Jessie remembered a story her mother told her about Annalea's days as a school cook. "Threw a pot of scalding soup at a some fool making fun of her cause she ain't got but four fingers. Annie surely showed him how four fingers can swing hard as five."

Annalea was still touchy about her missing finger.

"What you mean: How come I got four fingers on this hand? I'm lucky I got four, chile. That de-fense plant took more than fingers from some folks. When I first got to the plant, there was this girl name of Sissy working the table with Sara Flynn. Chile wasn't nothing but a baby, two years younger than Plum and she was just twenty. That Sissy was a sho-nuff country gal come to work in a de-fense plant straight from some dirt-water place down in Alabama. And poor thing, she couldn't talk right. Always sputtering: 'Yeah . . . Yeah . . . Yez'um, Miz Lady,' any time Patty O'Halloran got close to her. Patty had a way of sneaking up behind you anyways. I guess Sissy just allowed being scared of white folks to cancel out her good sense. One time Patty was watching her so close, the chile got flustered and forgot to tie the glove back on her sleeve. She was sposed to weld the side of a casing and slip it back on the belt when Sara Flynn finished. Had it rehooked and was starting to swing it to the conveyor when hot metal dripped right down her sleeve. Lord, we didn't wait for that chile to stop screaming. The whole place smelt like burnt flesh. When we tore that sleeve, we could see where the metal had ripped tracks clear to her elbow. Patty was pointing and laughing, talking bout: 'See, that's what happen to dumb clucks. Peeled right down to the fat.' Chile, I thought Plum was gonna go after that heifer. That Plum sho scared me. I thought I was strong from working them fields, but Plum, she could do the work of two men."

In Jessie's eyes, Annalea was still strong. From Mavis' tales of Annalea's frailty, Jessie had assumed she'd have to carry Annalea from one room to the next. Not so. Annalea used that walker the way a horse used a strong kick to ease out the sides of its stall. It held her all right, but it didn't keep her temper down. She wasn't a large woman, but she carried the illusion of size. As Mavis had said, she was bony, but the muscles in her arms and legs were knotted into lumps, and veins roped her hands and neck. If she had been male, she would have been called bantam weight. As a woman, she was simply a little odd, her head, hands and feet rough cut and a bit too large for the rest of her body. In a way, Jessie and Annalea were a matched pair. Maybe that's what Annalea saw in Jessie—something that made her different from all the other children, something that set her apart from her own kin.

Nevertheless, there they were—an old woman who looked a little different and a young girl who acted different. Even at a family gathering, Jessie could be found opening trunks of old clothes and junk, or rummaging through a stack of pictures, like the ones Annalea hoarded. "How come you always got to be poking your nose into somebody's business?" Mavis would ask. Jessie had no answer for her. She simply needed to know what had happened before she was born. Some children are like that, uncomfortable with the notion that the world started before they arrived, or simply unable to accept the idea that some things happened without them.

That summer, Annalea served Jessie's curiosity very well. That summer, Jessie found herself in the right place at the right time. One day, she found Annalea on the floor in one of the back rooms. Jessie hadn't heard her fall, and when she looked in the room, nothing was disturbed. Annalea was simply sitting on the floor, her walker a few feet away from her. From the looks of things, she had opened one of the boxes and pulled a blue felt hat from its contents. When Jessie saw her, she had the hat crushed against her mouth as if it could choke back the sound of her tears. But Jessie saw her shoulders heave, and heard the strangled noise escape her throat. Moving quickly, as if they suddenly had been summoned to a meeting, Jessie pulled the walker in front of Annalea and pried the hat from her hands. Jessie began to help Annalea to the door, and for the first time since arriving at the house, the girl noticed the old woman's frailty. Annalea's shoulders seemed no more than bony extensions, like the useless wings on an old brooding hen, and her steps were so labored, Jessie almost carried her into the hall. When they reached the bedroom, Jessie found herself automatically gathering cushions and shawl. And through it all, Annalea wept as if she'd just discovered something was lost.

After Jessie got her settled, she made her a cup of chamomile tea, and while Annalea sipped it, Jessie offered her the felt hat.

"It were Plum's," Annalea whispered. "Always had that old beat-up thing with her."

Jessie placed the hat in her lap.

"Ugly, ain't it? All by itself, it just ain't much of nothing. Bout the onliest time I don't recollect her wearing it back then was the first time I saw her. I met Plum the first day, you know. The supervisor was splaining to me all them rules bout safety and personal inspections, meaning they could search your body anywhere they took a notion to. I was sitting there when Plum busted in.

"She said: 'I ain't bout to take these here curl papers out my head for no job!' Chile, I couldn't believe what she was telling that man. Um-um-

um. Had these strips of newspaper tied all in her kinky hair. They was bouncing like flames some swamp woman had conjured up." Annalea laughed so hard, Jessie had to get her another cup of chamomile tea. "I swear," Annalea continued, "Plum looked like Buckwheat 'scaping from the Little Rascals. But she wasn't in no funning mood one little bit.

"Plum said: 'You crazy if you think I don't mean what I say. And while I'm at it, ain't nobody gone be sticking they fingers all up inside me neither. Talking bout I'm smuggling something outta here. Do I look like some kinda spy?'

"Now I tried not to smile," Annalea told Jessie. "In my way of thinking, Plum did look like first one thing then another. That was the way Maw-maw woulda put it. But Plum didn't care how she looked. She told that old supervisor: 'I know what you white folks is up to. Playing stink-finger ain't nothing but another way of making colored folks think they got no say in what goes on."

"That supervisor just reared up and shouted: 'You got a grievance? That's what the Union's for!"

"Plum just got right up in his face and yelled right back. Said: 'I don't see no Union out there stopping nobody from looking all up under my dress! That Union ain't done diddly-damn for ME!' Then she slammed her hand on the desk.

"Chile, when Plum slapped the desk, I tell you I bout jumped outta my skin. I spected that supervisor to go upside Plum's head or drag her out that office so the straw boss could beat her. In the Delta, black folks kept their signifying close to home. When folks got uppity, the boss man gave them the short stick. But didn't nothing of the sort happen to Plum. So after that first week, I just followed everything she told me.

"Plum would say: 'Walk straight. You ain't in no field now.' That was the way Plum splained the job. Straightforward, you know. So it were simple. She'd say: 'Gauge the weight of the load. Let that sucker slip on the hoist. Don't be lifting it up. It ain't spoze to kill folks till it leave from here. So just loosen up, girlfriend. They ain't tagged us as the enemy. Yet."

"Then Plum would smile, all toothy, and stick out her hips. And that supervisor, he be looking, then play like he looking all up on the wall trying to see if there was some kinda rule to cover what Plum was doing. Oh, they had the slogans, alright. Spozed to make us all stand up and salute the flag. LOOSE LIPS SINK SHIPS. KEEP YOUR POWDER DRY. PACK 'EM TIGHT—THE BOYS DEPEND ON YOU. But them signs didn't hardly mean nothing. They was just a way to keep folks' spirits up. The signs we had in the plant, them signs was the ones that meant something. DON'T CONTAMINATE—WASH HANDS THOROUGHLY—THE COUNTRY'S FIRST DEFENSE IS YOU! I read 'em every day. Always telling you to do something or other. BIND CLOTHES SECURELY—KEEP HAIR AND FINGERS CLEAR OF MACHINERY—THAT MEANS *YOU!* Them was the real signs. Um-hum. Them signs meant business. And always something bout *YOU* in em. The straw boss was always checking cause of them signs. Even the Union inspectors. Checking to see who was gonna be put on call and who was gonna get docked pay. Plum said they was just coming after us to pull what little money we was gonna make, but I told her that leastwise, there was no signs talking bout NO COLOREDS ALLOWED. That's what they had put up in the South in them days. I seen 'em all my life, chile. But up at the plant, they wouldn't tolerate that, not with the war going on and them needing colored women to work longside the white ones. One time at the Union meeting, the foreman even said: 'I best not hear of nobody putting their personal biases in front of this nation's safety.' He was talking to the white women on one side of the room, so I spect he didn't think us colored women had no personal biases. I spect I didn't have none at first. But if I'd had, I mighta kept my finger."

"How'd you lose it?" Jessie asked.

"In them machines, chile. Machine just mashed it. I stood there and watched it and didn't let on. Didn't nobody know."

"But if Aunt Sara was there."

Annalea grunted. "Yeah . . . Well, she was and she wasn't."

"I told you she was crazy," Mavis said over the crackle of phone wires. "Don't know what she talking bout. And Mama said, you better quit asking her all them questions. Mama said it ain't none of your business."

"Weren't none of Sara Flynn's business, and I wouldn'ta said 'boo' about it if it wasn't for Plum. Me and Plum, we worked one side of the line, and Sara Flynn and Big Myrtle worked the other side. Sometimes, I didn't hardly see Sara Flynn the whole day. All I saw all day was them bomb casings hanging on the pulleys like a line of dirty clothes. And the noise could lift off your skull. Smells too. Honey, you ain't never seen nothing like that 'ssembly line. Go on in that room by the stairs. I got me a box in there with some pictures."

Jessie followed Annalea down the hall, her footsteps slipping in behind the thump-thump of her walker. Jessie remembered the summer she and Mavis had visited the zoological gardens. They had watched a land turtle climb a wooden ramp, the sound of its shell hitting the floor with a thump as it dragged itself upward: thump-thump-swish, thump-thump-swish, the smaller turtles pushing and climbing over it. While Annalea mimicked the turtle down the length of the hall, Jessie forced herself not to hurry to that room and its box full of promises.

"Be careful, chile," Annalea told her. "Some of them boxes ain't been moved since I brung 'em here. Open that one." She aimed a leg of the walker in the general direction of the appointed box. When Jessie spread the top of the box, the musty air brushing against her face smelled like soiled underwear. "That be the one," Annalea said. "Look under them pictures there. Yeah, that's what tells you all bout Plant #4."

The ink had faded to a pale green, almost golden in places, and the print was barely legible. If Jessie looked closely, she could read the warnings: THE ENEMY IS WATCHING YOU it said, and under this heading, the drawing of Japanese and German spies lurking over an assembly line of women. The room was cut into quarter sections by conveyer belts that were banked on either side with slab-like tables. The belts had been placed in a U-shape pattern, the ends moving out of and returning to a hole in the wall that seemed to be filled with fire. The whole room held the illusion of fire. Jessie could see welding torches at each of the tables along the belt. All the workers were in attendance to the metal forms suspended from the conveyer belt. The figures in their hooded uniforms looked alike—anonymous, as Annalea had said—except for their instruments. Some had eye scopes banded about their heads. Others wielded acetylene torches, and others used cranes to help them push against the rough-cut metal shapes. On one side of the room, a wall held the poster of Uncle Sam pointing his finger: UNCLE SAM WANTS YOU, it said, and on the other side, a poster answered, PRAISE THE LORD AND PASS THE AMMUNITION.

"Chile, the only thing hotter than that room be the sun down in Mississippi. I don't know how we stood it, but we was so young in them days, even Sara Flynn, wasn't nothing to hold us back. The whole world was at war, you know. Some of them boys danced in that USO one week, and got killed over there in the war the next week. The president was always on the radio saying, 'WHAT ARE YEW DOING TO HELP WIN THIS WAHR?' Well honey, if we wasn't making the bullets and the bombs, we was buying ration stamps and pulling down the shades for air raid drill or going out to the USO. That's all there was in '43. Sometimes I thought the world was gonna come to an end. I'd watch everybody on the line—all of us welding and cutting and hoisting them bombs and shells, and I'd think: What them boys fighting for? Especially the colored ones? I seen 'em, you know. Them boys going off to war. Going off to fight with them bombs we was making. It sho was hard to tell 'em what kinda work I was doing. Ain't no easy way to tell a body you making something that could kill 'em as quick as do the killing for 'em. Some I didn't tell. Some I just made up like I didn't know what I was doing. Some like Toby . . ."

Annalea sighed and looked at the faded brochure, then looked at Jessie as if she were a stranger. Abruptly she turned and thumped off toward the kitchen. Jessie put the box back onto the stack of other boxes, but not before she pocketed several yellowing snapshots. Then she joined Annalea. She found her digging around in a tin of coconut macaroons, mumbling about how the coconut got stuck between her teeth. She seemed to know Jessie was watching her, but she seemed equally determined not to know it also. Annalea poked and poked, and Jessie watched the loose skin of her arms swinging as she dug around in the cookie tin.

Jessie thought: *"I might be determined, but I'm not stupid."* She let several days pass before approaching Annalea for more stories. Her plan was simple. She told Annalea she'd help her put the rest of the photos and memorabilia in an album. "Ain't no use in leaving them to get all faded. This way, they'll be easy for you to reach." To her surprise, Annalea readily agreed, and the next time Jessie went grocery shopping, she bought the thickest scrapbook she could find.

"The straw boss we had was this old white woman named Patty O'Halloran. Ain't that something? She went by the name of Patty, and in them days, we called them white folks Paddies," Annalea laughed. "Well Patty, she was crew boss for the swing shift. That's the one I worked. Two to midnight, with a hour for lunch, breaks in between, and overtime. When I come on, the sun just be thinking bout slipping low to the ground but still be hot enuf to raise up and beat you. Mind you, it weren't like the Delta. That Mississippi sun could ride your back like a drunk what's done passed out from corn likker. But that sun up North did have a weight to it though. Come winter, it was so cold, you be wishing you could member how the heat felt. When we left that trolley stop, we had to bust that wind walking past all them DeSotos and Fords and Studebakers some of them white women was driving. But it didn't matter if you was driving some jalopy or walking. Once you got to the 'lectrified fence, that gate guard could keep you out there checking your badge, careful like he didn't believe colored women was spozed to be working in that plant. Then he let us walk the last bit of open ground to the tunnel where the locker rooms was. When we was in the open, we laughed and talked real loud, cause we knew, soon as we got to that tunnel, wasn't no more laughing. Straw boss saw to that.

"Now I can't tell you whether I liked Patty O'Halloran or no. When I first seen her, she was just another old white woman to me. Useta walk up and down the line, clicking her stopwatch like she was timing us. They kept the radio on through the whole shift. That's all we heard over them loudspeakers—that radio with the Andrews Sisters and the big bands and President Roo-sevelt telling us to help win the wahr. Only one seemed to be put off by it was Plum. Plum just listened to that radio so she could find out when them USO dances was gonna be held. Soon as we'd get back to Miz Freida's rooming house, Plum would commence to aggravating for us to go to the dance. She couldn't do nothing bout it during the shift cause Patty O'Halloran was watching us so. I spect Patty didn't have Sense One of why the colored women was working in the plant. Every time the President come on, she'd watch us close like she spected we didn't understand what he was talking bout. I understood readily enuf. I understood he was trying to tell me why my Hadley got killed overseas. And Sara Flynn understood. She lost two of her boys over there. Eighteen and nineteen, they was. Bout your age, chile."

"Girl, we just three or four years younger than your brothers who died in the war," Jessie told Mavis. "Ain't that something? They woulda been thirty by now! Older even! My mama ain't but thirty-four. How old's your mama?"

"None of your business," Mavis snapped. "And Mama said you getting too nosy. She called your mama and you gone be in big trouble snooping round that house, Jessie Crawford."

"Jessie, I want you to behave yourself," her mother said. "I can't spend all my money on this phone and I'm tired of hearing Sara Flynn complaining all the time. Sara Flynn's got enough trouble with Mavis. She don't need no more with you. You understand me, Jessie?"

Jessie tried to soothe the tone of patient tiredness in her mother's voice by saying, "Yes ma'am," and "No ma'am," in all the right places, but by the time Mae Willie Crawford reached the point of calling upon her daughter's sense of Christian spirit, Jessie had already figured out how to lead Annalea back down that long road to Plant #4.

"You know, fore I left that plant, I got myself acquainted with Patty O'Halloran. Patty wasn't too bad for a white woman. She just hadn't been round colored folks before. Only thing wrong with her was she had this body odor. I mean, all of us smelled like sweat and sheet metal, but Patty kinda smelled like her monthlies and whiskey. And they talks bout us colored folks stinking," Annalea muttered.

"Patty was always watching us, talking bout how she was trying to make certain we did our jobs. She didn't bother me much cause I was useta white folks looking over my shoulder while I worked and they looked. I sho had enuf of that in them cotton fields. But Patty had it in for Sara Flynn. In point of fact, Patty had it in for all the old women. Stayed on Sara Flynn's back like white on rice. Said she was too old to be working in some factory. Sara Flynn wasn't too old. Oh, she looked bad and all, but Sara Flynn had half-growed chillun and that's bound to make any woman look a little peaked. Now quiet as it's kept, I'm older than Sara, but white folks generally don't know how old Negroes be. They just picks them a age and stays with it. Patty O'Halloran picked a sho-nuff age for your Antie Sara. And to make matters worse, Patty was always pairing up Sara Flynn with them real young girls. Trying to get her into trouble. I spect that's what went wrong with Sissy.

"I member standing by the airlock watching them load Sissy in the ambulance. That airlock was a kinda space tween two double doors where it stayed the same temperature all the time, but soon as you stepped through that door into the 'ssembly room, that heat slapped you SMACK. When I looked back, there they was—all them women lined up—nearly fifty or sixty in that room and bout half of them colored. That room was hotter than them cotton fields, I tell you. They had us working off a conveyor belt. They'd run them pieces of shell casings by us and we'd pull them off the belt and seal them together with 'cetylene. Then we'd put 'em back on the belt and they'd go to another room where some women put them up against the rotors till them seams was smooth. They had five 'ssembly rooms like that. All of them connected to the coating shed. I don't know where them bombs went when they left the coating shed. Tell me, they had another plant where they put the dynamite in 'em, but I didn't never see it. All I saw was Plant #4, and that belt sending out them shells like there was no end to it. I did twenty or thirty a day. Worked under that big sign saying PRAISE THE LORD AND PASS THE MUNITION. Sometimes I felt the Lord coulda passed some of that munition on to somebody else. Sara Flynn sho-nuff did. When they put Sissy on that ambulance, Sara Flynn started falling apart, but Plum got to her fore Patty O'Halloran could. Plum was holding her up. That's what I saw when I looked through that airlock. Plum holding onto Sara Flynn like she was gone break or something."

Just telling it seemed to make Annalea break. Whenever she grew tired, Jessie would pick a room and browse through one or two of the boxes on top of the stacks, adding pictures to the scrapbook as she came across them. By this time, Annalea seemed to ignore her snooping, and Jessie was so bent on finding new bits of evidence, she almost forgot the photos she'd snitched from the war poster box. It took Mavis' irritating voice to remind her of them.

When Jessie first picked up the phone, all she heard was an ear-splitting wail, a cry of anguish that was so loud, it almost drowned her Aunt Sara's words. "I am surely disappointed in you," Sara Flynn said. Mavis sputtered in the background and there was a moment of static as she tried to grab the phone from her mother, but Sara Flynn did not relinquish it. "Jessie, what we gonna do with you?" Sara Flynn asked. "We expected you to behave better than this. You know Annalea's not well."

"I'll fix you for this!" Mavis screamed. "I'm gonna get you, Jessie

Crawford. I'm gonna get you, heifer. YOU HEAR ME?"

"Jessie, this is your mother. Do you hear me?"

Jessie shuddered at the thought of the three of them hovering around the phone, but she simply said, "Yes, Mama." She didn't add she could have heard her mother a lot better if Mavis hadn't been screaming: "I won't go! I won't!" over and over again. "Mama, I'm alright," Jessie said. "Me and Annalea don't need no company."

Her mother seemed to pace her words as if Jessie had suddenly grown retarded instead of disobedient. "We are not asking what you need, Jessie Crawford. I did not raise you to cause this kind of trouble. You went there to help poor Anna, not upset her. Sara Flynn's planning on being there next week, so you stop bothering Annalea, you hear me?"

Jessie said, "She's not upset, Mama," but she thought: *"Next week? Lord, I gotta move fast."*

Sara Flynn took the phone again. "Whatever you're doing, I want you to stop it right now. Annalea don't know what she saying half the time. And don't you be snooping round in her house. That's her private business. What you been up to anyway?"

Jessie said, "Nothing."

"Sometimes I don't understand you," Sara Flynn said as Mavis screamed, "You just bet not be messing up, Jessie Crawford! You just bet NOT!"

Sara Flynn said, "HUSH!" And over the sound of Mae Willie Crawford's complaints added, "Sometimes I don't understand either one of you."

Jessie wondered just who she meant.

"Family do get outta hand," Annalea said. "When I was growing up in Mississippi, fore the war started, I didn't have no idea I wanted to see something outside of the Delta. Then me and Maw-maw went down to the station four times seeing menfolks off. Two of them brothers of mine. I didn't have it in my mind to be going nowhere fore Hadley got killed, but one day, me and Maw-maw went into town to get them ration stamps. We had to get them at the post office cause we lived outside of town a ways. Instead of helping Maw-maw count her stamps, I caught myself staring at this big poster of Uncle Sam with his finger jutting straight out at me. UNCLE SAM WANTS YOU, it said. I thought to myself then, 'Why they got to end everything with YOU? But still and all, I fixed myself on finding out what Uncle Sam wanted with me.

"And chile, I was so scared the first time I walked into that plant, all I membered was that poster of him pointing his finger at me. But Plum said: 'It ain't nothin but a job, girlfriend. Ain't nothin but some hauling and lifting.' So I figured it was gonna be like back home. I was sho wrong.

It was all upside down and turned inside out from the beginning. 'From the git-go' like Big Myrtle useta say. But she always took everything from the git-go. Come from them years she worked the Chit'lin Circuit, I guess. You know, them folks didn't make nothing but nickels and dimes trying to bring a little sweet music to colored peoples down South. Sometimes folks would give 'em food steada money, or put them up for the night, in the barn if they didn't have no other room. Big Myrtle was over six feet tall, so wouldn't nobody mess with her. Just having her on the line kept us from getting in trouble sometimes. And Sara Flynn said if Big Myrtle hadn't been staying at Miz Freida's, folks woulda made more trouble for us. Some folks didn't think much of colored women working at the plant. At times they'd ride by and thow things out they cars when we was sitting on the stoop in front of Miz Freida's. That was the rooming house we lived in. Miz Freida fixed food Delta style, and down the street was a pawnshop where colored folks took their fine clothes for the Jew to sell. Big Myrtle near-bouts lived in that Jew's store. When it was hot, we'd be on Miz Freida's stoop. If Big Myrtle didn't wanta talk, she'd clamp that raggedy mouf of hers shut, but if she got the notion, she'd yell at the folks peskering us. 'What you think you doing?' she'd ask 'em. Chile, she had a voice low like a man's and when she'd been dipping the snuff to keep her gums from hurting so, she could out-bass many a man. But she could pull in the mens too, Big Myrtle could. She was a pistol on that dance floor. I swear, tween Big Myrtle and Plum, Toby was almost too scared to talk to me."

At that point, Annalea clamped her lips shut and closed her eyes. Jessie thought she was about to fall into one of her sleep states, or slide out of the subject into another one the way she did sometimes—easy like those cottonmouth snakes she talked about. Too many times, Jessie had listened to Annalea dance from one memory to another as if she were still changing partners at the USO, so this time, Jessie took a chance and pulled out the photos she had exhumed from the box that day she'd caught Annalea weeping. She thrust the picture of the young soldier into Annalea's hands. Annalea shook her head, but didn't say anything. Jessie handed her another picture, but when she tried to retrieve the snapshot of the soldier, Annalea carefully placed it on top of the new photo and continued to stare at it. Jessie waited. She had a question all framed in her head, but she didn't have the words to ask it. After the ultimatum of that last phone call home, Jessie had studied those photos. It hadn't taken much doing to see that the soldier with his gate-mouth smile looked so much like Mavis that, for a moment, Jessie thought he might have been one of Mavis' dead brothers. But the photo was signed: Love as always, Toby Ward.

"Who's that?" Jessie said quietly.

"I spect that's Toby," Annalea answered. Even though she frowned, she looked at that photo as if it were as familiar to her as the smell of her own breath on the pillowcase. Then she whispered, "Lord, Lord . . . he weren't nothing but a baby."

"Who is he?" Jessie repeated.

"One of them soldiers, chile. I didn't meet Toby till after Sissy got hurt. You member I told you what happened to Sissy. We all knowed what happened was her fault, but we couldn't help but feel sorry for her. They was always telling us to be careful round the plant. Signs up everywhere. Some of 'em weren't no more than slogans, stuff them singers like the Andrews Sisters were liable to be telling folks about. They was kinda catchy though." Annalea leaned back and closed her eyes once more.

After a while, Jessie made a little noise in her throat and Annalea asked, "Where was I?"

"Toby," Jessie said.

"Oh, we was something," Annalea said. "We'd go down to the big dance hall down by the bus station. That's where the USO was so the soldiers could find it right away. Course, there was another one over by the Red Cross building, but that was uptown and the white folks went there. We didn't frequent that one much a'tall. They had them dances every Saturday night, you know. We couldn't go every week. Some weeks, we was still at the plant when the dances was going on. But some weeks, we just had time to hightail it home, thow on some clothes, and put some Lov-Ere on our hands to smooth out the rough. We'd get there just fore they played the last song. Some weeks, we didn't need more'n the last song. Some weeks, we didn't even need no soldiers. We just took to the floor ourselves. I always had to have myself a dance with Plum anyhow. She was the one who learnt me dancing. First time she saw me Lindy hopping up and down like they do in Delta country, she just took me over to the side and looked me straight in the eye. 'What you trying to do? Stomp down some cotton? You moving too much, girlfriend. Just lay back. When the cat sticks his knee up next to your koochie, just ride it. Make that saxophone do all the work. That's all the dancing these here soldiers need.'

"Then she took me through a slow dance, and I tell you, I ain't never danced with nobody else the way I danced with Plum. Um-um. I always had to have my dance with Plum. Even when the others commenced to teasing me bout hugging the wall till she drug me on the floor, it didn't matter. Course there was Toby . . ." Annalea sighed, and for a moment, Jessie thought she'd lost her again. But this was the third time she'd mentioned the name Toby, so Jessie was determined to keep her talking.

Jessie grunted and Annalea dismissed whatever stray thought she'd hooked onto by rubbing the swollen knuckles of her stiff fingers.

"Yeah, Toby . . . Not that I encouraged Toby, mind you, but it was kind of hard to be rid of him. Him being Big Myrtle's boyfriend and all. Leastwise, that's what she told us when she introduced him. Plum had found Big Myrtle a room at Miz Freida's same as she had for the rest of us when we come to work at the plant. Plum knew everything there was to know alright. And when Toby found out Big Myrtle lived at Miz Freida's, he come running. At first, all Toby wanted to do was be near Big Myrtle. But it was Plum who put some stuff on it. Plum wanted to know what Toby saw in Big Myrtle and she wouldn't rest till she found out. See, we useta trade off dresses. Leastwise, me and Sara Flynn useta trade off dresses. Wasn't no use in trying Big Myrtle's dresses, and if Plum wasn't wearing trousers, she was wearing them loose dresses didn't have no shape a'tall to them. But we all traded them rhinestone pins. Made us look like we was Diamond Lil, they did. Toby liked them pins. He'd say: 'Sweets, you lit up like Broadway.' Toby came from Noo Yawk, so he was likely to know what he was talking bout. And he be the first one to call me Sweets. He'd say, 'Sweets, you the prettiest thing round here.' Say it right in front of Big Myrtle. She'd stand there with her face all puffed up like she been fighting Joe Louis. I guess that's when Plum got a mind to put some stuff in the game."

Annalea slid Toby's picture under the other one she was holding. Toby was in that snapshot too, but so was Big Myrtle, Sara Flynn, Annalea, and Plum. It was a Boardwalk snapshot, and they were all grinning, cheek-to-cheek and posed somewhere between a tango and the cakewalk: two women on either side of Toby who was trying to embrace them all. Jessie took the pictures and began pasting them onto an empty page of the album.

"I spect Toby knew he wasn't coming back from that war," Annalea muttered. "A lot of them did, you know. But Toby wasn't like them others. If the truth be known, we shoulda been calling him Sweets. He sho was sweet on that dance floor. Plum was the onliest one who could outdance Toby, but Toby had a way about him. He could figure-eight, belly-grind, and make you dip smooth like in the movies. One time down in Mississippi, I saw some snakes doing they dance. Hugging and crossing over. Moving like water. Honey, Toby coulda showed them a thing or two."

Jessie aimed for the big question. "How come he looks so much like Mavis?"

Annalea shook her head. "Lord chile, you sho got the questions. I thought that was something I done put behind me. Us women, we tried to put it behind us from the git-go. Some things just ain't easy, though Toby had a way of making things seem easy. Now me, I raised such a fuss when Plum tried to put me up to doing her dirt. I figured Big Myrtle was like family. We was all like family. Maybe that's why Big Myrtle never said nothing to me. Just was all the time watching me. Looking pitiful sad and lovesick. Sneaking off with Toby every chance she got. I come upon 'em once. They wasn't doing nothing, just laying up in the bed, and wasn't no reason for me to be asking questions. I done had me one husband and that one be enuf. But Plum, she was the one with questions. Always carrying on bout how Toby just some man to pull the wool over our eyes. Got to the point, she was pret-near driving me crazy. Sara Flynn tried to talk some sense into her, but Plum was of one mind. Then Sara Flynn tried talking to Big Myrtle. Problem was, both her and Plum was way past talking, both of 'em jealous of what they thought I was doing with Toby. Sara Flynn told me she was scared we was all gonna get fired the way we was watching each other all the time, but there was nothing I could do to help. Leastwise, I didn't think there was. Then I up and lost my finger. This finger here . . ." Annalea held up her left hand. The stump of the missing ring finger was gnarled worst than any of Annalea's other arthritic knuckles.

"I guess I wasn't paying no attention, thinking bout me and Toby. Thinking bout how Big Myrtle and Plum was taking it all. I was reaching up to hook a shell casing when it bucked. Weighed about fifty or so pounds, so I had to slip it on its side. But it slipped on my hand instead. I grunted or something. I don't know. Felt like something done stepped on my hand. Like something done tried to chop it up for kindling. I knew Plum was holding up the other end of that shell and waiting for me to say something, but my jaws was locked. All I could do was empty all the life outta my face. Sara Flynn yelled to Plum to lift the end. Sara looked like she was staring at Sissy all over again. Big Myrtle was too far away, but she spit her snuff in the coffee can and start humming: ' . . . *blind man standing at the pool, crying, ohh Lordy save me . . . blind man stood at the well and cried . . .* ' The black women joined her and the white women come up with they own hymn. You'da thought we was warring, what with 'Lord Lord' and 'Jesus Christ the King' calling out from one end of the room to the other. Patty O'Halloran was trying to figure out how to stop it. Wasn't that Patty was against religion—she was as much Catholic as any Irish—but when the colored women was singing, she act like they was pushing her out the way. Course if it was left to Plum, they woulda been. Plum got that bomb offa me. Got them gears groaning and pulled up on the hoist. Weren't no more than a hiccough in the belt, but we could see the Patty noting the time. Weren't no time a'tall. Not enough to dock nobody. Not enough to call the supervisor or stop work like they did for Sissy. Only enuf time for Patty to screw her face into trouble. So Plum yelled, 'They calls this crap e-quipment?' Everybody knew Plum was covering for me. Patty couldn't do nothing cept click her stop watch and walk down the line.

"I was almost ready to leave work when I took sick. I had said to myself: Lord, just let me make it through this here shift. The Lord heard me, but he didn't give me one minute past that time clock. I beat it for that toilet. Big Myrtle was already in there. I could hear her in the next stall. You know, by that time, Big Myrtle was getting sick on a regular basis, and we always had to wait for her when the shift was over. Sara Flynn and Plum was outside waiting on Big Myrtle like always, cept that day they was waiting on me too. I just couldn't seem to get outta there. I was stuck at that sink. See, I'd worked the whole shift without taking off my glove and by the time the shift was over, that glove was stuck to my skin and the finger was heating up inside it. I had to peel that glove offa me. I run some water over it and kinda rubbed on it. After I rolled it part the way down, I could see the joint of my finger. Chile, this finger was swole up twice its size and had the sickness colors running through it. Reds and blues and greens. Reminded me of them shell casings. You know, like when they first come down the line and look more like pig iron than they do bombs. But you'da thought somebody shot me dead, cause when I snatched at that glove, trying to get the last little bit offa me, I hollered like a bullet had done hit me. I guess Patty had to fight Plum to get me outta that toilet into the dispens'ry. And course, Patty found Big Myrtle too, all curled up over the toilet stool, sick to her stomach.

"When I come to, Plum and Sara Flynn was arguing with Patty O'Halloran, and this white doctor was moving tween me and Big Myrtle trying to care for both of us at the same time. I looked up on the ceiling and for the first time, saw that munitions sign spelled out. It said: PRAISE THE LORD AND PASS THE AMMUNITION AND WE ALL LIVE FREE. Onliest thing free in that room was noise. Big Myrtle was moaning and Sara Flynn was yelling bout how we had our own doctors and could take care of our own. That was sho-nuff true. We all lived in this house taking care of each other long after that white doctor put his pills away. But Patty O'Halloran wasn't bout to let the whole thing slide. Plum come over and tried to pull me to my feet and Patty snatched me away from Plum. I thought they was gone fight sho-nuff, but the doctor broke it up and Patty started asking all kinds of questions. First me, then Big Myrtle.

"It wasn't that I told her nothing, mind you. Colored folks useta keeping things in. It's the onliest way we done survived white folks. But some white folks got a way of figuring out things. And one woman be more liable to get her a sense of what's happening to another. Patty saw that doctor was upsetting Big Myrtle looking at her like he ain't never seen some stovepipe of a colored woman what got caught in the family way. So Patty made that doctor leave the room. Told him, 'OUT!' and pointed her finger like Uncle Sam. Then she commenced to talking bout how much sick leave I had coming and asked Big Myrtle, 'Why didn't you tell me what was going on?' Big Myrtle just couldn't bring herself to talk to that woman, so I told Patty she hadn't never bothered to ask nobody. 'Well I'm asking now,' she said. I didn't say nothing. I just looked at the ceiling and hung onto Big Myrtle like she wasn't but as tall as I was. Patty said, 'I don't suppose I'm ever gonna understand you people.' I just laughed and said, 'No ma'am.' Patty O'Halloran mighta been a nasty-smelling white woman, but she fixed it so we kept them jobs long enuf for me and Plum to buy this here house. This be where we moved—me and Plum and Sara Flynn and Big Myrtle."

"Where Plum and Big Myrtle now?" Jessie asked.

"Chile, you ain't got to know everything," Annalea said. "Make do with what you got. That's what we did, honey. Me, Plum, your Antie Sara, Big Myrtle. All of us back then learnt how to make do."

Jessie felt the question she'd been saving press its way into her mouth. "Annalea, you be my cousin?" she asked, ready to accept Annalea one way or another. She remembered a time in the fourth grade when she'd had a friend who was in the seventh grade, a friend who had been generous enough to let Jessie call her "play sister." But until now, no one had asked Jessie to pretend anything with Annalea. "You be my for real cousin?" Jessie repeated.

Annalea laughed. "I spect I'm bout as much family as you done ever had," she said. "Just you ask Sara Flynn. Ask your Antie Sara." Jessie waited for more, but Annalea merely stared at an open page in the photo album, then turned her eyes to the wild roses climbing the edge of the toolshed in the yard out back. Jessie was breathing in deep gulps as if she'd been working hard. "You ask Sara Flynn," Annalea said again. Jessie stood up and started for the door. On her way past Annalea's chair, she leaned over and kissed the old woman's sparsely covered head. "Just don't tell Sara Flynn I told you nothing," Annalea added, but Jessie had turned and walked out of the room, leaving behind all of the codes of silence, the rules of behavior. The door sucked the noise out with her.

The day Sara Flynn arrived, Annalea heard her and Mavis slamming suitcases onto the driveway and calling to neighbors. She pushed her walker to the window and opened it, letting the scents of rosemary, azalea, and buttercup mix with the musty odors of her toilet water and face powders. If they were going to leave her with Mavis, a child who seemed to be put on earth just to make sure there was no rest for the weary, the least she could do was hasten her own death with the croup, which was sure to be floating on the humid summer air. She listened to the sound of the taxi pulling out of the driveway. The front door slammed, and for nearly half-an-hour, she heard the buzz of voices in the dining room as Jessie answered questions. Then footsteps thudded down the hallway. Annalea tuned out the world. With Jessie gone, she didn't have to listen to anything she didn't want to hear. Annalea waited.

"You promised!" Sara Flynn screamed in her good ear. "You promised you'd never do this. What about that child? Here you are, running your mouth like you ain't got nobody but yourself to worry bout. I told you to keep your mouth shut. I told you fore Plum died. Told you how it had to be and you said you'd understand. You promised, Annalea."

As the voice vibrated against her hearing aid, Annalea closed her eyes and rubbed her tongue around the outside of her gums. None of it was her problem. What could Sara Flynn have been thinking, leaving her stuck with that nosy child in the first place? Better to have left her with Mavis, which was as good as leaving her alone. *"Lord knows, I done gave Sara Flynn more than enough reasons to leave me alone,"* Annalea thought. But she chased away the reasons Sara Flynn might have had for abandoning her, her mind whipping from one idea to another until her eyes seemed to be following the flutterings of young birds flying past the window in wild patterns, as if the sun had brought them to some sort of madness. And while folks laughed to see sparrows chasing each other under the blue sky of a summer afternoon, they clucked their tongues at the sight of Annalea stuck in that window. From a distance, no one could tell Annalea had a thing on her mind. From a distance, she seemed to be just another old woman, the splotches of pasty skin seeming to grow larger as she slowly rocked away the heat of another summer's day.

The Woman Who Would Eat Flowers

CORA KAY WAITED until the old woman moved the broom a whisper away from her big toe before she yelled, "Don't be sweeping my feet! That broom mess my feet up from where I was going."

Kei-Shee mumbled something that probably sounded like "Shade-down," or "Chinatown," to most folks in the Flats, but Cora Kay's ear had been trained to understand a few Chinese phrases, and she knew when she'd heard one of those curses Kei-Shee muttered whenever she had the chance. That chance didn't happen very often, because it wasn't very often that Wu Yeung Lee allowed his mother to come out of the kitchen. In this respect, he was a good son, and she, obedient as any old-world Chinese woman, never entered the front part of Wu Fong's Eatery without her son's permission. In fact, through three generations of Chinese owners, none of the black folks in the Flats had seen any of the Chinese women waiting tables in Wu Fong's. Retired railroad men told stories about how their fathers had not seen old man Wu Fong's wife in the front of the restaurant when Wu Fong himself ran the place. Only men had waited tables until 1946, when Wu Fong's grandson, Wu Yeung Lee, hired Cora Ivory. Cora Kay had made the front of the Eatery her domain, and as she sat there, watching Yeung Lee's mother sweep the floor with a heavy straw broom, Cora Kay Ivory exercised her reign over this kingdom.

"You can just swallow that spit," she told the old woman. "You think I don't know what *shyä-dan* means? I ain't no lazy chicken, or whatever it is you be saying under your breath. And I ain't gone sit here and let you sweep me into my grave with that broom neither."

The old woman looked up and grinned, her one ragged tooth hanging like a loose nail from the top of her mouth.

"You know what I'm talking bout, don't you?" Cora Kay shouted.

Kei-Shee began swinging the broom back and forth as if she were getting ready to dance by swaying to the music. She moved closer to Cora Kay, swaying and grinning, the boom hissing against the wooden floor like the swish of a ball gown. Even though Kei-Shee had no ball gowns to remember, she remembered the brothel in San Francisco where she'd been trapped until, at eighteen, Yeung Lee's father had found her. And if she thought about the music of Chinatown streets, its nightlife similiar to the stingy row of cafes and jook joints on either side of Wu Fong's Eatery, she could not stop her memories. But Cora Kay's knowledge of street life was too recent, so she did not move. There was nothing in Kei-Shee's muttered oaths that would have made Cora Kay budge. Moving would not enter her mind until the wall clock reached 4:00 P.M., which was when she was officially bound to begin waiting tables. Even then, nothing moved Cora Kay if she didn't want to move—a trait she kept intact until she encountered a skinny little hobo named Clarence Henry, but that was yet to be. At the time, Cora Kay was about the business of polishing her nails, and the notion of pulling her body from its slumped position was no more a part of this ritual than sweeping floors was a part of waiting tables.

Cora Kay watched Kei-Shee and cast a few oaths of her own. "You can grin all you want to, old lady, but if you come near me with that broom, I'm gone make you a picture up on that wall, you hear me?"

Kei-Shee made the sound of a broom singing to itself—"Säu, säu"—her eyes glittering as she moved closer to Cora Kay's feet. "Don't be sweeping my feet," Cora Kay warned her again.

The old woman did a little hop-step and turned within inches of Cora Kay. The broom went back and forth, back and forth, and on its third swing, the one that most certainly would have made contact with its target, Cora Kay picked up a soy bowl of salt and flung it across the room—not at the old lady, but not away from her either.

The kitchen doors slammed open. Yeung Lee stood there, his machete knife already slick with a coating of duck grease. He glared first at his mother posed stock-still in the center of the floor, the broom frozen midway its downswing, then at Cora Kay, languishing in the third booth from the door. Neither woman acknowledged him until Yeung Lee yelled, "Mü-chin! Hwēi-chyu!"

The old woman nodded to her son and began shuffling toward the kitchen, dragging the broom behind her. When she reached the door, she turned and said, "Dzäi-djän."

Cora Kay stuck out her tongue. "So long yourself, you old bat."

Then she turned her frown on Yeung Lee. Although his lip curled once, he said nothing. But in the space of that look, the two of them wrestled with what little understanding they had growing between them. After a few moments, Yeung Lee marched back to the kitchen, cursing as he entered—his queue unleashed from its usual nest under his hat and quivering against his back. Cora Kay returned to the task of lacquering her nails. Seconds later, Yeung Lee's daughter, Tea Rose, resumed the sweeping her grandmother had abandoned. In the doorway, Kei-Shee waited to see what went on between her granddaughter and Cora Kay. She could have saved herself the trouble. Both girls set their expressions to appear as if they were alone in the room.

Tea Rose melted into the broom, its sweeping consuming all of her attention. She was a plump girl, about as old as Cora Kay, with a round face sharpened by the pinched set of her mouth and downcast eyes. Cora Kay was surprised at how the girl seemed to straddle two worlds. The way Tea Rose walked, like her speech, belonged to Kei-Shee, not the Flats, yet when she was out of Kei-Shee's sight, Tea Rose could be as much a part of the Strip as Cora Kay. Still Cora Kay was always amazed at how the girl scuttled away from the center of things. The day Cora Kay had moved into the spare room in the crook of the upstairs hallway, Tea Rose had stood just outside the door. At first, Cora Kay did not realize the girl was there. Then she'd seen a shadow, a movement like a falling leaf, or a cockroach hovering on the other side of the doorjamb. Cora Kay hated roaches, so she'd waited to squash the bug, the shoe in her hand raised at just the right level to make contact before the thing sensed danger. Nothing else moved, and as Cora Kay was about to relax, Tea Rose spoke. "You come live here?" Tea Rose had asked. "Your mama come live here?"

"I ain't saying nothing till you out from behind that door," Cora Kay had told her. But the girl had sidled down the hall.

The next chance she'd had to talk to Tea Rose was while the girl cleaned the hallway. Without breaking her rhythm of wiping down the walls with a damp rag, Tea Rose had asked her, "What name you have for papers?" Cora Kay had told her. The rag had slapped the wall once, twice, before Tea Rose had tried repeating the name. "Don't like that," she'd said finally. "That name only one you speak?" Cora Kay had shrugged. The rag had slapped-slapped, louder this time.

"My mama calls me Cinnamon," Cora Kay had said. "It's cause of my coloring. But she the onliest one I allow to call me that."

Tea Rose had begun to rinse the rag. "Sēn-nà-mēn," she'd said, moving to a new section of the wall. "Don't like that," she'd said, and once more, slammed the rag into action. "I call you Hoisin. Chinese spice.

Hoisin same brown-red, like you. I say Hoisin." The rag had echoed the name as Tea Rose worked her way down the hall.

"Chile's always cleaning," Cora Kay told herself. *"Moving like one of them church folk who seen the spirit and can't speak up right."*

Not speaking up was hardly one of Cora Kay's faults. Even the act of blow-drying her newly applied nail polish was a form of speech, each puff a challenge to whatever thoughts anyone might harbor about assigning her to sweep the floor. Cora Kay blew two puffs of air on each nail, then extended her hands to gaze upon the perfection of her rust-brown fingers, their coral-red tips the same shade of polish Tea Rose would secretly spread on her toenails later that night. Cora Kay repeated the blow-drying process until each fingernail received some ten puffs of air, but as Yeung Lee had found out by the end of the first week of her employment, she'd still spend the next several hours of work avoiding any direct contact between fingertips and dishes of food. Some nights, her fear of ruining her nails drove her into making Tea Rose place the orders on a tray, then forcing the customers to pluck their own food from tray to table.

Now, as Tea Rose swept, Kei-Shee lurked in the doorway and clicked her tongue in disapproval of both girls. The old woman hunkered there until the minute hand made its usual little jump-click sixty seconds before the hour, then she turned back to the kitchen. Just as the clock pinged its first count of four, Cora Kay pulled herself away from the booth. Strolling toward the front door, she dropped the bottle of nail polish into Tea Rose's cupped hand. Tea Rose closed her fingers over the gift, flicked her pile of dust under the nearest booth, and scuttled into the kitchen without looking once at Cora Kay, who had already reached for the CLOSED/OPEN sign stuck in a corner of the front window. On the fourth chime of the hour, she flipped the sign, announcing Wu Fong's was ready for business. Then Cora Kay Ivory turned her back on all who entered.

Turning her back was how Cora Kay had learned to deal with the narrow little world of the Flats, and in the execution of that act, she fit right into the pattern of Wu Fong's Eatery. Wu Yeung Lee and his family had become masters at being both a party to, yet outside of the crumbling district of tar-paper shacks, tenements, and factories, interrupted by a sprinkling of bars, jook joints, and cheap stores that spread across the flatlands into a neighborhood of sorts—all of it belted together by the skinny street known as the Strip. Yeung Lee, like his grandfather, Wu Fong, held a thriving business for black folks who the law said couldn't eat in the same place as white folks. Everyone knew they'd all get the same service at Wu Fong's, regardless of their color. But while everyone knew the street side of Wu Fong's Eatery, few people knew the folks inside the restaurant.

Like most of those who lived in that part of town, Yeung Lee and his family had earned their living from the railroad at one time or another. In the 1800s, when the railroad was being built, Yeung Lee's grandfather, one of the few Mandarian Chinese to come West, had been a cook for the Chinese workers the railroad company had refused to feed, as it had done so willingly for their white co-workers. Later, when the company bosses ordered Wu Fong to cook for the bucket brigade of black men hauling stones from Cobbler's Creek, he'd fed them as well. And when the railroad finally had finished laying the east-west track cross-country, the occasion for that famous picture of the hookup of tracks at the California-Nevada border, publicity did not include the Chinese or black workers who'd labored for the companies. Company policy had split those men into racial groups as clearly as the tracks had split the land. Cora Kay didn't know it, but her grandfather, who had worked in the train yards most of his sixty-one years of life, had been one of the men fed by Wu Fong. And his son, Cora Kay's father, had died following an accident in the yards. After that, Cora Kay and her mother had lived in one of the shanties at the edge of the tracks, where hoboes had been setting up camp since the Great Depression.

In those days, black men headed north the way geese travelled the migratory patterns into Canada, but unlike the geese, those men had no intention of returning to the breeding grounds south of the Mason-Dixon. Some left home in the rickety wooden Jim Crow part of the train, the only part colored people were allowed to ride. Others travelled as best they could, grabbing a passing train like the wind grabbed the sound clacking in its wheels. And for the women in the shanties, those men often represented their tickets out of town. When Cora Kay was sixteen, her mother had given her a choice.

"Cinnamon, ain't nothing here for us," she'd said. "Ain't no needa staying here listening to them trains come and go when we could be the ones doing the going. I got a man wants us to come along to Chi-town. Come with me, Cinnamon. Come with me, baby girl."

But Cora Kay had chosen Wu Fong's—"a steady job where I ain't grabbing holt of no freight car and cooking beans on no tin plate."

"Ain't nothing for you here," her mother had repeated.

"I don't know what's here and what ain't," Cora Kay had told her, "but I don't aim to leave fore I find out."

"Well, you ain't gone find out working for that Chinaman. These white folks ain't gone do nothing but give that Chinaman a hard way to go and a short time to get there. They don't even let them men bring they wives over here. That's how come there ain't nothing but that old woman and that chile working in that Chinaman's restaurant."

After she moved into the room at the top of the stairs, Cora Kay discovered the loss of her mother gave her something in common with Tea Rose, whose mother had been forced to stay behind when Yeung Lee returned to the States following his obligatory trip to China to find a bride. Under immigration laws that made it nearly impossible for a Chinese worker to bring his wife into the country, Yeung Lee had returned with his child, but if the truth be known, he had listed six-year-old Tea Rose as male, and given her the name Hēu-hwēi, or Sorrow. Like Cora Kay, Tea Rose had grown up in the sorrow of the Strip, with its gambling men and hoboes, railroad families and Christians. When she was younger, Tea Rose had fled to the Eatery's roof to escape school and the taunts of children singing: "Chink, Chink. Chinaman, eat dead rats. Chew them up like ginger snaps." From the roof, Tea Rose could watch the orange clay hillside for the first sign of smoke from inbound trains that, her father once told her, might be the one bringing her mother from China. Until her father hired Cora Kay, that view of the train yards had sustained Tea Rose.

"What you looking at that mud hole for?" Cora Kay had asked. "My mother come sometime this track," Tea Rose had answered.

"Don't hold your breath," Cora Kay told her, but when Tea Rose's father sent the two of them to gather day lilies, chrysanthemums, and sweet flower grasses growing in the meadow near the Hodiman Road shantytown, both girls would stare into windows of trains that were slowing down to make the approach to the station. Those outings made Cora Kay pull on the memories of her mother's cooking, and she would include coltsfoot and fireweed in the bundles of herbs she and Tea Rose gathered. Although Cora Kay had brought a large box of ground cinnamon in an effort to teach Yeung Lee and his family how to say her nickname, that box remained untouched on the pantry shelf. But Yeung Lee used the selection of wild herbs she'd picked in the meadow to spice his soups and stews, and in doing so, added another reason to the list of those he'd concocted to rationalize hiring Cora Kay.

Still, some folks on the Strip claimed they never understood the whys-and-wherefores of how Cora Kay came to work at Wu Fong's Eatery, even though everyone knew that, in 1946, Cora Kay had been the first black woman in town employed to work right out front in a business that was not owned by someone who was black.

"She young, but she sho know how to take care of herself," Dee Streeter said. "I spect that come from being raised in shantytown."

Dee was sitting in a booth with LuRaye Turner and Patsy Granger.

At least once a week, on those nights when they couldn't bring themselves to go home and cook in a second kitchen after a day full of kitchens out in the Belmont District, the women stopped by Wu Fong's for take-out. They were usually sitting in one of the front booths next to church ladies like Sister Vernida Garrison, the Ladies' Aid president, or Hattie Lou Pritchard, the doctor's wife, both of whom regularly brought Yeung Lee some of their Christian literature to heal the heathen ways they were sure infected the place, along with cockroaches and rats. Aside from spearheading a drive to get the city to tear down the shanties, these family women were among the first customers in the Eatery, and quite often they took it upon themselves to try "talking some sense into Cora Kay."

"Chile, that Chinaman's got you waiting tables every night. Go to school so you can get a good job," Sister Garrison would tell her.

Cora Kay would flick Sister Garrison's order of pork fried rice off the edge of her hip so quickly, rice skittered away from the plate and danced toward the end of the table before bouncing into the woman's ample lap. Cora Kay had no patience with these women. It was their children who'd run her home from school. "Your mama's like the railroad track," they'd laughed. "She been laid from one end of town to the other." They had teased her about what went on in the shanties the same way they'd picked on Tea Rose about being Chinese. So when Cora Kay reached the service window, she'd let Tea Rose know the church ladies had descended by writing the Chinese symbols for "religion-up-come" in the patina of grease covering the counter. In one way or another, those women paid for their cruel offspring.

"Lord, it's a sin and a shame that chile's mama up and left her by herself," Doc Pritchard's wife mumbled, her back teeth grinding sour against the extra dash of Szechwan vinegar Cora Kay had sprinkled on her order of Heavenly Greens. "That chile ain't got but one nerve and no manners," the doctor's wife added.

"And that Chinaman don't pay her enuf for room and board," Dee sniffed. "She got to live upstairs in that back room of his."

"But he do give her a place to stay," Patsy Granger muttered. "Out in Belmont, that white woman didn't even want to give me a room to myself. Said I had to share it with the wet nurse." Then Patsy took another sip of tea and complained about how it was so strong, "it burns clear through your throat like red-eye likker."

"May be a job, but Cora Kay do smell like food all the time," Sister Garrison said. "Garlic and onion. Trashy smells."

"Beats some other smells," the women grunted, all of them inching toward the first twinges of heartburn they'd suffer from that hefty dollop of Mongolian fire oil Tea Rose put in their pepper rice soup.

"That Chinaman don't seem to mind them smells," LuRaye noted, a hint of the devil in her eyes as she burped sweet-and-sour chicken.

The other women said, "Um-hum," and "I hear that," and stared at Cora Kay sauntering between tables, her age almost hidden behind a shabby dress that was permanently stained with the grease of fowl, pork, and fish. Then they turned their attention to the service window, where they could see Kei-Shee and Tea Rose, and behind them, Yeung Lee chopping onions, chicken, and strips of pork on the butcher's block, his nostrils flaring with anticipation of the cut—the thunk of his machete knife and the gleam in his eyes as sure and definite as anger. That view prompted all sorts of comments about just what might be going on in those rooms at the top of the stairs. Though the women were unwilling to admit it, more than one of them had examined that six foot tall Chinaman with more than food on her mind. They all had noticed how Yeung Lee's eyebrows grew together over the bridge of his nose, like frayed bird wings—"wild like the night owls up in the woods," some said—and how his hair, with its waist-long queue, was black as light trapped in the deepest part of a well. Cora Kay could have told them how Yeung Lee's eyes changed from liquid darkness to smoke, and how his voice was ribbed with silk when he looked up from the storage shed behind the restaurant and called to her while she stood in her bedroom window, the moonlight fashioning her rough cotton shift into a shapely garment. Cora Kay could have told them this if she were of a mind to speak to them. As it was, she simply watched them load their dinner plates with questions.

"You see them eyes?" they whispered. "Them eyes cut right through you," they told each other when they felt him stare at their hips as they slid out of a booth. But more than one woman had tried to provoke a smile that raised the dimples on either side of Yeung Lee's Fu Manchu mustache and goatee, then fantasized herself trapped in a Charlie Chan spy scene, Yeung Lee bargaining for her body with sacks of jade or opium just as some beautiful black man, like James Edwards or Canada Lee, rushed through the door to save her. Their dreams were always cut short by Cora Kay's presentation of the bill.

"Don't give you no time to finish eating," they sniffed. "Always there asking for money, like we trying to get by without paying."

"Honey, that girl just too sloppy. Don't know what no man would see in her."

But if the women were curious, the men were outright baffled. It was a known fact that Wu Yeung Lee's daughter, Tea Rose, was old enough to wait those tables herself. And if Yeung Lee was trying to be so careful about hiding his daughter from their eyes, why hire Cora Kay to tempt them? Others said the reason was as plain as Cora Kay's wide hips and Yeung Lee's roving eye.

"Is you blind?" men like Butler Sykes would cackle. "Take yourself a look at Cora Ivory, then ask why that Chinaman wants her round him."

And his railroad buddies, Maroon-Willie Evans, Lip Wooten, Whitaker Yarrow, and the other men who ran the road, would nod their heads. Like them, Butler Sykes came home for a layover ready to see his woman, and ready for a scam. But like most of the married men, Butler didn't let go of the road just because the train had pulled into the station. Unless his wife caught him, he spent the first hours of his layover with the unmarried men, combing the Strip, and later, coaxing his friends into a little game in the room in back of his wife's funeral home. The problem was the funeral home game usually involved high stakes, and although gambling and women were almost second nature to railroad men, most of them didn't want to lose their entire paychecks on one game. Running the road meant having to sit on their feelings and memories of home until the train pulled in, and they wanted a little something in their pockets once they left that train behind them.

Necessity had taught the men to be careful about separating home and the railroad. When they dressed for work—checking shoes for rundown heels, double-checking facial hair, or checking for the least hint of manly scents that had to be removed before the head conductor finished his white-glove inspection—they'd had to shed all memories of home. To carry that memory past the threshold of the trains was dangerous. One racist remark too many, and home could grab a man's throat and rip it open—"Just come tumbling out fore you can snatch it back," Whitaker Yarrow would say. So while they had to scramble aboard the train, once they were released from duty, they were ready to run a game. Still, nobody played on an empty stomach, and they knew that, next to the chitterlings and collard greens folks loved to buy at Rosie's Bar-B-Q, there wasn't a better place to eat on the down side of town than at the restaurant owned by Wu Fong's grandson.

Maroon-Willie, chowing down at Wu Fong's, would praise Yeung Lee's cooking as he remembered serving under a vicious captain in the Merchant Marines, and how, mid-voyage, he had abandoned ship to escape the captain's wrath, thereby earning the name Maroon. "You sho get your money's worth at the Chinaman's," he'd tell the others. "Ain't like in the Merchant's when you be eating green chicken gizzards, or thowing up food done spoilt past rotten. They oughta have that Chinaman cooking on them boats. Make the Boss Cap'n eat that other slop himself. That's how come I'm running the road. Means I ain't never too far from eating good."

"Food's good, but that woman's got an attitude," Butler said.

"Still it be betta than some offa places," Lip Wooten told him. Lip had been running the road so long—some said before A. Philip Randolph started the Brotherhood of Sleeping Car Porters—that he'd grown gray-haired and bent-back. The other members of the Union protected him because he'd lost his strength, and the use of half of his mouth when he was hit in the face with a blackjack during a railroad strike before the war. They took up the slack when he doubled under the leadweight of a suitcase, or caught flak from white conductors who mimicked his thick-lipped speech.

"We'all ain't jus a membah of the Brothahhood," Lip added. "The Brothahhood be like fam-bily, but we'all still gots ta beg fuh food on that train. So longs ah git mah food heah-ah, don mattuh how Cora Ivory be actin'. See, ah members time when we'all pullup to Sa-town an they say: 'Don serv niggahs back heah-ah.'"

"Yeah, they say that in Chicago," Maroon-Willie nodded. "They say: 'Don't serve niggers here.'"

Whitaker laughed and said, "Well, Maroon, you and Lip shoulda told 'em: That's OK . . . we don't eat 'em neither.'"

Everyone howled at that inside joke, but the laughter died quickly when Whitaker added, "I still don't see why ain't no Chinawomen waiting tables." And until someone like Maroon-Willie said, "Pass me some more of them garlic ribs," they'd all look at the hip-riding tightness of Cora Kay's soiled dress as she leaned over to pick up a tray of dishes from a table. And they dreamed of train stops where fancy women catered to them.

While churchgoers and family folk were among the first round of customers at the Eatery, the railroad men and the rest of the night trade took over the place after dark, when flickering neon lit up the Strip from the Flame Bar's dancing lights at one end, down to the Glass Bar's Seagram's sign blinking at the opposite end. From that time till an hour or so past midnight, Wu Fong's Eatery belonged to the night crowd. And every night, those folks found Yeung Lee at his chopping block, the machete's blade hissing toward its target with unerring accuracy. Every night, while Cora Kay sidled from table to table, her skin most often as oily as the plates she piled on the counter over the sink, Tea Rose sat in the back room, filling orders and folding dough for fortune cookies, while her grandmother listened to radio tales of the Shadow, the Green Hornet, and the Fat Man. Between episodes, Kei-Shee washed dishes, stirred fresh noodles into the ever-present pot of broth, and checked the bin of rice. At times she muttered some oath to rid the room of spirits, or to warn Yeung Lee of trouble. And even before Clarence Henry showed up, there was plenty of trouble on the Strip that could touch Wu Fong's.

Not that any owner of Wu Fong's had been unfamiliar with trouble. So many shady types had frequented Wu Fong's that the police simply cruised through the restaurant from time to time. It was not uncommon for a family of church folks to watch several tables of gambling men scramble for the side exit, or rush for the pantry in back of the kitchen, where the dim outline of a door was barely visible under a grease-stained bamboo curtain. For the generations of Wu Fong owners, this activity became a sort of stock-in-trade. The old man, Wu Fong himself, had likened it to the days of the Tong gangs back in China. He had neither encouraged nor obstructed this New World version of gangsters. He'd just learned their games, and in some ways, played them better than they had. That was one reason the restaurant had survived. Soon after opening his business, Wu Fong had hung up a scroll painting of a Chinese farm with a grass-writing motto:

> *In a land where no rice grows, the man with full baskets*
> *is the cold wind biting the beggar's coat.*

During his gambling days, Wu Fong's baskets were full, and for the white men, gambling with the same odds against the wind, that presented a problem. Gambling was a thin vein that ran through all the railroad men and gold miners, and the year he opened, Wu Fong had tried his hand at a bit of back-room gambling behind the restaurant's kitchen. His luck with cards had doubled his income. "Hit good pü-kē-pái," he'd said. "Dä-djïr-pái." But new money does not go unnoticed, especially in places like the Flats. Wu Fong's luck had almost cost him his life. One day the cops had raided a game and not only had destroyed the back room, but most of the restaurant as well. From that point on, Wu Fong confined his card playing to close friends, and when he did not have outside players, he'd used his family. And so it was that Yeung Lee inherited his grandfather's card luck, a skill he'd passed to Tea Rose. And it was Tea Rose who perfected Cora Kay's beginner's luck, and later, Clarence Henry's fool's luck.

"Hoisin play low, win lump money," Tea Rose would tell Cora Kay.

They'd practice on Sunday afternoons, when the restaurant closed at ten to accommodate the sensibilities of their Christian neighbors. At first, Tea Rose would come to Cora Kay's room. Later, when Yeung Lee became more comfortable around Cora Kay, he joined their games. He'd move the cards in a fast shuffle that spread them in an even pattern across the table, like the Chinese fan he'd brought from the old country, the one he'd given to Cora Kay a month after she'd come to work for him. He'd move the cards with the same speed as he moved that machete knife. Between games, he'd offer a trick, closing his eyes and saying, "You think one card. I tell you number written that card." No matter what Cora Kay did, Yeung Lee picked the right card every time.

"We oughta sit in on a real game," Cora Kay told him.

"No, no. I not allowed go play some pü-kē-pái card here."

"We could make some big money," Cora Kay reminded him.

For a moment, his eyes blinked with interest, but he had made his father two promises: He would not gamble, and he would not cut his queue. "Make lump money downstairs," he said, and folded the deck.

"Make lump money downstairs," Tea Rose echoed.

That stubbornness persisted until Tea Rose saw Clarence Henry. In fact, it was Tea Rose who spotted Clarence when he first came in the restaurant. She and her grandmother had a better chance of observing the comings and goings of both the restaurant and the street than Cora Kay did. Kei-Shee, occupying the woman's stool, sat high enough behind the kitchen service window to be in direct line with the front door and the street beyond. If the old woman signalled the approach of the police with, "Um cha hwēi-lai!", Cora Kay would quickly hide the cash box under the bin of fortune cookies, while Tea Rose helped her father open the door for the gamblers to scoot through. All of that was just a simple courtesy. Usually the law was after bigger fish, big-time gamblers like the district boss, John Gionio, who ate at Wu Fong's on a regular basis. The cops really didn't bother to harass the Chinaman, who, after all, was legally forbidden to give testimony in court by reason of a dusty 1800s edict.

"I no Emancipated! Dzēu-chyu!" Yeung Lee would shout when the cops burst through the door. And when the flurry died down, he'd feed them dishes of noodles and rice, and after a decent interval of delay, bow them back to their patrol cars.

But despite the traffic of Gionio and other up-and-coming hoodlums, the regular trade pretty much remained the same, and the service at Wu Fong's was dependable. Yeung Lee's generous bowls of sticky rice, the thin noodles in their broth of chicken feet and ginger, the pungent oxtail stew, or roast duck garnished with turnip roots, broccoli, and the leaves of sweet mustard and dandelion kept folks coming back. But just as Yeung Lee's knife cut-cut on the chopping block, those living above Wu Fong's, including Cora Kay, remained cut off from the world—East or West. And until Clarence Henry showed up, folks took it for granted that Tea Rose would be confined to the back room while Cora Kay waited tables out front.

"What's that Chinaman saying?" the railroad men would ask when

Cora Kay served their food while Tea Rose peeked out at them from the kitchen. "He saying it be alright to have colored women working they butts off whilst he hides his own women in that back room?"

Wu Yeung Lee offered no answers, and neither did Cora Ivory. And in a way, Cora Kay made matters worse by ignoring the men.

"Ah spect Cora inna puttin out fuh the Chinee-man," Lip muttered.

"You just mad cause she ain't putting out for you," Maroon said.

"Ah don need it. Mah woman waitin fuh me at home heah-ah."

"Now Lip, where else that ugly woman gone be?" Whitaker asked.

"Don't be funning at Lip. All of y'all mad cause Cora Kay don't pay none of you no attention," Butler reminded the men.

They nodded. Certainly, all of them had tried to put a hit on Cora Kay at one time or another. Nothing seemed to impress her, and though the men boasted of seeing better looking women, all of them agreed that with her single braid of kinky rust-colored hair, thick ankles, and skin dusted a silk brown tinged with the light of an October's sunset, Cora Kay wasn't exactly an ugly woman. Her long legs and wide hips earned her the nickname, "High Pockets," and the men followed the sway of her ass while she waited tables. But none got close enough to do more than watch. The fact was that like any woman who kept herself a mystery, the men couldn't stay away from Cora Kay. So until Clarence Henry tumbled out of that freight car and got himself a room at the Proctor Hotel, where the unmarried railroad men stayed on their layovers, all they could do was keep a close watch on Cora Kay. They should have watched Tea Rose. Clarence Henry did.

The fate that brought Clarence Henry into Wu Fong's Eatery was as straight as the railroad tracks that brought him into town. Everyone knew railroad men were partial to the Chinaman's because old man Wu Fong had fed their fathers, but they also knew Wu Fong's was one place where it didn't matter if a man was running the road on a job, or running to get away from where he'd been. Clarence Henry was running when he hit town. Butler Sykes spotted Clarence when he and Maroon-Willie were taking a break at the end of a trip. They were standing in the doorway of the train when it slowed down to make the bend where the tracks spread away from the main line on the town side of the hobo camp. Seeing Clarence made Butler elbow Maroon-Willie, and Maroon-Willie inched away from the door to pass the word along so other Brotherhood members could watch out for Clarence once the train was in the yards. That was when Butler swears he saw Cora Kay Ivory romping in a field of wildflowers with somebody wearing a small brocade hat—"a tassel on top like the Chinaman's," Maroon-Willie later offered. Cora Kay and Yeung Lee would have laughed to know the rumors about them were as thick as the egg-drop soup Yeung Lee served at the restaurant every Saturday night, but not everyone trusted what the men claimed they could see from a moving train.

"No, it were sho Cora Kay, and she were a sight," Butler said when the other men questioned him. "Had on one of them long dresses, like the women be wearing when they go to the dances. Cept it was broad daylight, and them weeds and flowers so tall, she couldn't hardly move. And somebody else was with her—though I couldn't rightly tell who."

"Well, I sho caught me a glimpse of something in the field cross from the processing plant. And that Chinaman's car was parked up by a tree over near Hodiman Road," Maroon-Willie added.

"You mean that DeSoto?" Whitaker asked. Butler nodded, but Whitaker shook his head. "Naw, naw . . . can't be."

"Ah heah-ah them Chinee-mans shooes it off like a pistol," Lip said. "Heard that myself," Maroon added. And all the men looked at Yeung Lee with a new bit of understanding glued to their eyes.

Still, Maroon-Willie and Butler had to admit they never had a clear view of whatever was going on in the field, because that was the same moment Butler saw Clarence Henry, limbs thin as a praying mantis', push himself out of a boxcar, and climb the ladder to the roof. Clarence had left that car intent on scrambling across the flatlands toward the town's black section, but when Butler spotted him, slipping two steps ahead of the yard bulls, he'd set Clarence on a straight line into the Black Belt, set him up the way he'd set up other black men who'd fallen off trains looking for work. Of all the railroad men, Butler had more pull than most, not only because his wife, Aleeda Grace, owned the colored funeral home, but also because he was the spokesman for the local Brotherhood Union. Butler's layover hadn't ended before he'd found Clarence a job working from 5:00 A.M. to midnight at the boxer's gym. There, Clarence cleaned up the resin and sweat of would-be prizefighters, white boys who had hopes of knocking the spit out of some black kid who wanted to be a champ like Jack Johnson and Joe Louis. But Clarence wasn't interested in fighting.

"It just be a job," he told Butler and the others when they came back to town that next weekend, and picked him up at the Proctor. "That job do for now, but I got me some plans."

They watched him straighten his square knot, then pull a loose thread into the inside seam of his shirt. It didn't take much for them to figure out where Clarence had bought his duds. On the train, the men hid behind their uniforms the same way Clarence hid behind his mop and stacks of towels at the gym, but when there was a need to get dressed up, almost all of the men who lived in the Flats had bought swank clothes from Hoffmeyer's Pawnshop at one time or another. Those clothes helped them lose the leather-tight grins they'd learned to click into place when they boarded the trains, or shined shoes downtown by the courthouse, or chauffered cars in the Belmont District—or like Clarence, stacked towels at the gym. For Clarence, Florsheim shoes had replaced the beat-up work boots he'd been wearing when the men had found him in the train yards, but his one-button rolled-lapel suit, with peg-legged trousers and jacket nipped at the waist, was, as Butler said, a dollar short and twenty years too late.

"Clarence, my man, peers to me you all dressed up and no one to fuck," Whitaker told him. The other men laughed and pulled themselves taller inside the black tailored pants the railroad bought for them.

But Clarence merely grinned at himself in the peeling mirror of the hotel's chifforobe and said, "Ain't nothing but a little bit for now." Then he smoothed each eyebrow into a velvet arch. "Just you wait and see what this brings me. My hands itching for some cards."

"Well, Slick, you just be sure that itching don't bring you a one-way ride out of town," Butler said.

Clarence kept smiling. "I come in on that train, so I can go out the same way." Then with a hairbrush in each hand, he plastered strands of hair against his skull, his hands moving so rapidly, the brushes crackled against kinky hair as if they were copying the sound of train wheels. The whistle of a southbound train had made Clarence Henry shudder until he was old enough to figure out his worry was just an urging to leave on one of the trains that passed the sharecropper farm his father worked, or closer still to the Louisiana-Arkansas state line, where Clarence finally had jumped a northbound freight after its whistle had roused the urge to move once too often.

"Listen to the man," Maroon-Willie snickered. "He don't know he can leave this town riding in a pine box steada the boxcar."

"And don't think that train gone be waiting for your black butt neither," Butler warned.

"That train wouldn't get nowhere if it wasn't for a colored man named Elijah McCoy," Clarence said.

Lip slapped his knee and hooted. "Thazz right. He the one be invent-ah fuh them steam fits. Call 'em The-Real-Mc-Coy, they do. Then come long them other cullard boys. Them call Winn and Woods, an they make 'em bettah even fore Mc-Coy."

"How you know so much?" Whitaker asked. He was really asking Clarence Henry, but for once, Lip Wooten had answers and he wasn't about to be outdone.

"Ah be readin aftah y'all be talkin," Lip said. "Sa'more cullard boys invent-ah fuh the rail too. Burr an Jackson an Purvis an . . ."

Clarence interrupted him. "Man, I ain't got no time to be standing here whilst you list all them cats. Less you got somebody inventing fast cards, there's a game out there with my name on it. And in case anybody ask, you can tell 'em my name is Lucky. As the song goes, *I guess I'm just a lucky so-and-so*." With that, he strutted out of the room and left them to close the door behind him.

As they headed for Wu Fong's, Whitaker told Butler, "You gone help one poor boy too many one of these days."

"Aw, he ain't doing nothing but blowing off steam," Butler said.

"I don't know," Whitaker muttered. "I seen boys acting half that bad jump up in your face asking for death."

With as much travelling as Whitaker had done on the railroad, he had reason to be suspicious of drifters like Clarence Henry. But who was to say why Kei-Shee never trusted Clarence? Perhaps she remembered San Francisco and the gold miners. Perhaps she remembered the gamblers who frequented the brothel where she had worked off the price of her ticket from China until Yeung Lee's father had brought her to town as his bride. Perhaps. At any rate, she was the one who overheard Tea Rose mutter, "Shēn-yan-sē-dē." So Kei-Shee turned to see just what patch of black skin had caught her granddaughter's eye, and made her lose all of her senses by speaking without permission.

Kei-Shee, who had been both teacher and mother to Tea Rose, was worried about her granddaughter's future. Not long before Clarence Henry arrived, Kei-Shee had tried talking to Yeung Lee. Len Poo Yen, the laundryman's son, had been killed two years before in the invasion of Normandy, and only the month before, Kei-Shee had urged Yeung Lee to put more money aside for a trip to China, or at least to the West Coast where young Chinese bachelors dreamed of finding a bride who already lived in the land of the Gold Mountain. Kei-Shee sensed the problems of finding a suitable husband for Tea Rose any place near the Strip, and the minute she saw Clarence Henry, she muttered, "Hēi-fon Kwei!" with such a vengeance, Cora Kay almost dropped the stack of dirty dishes she was putting on the counter.

For once, Cora Kay gave all of her attention to the restaurant. When she turned around, she saw several of the men from the cattle yards, high on their weekly pay and eating as much as they could before they had the rest boxed up as take-home for the family. She knew Kei-Shee would not have used them to mutter an oath about "foreign-black-devils." The old woman called working men, "Häu-kàn rēn,"—good-look-men. Cora Kay saw them sitting near Sister Garrison and Doc Pritchard's wife, who were downing their usual Saturday night helping of shrimp fried rice. She was sick of throwing Christian pamphlets in the trash after they left, but it would be too much to hope the old woman was referring to them as "foreign devils." Other than one or two kids picking up take-out for their mamas, she only saw Maroon-Willie, Whitaker, and the usual crew of railroad men fitting themselves in a booth. True, they were loud and would try to cheat her every chance they got, but Butler Sykes' wife let the Chinese use her funeral home if one of them died, and none of the other men would have made the old woman spit out the words, "black devil." Then Cora Kay saw Clarence Henry—"six shades blacker than night," her mother would have said. When she turned back to Tea Rose, she knew by the look in the girl's eyes that she'd spotted Kei-Shee's "Hēi-fon Kwei."

At first nothing set Clarence apart from the others except his old-style pin-striped suit, its slightly musty odors marking its pawnshop origins. But mothballs could not compete with half a night's work already weaving the smell of onions and soy sauce into her clothes and hair, so Cora Kay had to look for some other sign. Clarence was a bit thin for her taste, his face a little too broad and his eyes somewhat shifty, but when he smiled, the chip in his front tooth made him look young and old at the same time. It also made Cora Kay remember a time when she was a little girl, before WWII, and a man who used to visit her mother. He had given her candies, and promised her a trip to the circus when he came back that next spring. But the war had started, and he'd never returned. Still, she recalled his laughter and how he'd told her he'd broken his tooth riding in a rodeo in some town out in Oklahoma where all the folks were black.

"Don't be telling that chile all that devilment," her mother had said. "Whoever heard of such a thing? A town with no white folks in it and all the black ones riding horses like in them cowboy movies."

But the man had insisted there was such a town, and he'd gone off to find it, taking with him the devilment in his smile.

Cora Kay leaned across the service counter to signal Tea Rose, and once again, Kei-Shee muttered, "Hēi-fon Kwei!"

"Shut up, snaggle-tooth. I ain't studying bout you," Cora Kay told her. But she kept her voice low in case Yeung Lee looked up from his chores of splitting celery root or cracking a duck's back with one stroke of his knife. "Why you always got to be flapping your lips?" Cora Kay hissed at the old woman. "Why you always got to be taking a look-see at what I do? Look-see, djäu. Humph! You think I'm seeing something? Think I'm looking at something to talk about?"

Then, satisfied that she'd given Tea Rose as many clues as she dared, Cora Kay started to worm her way between tables and booths, ignoring customers who signalled her as she aimed for Clarence Henry. Kei-Shee grumbled as she watched Cora Kay's progress, and had it not been for the old woman's mutterings, Yeung Lee would not have looked up from his chopping block. When he saw his daughter was also staring at something in the front of the restaurant, Yeung Lee went to the service window. And that was how, in the early spring of 1946, trouble came between Clarence Henry and Wu Yeung Lee. To his credit, that trouble was not all Clarence's fault, despite what anyone in the Flats might say. With Tea Rose's help, he unknowingly took a roundabout way of raising the Chinaman's hackles.

Clarence had made the right call when he claimed to be a lucky so-and-so. By the time Yeung Lee came to the service window, Clarence had started talking to Cora Kay, who was standing in the aisle. He'd had to turn around to talk to her, and in turning, saw Tea Rose staring at him, her round face perfect in its moon-shaped wonder. Of course, he also saw Yeung Lee—it was hard to miss the big Chinaman—but Clarence Henry believed in his luck, so he'd continued to stare at Tea Rose. It didn't take Yeung Lee long to discover the target of his daughter's admiring glances was the same beaming black face that held Cora Kay's attention. It was doubtful whether Yeung Lee tried dividing his anger equally between Cora Kay and Tea Rose, or whether he was aware of how tightly he gripped the knife's handle, or that he'd begun to shift his weight so his next step would lead him out of the kitchen. But none of it mattered, because at that moment, Clarence's luck held true. Just as Yeung Lee reached the kitchen door, machete in hand, the police burst through the front door on one of their routine raids of joints along the Strip.

The regular customers had practice at timing their scramble, but without knowing where the rear exit was, Clarence tried running toward the front door. Immediately he was turned back by the onslaught of cops. At one point, Maroon-Willie tried to reach him, but Clarence vaulted across tables to the other side of the restaurant. There the church ladies beat him back with their purses, and the cops would have tagged him if Tea Rose hadn't snatched him into the kitchen. Yeung Lee already had the pantry door open, but Tea Rose took Clarence through the alley to the storage shed, where she locked him in as tightly as her father had locked in the burlap-covered bales of rice and tea freight trains brought him from the West Coast.

And while her father cleared the air—shouting: "Here not allowed Tong! Here not allowed suckee yä-pyän! Not allowed card men! Here belong only honest man!"—Tea Rose let the confusion help folks forget she'd neatly placed Clarence Henry in the storage shed. The whole business might have gone unnoticed if Yeung Lee hadn't been suspicious already. But he was, and long after the cops had left, he watched the two girls. So it was much later, after the Eatery had closed and Yeung Lee and his mother were snoring in unison, that Tea Rose was able to release Clarence from the storage shed.

"Where you going?" Cora Kay whispered. Tea Rose was at the end of the hall when she stopped her. "Make water," Tea Rose said, as if Cora Kay suddenly couldn't remember they were forced to use chamber pots at night like almost all of the folks in the Flats.

"What brand of truth you giving me?" Cora Kay asked. Tea Rose's eyes were like a night breeze flowing past her, a splinter of light caught in the cinders of coal piled at the edge of shantytown. "What you up to, girl?"

Tea Rose said, "I make someone belong-safe when cops come chyu-djēu."

For once, Cora Kay was impatient with the spider web of Chinese woven into English. "Where is he?" she hissed. "Where is he?"

Tea Rose bowed her head and moved away in what Cora Kay called her cockroach steps. Still, Cora had to walk fast to keep up with the girl, and Tea Rose, in her usual determination, never looked around to see how far away Cora Kay was.

When Tea Rose opened the shed, Clarence was a deeper shadow huddled in a corner and sleeping as if darkness were a solution to his problems. Tea Rose waited until Cora Kay closed the door before she lit the lantern, then they both watched Clarence rub sleep from his eyes. For a moment, the three of them inspected each other. Tea Rose drank in images of Clarence as if he were a vision she'd seen those nights when she'd escaped to the roof where, if she looked at it long enough, the sky's darkness seemed as thick as flesh. And Cora Kay stretched out toward something her mother told her about how a man smells when he awakens—the softness in back of his neck, the pillow of his shoulder. She fought to see Clarence for what he was—his razor-boned frame too loose and slippery to stay in one place. What Clarence saw was Cora Kay's skin under its red-brown covering—not just the patch of cinnamon the railroad men had dreamed when she served their food off her hip in the same way some women carried babies, or what made Yeung Lee remember a tapestry where dragon fire licked the edges of the ocean. But no vision pleased Clarence more than Tea Rose. Her hair, purple-black, softened and darkened a face so pale, he'd seen her clearly even before she'd held up the lantern. Whatever Clarence saw in her face made him shudder as much as a train's mournful whistle had. And those eyes, their lashes brushing down just before he could discover the secret they held. Already he was touching her—the sweet skin behind her knees, the small of her back, the inside of her thighs where the rush of smells would fill his head and leave him drowning.

"You gone get us killed," Cora Kay said to both of them. "Yeung Lee gone come out here and chop us all to little pieces the way he chops up them ducks. Y'all must be crazy. I'm outta here." She moved toward the door, but Tea Rose stayed where she was. "You hear me, girl?" Cora Kay asked her. "Your daddy don't play. Specially with the likes of that," she added, nodding toward Clarence Henry.

But Tea Rose was well past reason. "What name you call?" she asked Clarence. "What place you live? What place belong your wife?"

As Cora Kay left the shed, she rightly assumed she had trouble on her hands.

It wasn't long before Tea Rose and Clarence were meeting in secret on a regular basis. In fact, the two of them were at ease with the mess they were creating. As long as Tea Rose knew when Clarence was going to meet her, she easily assumed her expressionless pose behind the service window. Cora Kay, on the other hand, had to act as if Clarence were a piece of woodwork when he came into Wu Fong's with the railroad men.

"Well Slick, she sho got your number fast," Whitaker told Clarence when Cora Kay barely stayed long enough to finish taking their order.

"Um-hum," Maroon-Willie added. "Come on strong the first time she seen you, now turning you cold as a tombstone."

"Hey, y'all know this cat's the best thing she seen since Wonder Bread," Butler laughed.

"Yeah, the butt enda bread," Lip said.

The others laughed, but Clarence said nothing. Like Cora Kay, he was relieved that the jokes reached Yeung Lee. After a while, the Chinaman stopped staring at him each time he came into the restaurant, so Clarence figured he was home free. But he didn't have to make excuses for the noises Yeung Lee heard drifting into the upstairs windows long after closing hours, when being with Cora Kay made his eyes glint black as the stones at the bottom of the creek. When Yeung Lee heard laughter, Cora Kay would hold him closer and say, "It's them foxes. They useta come right up to the door when I lived in shantytown." And when the shed door creaked against a rock Tea Rose hadn't kicked out of its path, Cora Kay would say, "It's them trains. Must be breaking in a new yard crew. Some ain't good for nothing."

After a while, Cora Kay began to look more strained than Tea Rose. Yeung Lee told her, "I no send you for flower-pick. You tired out work maybe."

"We need some place not for work," Tea Rose said. And after she'd gained her father's permission to return to the meadow, she told Clarence almost the same thing.

"We need some place invite me, huh?"

Cora Kay moved away from them. It wasn't that she wanted to leave them alone, but she simply did not want to hear Clarence's answer. More than once, they'd said too much around her. And once, when they'd been in the meadow, she'd seen them sink into the tall grass. She'd wandered away to look at the shadows of Indian Hills, visible on the horizon some thirty miles south of town and tinted pink by the sun, like the clumps of pale agates she used to find at the edge of Cobbler's Creek. The creek was like a bright silver guardrail guiding the way toward the valley. She'd searched the valley for a while, then turned back to where she'd last seen Clarence and Tea Rose. At first, the meadow had seemed empty. Then she'd spotted a slight depression in the grass. And with her hand shielding her eyes, she could see the two of them pillowed by wood violets and chicory bending under the weight of their bodies. A sparrow rustled the branches of a sycamore, and the flash of light was trapped in the movement of Tea Rose's arm curling toward Clarence Henry. If the wind blew just right, the grass spread back to its raw side and Cora Kay could clearly see them both: the smooth slant of Clarence Henry's back, humped marble-black like the rocks the railroad had used to shore up the trestle, and Tea Rose's legs, bent in that crooked way women assumed when they opened their bodies for birth or love. And the two of them moving, pulsing like snakes, or the very grass itself, flower petals falling in the wake of a breeze.

It wasn't as if the sight surprised Cora Kay—she'd witnessed more than that in shantytown—but the wonder of watching Tea Rose open herself to Clarence kept Cora Kay fixed on the scene. Later, she wished she'd had the sense to turn away, because it was at that point that, somehow, Cora Kay began to feel responsible for the conspiracy that hummed between those two. And it didn't take long for her part in the act to come due.

"Hoisin, you make card men say yes for lump money game?" Tea Rose asked her. "Henry C. good card man," she said, reversing his name, Chinese fashion.

"Humph. Good for nothing," Cora Kay snorted.

"No. Make lump money. Big game when Fù-chin fall-sleeping."

"Your daddy don't sleep that sound, and the onliest thing Clarence gone buy you is a space in the graveyard," Cora Kay told her.

But in the end, she found herself setting up the game. *"I'm running a fool,"* she told herself, but she'd seen Clarence Henry double-shuffle cards, his long fingers tapered like ribbons, so graceful, they seemed to flow into the act until cards and hands moved as one. Clarence had told them more than one story of how some redneck card player had been tempted to break those fingers just to erase their image from his memory. Cora Kay had to admit Clarence could move cards almost as well as Yeung Lee, but she still had her doubts about setting him up with the big-time gambling men.

"Takes more than the nerve of a brass monkey to shine in that game," Cora Kay told Clarence.

"Do I look like I'm short on nerve?" Clarence asked. "Besides, what I don't know, my woman know."

Cora Kay eyes went from Clarence to Tea Rose. Tea Rose grinned. "Man, I think you musta hit your head when you fell off that train," Cora Kay said. "You think they gone let some Chinawoman come to a game with you?"

"Um-hum. And be glad for the gamble," Clarence laughed. Moving from the South to the North had been his biggest gamble, so a city game seemed like a piece of cake. His instinct always told him when to push for a bet and when to fold. Now it told him to bet. "You just tell 'em Tea Rose is ready. Can't be my doing, else they back off. You just pass the word at Wu Fong's."

"Hoisin, I have shing-yün, much luck. We make lump money," Tea Rose said. "Invite you come big house."

"Not me," Cora Kay said. "I ain't going nowhere. Not to that game or some house you think you gone get. I'll do this and no more."

So the next time Cora Kay served the table of railroad men, she let Tea Rose's little firecracker drop. Clarence Henry's luck seemed to be spreading itself around, because not only were the railroaders there, but John Gionio and a few big-time gamblers were in the next booth. Cora Kay said it loud enough for both groups to listen. For a second, all conversation came to a halt.

"Maybe y'all didn't hear me right," she said. "Maybe I oughta be serving you them fortune cookies early."

Gionio bathed her in one of his dog's-head grins. "If there's some other gentlemen interested, then you can bring us a couple dozen thousand-year-old eggs. They gonna need that much luck."

Cora Kay looked at the booth full of railroad men. Clarence didn't signal until Butler and Whitaker nodded. Maroon shrugged, but Lip looked confused, so Cora Kay figured he wasn't coming. No matter. She already had enough players. "Thousand-year-old-eggs," she said, as if she were writing down a regular order. "I guess we can get 'em to you a little after midnight."

"But you make sure that Chinawoman washes the grease off the money fore she hands it over," Gionio said, then patted Cora Kay's hip as if he were stroking a horse's flank.

Cora Kay smacked him with her pencil, and the sound of the wood whacking across Gionio's knuckles was almost as sharp as the crack of Yeung Lee's machete on his chopping block.

Gionio laughed and leaned away from the booth to catch Butler's eye. "I'll take that broad for my table," he said.

"You take what you get," Clarence snapped.

Butler hunched Clarence. "Don't pay no tention to him, Mr. Gionio. He just selling buffalo chips."

Later, Butler had a few choice words for Clarence. They had left the restaurant and were walking toward the funeral parlor where Clarence and the others would help Butler set up the gaming table.

"Man, why you want to front-off somebody?" Butler asked Clarence. "Ain't you got no better sense than to rile that white man? Watch your mouth. You asking for trouble."

"Trouble be my name, asking be my game," Clarence said.

"Well, Sporting Life, you best be asking for the right cards tonight," Whitaker told him. Maroon said, "Um-hum," wagging his head.

But Clarence just threw back his head and laughed, showing a row of sharp, even teeth. Whitaker sighed. Like most black folks born in Dixie, he remembered how death could as easily knock at his door in the form of a posse as it could creep up behind someone caught in the wrong place by accident of forgetfulness. All night, Whitaker was afraid he'd be caught in Clarence's accident of forgetfulness, so he kept his eyes peeled for trouble.

Trouble didn't come until late in the game. By all rights, Clarence and Tea Rose should have bought themselves out of the play at least an hour before Gionio started chomping on his losing streak. Perhaps it was knowing the pile of winnings in front of them meant they'd passed the point of no return, or perhaps it was the thick air that left them groggy and overconfident. Certainly the back room of the funeral parlor carried that smell peculiar to any house of the dead. As night crept toward dawn, the scent grew heavier—even with the blue smoke of tobacco and whiskey fumes, even with the card players' body odors in a neighborhood where the usual odors rising from cattle pens could reduce folks to lizards scurrying for a place among the rocks, and spitting words at each other when they couldn't find their real targets. Gionio was losing, and he needed a target.

"Leda got some fresh blood in here?" Gionio asked Butler.

"I don't be asking my wife who she burying," Butler said.

Gionio looked at the cards in his hand. "Whatever she's burying turned rancid fore it died." He looked around for a response.

Everyone intently studied their cards. Whitaker worried the end of a cigar, and Butler rubbed the stubble of his beard, while the dealer, Hugh Spalding, Gionio's cut-buddy who controlled the city's water rights, sliced his forehead into a frown that was deep enough to fold skin over skin. Only Clarence seemed at ease—Clarence and Tea Rose who was sitting right behind him. Tea Rose was wearing flowers in her hair, and each time she leaned forward to gaze at Clarence's hand, the petals quivered. Tea Rose's usual grease-stained smock had been replaced by a shantung dress, slit up both sides and so tight, it seemed to dance across her hips of its own accord, music or not. Gionio tried to imagine her naked and spread under him. When she leaned forward, and coached Clarence to ask for three cards, Gionio heard her whispered signal of "Yău-săn-gē," as "Y'all singing." Tea Rose felt him staring and looked up. Gionio could only see half of her eyes under their slanted lids. He didn't like anything hidden, especially something Chinese.

"Maybe we oughta tell Leda to get another coffin ready," he said. "Something's turning rotten sure as I'm sitting here."

Nobody responded. Hugh dealt against each player's discard. Butler called and raised the ante. Everyone threw in money, except Maroon and Whitaker, who folded. The play should have gone smoothly, Clarence hadn't been listening to Gionio's lament. Although Whitaker said, "Take it easy, man," Clarence raised the bet again before he called in the hand. Butler shook his head, Hugh folded, and Maroon-Willie looked around the room as if he were searching for a pool of water to throw himself into. That left Gionio and Clarence in a face-off. Like the motto on Wu Fong's grass-writing scroll, Gionio's look was colder than a wind biting a beggar's coat.

He said, "Lay them cards out careful, boy."

"Any way you want 'em," Clarence said. "Read 'em and weep."

Gionio pushed back from the table. "I don't weep for no niggers. And don't think you gone get rich off me, boy. I'll be here when they done buried your black ass six feet under in a pauper's grave."

It's anyone's guess as to whether John Gionio ever looked at Clarence Henry's winning hand. It would be a shame to think that big-dog spread of aces high, nine low mixed suit went unnoticed, but none of the players had time to attend to cards right at that moment, because Gionio came up from the chair with his gun drawn. The table spilled onto Hugh's lap, and Maroon raced Whitaker to the floor. It was probably Butler's alarmed cry of "John!" that stopped Gionio, who wasn't averse to killing, but had long since hired others to do his dirty work. So he looked at his gun. For Clarence, that hesitancy was another bit of luck. He and Tea Rose wasted no time leaving the room. One scoop, and the money was in his hat. Two steps, and Tea Rose snatched him through the door. Three steps, and before Butler could finish saying, "Ga'damn black mothah . . ." they were in the alley.

As Clarence well knew, running was an art only survivors lived long enough to brag about. Between his knowledge of the streets, and Tea Rose's history of clearing the restaurant during a raid, they were halfway to Wu Fong's before Gionio could call his boys. But both of them knew how small they'd carved that lead. They needed help. Tea Rose sprinkled Cora Kay's window with pebbles four times before Cora Kay lifted the sash. When she saw Tea Rose's panicky look, and the hatful of money Clarence was showing her, Cora grabbed her clothes and sneaked past Yeung Lee. By the time she reached the back door, by the time they told her Gionio was following them, she knew they would get nowhere on foot. And Yeung Lee's DeSoto was so conveniently parked by the storage shed.

Clarence's years of running had not put him in a place where he could have learned to drive, but once behind the wheel of the car, he had no recourse but to pretend he knew how. It had seemed so easy when he'd watched other men doing it. He fiddled with the gears, and keeping both feet on brake and clutch, waited for something to happen. Cora Kay stared at him as if he'd ordered some odd combination of food, like sweet-and-sour ribs sprinkled with fried shrimp. She tried to be patient. "Put it in gear, Clarence. Move your feet, man."

By some accident, Clarence popped the clutch and stomped the accelerator. The DeSoto lurched forward, stopped, lurched, stopped.

"Hit that stick again," Cora Kay said.

He snatched it back and the gears screamed so loudly, Tea Rose slid to the floor, certain her father would wake up right at that moment and find them. She needn't have worried. Yeung Lee didn't wake up until Clarence had ground the gears for the third time, and Yeung Lee didn't reach the window until the car had rolled into the Mission Road intersection. They might have heard him shouting if Clarence hadn't been shoving the gears again. Cora Kay leaned over to see what his feet were doing. Her head was so close to his crotch, Clarence almost unravelled. He slammed his foot against the accelerator once more, then, in an effort to hide his rapidly growing erection, lifted his leg from the clutch, and the car shot across the intersection as if it had been blown from one of the cannons circus stuntmen used to propel a body into the air. That move slammed Cora Kay into the dash, and nearly took off the top of her head. She moaned and sat up. The bundle of sage Yeung Lee had hung from the rearview mirror quivered.

Cora Kay managed to say, "Jesus, you bout killed me."

And Tea Rose shouted, "Hwēi-lai! Hwēi-chyu!" Those were the first words she'd spoken since they'd climbed into the DeSoto.

"What she saying?" Clarence asked.

"She saying: 'Go back,' Cora Kay told him.

"I got to get turned around," Clarence said. But the car hit the first set of train tracks, and galloped from track to track before it died midway the inbound line. Clarence yelled, "Shit!", but he had definitely passed the danger of his erection. Now he was sweating. He tried the motor again. The DeSoto protested. Tea Rose bounced up and down as if her backseat action would start the engine. Cora Kay wanted to wallop the girl.

"Why the hell am I here?" Cora Kay said to no one in particular.

She could smell the whiffs of sweet-sour cow manure, and the moldy yeast of grain elevators and old warehouses. On the other side of the tracks, she saw the beginning of the narrow streets that lead to shanty town where the road curved downhill toward the back side of the train yards. This wasn't her idea of coming home again, but then, none of it had ever been her idea. She turned to say something to this effect to Clarence when lights reflected in the back window caught her eye. Cora Kay blinked. There were all sorts of visions she might have imagined seeing, but none of them involved Yeung Lee waving his machete, and running down the road in front of several oncoming cars, motors churning on a low growl.

Clarence moaned. Tea Rose yelled, "Fù-chin! Fù-chin!" as if none of them could have recognized her father.

"Shit! And Gionio behind him! That does it!" Cora Kay shouted. "That's it! You see what y'all done done? First the car, then them damn gamblers chasing you. Now you got Yeung Lee ready to kill us. What else could . . ." she began. And as if it had been waiting for that question, an inbound train's whistle screamed twice.

Clarence yelled, "Shit fucka-roony!" and leaped out of the seat. Where his feet had clumsily sought brake pedal and clutch, they easily found ground level and headed up the tracks without missing a step.

Cora Kay screamed and pulled at the door latch. For want of an quick escape route, Tea Rose merely screamed, a long protracted sound like nails scratching glass, a sound that bypassed all of her language problems. Once more, a train answered, this one on the outbound track. Now, all of them abandoned the car. Cora Kay panted and looked both ways. Town was out of the question, and going up the tracks would merely put her in the station. Clarence had already doubled back, and was diving into the car to retrieve his hatful of money. "Leave the damn money!" Cora Kay shouted. But he stuffed some in his pockets, then

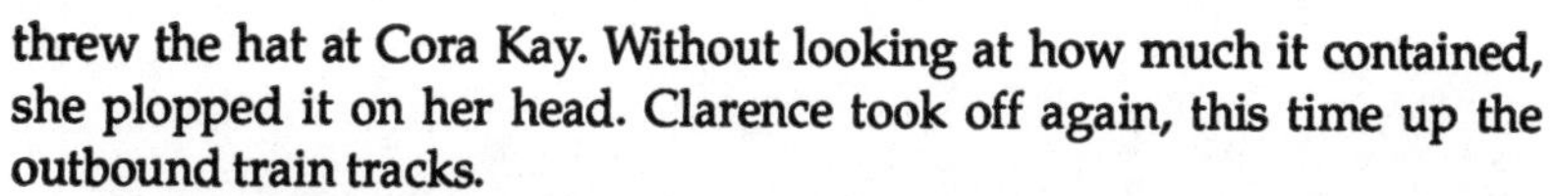

threw the hat at Cora Kay. Without looking at how much it contained, she plopped it on her head. Clarence took off again, this time up the outbound train tracks.

Cora Kay turned to Tea Rose. "Com'on!" she yelled, trying to grab the girl to get her moving. "This way!" Cora Kay shouted. And she heard Yeung Lee shout something too. He was closer, close enough for her to see his queue streaming, like the tail of a stallion in full flight from the headlights of the cars behind him. And his machete blade picked up the glare of the car lights. He yelled again. This time, Cora Kay clearly heard him shout, "Dji-nyü!" She vaguely wondered just who he was calling a whore, but the approaching train whistles told her it didn't matter. The cars behind Yeung Lee added their horns to the noise. Cora Kay snatched at Tea Rose again. "Move it!" she yelled, and started running. Out of the corner of her eye, she saw Clarence had turned back one more time. Tea Rose was already running toward him when Cora Kay hurled herself into the row of jimson weed, skunk cabbage, and foxglove growing at the edge of the tracks.

Cora Kay cut diagonally across the tracks and slipped into the underbrush separating the railroad yards from shantytown. The ground was wet and she slid down the embankment, past someone's outhouse. Behind her, the shouts of men grew louder, and the trains were rumbling nearer. When she entered a rut between the shanties, she heard gunshots, then a long crunch as first one train, then the other, chewed Yeung Lee's DeSoto. Cora Kay's headlong plunge took her right into the arms of Sister Vernida Garrison and her little band of Ladies' Aid volunteers finishing their nightly shantytown mission. Sister Garrison didn't know whether it was man or woman falling into her arms—the hat askew on a hard, lumpy head, the face covered with stinking mud, and the dusty prickles of poisonous plants clinging to the arms that enfolded her.

"Lord help me! I been kissed by the evil eye," she screamed.

Folks say Vernida Garrison was never quite the same after Cora Kay Ivory plowed into her that night. Certainly Yeung Lee was never the same. Only the food was dependable—and Yeung Lee's anger as his machete sliced the air, and he muttered about the black-foreign-devil who wrecked his car and took his love away from him. Folks who ate at the Chinaman's waited to see if Tea Rose and that badass Clarence Henry ever returned to the Flats. Like Yeung Lee, they were disappointed. No one saw Tea Rose after that night, but folks on the Strip frequented Cinnamon's Bar, and if they were real nice she'd speak a few words of Chinese while she poured their drinks.

Amazing Grace and Floating Opportunity

IN THE LATE MORNING SUN streaming through the upstairs windows of the Home of Perpetual Rest, Aleeda Grace Sykes was oiling her body. On the outside wall of the building, a mural depicted a Black Jesus blessing the children, the hills above Him partially hiding the second floor windows in dark green shadows. The mural distracted anyone's attention from the windows, but inside the house, Aleeda Grace had a clear view of the world.

It was one of her pleasures, standing there in the eye of Christ, so to speak, while her kingdom stretched out below her across the flatlands to the railroad yard and south toward the city center. There, the skyline was unbroken except for three ugly red-brick apartment buildings the city referred to as Public Housing Projects. In Aleeda's eyes, those buildings were no more than high-rise versions of mortuary trays, little cubicles waiting to be filled with poor black folks. After the first three were built, her husband, Butler, had warned her of the impending doom. Before the Projects were started, everything had been simple. Butler, with seniority on the Sunset Limited, was a member in good standing in the Brotherhood of Sleeping Car Porters and the Youngfellow Festival Singers, and she was owner of the Home of Perpetual Rest, a matron in the Ladies of the Morning Star. Now the foundations for three more buildings were in place, and surveyors were standing on their doorstep, flagging the very ground that held the funeral parlor. Aleeda was beginning to think there was no escape. Except for those who had managed to buy houses on

Cottage Grove near the uptown end of the Flats, most folks had lived and died in the wooden houses and tarpaper shacks of the flatlands. But like the new folks moving into the Projects, Aleeda Grace stood a good chance of being stuck forever in the Flats.

Everywhere she looked, there was some reminder of the Projects, especially mornings when trucks ground their way past the Home to the building site. That rumbling sounded so much like the noise of the freight trains, it set her to thinking about her husband and his job on the railroad. The Projects now stood between her place and the train yards, but over the years, she'd imagined that, if the light was right, Butler could look back and catch the sun glinting off the cross fixed to the roof of the funeral parlor. She hoped that cross had comforted Butler as much as hearing the long pull of an approaching train's whistle allowed her a moment's peace from worrying about where those trains might have carried him, and what he'd had to do while he was away. And she hoped his last shift had been easy enough to let her tell him what she had to tell him when he returned.

Aleeda Grace filled her palm with a mixture of mineral oil and jasmine, and slowly, as if each inch of skin represented the distance from her bedroom window to some spot on the horizon, began to rub the oil in place. Her body was sable brown, dark as an afternoon shadow under a palm tree, or the mud clay that lined caves men had plumbed for precious stones. For a moment, she let the morning sun warm her skin and listened to the radio gospel choir singing, *"Jesus is the light of this world"* against a clatter-bang of dishes as her second daughter, Viola, cleared the breakfast table. Judging by the aroma of the stew pot mingled with the last of the breakfast odors, Viola had already started dinner. More than that, she had set up a canopy of smells to cover the ever-present scents of formaldehyde and chloride from the embalming room. Aleeda had taught her daughter well, but covering odors was a small price to pay for a successful business.

As the pitch and swell of noises from the first floor rooms reached her, Aleeda shook her head and sprinkled a few extra drops of jasmine into her hand. Then she pulled the palmfull of oil from her left breast to her fingertips and out toward the center of town where John Gionio, the district straw boss, was having his morning coffee. Aleeda rubbed and kneaded her skin, spreading the oil down the length of her arm, fingers flexed in anticipation. Another palmfull and she turned her attention to the other arm and north, where Vinnie Loemann's junkyard rested in the pale light of morning, his black Cadillac the only piece of gleaming metal in that mass of rusty pipes, broken machine parts, and rotting tires. She looked past the thundering whine of construction equipment toward Vinnie's place, and frowned. She could imagine any number of locations more pleasant than Vinnie's as a boundary for the colored district. But if she'd drawn a line from her right shoulder to Vinnie's, and another line from her left shoulder to Gionio, she would have sketched in the north and south boundaries of the Clayton District, that wedge of the flatlands splitting the city by color: black folks on one side of the line, whites on the other.

Aleeda grunted and began oiling her back. That gesture prompted a change in the direction of her thoughts. Behind her, the outermost boundaries of the Clayton District ended with the intersection of Mission and Kingshighway, where the trolley line was finally being extended into the Flats, and crews were widening the narrow roads into full-fledged streets. Eventually, those streets would rise up to meet Indian Hills and the Belmont District, where the white folks lived, and where Aleeda Grace Sykes had her heart set on moving. A real house in Belmont with a yard so neat, it looked like it had been painted in a coloring book. That, and the funeral home in the Flats—that was her dream. "You don't wash your feet in the same water you drink," she'd tell Butler. Still, she knew the color line had been impenetrable. There wasn't a black person living in an American city in the middle of the twentieth-century who did not know that. This line was no child's game of "one-potato, two-potato," "step-on-a-crack," and "ollie-ollie-oxen-free." This line was an invisible barrier that no one in the Clayton District had thought about crossing, at least, not yet. Aleeda Grace had it in her mind to do something about that.

"You want some more coffee, Mu'dear?"

Viola was at the door, breathing shallow in a way that did not allow Aleeda Grace to know how long she'd been standing there. Aleeda stifled an impulse to cover her nakedness. It wasn't a question of modesty—both Viola and her other daughter, Dora Emma, had begun to assist in readying bodies for viewing almost as soon as they could walk—it was simply a matter of not being properly dressed. Viewing bodies was one thing. But viewing their mother was another situation altogether. And Vi was well aware of that.

Without turning away from her daughter, Aleeda said, "Hand me that velvet robe over there."

As the girl hurried toward the bed, Aleeda plucked up a linen towel off the chaise lounge and began wiping oil from her hands, all the while staring at her daughter. Like the rest of the Sykes women, Viola had inherited Butler's height as well as Aleeda Grace's width. Aleeda watched her bending to pick up the robe, her small waist pulled into the swell of her hips until the plain black dress seemed to strain against the curve of her body. She wondered if her child had gained weight, then spent an idle moment measuring her for a coffin. After more than two decades in the business, the thought really did come to her subconsciously, but she tried to reject it as quickly as it had appeared. Up to this point, she'd buried four family members: her parents, her brother, Albert, and her year-old son, Butler, Jr. Four were enough.

When Viola offered her the robe, Aleeda let her stand there for a moment, the garment falling in soft folds from her awkwardly extended arms. Aleeda carefully cleaned the oil from each finger as if she were putting on gloves. During the whole ritual, she never changed her expression, and finally, the directness of her look caused Viola to lower her eyes. Aleeda smiled at her daughter's discomfort but did nothing to ease it. She knew Vi's abrupt appearance in the doorway was her own way of needling her. She remembered how Viola and Dora Emma were always cooking up a game of "pray-for-the-dead" with the neighbor kids, a game that became especially loud when they knew she was at the desk near her office window. And Viola had always been the one buried under leaves, the others kneeling beside her, chanting, *"Pray for the dead, pray for the dead, and the dead will pray for you."* It had been a stupid game, made up to tease folks who were superstitious about raising children in a funeral home, but each time Vi exploded from her grave of leaves to tag one of the others as "It," Aleeda was reminded of how John Gionio and Vinnie Loemann had tagged her when she'd tried to play dead.

Finally she accepted the robe from Viola's outstretched hands, and said, "You can take that coffee back downstairs. I got no time for a second cup. Anybody call?"

"Just two," Viola answered as she gathered the coffee service onto a silver tray. "Dora Emma. And Mistah Loemann . . ."

Aleeda grunted. "Humph . . . MIStah Loemann can wait."

Viola took silent note of which phone call her mother had singled out. She wondered how long it would take her mother to forgive her sister for moving to St. Charles county, or better yet, for screaming insults about the funeral home on her way out the door. *"Could at least say her name,"* Viola thought. *"Ain't like she's dead."* Still she knew her mother's stubbornness could bury the living as quickly as she buried the dead.

Watching Aleeda Grace finish dressing, Viola remembered the countless times they had received bodies so brutalized in their passage toward death, no one had believed the casket could be opened for viewing. She had watched Aleeda work her miracles of special formulae and makeup combinations that white morticians would not have tried even if they had been forced to bury Negroes.

"Colored folks just takes a little while longer," Aleeda had told her daughter. "They skin is special. Runs the range clear from coal black to whatever degree of white they got in they blood, and all them browns and reds and yellahs in between. So you got to mix things just right. Too much zinc, and the body turn black and hard like some piece of tree stump what's been petrified in the sun. And if you don't stir in that 'maldehyde and alcohol just so, they turn all ashy-dry like a dirt floor. You got to be careful, cause folks want to know it's they relatives they be looking at, not some chewed up piece of something look like it ain't never been human."

At those times, Viola had regarded her mother with awe, a feeling that both pleased her and frightened her into believing she could never live up to Aleeda Grace's expectations. That fear was the cloak of her mother's life, the winding cloth every mother passes to her daughter as surely as she delivers of herself a body patterned after her own. And in Viola's case, that cloth had been twisted tight by the institution of slavery and the racism that accompanied it. What black women passed to their daughters was a sense of survival that was both outrageous and cautious, one that kept them in the middle of life yet removed from it, lest they become consumed by its cruelties. In a way, that kind of control explained Aleeda Grace's adjustment to the undertaker business. But that control had escaped Viola's sister, Dora Emma, who had fled the house thinking that if she stayed, she would inherit her mother's way of looking at death as something that must be attended to by the living. Viola had stayed, and though she was no match for her mother, she was as stubborn as Aleeda Grace had ever been. She knew she had taken from her mother something more than color of skin, or hair, or vagina, breasts and belly, but she did not have a word to put on whatever else had been passed to her. That was still waiting somewhere, close by.

Viola said, "Mu'dear, I fed the fish and dusted up round the fountain. I got the card tables stacked up and the chairs put away. But I need to label them jars in the back room and get the crates set out. You want to see 'em?"

Viola pulled a bundle of apothecary labels from her pocket. Aleeda could see her precise schoolgirl scroll, the *l*'s and *r*'s looped and arched in a perfect symmetry of names: mercuric chloride, alum, potash nitrate, alcohol. It was as close as Viola could come to hinting at the need to begin packing. She chewed the inside of her lip and waited for her mother to answer.

In the pale light of that velvet-cushioned bedroom, Aleeda studied her daughter's face. "Stop gnawing on your mouth," she told her.

"That's a bad habit. And don't be rushing me. Ain't no need of being in an all-fired hurry to get the moving started. The sand ain't settled in the bottom of the glass just yet. I still got time to do me some talking."

"I'm just saying we ought to get started on the back rooms," Viola continued. "I got all the needles cleaned and the fluid jars emptied. We gone have to replace some of them canisters and half them chemicals can't be bottled."

She clicked off her duties as efficiently as Aleeda Grace had ever done, but the girl's very efficiency made Aleeda move toward the window and stare at the grounds below. Construction workers had clawed a cut-back trail through a grove of trees that had separated her property from the tail end of Mission Road, and at the road's end, where Aleeda had dug up the remnants of her flower garden, engineers already had planted new signs designating the path as Mission Street. But the scraggly patch of dirt still carried the imprints of Aleeda's trellis poles and flower beds.

"I told DuBois to have the car ready bout four-thirty, but he ain't had no time to clean the embalming room. I could do it," Viola added.

Aleeda sighed and turned to her daughter. "Viola, if you want something to do, go out to the greenhouse. I spect them callas and valerians need watering."

Viola nodded. "You gone call Dora Emma?"

"And don't forget to prune them roddies. They get outta hand."

Viola said, "Yes Mu'dear," in that patient voice Aleeda hated so, but she had no sooner left the room when Aleeda Grace dismissed her by turning back to the window, her thoughts centered on the construction site once more. As she peered through the haze of smoke that seemed to hang eternally over Vinnie's junkyard, a fly buzzed the scent of her body oil. She slapped it between her open palms, then quickly wiped her hands on the linen towel she'd draped over the back of an ornately brocaded chair. Just as quickly, she rubbed a fresh dollop of oil into her hands and worked the liquid from her shoulders to her waist. Her breasts were heavy, pendulous without the eight-hook brassiere she'd worn almost every day of her adult life, and her stomach, though round and loose with the stretch marks of six births, three of them stillborn, led to the gentle slope of her pubic bone where a nest of kinky hair puffed up with its own importance and glistened with oil. But Aleeda remembered being slim and small-breasted, so light on her feet, she'd almost managed to slip past Vinnie Loemann the first night she'd met him. That was twenty years ago, and now she had no way of slipping past Vinnie or John Gionio. What she wanted to do was slap the two of them between her hands as she had done with the fly, but if

Aleeda Grace Sykes knew anything, she knew it was she who was trapped.

So she threw the towel back onto the chaise lounge and sat down. For a second, she stared at the dresser and the gilt frames holding the pictures of her children: Viola, Dora Emma, and in a small rosette frame placed apart from the others, a picture of Butler, Jr., taken at his funeral, a host of angels superimposed on the print above the tiny casket. That photo made her turn away and begin oiling the lower half of her body. The past was the past, and she meant to keep it that way. With short, deft strokes, her fingers probed from hip to thigh, feeling for the length of muscle under the fleshy layer beneath the skin. As she worked toward the calf, she flexed her foot, testing the tension and give of tendons at the back of the knee, the cartilaginous thread between ankle and calf. With each movement, she rubbed at the troubles caused by the babies she'd lost, the disappointment caused by Dora Emma, the sadness of her son's death, and the despair of her husband's railroad job.

Somewhere along the westbound line, the Sunset Limited, Butler's train and another source of her discomfort, was racing toward the city. For a second, she toyed with the idea that if Butler had stayed at home, maybe her babies would have lived. Just thinking it made Aleeda laugh. Butler Sykes had been a railroad man when she married him, and nothing she'd done, not the funeral home nor the babies, would have changed that. By the same token, nothing he'd done would have changed her. For years, folks had suggested her life would be easier if she gave up the Home of Perpetual Rest, if she simply allowed herself to be wife to Butler and satisfied that he had a good job running the road with the Brotherhood of Sleeping Car Porters. The Brotherhood was a powerful Union, but the world had yet to be challenged by sit-ins, and schools were still five years away from desegregation. As much as she loved Butler, Aleeda knew the only difference between what he had to do to keep his job and what she had to do to keep the Home was simply a difference of which white men called the shots. It was the one continuous argument she had with Butler—how he answered to the Brotherhood and the Boss Cap'n of the Limited, and how she answered to Loemann and his boys.

Butler would say, "Leda, I know you ain't done nothing wrong, but them folks got a holt on you and when white folks get to mixing in your business, wrong got a way of being there."

Aleeda Grace would smile and remind him of how he had to leave that kind of talk waiting on the station platform when the Boss Cap'n yelled: Al'BOARD! "Onliest thing this world be telling folks like us when to push and when to hush," she'd say, not bothering to add that it was a distinction she'd learned the day she'd tried to hide from Vinnie Loemann. And now, if making that distinction meant placing the funeral parlor over the Sunset Limited, so be it.

As owner of the Home of Perpetual Rest, Aleeda Grace took death as a serious business, something you prepared for and finally embraced with all the God-given love you could muster. Her funeral parlor was always open for inspection, and she dared anyone to find a better place to bid farewell to their recently departed—either through the front door where the light from the clerestory fell upon the usual funeral home version of clay angels circling a fake marble fountain, or through the back door where an iron grating protected the dead from the living. Not that her clients had much choice in the matter. For years, the Home had been the only funeral parlor in the city catering to colored folks. "We lay these Negroes out better than what they knowed when they was living," Aleeda would say. "I make sure they leave this world in style." And that was where Butler provided his services. His observations of the posh trappings aboard the Sunset Limited were not wasted. He had brought his wife similiar patterns of crystal and china. Their bedroom had taken on the decor of the Limited's finest coaches: fringed velvet throws, ornate headboard, cut-glass lamps—and by Aleeda's bed, fresh every morning, Butler arranged to have a single red rose in a thin-stemmed vase. Aleeda carried this elegance into her funeral parlor. If folks had known any better, they would have sworn they were visiting the sitting rooms of the Vanderbilts or Carnegies instead of the viewing room in the Home of Perpetual Rest. Those who were jealous accused her of putting on airs, but everyone knew Aleeda Grace Sykes paid just as much attention to what went on in her funeral home as she did to what went on in the family rooms upstairs. In truth, Aleeda was as careful with the bodies she buried as she was with her own body and the daily ritual of oiling her skin.

Still, any thought of problems with the funeral parlor could break her routine. As she shifted her attention from oiling her left leg to her right leg, she was aware that the creak in the floorboards was caused by a slope in the wall between the reception area and the casket room. If her calculations were correct, that wall had begun to slope two years ago when the city broke ground for the first buildings of Project housing that would soon overrun the Clayton District, including the Home of Perpetual Rest. She shook her head and chewed the inside corner of her mouth. She could see Gionio's trucks making their circuit around the construction site, dust swirling like small tornadoes in the trail of tire tracks. It was not a pretty turn of events to have her life come to this dilemma—how some city planner's redlining of districts would finally bring her, head-on, to the end of being manipulated by the likes of Vinnie Loemann and John Gionio.

In a way, it was fitting that she should have been the one to clash with the city's political boss and the underworld. Aleeda Grace had become the city's first and only black woman undertaker because of an earlier confrontation of a similiar nature. Certainly, before that night in October 1928, when she'd met Vinnie Loemann, Aleeda Grace had never contemplated being close to death, much less owning a funeral parlor. That night, she was just another twenty-four-year-old kitchen maid looking for a little bootleg hooch to warm her on the long walk from the Belmont District to the carriage rut that, in those days, folks called Mission Road. It was well known that Isaac Cuzzens not only buried the colored, but made the best gin in town and ran a clean gambling room in back of the parlor. Aleeda knew it better than most, because she and her brother, Albert, occasionally helped Isaac bottle some of his booze. So she'd stopped at the back door of the Home of Perpetual Rest. She'd arrived just in time to witness Isaac's death.

"When I heard all that shooting . . . pop-pop-pop like somebody broke wind and busted all the buttons on they pants, I hid myself in a coffin, honey. I just laid there and played like I wasn't in that room a'tall. Weren't much of a funeral parlor in them days," she'd tell folks, "but I wasn't much of an undertaker neither. Sort of picked it up for a song and dance, you might say." Then she'd chuckle over the memory of how she'd skittered into an open casket, playing dead until the smell of garlic had made her to open her eyes and laugh at a gunman "with a nose long as the gun he was holding," she'd told folks. "I laughed so hard, that long-nose hoodlum couldn't do nothing but look at me with his mouth hanging open like a broken gate." But she'd neglect to mention that it had been the gunman's boss, John Gionio, who had signed over the deed to the funeral home. That neglect had turned into a habit, and even after she'd married Butler Sykes, she'd waited two years to tell him about the arrangement she had with Vinnie and his boss. In those days, she had thought she'd look upon the end of that arrangement with relief. Now that the end had come, it carried complications.

The thought of those complications made her move as if she'd heard someone call her name. Applying the oil slipped from being a leisurely process to a task as perfunctory as readying a body for a service. And Aleeda Grace moved from being a small, slightly plump woman enjoying the first private hours of the day to the short pigeon-breasted woman known, and sometimes feared, throughout the city as the colored proprietress of the Home of Perpetual Rest.

Downstairs, the radio was quiet, so she knew Viola had nearly finished tidying the kitchen and was expecting her. The two of them had quite a bit to do before she finished her business with Vinnie and Butler came home. As she pulled herself into the stays, hooks, and girdle of middle-class trade, Aleeda ran through the little speech she'd prepared for her husband. She knew he wouldn't be so keen on bucking Gionio and company alone. Working with the Brotherhood over the years had lulled him into believing every struggle needed an organization. Those same years had taught Aleeda never to trust organizations. In fact, those years had taught her to fight them. Her battles had begun the day she'd decided to throw in her lot with Vinnie Loemann, and she was still fighting them: the Loemann boys and their underworld connections, city hall undermining any move she made with its taxes and rezoning schemes, and the funeral parlor business, more specifically, the male undertakers who had never quite accepted the fact a woman owned the Home of Perpetual Rest.

"UNDER do seem to be my middle name," she thought as she tugged her waist cinch a smidgen tighter. "I'm under this one and under that one. But I ain't bout to go under just cause some crooks think they got they hands on this property." Having said that, she smoothed her hands down the curve of her hips and checked her image in the oak-framed mirror. Pleased with what she saw, she started down the stairs.

Her dress might be considered old-fashioned, with its dark gabardine skirt and white blouse, watch pinned to the left breast pocket, but everything else about her was moving toward the future. The funeral business was a constant reminder of how fragile years could be, and Aleeda Grace had no intention of being left behind tending the dead while other folks staked their claim on the years to come. She paused midway down the stairs where a clear glass square in the tinted window allowed her one last look at the flatlands. Even if she wanted to keep the Home, in a few months, the Projects would block her view of the railroad yard. What she saw now was a raw swatch of land littered with lumber and piles of bricks stacked like ancient tombstones, the construction cranes hanging above them like the bones of dinosaurs. *"Ain't nothing new never gone be here,"* Aleeda said to herself. *"There's always gonna be death in this place."*

She watched a crane lower a steel girder onto a foundation at the project site, and the sunlight, eager to claim anything shiny, bounced off the blade of the girder toward the train yards. Aleeda was staring at this trick of light, trying to guess which track would hold the in-bound Sunset Limited, when Dough Boy appeared at the foot of the stairs. The connection was all too obvious. Dough Boy's appearance and the light from the railroad yards, both there to remind her of Butler's impending arrival. In the old days, until the beginning of the war when the big city factories claimed them, colored folks were always hopping off the north-bound trains to work in the packing house or the railroad yards. Some of them entered town by hitching rides on freight cars, while others bought a ticket for the overcrowded Jim Crow car that was hooked onto the back of the train. "They specting to find heaven starting somewhere here and spreading clear up to Canada," Butler would say. DuBois Rutledge had been one of those lost souls Butler had brought to their doorstep, and he had stayed with them. Aleeda, put out with having the young boy stumbling underfoot and eating everything in sight, had given him the name Dough Boy.

"I'ma make my pickup now," Dough Boy told Aleeda. "Go over to the barber shop, and down by the pool hall, and over to the . . ."

"I know your run," Aleeda interrupted. "You don't have to tell me every place you stop."

"I needs to keep it in my mind. Mistah Loemann . . ."

"MISTAH! What you mean: Mistah? Second time I heard that today. You mean, Vinnie Loemann, don't you? Vinnie. Right?"

Dough Boy used his cap to polish the newel post. "Miz Aleeda, you knows I always calls him Mistah Loemann. Specially since he carry on so bout wearing a suit and all."

Aleeda said, "A suit?" and stared at Dough Boy. It was beyond her why Butler had tolerated the man for so long, but for some reason, Butler felt responsible for Dough Boy, almost as if he, himself, had sent that poor little fat boy out of a bilge-water town in Georgia to search for heaven and, instead, left him in the Home of Perpetual Rest. *"Left him to drive me crazy,"* Aleeda thought. "What's Vinnie Loemann's suit got to do with anything? You want a suit, there's plenty in the back room."

"Them suits for dead folks," Dough boy whimpered. "Don't be putting me in no dead man's suit. I wants me a suit, I buy one from the pawnshop, less'n I can afford one of them worsted wools from Oscar Flowers' place. No 'suh, won't be no suit what's split up the back so's ol' man death can come a-cawling."

"Get on outta here," Aleeda told him. "Go on. Make your pickup and get on back here. Wasting my time talking bout what suits be for dead folks and what suits ain't. What's dead got to do with it? You work in a funeral parlor."

Dough Boy said, "Yes'um, yes'um," and scurried toward the side door.

Aleeda inhaled and put her hands on her waist, her thumbs pushing against the small of her back. As she stood there, probing for her muscles, she heard the side door open and close, open and close, as if Dough

Boy couldn't decide whether he was coming or going. She shook her head, then slowly eased the air from her lungs. And when she finally felt her back muscles relax, she pulled herself upright and descended the stairs, her head held high in a debutante's practiced walk. Under that pose, both the righteous and the earthy sides of Aleeda Grace glided toward the first floor foyer, where the fountain recycled its water with a soft gurgle of sound, and the carpet released the sour smell of must and decay. Her earthy side stood in front of the fountain and admired the bright shadows of goldfish sparkling in mirrored reflections of water like bangles on an evening dress. That side held her fingers above the water and wondered if she could find a swatch of silky material in the same rippling shades of blue and emerald. The business side leaned toward the righteousness of Aleeda Grace and reminded her to have the goldfish flushed before the rest of the hallway was dismantled. She flicked the water from her fingers.

"Nothing lasts forever," she said, and for luck, rubbed the backside of an angel dancing along the edge of the fountain.

"Talking to yourself, Leda?"

John Gionio was sitting in one of the Spanish highbacks close to a potted palm by the door. Both the fountain and the chair's latticework almost hid him from view, but Aleeda knew the voice. His nasal twang was unmistakable, distinct even among a city council full of other chicken-neck members who had never crossed the state line. When Aleeda stepped away from the edge of the fountain, Gionio was clearly visible: the vest of his signature three-piece suit tightly buttoned across his bony chest, his long legs stretched away from a body as thin as a hunting dog's tail. She wondered how she could have missed him when she was on the stairs. Then she remembered Dough Boy's comments about suits.

"So you the one putting high-tone ideas in that boy's head."

For a second, Gionio looked confused. Then he laughed. "If you're talking about your flunky, I don't have the time it would take to put an idea in his thick head. But maybe I've got time for you."

"You calling me your flunky, Johnny?" She let one corner of her mouth assume a smile because she knew Gionio did not want her calling him Johnny. "I don't recollect doing no fetch-and-carry for you. We been real careful bout that, ain't we?"

Gionio uncrossed his legs and leaned forward, elbows on his knees, and head in his hands as if he were mulling over some great scheme. As he spoke, he rubbed his face—"*smooth as mausoleum marble,*" Aleeda thought, but she remembered earlier years when that pointed chin was shadowed under the stubble of a beard.

"Leda Grace, I am sorely vexed this morning. Here I am, your Councilman, come to call on a member of his constituency, and I'm addressed in this offhanded manner. So little respect." He shook his head and smiled at Aleeda. "That kind of behavior does make it difficult for me to serve your best interests. It puts me in a . . . How can I say this? . . . a position of not knowing what to expect from you. It forces me to question how long it will take me to teach you your place in this life."

"This be my place," Aleeda hissed. Her gesture encompassed the waiting room. "Ain't that why you come to talk to me? Bout my place? I expected Vinnie to be the one come a-calling for them papers. That's what you after, ain't it? Them papers what be carrying the name Aleeda Grace over this here address."

"Ah yes, an address. An abode. A residence." Gionio stood up. "Come outside, Leda." He saw her hesitate. "It's OK. My car's waiting for me, so I have to be going. But I want to show you something before I leave."

At the curb, Gionio's black Packard, long as a funeral hearse, almost pulsated under its coat of wax. Although the trucks had been moving for only a few hours, the air was gritty-thick, but dust slid right off the car's finish. Aleeda pulled a perfumed handkerchief from her sleeve, and sniffed it. Gionio seemed unaware of the grainy air. He carefully donned a gray hat, pale as his closely shaved skin, then ran his hands along its edge to make sure the curl of the brim was just right. The hat, like the Packard, seemed spotless, almost as if the dust did not dare settle on it. Aleeda flicked a few grains off her blouse.

"Look at this," Gionio said. "This is progress. A chance for new houses, new jobs. And all for your people." He motioned from the sweep of road to the construction site.

Aleeda followed the direction of his gesture. Where the houses had been razed and the land staked out in grids marked with red flags, she saw the backs of black men bent over shovels and bowed under heavy loads of wooden planks. The white men were positioned behind the wheels of trucks, or operating derricks. But she had to admit that in a way, Gionio was right. There were four black men for every five men sweating under the direct rays of the sun. However, Aleeda Grace also knew that only the machine operators had the protection of a Union, and by her count, none of those men were black. Like Butler always said, there were white folks who still didn't have it in their minds to allow black men to have a Union.

"I see 'em out there," Aleeda said, "but I bet they don't all be making the same wages? How much you want to bet? Cards or dice?"

Gionio laughed. "I deserved that. Still don't miss an opportunity to float a game, do you, Leda? Can't get money off your mind?"

"Can you?" she asked.

"I take it upon myself to stay clear of another man's business. That means, I do not question his money and he does not question mine. That's why it's me come to see you this time, not Vinnie. And that brings us back to this." He turned his gesture to the entrance of the Home of Perpetual Rest. "As you notice, Leda, it has no address."

Two zeroes were affixed under the wooden letters designating the funeral parlor, and although the outline of the missing number, a seven, was still visible, Aleeda knew folks allowed that triple digit number to cause havoc with their daily bets. "Don't tell me you done waited all these years to be throwing some number up against me, John Gionio." She let the laughter swell in her throat and when it spilled over, it nearly covered the whine of a truck revving up its motor. "Don't that beat all. City boss hitting the numbers."

Gionio adjusted the tie around his scrawny neck, and squared his shoulders. "Leda, you know I do not play the numbers. I leave that to other folks. Or have you forgotten?"

"I don't forget nothing, Mr. Johnny Gionio. I don't forget where I be and why I be there. I don't forget everybody knows where to find me. Folks got something to bring me, they come right here. Don't nobody get lost looking for me. That address be as plain as the nose on your face. You just ask folks. They tell you where Butler and Aleeda Sykes be living." She paused. "And where they gone stay till I say it's time to move," she added.

But Gionio did not take the bait. That caused Aleeda Grace to break out in a sweat. The weather wasn't hot, but Aleeda's temper heated her scalp until a small trickle of perspiration escaped her hairline and made its way toward her cleavage, which was only slightly hidden by her blouse. Watching it track across the plush mound of skin rising at the neckline of her blouse, Gionio remembered he had an early luncheon meeting.

"You're a handsome woman, Leda Sykes. I've told Butler that many times. Be a pity to see you lose everything." He reached over and with one finger, thin and white as a candlewick, caught the droplet of sweat just before it disappeared. "Yes, a shame," he added, and smiled as he rubbed the moisture between his thumb and forefinger.

Aleeda's blush, darkening her lips and the rims of her ears, held the undertones of a bruise, but Gionio, seeing her only in one shade of black, took no notice of it. However, he did notice Aleeda flinching from his touch. "You pulling away from me, Leda Grace?"

"You don't scare me, Johnny. You can't do nothing to me."

"I wouldn't think of harming a hair on your lovely head," he smiled.

"We go too far back for that. No, I would not do anything to you. But you've got till tomorrow morning, Leda. The game is over. I'm calling in the bets."

"I ain't going nowhere without my due. It's gone take more than them trucks to get me outta here. Everything I got is here."

"You'll go," Gionio said. "And you'll be happy to get out with what little you have left." He turned and walked to his car.

At the curb, he looked back at Aleeda. Even without the dust from passing trucks, the Home was badly in need of paint. One side faced a block-long string of condemned buildings, while the side with the mural faced the construction site. There, his trucks were lined up and ready to roll. But for several blocks in the other direction, the only habitable buildings were the funeral home, a bar-b-que stand, a Chinese restaurant, and several rundown bars. Gionio owned them all. *"All this end of town ever offered,"* he thought and waved at Aleeda.

The Packard was just nearing Kingshighway when Aleeda reached the bottom of the staircase. By the time it turned onto the thoroughfare she was at the landing—four buttons already loosened on her blouse, her watch in her hand. Viola stepped into the hall to see who had slammed the front door. Almost before Viola said, "Mu'dear?", Aleeda snapped, "I'll be in my room!"

Clothes began to fly away from her body seemingly of their own volition. Her blouse lost its shape and fluttered to the floor like paper ripped from a packing box. When it sailed from Aleeda's hand, the sleeves already hung in tatters from the shoulder seams, and buttons scattered across the tiles like bright stones. "Son of a bitch!" Aleeda muttered, and slammed her belt against the back of the chaise lounge. "Son of a bitch!" and the memory of Gionio's mouth filled that space she'd left sealed for twenty years. She clawed at her breasts, and the hooks on her bra, crooked like thin wire fingers, bent outward under the pressure. "He never even asked," she cried and hugged herself close as the anger scratched her throat. Then it burst through, and Aleeda began to sway, moving back and forth as if she were pushing against some invisible barrier. With a hoarse moan, she kicked off her shoes, flinging them against the wall. Only then did she release herself from her own embrace, and then, it was just to tear at the rest of her clothes. They resisted her frantic movements, and that proved to be almost too much for her. She stood still for a moment, inhaling, chewing the familiar crinkle of loose skin inside the corner of her mouth. But it did not hold its taste. It had become something else that would not do her bidding. She swore again, and bit down. The red stain spread its odd sweetness across her gums and teeth, then stained her lips.

What had he said that night? "You are too impatient," he'd said. "Take your time," he'd said. But the cramped space of the casket had pushed against her, and the smell of satin lining, moldy even before it had spent time under a mound of earth, seemed to pull in air faster than she could breath. So she had urged him on, riding him in that house of death on the promise that he would never again ask so much of her. Now she stood in her bathroom, half dressed, and felt the imprint of his finger as if he'd left a scar. She leaned over the toilet and spit and spit until she could not longer salivate. Then she rinsed her mouth with tap water and spit until the water was no longer pink with blood.

She examined her face in the mirror. Her reflection hadn't changed much. Just the streaks of anger in her eyes, and her injured pride still deepening the color of her cheeks, the rim of her nose.

"Come in here looking like death eating soda crackers on a rainy day," she mumbled. "Come in here like he own somebody. Come himself. Mr. Big-shot Johnny. Couldn't even send Vinnie Loemann."

It had been years since Gionio had tried to do his own dirty work, but longer even since Aleeda had failed to do what she had set her mind to do. *"I done buried folks badder than that,"* she told herself. *"Don't you try to play me cheap, Mr. Johnny Gionio. I knew you fore you was who you think you be."*

She leaned forward, plugged the bathtub and turned on the water tap. *"It ain't over yet,"* she told herself. Butler was still to come home, and the week's receipts still to be counted. Maybe it was time to review all of the books, especially the ones she kept for her own records. It almost worked, all that talk, but somewhere in the mirror, she saw a hesitancy that said Gionio had nothing to lose. "All he's seeing here is a set of zeroes," the mirror told her. She turned away from that reflection. "It ain't over yet," she repeated. Then wrapped up and breathless, she stepped into the bathtub's shiny white basin. At first, the porcelain was cold, but soon, water lapped at her feet. She crouched down and watched the water seep through the mesh of her stockings, then soak the hem of her skirt until the material, thoroughly wet, ballooned around her waist. As the tub began to fill, the billowing skirt floated higher than her waistline, higher even than her breasts. Finally, she turned off the tap, closed her eyes, and let her arms rest just above the water. Steam began to fill the room and the kinky-thick hair that she'd coiled that morning at the crown of her head began to absorb moisture and burst free of its pins. Enthroned in the claw-footed tub, her arms spread out and her hair pushing its way to freedom, she looked somewhat like a vengeful frog. At least, that is what Viola thought when she entered the bathroom.

The water had been running, so Aleeda Grace could not have heard her daughter knocking softly at the bedroom door. Viola had come upstairs with a tea tray, and it was the rattling of cup against saucer that made Aleeda open her eyes. When she glared at her daughter, the anger was still blooming in her eyes. Viola picked some spot on the wall to look at and whispered, "Tea, Mu'dear?"

Aleeda stood up, water dripping from her wet skin and clothes, steam falling away from the muscles of her shoulders and back like a veil. Even Viola, who was accustomed to her mother's spells, as Aleeda's temper was called, had never seen her so disheveled. If they'd been playing "pray-for-the-dead," Viola would surely be tagged "It." Aleeda snatched at her skirt again. This time, it gave way, and she threw it at Viola. The girl stepped back just as the skirt plopped to the floor. Steaming the way it was, Viola was reminded of the first time she'd seen her mother preserving the eviscerated section of a corpse.

"Maybe you need some sherry," she told Aleeda, and rushed out of the room.

"Chile, you better bring me some scotch!" Aleeda yelled. "I ain't ready for no tea party. You hear me, Viola?"

But Viola was already gone. Aleeda pulled at the stocking clips and side snaps of the girdle, then unwrapped it from her waist and tossed it onto the waterlogged skirt. The stockings were a bit more difficult because both her legs and the hose were wet, but after sitting down in the tub once more, she managed to remove the nylons. Both were snagged with runs trailing their length. "I'm used to silk!" Aleeda shouted. "Silk and folks that know what respect means!" The bathroom tiles returned her words in hollow echoes. Aleeda knew it was time to cry, but she'd used all of her tears long ago. Besides, crying never got her anywhere. She had come from generations of women taught not to cry. "What good was crying for a slave woman?" her mother would have asked. So Aleeda Grace leaned into the steamy water and cursed until the anger soaked away from her. She was still cursing when Viola brought her the scotch.

The girl picked that spot on the wall to stare at again. "You alright, Mu'dear?" she asked.

Aleeda turned on her as if she'd just spoken in a foreign language. Then she said, "Pour me a glass of that scotch, and hand me them bath salts. This water don't do nothing but bring up all them smells from downstairs. I spect that smell done soaked clear through the roof beams of this house. Maybe it'll scare all that construction mess away from us."

Viola handed her the glass, and sprinkled jasmine salts into the water, managing all of it without seeming to look directly at Aleeda. "I don't think them smells gone keep them folks away, Mu'dear."

Then, as if confirming what the girl had said, a muffled explosion shook the house, and water sloshed at the edges of the tub.

"Can't even let me take a bath in peace," Aleeda snapped. "Them Projects must be bigger than I thought. Big enough to make ol' Johnny come a-calling all by his lonesome." She had her eyes half closed when she realized Viola was still waiting. "Go on downstairs, Vi. Dough Boy's gone be back pretty soon."

"You alright?" she asked again.

"Viola, I'm just fine long as you don't fuss over me. Now go on. Stack bottles in the back room. I don't care what you do. Just let me finish my bath fore they blow this house up under me."

Aleeda closed her eyes once more. Now that she was listening, she heard the foreman's whistle signal the second explosion. And again, the house rocked, its timbers creaking as if it too were signalling the end.

"Don't nothing stay the same," Butler would say. "Black folks got to move along like everybody else. This here is 1949. Them soldiers didn't fight in that war overseas just to come home and sit in the back of some train, or live in a tarpaper shack. Everything's gone change. This town long with the rest of it. They digging up half the Flats for that Project business. Where you gone be when there ain't no funeral home? Where you gone be when Vinnie and Johnny G. leave you high and dry?"

Aleeda had laughed away his concerns. She knew you didn't have to be brilliant to figure both Gionio and the Sunset Limited would reach their end long before there was an end to the funeral business. For years, she had watched Butler come home tired after walking car to car from Union Station to the Coast on a train where a black man was known only by his first name, if he were lucky enough to be recognized as a grown man who had any name at all. Aleeda hated what that job did to him. Despite A. Philip Randolph's Union, the only black folks who pulled themselves up the wrought-iron stairs of the Limited's sleeping cars were pullman porters. And all those years, she had watched him dress with the notion of keeping his smile in place as if he really did enjoy the act of waiting on white folks, as if there really were nothing else in the world except the Sunset Limited and the time he spent on it. It was the same smile she found herself wearing when Gionio paid his visit, but she was planning to discard that smile, the Lord willing. Butler had put up with that nonsense because of the Brotherhood. Aleeda had put up with it because she expected a payoff.

"Mu'dear, DuBois come back. Mu'dear, you hear me?"

Aleeda must have fallen asleep, because when she opened her eyes, she didn't know quite where she was at first.

"DuBois come back," Viola repeated. "He only got half the receipts." She held out a box for Aleeda's inspection. The box contained slips of paper scrawled with lists of figures and letters arranged in a shorthand coding only Aleeda was supposed to see.

"Viola, I don't care where you got them number slips, you take them outta here. You understand me, chile? You know better than to bring them things up here. What have I told you? Upstairs is for family. Don't be bringing that mess upstairs."

"But DuBois don't know what to do, and he got somebody . . ."

Aleeda stood up and grabbed a towel from the rack. "Dough Boy don't know how to tie his shoes in the dark without a flashlight and a map," she said, knotting the bath towel around her torso. "You know I told you I don't never want to see them things anywhere upstairs. You go put that stuff in the office. This here's a respectable house, and I intend to keep it that way."

"Mu'dear, everybody knows bout . . ."

Aleeda Grace interrupted Viola by clutching her shoulders. Although she was shorter than her daughter by several inches, standing inside the bathtub gave her height. She began to shake the girl. "Folks know what you want them to know!" Aleeda said. "You think somebody be asking Doc Pritchard where he gets his money? You think folks be talking bout how Cinnamon Ivory got that tavern? Or Reverend Blankenship keeps his church? I run a funeral parlor. That's all. You hear me?"

Viola felt herself beginning to unravel, but she said in a steady voice, "Yes Mu'dear. I hear you."

Aleeda Grace stared at her for a moment, then released her. "What you waiting for? That box ain't gone walk outta here by its lonesome."

"What I'm gone tell DuBois?" Viola asked.

"Tell him to go back and get the rest of them receipts. And you go with him. You can pick up your pappa from the train station on the way back."

"What I'm gone tell Mistah Loemann?"

"Who?"

"Mu'dear, I tried to tell you, DuBois got Mistah Loemann with him. He's downstairs. I gotta tell him something or he's liable to come marching up here."

Aleeda stepped out of the tub and quickly wiped her feet on the bath mat. "If Vinnie Loemann comes up them steps, there's gonna be hell to pay." She wagged her finger at Viola like a schoolteacher disciplining a forgetful student. "You go down there, and you tell that ugly little bow-legged monkey to keep himself in that waiting room. Don't know what he's doing here so early anyway."

She swept past Viola and sat down at her dressing table where she began brushing her hair, digging in as if she were trying to rid herself of something that was worming its way toward her scalp.

Viola cleared her throat. "Mu'dear, don't be mad at DuBois, but Mistah Loemann ain't in the waiting room."

Aleeda threw down the brush. "Well, where the hell is he, Viola?"

"He sitting in the viewing room. Say he wants you to open up the back. Say he got to take all them chairs and tables back over to the warehouse."

"He better take his ass back out to that junkyard. You tell him . . ." Aleeda began. Then she heard a truck roaring past and thought better of it. "Tell him I'll be down directly. Give him a glass of scotch—this scotch, not the stuff I keep for your pappa's friends—give him a glass of scotch and tell him I'll be down directly."

Viola nodded and poured the drink. Just before she left the room, Aleeda stopped her again. "Viola, you leave that man in the viewing room, and lock the door on him. Then you and Dough Boy go straight out and get your pappa. It's quarter past four. That train done come in by now."

"Mu'dear, I . . ."

"Do what I say, chile. At least, this once."

When the girl had gone, Aleeda looked at her face in the mirror. If Dough Boy had not picked up all of his receipts and if Vinnie had accompanied him on his run, then it only stood to reason that Vinnie had pocketed some of the slips. Aleeda kept staring at her reflection until her nameless self took over, the part of her that had learned to deal with grieving widows, bad gamblers, and Vinnie Loemann. Then she pinned her hair into a crumpled nest at the top of her head, and finished dressing, smoothing the mixture of oil and jasmine over her body without thinking of how much went where. This time, the ritual took only a matter of minutes. This time, the noise of trucks and tractors moved her from limb to limb as if she were slapping paint against the side of a house. Twice while she was dressing, the sounds of earth movers and jackhammers seemed to be on the porch outside her front door. "If they coming to get me, I might as well dress up like I been expecting them," she said, and put on a lace-front blouse, drop earrings, and silk hose. Then she went downstairs to take care of Vinnie Loemann.

The key turned soundlessly in the well-oiled lock, and for once, she blessed Dough Boy's ready obedience to follow her orders to the letter. She opened the door only wide enough to slip through and push it shut again. Vinnie was perched on a railing in front of a closed casket Aleeda used to show customers what kind of merchandise they could buy. He was engrossed in a game of solitaire, his playing cards spread out on the coffin lid, and loose cigarettes lined up on its rim as he bet against himself. Aleeda was sure he was cheating. Cheating was as much Vinnie Loemann's nature as being thickheaded was Dough Boy's nature. But there was nothing in Vinnie's nature that would make him volunteer to be with Dough Boy, numbers receipts or not. Aleeda Grace waited long enough to see Vinnie peek at a hidden card, then she stepped away from the door.

"I can't understand a man what cheats when ain't nobody playing with him."

Vinnie turned, the card still in his hand. "I'd let you play with me, Auntie." He slid back his thin upper lip and grinned, exposing teeth so laced with rot, they looked like corduroy.

To Aleeda Grace, cleanliness was a ritual that, next to death, she observed with the fervor of an evangelist. Everything about Vinnie went against that principle: his teeth, the cracked skin on his lower lip, the scarred crown of his balding head, the hairs creeping out of his ears, and his clothes, wrinkled from the grungy shirt collar to the pants' cuffs. In all ways but one, Vinnie Loemann was a cheaper duplicate of John Gionio. The only difference was that Vinnie didn't bother to wash off the dirt he dabbled in all day. In fact, he seemed to make a conscious effort to spread it around. Aleeda winced at the sight of the empty scotch glass leaving a ring on the hardwood surface of the coffin. Vinnie saw her looking at the glass and handed it to her.

Aleeda was careful not to stare at the rims of dirt circling his fingernails. "I'd offer you another drink," she said, "but I don't spect you gone be here that long."

Vinnie pulled his fingers through his rubbery clumps of hair. "Up to you, Auntie. I don't leave till the Man tells me. Could be awhile." He pulled the cards together and listlessly shuffled them.

"My name is Aleeda Grace. Miz Sykes to you." She put the empty glass on the floor under the guardrail. "If you here to pass the time of day, don't bother. I got some work to do. I need to count the week's receipts. Vi tells me some didn't come in. You know anything bout that?" Vinnie shrugged. "My daughter tells me you the one come to fetch them gaming tables," Aleeda continued. "How come you need to be following Dough Boy all over town if you just come for them little piss-poor tables?"

Vinnie leaned over the edge of the rail and put his face close to hers. "Now Auntie, ain't nothing piss-poor in this business. You know that. I had to do me a little checking. Had to find out just where that fat boy makes his pickup before you move outta here, so I followed him. Got it?" He pulled a set of folded papers from his suit pocket and waved them in front of her face. "And the way I hear tell, you gonna be moving pretty soon—right, Auntie?"

The movement of the papers only made his bad breath spread faster, and the familiar odor of stale garlic caused Aleeda's stomach to lurch. She realized she hadn't eaten since breakfast, but she knew one thing for certain—she wouldn't eat as long as Vinnie Loemann was in her house. "I done already said once today I can't sign no papers without my husband, so you might as well leave now."

"Why? You the only one got to sign it. And if you waiting for your old man, like I said, could be a while."

Aleeda felt her heart thump against her chest wall. She told herself it was the garlic smell and her empty stomach. But if that were so, why was Vinnie grinning at her, his top lip disappearing into the gummy ridge above his teeth? "The Sunset Limited is never late."

Vinnie let out a snort of sounds that passed for laughter. "Not unless it hits a snag," he sputtered. "A little accident."

Now Aleeda wished she kept the glass in her hand, because at least she would have had something to clutch instead of digging her nails into her palms. "What the hell you mean, white man? Don't you shit me."

Vinnie went back to shuffling cards. "Careful, Auntie. The Man just called for one accident today, but that don't mean I got to stop counting past one."

Aleeda watched the cards fall from one grubby hand to another as Vinnie's fingers quietly moved the order of the deck without seeming to be interfering with the flow of cards at all. She thought of the many times she'd gambled with him, how good he was, and yet, how much he had to rely on someone else to give orders. That someone could only be one man, but she knew neither she nor Vinnie would actually say his name. No names—another of her agreements, one that she had not foreseen as trouble that night in 1928 any more than she ever could have foreseen putting Butler in danger. She heard her voice quietly asking, "What happened?" but Vinnie kept shuffling cards. She repeated the question twice before he answered.

"Happened?" he repeated. "Lots of things happen." He held out his hand, the cards stacked face down in his palm. "Who's to tell?" he chuckled. Without thinking about what she was doing, Aleeda cut the deck. The cards broke on the eight of clubs. Vinnie smiled, closed the deck, and shuffled again. "Can't never tell what's gonna happen on the railroad," he said. "Too many tracks. Man looks up when he should look down. Runs when he should walk. Win some, lose some." Again, he extended his hand. "Could be a man's luck just runs out," he said. "They tell me out there in the dark, ziggaboos look alike. What you think?"

This time, Aleeda split the deck on the ace of spades. "Aces and eights. A dead man's hand in a dead man's house." Vinnie's laughter scattered like the noise of foxes Aleeda used to hear at night when the stretch of woods still hunkered at the edge of the railroad tracks, and men like Gionio and Vinnie were still dealing in bootleg hooch instead of making plans with city bosses for high-rise Projects. "Like I said," Vinnie told her, "I got plenty time for that other drink."

As he began to deal the cards for solitaire, Aleeda tried to hold her vision still. The candle-shaped light bulbs cast a dim yellow glow on the polished oak panels, and where the wall broke for the double sliding doors connecting the viewing room to her office, the light made the wood shimmer as if the room were about to disappear. Despite the smudge of Vinnie's hand prints and the water stain from the scotch glass, the coffin also seemed to shimmer in that dim light. Even Vinnie's cards seemed to float toward the coffin lid. Aleeda had not been aware of how much the viewing room's panels blocked most of the outside noises until she heard the funeral car's gears grinding and the crunch of gravel in the alley as Dough Boy, once again, slipped the clutch. The car door slammed. Only one door, and the hiccough of metal against a stubborn hinge meant only the door on the driver's side of the hearse. No other sound. No footsteps striding down the hall in heavy brogans. No one calling her name from the foot of the stairs. Just Vinnie's cards slapping against the coffin in his unending game of solitaire.

Aleeda managed to keep her voice at its even pitch. "I don't like drinking in here," she said. "It's bad luck."

Vinnie fanned the cards and blew on them. "I see your point," he grinned, showing her the root system of several teeth.

"Why don't you go wait in my office? More comfortable in there." Vinnie did not move. "You can go over the receipts," she added. "At least, the ones we got. I'll come in and check the books when you finished."

Without waiting for his reaction, Aleeda moved to the connecting door. When she unlocked the catch and slid the door open, Vinnie's grunt let her know he'd tried to leave the room earlier. "Won't take you that long to tally them receipts," she prodded him. "I musta left something to drink on the sideboard. Make yourself to home." She smiled, knowing the temptation of free booze and the chance to invade the unguarded numbers box would be too much for Vinnie, no matter what orders he might have received. He began to gather his cards. "Just make yourself to home," Aleeda repeated. "I told Viola to leave them receipts right there on the desk."

Then she stepped back and opened the door wide enough for Vinnie to slip past without brushing against her. Nothing could save her from the rank smell that invaded her nose, odors collected off the debris Vinnie gathered in his junkyard: the smell of metal shavings and old rubber mingling with the sour sweat of his own neglect. She watched him head for the sideboard, and slid the door shut before he reached it. One click locked the door, but now that he was safely put with a bottle of cheap booze and an hour's worth of juggling receipts in his favor, there was no real reason to lock him in the room. Still she felt better with the key in her pocket. That feeling lasted only until she opened the iron grating covering the door to the loading dock. The alley seemed to be filled with black cars: Vinnie Loemann's black Cadillac on one side of the door, tip to tail with the hearse on the other side.

What Aleeda heard first was the sound of Dough Boy weeping. But only by putting her hands on the fender of the hearse, and squeezing between it and the building could she get past the hearse and far enough into the alley to see anything. When she was clear of the front fender, she saw the driver's door hanging open, but still could not see Dough Boy or Viola. The sounds, however, were unmistakable: Dough Boy's hoarse intake of breath like a note stuck in a pipe organ, and Viola's hum of pain broken by a garbled string of words. Although Aleeda knew what her child was saying, although she was almost close enough to distinguish the sounds, she refused to let her thoughts pick up the words. Then she was too close to deny them.

Over and over, Viola moaned, "Ohh, Pappa . . . no, no. Pappa, no." It was a chant, a keening that for a moment, left her alone in that alley with her despair. Aleeda knew that sound. She had heard it from girls turned into widows, and children turned into orphans. She had watched that cry rise in the throats of women unable to face what the next day might bring, and she could not say what pained her most—listening to her child sink into that grief, or waiting for the moment when her own grief would bring her down. She chewed the tender lining of her mouth and let her daughter lean into the cry, then she opened the side-service door of the hearse. Butler was stretched out between the coffin rails, Dough Boy and Viola kneeling at his side.

As soon as Dough Boy saw her, he called her name and fell, sobbing, into her arms. His weight almost pulled her to her knees, which had suddenly gone weak, but Aleeda drew back and very slowly said, "Dough Boy, stand up. Help Viola out of the car."

"Miz Leda, they done killed him."

"I know," Aleeda said, and looked past him to Viola. "Dough Boy, go on now. Help her." Viola, her face blurred by tears, turned toward the sound of her mother's voice. "Mu'dear . . ." She extended one hand to Aleeda Grace, but the other hand remained clutched around her father's wrist.

Throughout her time at the Home, Aleeda had always found it surprising that a body's weight did not depend so much on how a living person was able to move under his own power, as it did on how suddenly that power had been lost. Her heaviest bodies had been those who had not seen death coming. When she leaned forward to help Dough Boy raise Viola out of the hearse, the girl's body had given way to the dead weight of that kind of shock. "Com'on, baby," Aleeda pleaded. "We got to get your pappa inside. Com'on, Vi. Stand up, baby."

Viola silently allowed herself to be pulled across the floor of the hearse. Aleeda shifted her weight so she could release Dough Boy and embrace her daughter. Viola's body shook with sobs, and Aleeda hugged the girl as she had when Vi was a child and needed her mother to soothe a scraped knee. It wasn't enough. It was never enough, even with strangers, those who had come to her only to bury the dead and would not speak to her again until the next time she was needed.

"Miz Leda, what I'm gone do?" Dough Boy begged.

"Get Viola inside," Aleeda told him. "And get the big table over by the door. I'll roll the car down so's we can haul him . . ." She stopped. Viola, leaning against her, shook with another rush of sobbing. "Just go inside and get the room ready," Aleeda told the boy. "We can't leave my husband in this alley."

For a few seconds after Dough Boy had pulled her daughter away, Aleeda felt the imprint of Viola's body. Then she eased herself inside the hearse. Butler was already cold, his mouth drawn in the grimace of that last painful breath. She kissed him anyway. Black spores of dried blood were caked against his scalp, and one eye was partially open under a deadly bloom. Aleeda closed it and kissed both lids. She would have to use putty to fill in the space around the wounded eye. She reminded herself to use an understitch for his ear where the lobe had been torn away, and for his neck, near the collar where the skin was shredded, she would use silk and the length of his Youngfellow's scarf. "Everybody's gonna think you just stepped out for a time with the boys," she told him. "They gone say, there's Butler, ready for the Saturday chorale. That's what they gone say."

And she put her head against his chest. Viola had folded his hands the proper way, but when Aleeda leaned against them, she felt the give of broken bones in his rib cage and knew she'd have more work padding his figure to stay as upright and strong as it had been during his life. She kissed his hands, the fingertips where the blunt nails had turned bluish gray. Her mouth was surprised by the taste of salt until she realized it was hers, not Butler's—that it would never again be Butler's. "Oh my sweet man, I didn't know. Lord, I didn't know it would ever be you. I know I shoulda told somebody what I saw, but after all them years went past, I didn't think they'd do nothing. And Lord, I didn't know it would ever be you."

Although she did not brush her hand across her face, she knew she had managed to swallow her tears. The back of her throat ached as if she'd screamed, but she held in the sound. She knew she could not have stopped screaming if even a little escaped. "That train howls like a woman what's done found her man in the wrong bed," Butler would say when he bragged about the Limited. And he told stories about that train to anyone who would listen: Dough Boy, Viola, or the men who hung out in the afternoon swapping tales at Brown's Barber Shop. Viola still loved to hear her father talk about how the lonesome sound of the Limited's whistle moaned the Blues like it was calling W. C. Handy to rise up from his sickbed, and how, in the desert, the wheels thundered so loud, Mexican children waved to the speeding train and cried, "There goes Santiago's horses!" And always, Butler would smile and say that speeding train was "Taking me home to my baby." Then he'd squeeze Aleeda until she complained.

"I'm sorry, Butler. Lord, I'm so sorry," Aleeda told him.

But by the time Dough Boy opened the heavy doors to the loading dock, Aleeda Grace had gathered herself behind the mask of undertaker. Dough Boy rolled the cart to the edge of the dock, and Aleeda positioned herself at Butler's feet. She was prepared to push his body forward so Dough Boy could slide his shoulders onto the cart when suddenly Viola crawled in beside her. Aleeda might have protested, but Viola glared the way Butler did when he was really mad, and tightened her jaw until, in profile, the angle of her face was exactly like Aleeda's. For the first time that day, Aleeda had the good sense to bow to her daughter's will. Between the two of them, they lifted the body of Butler Sykes toward the door, where Dough Boy hoisted it onto the cart and clear of the loading dock.

Aleeda's check of what she would need was automatic, but she found Viola was already one step ahead of her—rubber gowns and gloves ready for the three of them. "Com'on, chile. Let's get his clothes off," Aleeda said. Dough Boy's mouth hung open, but he did not move. "Dough Boy, don't stand there. Help us strip him."

Viola nudged the boy forward. They tranferred Butler onto the morgue table, and Viola lined up the equipment in its proper place. None of this required much talking: Dough Boy quietly wept as he began to cut away Butler's clothes, Viola clicked the aspiration tubes into their proper vats, and Aleeda checked the jugs of chloride and formaldehyde solutions against her private formula. Aleeda quickly marked the areas for incisions: the groin, the base of the neck, the abdominal wall—the first set of syringes plunged deep into the bladder and intestines. She was setting up the initial injection fluids when she remembered Vinnie Loemann.

Aleeda peeled off her gloves and said, "Dough Boy, go get the Union boys. Tell 'em we got a shipment for the midnight train."

Viola gasped. "Mu'dear! No! Don't be sending Pappa off till we done had services."

"Hush, chile. Didn't nobody say your pappa was going nowhere. I said we had a shipment, that's what I said."

"What I'm gone tell 'em if they axs me why you calling for 'em?"

"Tell 'em just what I said, Dough Boy. Tell 'em we got a shipment."

"We ain't had nobody ready for shipment in a month, Mu'dear."

Aleeda glared at her. "Go on, Dough Boy. Don't let them boys get too drunk, else they won't be able to take care of business." She threw her apron onto the loading cart and walked from the room. Viola followed her, hurriedly peeling off gloves and apron before she reached the door. "Where you going?" Aleeda asked her. "You know better than to walk out of that room without washing." Viola didn't mention that Aleeda had done just that. But she didn't turn back either. Seeing that, Aleeda stopped.

"What did your sister . . . What did Dora Emma say to you on the phone this morning?"

Whatever Viola had been expecting out of Aleeda's mouth, this question was not it. She hesitated, then remembered her sister's conversation. That memory almost made her weep again. "She say Mistah Loemann . . . She say Mistah Loemann come by yesterday morning and give her some flowers. She say she ask him what he was doing in St. Charles county and he say he was waiting on the train."

Aleeda felt her teeth drive into the sore spot inside her mouth. "Did she talk to her pappa yesterday morning?"

"No ma'am. She say she waited for him, but he didn't get off the train. But Mu'dear, sometimes Pappa be so busy . . ." Aleeda was already walking away. "Mu'dear, where you going?" Viola called out.

"Don't leave your pappa by himself. I'll be in to help you directly," she added.

"But where you going?" Viola asked again.

"To do something I shoulda done twenty years ago," Aleeda said, then she walked in the kitchen and quickly shut the door.

Once inside the kitchen, she stopped for a moment until she heard the embalming room door open and close. Then she went to the sink and washed her hands in thick green soap, and after drying them carefully, once again, oiled them with her jasmine mixture. Next she pulled a wine decanter from the cabinet. Pinpricks of rainbows were reflected in the crystal facets as she polished the mouth with a clean dish towel. Then she removed two highball glasses and gave them the same treatment. From a little cubbyhole, almost hidden in the side of the cabinent, she selected a bottle of her private stock of scotch, and a bottle of pure-grade uncut Tennessee lightning. After filling the decanter half-and-half from each bottle, she set it and one of the highball glasses on a silver tray, and replaced her stock bottle in its compartment. But before she closed the door, she removed a small brown vial from the cubbyhole. Now she concentrated on the second glass. She rinsed it in a straight shot of lightning mixed with a healthy portion of powder from the vial, swishing the liquid around and around the circumference of the glass in movements as swift and sure as a woman controlling the warp and weft of fabric on a loom. Balancing the glass on her palm, she admired its perfection for a moment before emptying the excess liquid and placing it on the tray. Then she shook some of the vial's contents into the decanter. When she recorked the brown vial, she read the arsenic and chloride of lime label, and smiled as she placed it back in its cubicle. She was about to close the door when she had second thoughts about the other highball glass, so she rinsed it in enough Tennessee lightning to wet the rim, then closed the cubbyhole and headed for her office. Behind her, the kitchen looked as untouched and sanitary as it had when Viola had finished washing the breakfast dishes.

Having no wish to signal Viola as to her destination, Aleeda entered her office through a series of interlocking doors that allowed her to avoid the hallway. When she stepped in the room, Vinnie was a little surprised to see her come through a door that he'd assumed was a closet. She smiled at him. Just as she had thought, Vinnie had spent his time drinking the liquor she'd left in the office and tallying the receipts, no doubt with the total in his favor. "Not a bad cash crop," he said, but Aleeda let the belch of diesel engines slamming into second gear affect her hearing. According to the wall clock, it was time for the construction crew to be closing down for the night. *"All the better for what I got to do,"* she thought.

She carried the tray of drinks to the sideboard. "I thought I'd share a little of my good scotch," she told Vinnie. "Then I can check your tally, and while I'm at it, read them papers you flashing at me."

Vinnie grinned and dutifully pulled the papers from his pocket and waved them. He had an unlit cigarette in his mouth, but Aleeda knew he wouldn't light it. She'd once scared him shitless by dropping a smoldering match into an open crock of alcohol. From that point on, Vinnie was sure everything in the funeral parlor was flamable. If he'd had any sense of smell at all, he could have detected the odors of Murphy's soap and Neat's-foot oil Dough Boy lavished on the place in his daily cleaning. Or at the least, he would have caught a whiff of formaldehyde stubbornly clinging to Aleeda's clothing. But Vinnie, like Dough Boy, was short on senses of any sort. That's why Aleeda's next step passed without a hitch. Instead of taking the tray over so he could select his glass, she picked up both glasses and handed him the one she'd prepared for him. Then she poured them both a drink. In good faith, she sipped at hers and gestured toward the davenport.

"You want me to go over them receipts now?" she asked.

Vinnie's upper lip peeled back. "Could do that," he said, and put the highball drink on the desk. "And you could be signing these." He put the transfer of deed papers on the coffee table in front of her. Aleeda stared at the papers but said nothing. "Then I could have me another drink. Nothing like killing time," he laughed.

Aleeda nodded, picked up the numbers slips and the transfer papers and headed for her desk. As she brushed past him, Vinnie, half drunk on booze and a little power, rubbed her ass. If she'd had second thoughts, he'd ended them. Aleeda clenched her jaw and sat down at her desk. Vinnie was watching her, waiting for a reaction. She tried not to stare at his highball. Instead, her glance took in the sideboard, the vase of freshly cut flowers on her desk, the dozen or so ornate Greek urns perched on bookcases near the window, the periwinkle curtains behind their heavy drapes. But when she reached the window, she quickly shifted her gaze from dust clouding the window pane to the wall in front of her. There, photos hung with an orderliness that let her mind slip away from Vinnie and the room and the chaos outside the window. She scanned the display: shots of the African-American Betterment League, the Antioch newspaper staff, the Ladies of the Morning Star, the Black Star softball team, the Ethiopian Volunteers of World War I, the Steppers and Youngfellows and Daughters of the Underground Railroad, and of course, the local members of the Brotherhood of Sleeping Car Porters standing in front of the Sunset Limited. The Union picture brought her back to Butler, whose face in that 1931 photo was both handsome and innocent despite the suspicious glance he was casting upon the photographer.

Aleeda snapped open the deed of transfer papers as if she were flipping open a grocery bag. She pretended to read through them, then signed the last page, and leaned back in her desk chair, taking a sip of her drink and bathing Vinnie in a smile of conspiracy. The alcohol bit into her throat and knifed its way into the lining of her stomach, but she held her smile. Before she could sort out the tally sheets as if she were actually checking Vinnie's figures against her own, he had finished half of his drink and replenished the glass from the decanter. He settled himself on the davenport, scrunching against the horsehair and grunting slightly about its itchiness. Aleeda listened to him breathe, that raspy kind of breathing that comes with keeping midnight hours. Her tally sheet began to quickly fill up with numbers. Vinnie made a vulgar sound deep in his throat. Then he coughed: once, twice. Another drink, a gulp as he forced it down. Aleeda hurried the column of figures. Another painful cough. The breathing a bit more labored. The cough of something caught in his throat. A long inhale. Quiet. Only the scratch of her pen entering figures in their appropriate columns. Aleeda rubbed her eyes, the silence settling around her. She checked her balance sheet. Too many missing numbers. Vinnie had been a busy little man in his last few hours. She shook her head, then banded all the receipts according to her tallie, and locked them in her desk.

On the davenport, Vinnie stared at the ceiling in wordless surprise, his lips already flushed with blue tint. "Vinnie, you don't look much better now than you did when you was breathing," Aleeda told him. "Yeah, you do look a li'l peaked. Let's see if I can't do something bout that."

When Aleeda opened the door to the hallway, Viola was standing there with the cart. "The boys gone be here at ten-thirty, Mu'dear. We got five hours." She nudged the cart against the door.

Viola marked that moment as the first time her mother had been totally unprepared to react to something she'd done. Viola just kept leaning into the cart, until finally, Aleeda stepped aside, pulling open the door wide enough to let the cart through. But the door presented a problem. There didn't seem to be quite enough room to allow them to remove Vinnie Loemann's body. Then Aleeda saw how the frame had buckled near the point where the entire house was beginning to sag toward the construction site. By throwing her weight against the door on one side, and with Viola pushing the other side, the wood gave with a snap that echoed throughout the house, a sound Aleeda Grace swore she had heard more than once when Gionio's Construction Company trucks dragged their loads past the Home of Perpetual Rest.

The Return of the Apeman

THERE IS SOMETHING SAD about a moon that hangs low over the rooftops of a housing project, a certain sense of displacement, as if the moon has wandered off course and is about to be trapped by the upward thrust of buildings, the thick chunks of concrete jutting out of the earth like fingers about to claw their way into the sky. Most inhabitants of housing projects do not think about the moon. Ask the Apeman. In all of his years of roaming the labyrinths of the DeWitt, he seldom looked at the moon, even when its light seemed to hurt the inside of his eyelids after he'd turned his back on the night. For the Apeman, night was only the lengthening of shadows, the darkened doorways and corridors, the fluorescent glow of streetlights tinted by city planners to soften the potential anger of Project dwellers. For Apeman, night was only a swift movement from dusk to dawn and how evening dulled the color of his skin. In the flickering glare of passing cars his retreating figure seemed threatening, and after one swift glance, folks veered away from him.

If Apeman ever admitted he was conscious of the moon, it was only to brag about how, under the moon's light, no one laughed at him. Under its light, the room-sized bulk of his shoulders, the thickness of his forearms and thighs, the smooth roundness of his head brought him closer to a resemblance of those Nuba wrestlers from his ancestral roots.

Like them, he relied on his strength, looked upon it as being holy. And like them, his head, a seemingly immovable object, a planet in and of itself, was perfectly bald.

"Mah chile come into this world bald as a bat," Sadie Washington told folks. "All gums and no hair, honey. Just like some of them ol' timey pictures his Granny Easton got stuck up in her dresser drawer. Musta been something I et. All them chili peppers. Scart the hair right off his head fore he got here," she laughed.

And the doctors who examined him—at least those Apeman had allowed near him until, at the age of twelve, he had laid out the clinic's leading dermatologist with one punch—those doctors shook their heads. "A genetic weakness," they said, unable to explain why a throwback to the ash-coated wrestlers of the Nuba was a weakness. And more than that, unwilling to explain how the likes of the Apeman had appeared in a midwestern housing project some four generations after a Portugese slave trader had kidnapped his great-grandfather from a village tucked in the elbow of the Nuba Mountains. And that was too bad, because there were folks in the Projects who needed that explanation, dudes who liked to go toe-to-toe—or in Apeman's case, head-to-head—to prove who was top cat. One bout with the Apeman always changed that. After one bout, they had to laugh to show they meant no harm when they called him Apeman.

But in the moonlight, Franklin Dupont Washington, Jr., was the Apeman, and if anyone had doubts about his nickname during the day, they only needed to see him under the moon's light when his chromedome stood out in its hairless glory like a beacon among the lesser warning lights of no-neck, bullet-headed hoodlums who stalked the paths of the Clayton-DeWitt Projects. That perfectly cylindrical skull was a signal for his enemies to back-off, step-back, get-back, be-cool-fool. In another life, in the Sudan, his body might have been painted with the status of warrior, or in heat of the Brazil's Bahià, he might have been a great capoéira, but in the Projects, he was merely a product of the street and those who ravaged it. And because of it, Apeman had many enemies, a few friends, and only one love.

It was several months before Apeman admitted he was in love, and even then, when he found himself searching the line-up of windows at the south end of Building H-3, he was not sure that what he felt for Rochelle Putnam was love. Certainly he was aware that if the moon was right and the night grown gentle with silence, he might catch a glimpse of Rochelle before he climbed the stairs, and fell into his bed and a dreamless sleep. No—Apeman had no sense of the moon, but on those nights, Rochelle was most certainly aware of the moonlight, for it was by its light she saw Apeman turn the corner near the incinerators that served their quadrant of the Projects. From her window, she would watch him materialize out of the scramble of shadows. She knew it was Apeman because he was the only dude so bold as to strut his hip-broke walk smack-dab from the light to the shadows without looking over his shoulders. And he was always popping his fingers, humming a double-time melody the buildings picked up in a play of echoes like a doo-wah chorus. She could see the light glinting off his skull as he reached the end of the path then. And before he entered the building, he turned his head her way.

"Got his eye peeled on me and his nose open for the world to see," she'd laugh, a little hiccough of sound she cut short while her eyes still held amusement.

Some nights when Rochelle rocked her child to sleep, she deliberately waited until she saw Apeman cross that last stretch of crabgrass near the courtyard. Then she placed the baby in his crib, and slowly moved to the window, tugging the curtains to get Apeman's attention. Some of the windows were nondescript, but others, like Rochelle's, sported red lights, lampshades, or curtains. This telltale color was a favorite for Project dwellers, so without her movements, the window was merely another dirt-flecked glass square among the many squares set eight across and eight stories high in the more than forty buildings of the DeWitt Projects. Rochelle knew her movements kept Apeman from wasting time looking for her. After she went inside, she would tune her radio to an all-night jazz station and sit at her window, glass of milk in hand, before he turned on the light in his mother's kitchen. Rochelle could watch him pick his way through the refrigerator, sometimes drinking directly from a carton of milk or sampling cold left-overs. Impatient with his mother's scant offerings, Apeman would turn to the window. This was their last contact for the night. As Rochelle reached for the overhead light cord, she knew Apeman could see her, that under the false moon of a bare light bulb, she was the center of his attention. For a moment, she stood with one hand raised to the light, the other on her hip in a casual invitation. Then she pulled the cord and vanished from Apeman's view.

This went on for several months before Apeman gathered the nerve to speak to Rochelle. And then, it was the accident of Project living that brought them together. By the time the Apeman was fifteen, his mother had surrendered him to the rituals of manhood that dominated the Projects, and Apeman had mastered those rituals as easily as he had turned his back on school and changed his waking hours from daylight to darkness. His world became the groups of toughs that staked out regions of the DeWitt, drawing lines of demarcation as meticulously as bush warriors drew territorial lines in equatorial dirt. In this he triumphed, and he had the scars to prove it. Unfortunately, DeWitt gangs found their yield was less than any tribal bounty. "Ain't but a little something to keep on keeping on," they muttered, and Apeman kept on with the best of them.

But he promised his mother he'd go easy on the gang wars and stay clear of the law. In exchange for this, he shared her house and a few small chores he saw fit to perform, as long as his image as the baddest dude on the block remained intact. Taking out the trash was one chore he allowed his mother. In his eyes, there was a certain dignity about adding fuel to the rubbish piles that kept the incinerators hot. And it was there he made his first face-to-face contact with Rochelle.

It happened on one of those autumn Project days when the fine gray dust of parched soil had lifted off patches of grass that had tried, all summer, to become lawns. Spindly trees trembled under an overcast sky, and only a few errant crows bothered to hawk their displeasure regarding this state of affairs. It was afternoon, before the children swarmed out of schools and Project dwellers with day jobs returned home. Most others were asleep. They were the ones waiting for night before they left for work, or waiting, like Apeman, for the cover of darkness where they could "hit the streets and do the do," as he put it. He was standing by the incinerator, its open door warming his face with its eternal flame, its walls decorated with graffiti that ran the gamut from one-word epitaphs, like HAWK and CHO-CHO, to the full-fledged threats of WATCH OUT SUCKER and DEATH TO THE FUZZ. Apeman already had fed one bag of trash to the fire. Another lay at his feet, a trickle of sour liquid seeping from its soggy contents and drifting toward a nest of ants scavenging the debris in the corner of the building. During the day, their only rivals were cockroaches, huge winged creatures as scaly as their prehistoric brethren. Some days, Apeman scooped up the roaches and threw them, crackling, into the fire. He despised cockroaches because they were sneaky, scurrying into corners if he surprised them by suddenly turning on a light in a dark room. Rats were different. He preferred their boldness, how they stood their ground and put up a fight when cornered. Though he'd outgrown his years of rat hunting and no longer joined the younger boys in pursuit of that sport, he still carried a stick to beat back the occasional intruders who didn't wait for night to make their way from the sewers to the Projects. Rat fighting was another reason Apeman did this chore for his mother. But on the day he and Rochelle finally met, Apeman's rat stick was leaning against the side of the building under a scrawled directive that read: BRO MAN SAY CHILL OUT. And on that day, the Apeman was dreaming.

Apeman's dreams were not Hollywood perfect. He had no dreams of tract homes and 2.5 children, mortgages and block-long Detroit sedans. His were not the grand dreams of boardrooms and corporate images. His were not even street dreams of gangster suits and gang power. Apeman was dreaming of the ocean. From where he stood, he could hear the roar of traffic at the entrance to the DeWitt where Mission Street intersected Kingshighway, now wide enough to be called a boulevard. In regular intervals, the flow was interrupted by stoplights, and the rush of sound rose and fell as if some landbound ocean were following the patterns of tides. Apeman had never seen the ocean, but he knew it was out there somewhere, as real and endless as any life he imagined—as hopeful as a life that, in his wildest dreams, included Rochelle.

And while the Apeman dreamed, Rochelle descended the stairs. When she reached the sidewalk, she stopped to adjust her baby's jumper suit and hat. The wind picked up a swirl of loose trash, and she shielded the baby's eyes from bits of flying debris, then pulled the child close, rocking it, soothing herself more than her son. There were days when the regularity of buildings seemed to close in on her, days when she thought she'd suffocate among those square blocks, stacked like children's toys in sets of four-by-four at right angles and against the normal patterns of city streets. If she had stayed in school, if she had continued her fascination with circles and squares, angles and arcs, she might have realized that these Project, a forerunner in the field of urban redistribution, had been built as an experiment in low-cost living, an experiment destined for failure. But Rochelle only saw how few living things survived in the DeWitt, and she held her child closer to her breast as she prepared herself for the long walk across the compound past the taverns and bars along the strip to Cottage Grove and old man Feinstein's nickle-and-dime meat market. Only last week, the social worker had reduced her welfare allotment, so she reminded herself to count her change carefully and not spend so much time returning Feinstein's smile. "Can't eat that Jew's grin," she muttered, and headed for the main walkway.

Her path took her below the slight incline where the incinerators were housed. When she turned the corner, she saw the Apeman. He was still gazing into the milky-gray sky, a swirl of insects and ashes from the trash fire billowing around his bald head. In profile, his oversized features seemed chiseled from stone, like those giant heads on Easter Island, their faces turned toward some distant point of origin no one as yet has discovered. But it was enough for Rochelle to know Apeman's gaze was aimed toward some place outside the Projects. The intensity of his look washed over her, and she might have stayed there, holding the image as close to her as she held her child, except at that moment, a cockroach slammed into Apeman's ear and set him spinning in a wild dance. Looking back, even Apeman was willing to laugh, but at that moment, all he could do was throw himself into the battle between insect and man, that age-old war of bug against man the bravest and largest men sometimes lost. This one reduced Apeman to infancy and left him beating his face and ears, twisting his body and leaping, from a flat-footed standing position, straight into the air. He danced against the image of the roach, its crusty body brown as onion skin, crawling along the crest of his eardrum. He managed all this while gargling. At least, Rochelle thought it sounded like gargling. Her baby clapped his hands and drooled with a giggle of delight. Rochelle didn't quite know what to do. She had seen Apeman dance before, and while he sometimes looked more like a linebacker than a dancer, his movements were always in tune with the music. Now he jumped, pivoted, and flung his body upward as if the top half wanted to go in one direction while the bottom half fled toward another direction. The baby squealed and applauded. Rochelle stared and tried to put a name to what she saw. *"It ain't scrammin,"* she thought. *"Ain't no cops nowhere near here. And he sho can't be shootin no baskets. The onliest round thing up on that hill is his big fat head."*

While Rochelle groped for a word, Apeman lunged for the sky one last time. It was then he saw her, and in a movement so fluid, a passerby might have thought he'd planned it all along, he feinted to the left and jabbed as if she'd caught him shadow boxing. What else could he do? After all, how could the meanest motor scooter in all of the DeWitt explain how he'd been cut down by a cockroach? How could a dude even mention cockroaches to a foxy lady like Rochelle, much less admit the damn thing had flown right into his ear while he was dreaming? *"Dreaming is something for cats what ain't got no guts to do the do,"* Apeman thought. Then he walked down the slope, and as casually as he could—considering the fact he was still twitching with the memory of the cockroach's wing fluttering against his eardrum—he said, "Hey Rochelle."

The baby leaned forward to offer his pacifier to Apeman as reward for such a grand performance, but Rochelle simply smiled and said, "Hey yourself."

That was all they needed to begin what was to go on between them.

To say that Rochelle changed Apeman's life would be a mild statement. "Honey, she done turned that boy clean around," his mother told folks, her voice full of begrudging respect for Rochelle, who had done what she, his own mother, could not do. "You ought to see him. Making out over that woman like she some kinda young thing. Humph! Ain't even studying bout the fact she got that baby. I told him. Franklin, I said, it's more than a notion taking care of somebody else's chillun. But he never did listen to me."

Still, while Sadie Washington complained, she also breathed a sigh of relief that her son had not had any children he'd abandoned to the haphazard life of the Projects where, too often, luck seemed to depend upon which number was at the top of a list. Ask the social worker. Ask the numbers runner. Everything in the DeWitt was monitored by numbers. The number of people in each apartment unit was determined by the available number of apartments. Or so they said. Availability was determined by the budget line. Or so they said. And always, the number of available units depended on the number of social welfare workers available to screen tenants, which in turn was controlled by the number of social welfare applicants, the age of the applicant, and the length of time any one applicant could stomach all the red tape connected with the DeWitt. This equation seemed to have little to do with those who lived in the Projects.

"They got you comin and goin," Apeman's mother said. "Half the time, I ain't nothing but a dollar short and a day older. Just playing the numbers and killing time."

Apeman usually supplied his mother with her daily lottery numbers, his equations just as easily based on the number of casualities suffered in a gang rumble as on the number of men needed for temporary jobs on any given day. Those numbers, as crazy as any, had paid off twice in the last year, but when Apeman began seeing Rochelle, his mother decided to try her own equation.

"You play me a nickel on twenty-one-twenty," she told the numbers runner. "I got a feeling bout them numbers cause they be the sum of ages what my son got himself involved with. Now I ain't saying twenty-one be old, mind you. Even if the person got herself a baby what ain't no more than one year old itself. But if seven come eleven, then twenty-one got to come twenty, and that be my boy's age. So you just put this here nickel right on that number today. Don't see how them two's gone be together long enuf to play this more'n once."

But she was wrong, and as the reformed crapshooter said about the player who had no better sense than to depend only on luck, she just couldn't see for looking. She had never seen her son maintain his interest in anything for more than a few weeks, so she chalked up the days he spent with Rochelle as a time coming to its end. She thought: *"He'll move when he puts his mind to it."*

At first, Apeman echoed those thoughts. "Everything is everything," he told his mother. "I'll be back home directly. I just got me a little action going. Gone let it run for a bit."

But even after he began sleeping with Rochelle, living more in her apartment than his mother's, he couldn't see how the sweet pain of holding her set him up to make all the right moves. What Apeman saw was Rochelle's easy laughter. Knowing how the system could close in on folks and turn them stone cold with rage, Apeman was amazed at her lack of anger.

"She don't even talk about the dude what give her that baby," Apeman told his mother. "But he sho musta been lowdown to be leaving her by her lonesome. She ain't no bigger than that." He snapped his fingers. "You oughta see her. Don't let nobody tell her nothing."

"I see her," his mother answered flatly.

Apeman continued. "I tell her. I say: 'Shell . . . ' She don't like me to be calling her Shell but I calls her Shell anyway . . . I say: 'Shell, put that boy down. He almost bigger'n you.' She just laugh."

He closed his eyes and saw Rochelle laughing up at him, but his mother saw her son being lured away from her house by a girl who was no more than chest high to Apeman's six feet of bulk. And unlike the Apeman, she saw Rochelle's determination.

Where Rochelle was small-boned, with that tight-lipped appearance some light brown-skin women carried, the Apeman was dark, loose-jointed and oily, his body jiggling as if he were about to pull himself away from the glue that kept flesh to bone. And while Rochelle allowed the rules and report forms of Project living to bind her to an orderly routine, Apeman always appeared to be thrown together as if his clothes were too small, his movements too big. He had no routine, except hanging out, and to the cops, all that flesh on the move spelled trouble. To them, Apeman was too big and too black to be left alone. To Rochelle, Apeman's looseness made him seem vulnerable, and when he smiled, a gentle boyish smile that always surprised her, she could hear the quickening rhythm of her heart. To her, the warm smell of Apeman's skin—"like the way mah baby smells in the crease of his neck," she said—made her feel as if she could curl up against his side and, for the first time since she'd moved to the Projects, sleep without fear. At those times, just before she drifted into sleep, she would say his name and smile.

Although Apeman called her Shell, he was pleased when she called him Franklin, her speech sweetening the word with the soft lilt of South Carolina that was still in her voice. Until Rochelle, his mother had been the only one to call him by his birth name, and while everyone else made him feel as if he had to defend himself against that name, when Rochelle said Franklin, it seemed to fit him. Holding her kept him from drowning in the stark daylight of the Clayton-DeWitt with its endless forms to be filled in triplicate, to be stamped and carried from one office to another, to be signed and countersigned. Instead of the daily game of avoiding yet another office that smelled of cardboard, pencil shavings, and stale tobacco smoke, Apeman buried himself in the scent of Rochelle's hair and the odor of Fels Naphtha soap on her sheets. Usually when he awoke, she was up with the baby, but as soon as the child fell asleep, she came to him.

Sometimes she made him so happy, he ended their lovemaking not by falling away from her, but by picking her up and walking through the house still buried inside her, her legs still wrapped around his waist. Other days, she'd nest against his body and trace the old wounds that had keloided into shiny ridges like a warrior's battle scars. When she asked about the fights, she laughed to hear his voice rumble inside his chest like quiet thunder. And when the stories seemed too real, she kissed the wound as if he'd just received it. She dreamed of his skin the way Apeman dreamed of the ocean, salty and sweet at the same time while the air around it filled her head with a giddiness. Just placing her cheek against his broad chest pulled the tightness from her face and made her weep. Although he loved her kisses, if she cried he made fun of his battles so she'd laugh and he could laugh with her. They tried to laugh quietly to avoid waking the baby, but if the child began to cry, Rochelle let her son take her place on Apeman's chest, and the three of them would lie in bed watching the sky above the Projects settle into its usual winter mush.

They might have stayed that way forever, except one evening, just as the last rays of sun coated the buildings in a brutal shade of pink, Rochelle said, "Don't go out tonight, Franklin."

They were sitting on one of the four stone benches that had been planted in the stingy lawn space of the quadrangle. The baby was scrapping a bottle cap across the surface of another bench, partially obliterating the rough attempts at graffiti someone had already tried to carve into the stone. As Rochelle's eyes pressed him for an answer, Apeman looked at the buildings for help, but those walls only offered the usual graffiti: SWEET PLUM, ROBERT 168, and CATO LIVES painted over the outline of a running man and reduced to idiocy by some poor speller's curse of FUCH YOU! Apeman searched the sky. A plume of smoke wormed its way around the corner of one building, and somewhere in another section of the complex, an incinerator belched the rancid odor of burning cloth. Somewhere else, a dog barked, and the hoarse cries of teenage boys offered answers to the beast. Both sounds almost covered Rochelle's voice as she repeated her request.

"Stay with me and the baby tonight, Franklin."

Apeman leaned forward as if he hadn't heard her correctly. "The dude looked like he was faking his shots from the git-go," his friends would say later. At the time, whatever move Apeman wanted to make was cut short by the way the sun changed Rochelle's skin to a shade as brown as the biscuits his mother baked. Apeman missed his mother's cooking, but he willingly gave that up the day he decided to move in with Rochelle. Now he had to give up his turf of darkness as well.

The kids in the area were the first to know. They passed the word to Apeman's buddies, who sent it spiraling down the middle of the Black Belt as far as Feinstein's Meat Market. There, it dissipated in the front yards of houses with only one or two families, folks who believed they lived far enough uptown to ignore the bad vibrations that pushed out of the scramble of lives occupying the Clayton-DeWitt. But on the stretch of road frequented by Apeman and his friends, the news that he was shacking up with Rochelle leaked into the bar-b-que rib joints, record stores, and pool halls. The talk was sprinkled along the street like bits of newspapers, like the wine bottles, numbers slips, and rotting food that spilled into the alleyways behind the taverns and cafes. It rattled against the iron bars covering the windows of loan shops, and clattered in the rhythms of the stacked heels of hustlers parading the street that separated the Projects from Mission Street on one side, Kingshighway on the other.

"Mah man's chained to the bed," they laughed. "Rochelle done caught the Apeman by the short hairs," they said, and passed the word to the cleaning women waiting by Hodiman tracks for the #6 trolley to take them to their day jobs in the Belmont suburbs.

"Don't be ax'ing me what that boy doing," Sadie Washington told the women. "I ain't the one he got to be splaining something to. I got five more chillun at home. If the welfare woman come to mah house, I ain't got nothing to splain."

The women grunted "Ump-um-um," in the practiced code of folks who had been silenced by years of servitude. Their disapproval was picked up in the caws of crows sitting on telephone wires, and the hoarse barks of a scabby old dog chained to the junkyard fence.

Later, Apeman could hear a trace of it in the voice of the social worker who paid a surprise visit to Rochelle's apartment.

She said, "Perhaps you would like to fill out the change of residence forms, Mr. Washington."

"I ain't changed nothing," Apeman told her. "I just be helping out till Rochelle get on her feet."

The woman stared at Apeman. He was stretched out on the sofa, the only comfortable piece of furniture in the room. The baby, propped up against Apeman's belly, watched her, its eyes wide as a rabbit gone torpid. Rochelle had offered her the only other chair in the room, but the social worker preferred to stand. She'd placed herself in the middle of the room near a coffee table covered by a straw doily, an ashtray, an empty baby bottle, and several toys. Aside from a radio and a drooping rubber tree plant placed near the window, the rest of the room was empty. "Exactly how are you helping Miss Putnam?" the woman asked.

"He just watching the baby for me," Rochelle interrupted. "When I got to go looking for a job," she added quickly.

The woman sniffed. "And when do you look for a job, Mr. Washington?"

The baby's screams saved Apeman the trouble of arranging an answer. He tucked the child under one arm the way a quarterback would tuck a football. "I can't do but one job at a time," he told the woman, then flashed his Pepsodent grin and lumbered into the bedroom.

The door had barely closed before the baby stopped screaming. Rochelle smiled. Once, Apeman had fallen asleep with one of the baby's rattles glued to his forehead. He'd stuck it there to soothe the child, but when the baby had finally closed its eyes, so had the Apeman. Rochelle had spent hours icing the edges of the suction cup before she could peel it off his forehead, and it took weeks for the purple bruise to disappear. Even now, the baby sometimes said, "Rattle? Rattle?"—laughing when Apeman leaned over to kiss him.

"The baby be teething," Rochelle told the social worker. "But Franklin, he real good with him."

The woman turned her frowns from the bedroom door to Rochelle. "Well . . ." she said, momentarily stunned by the look she'd seen in their faces. It was that kind of liquid smile she saw in teenage kids when she caught some boy trapping a girl on a stairwell, or in an alcove of a building already teeming with too many babies. Sometimes she had personally escorted those kids back to school, but she couldn't imagine ever having to take these two to any school. In fact, she couldn't imagine Apeman in a classroom. What desk would accommodate him? What teacher would tolerate him? The woman sighed and placed a set of the appropriate papers on the coffee table. Although she said, "I expect you to include the names of everyone living in this unit," she knew the next time she came for a visit, Rochelle Putnam would simply hide the Washington boy.

"Dig it, I don't hide from nobody!" Apeman told Rochelle. "Don't be letting that white woman tell you different. She come in here with them papers all lined up like she some kinda general ready to throw us outta here. She mess with me, I put that bitch away."

Rochelle kissed him: lips, eyes, face, the top of his head, the small scar at the crown where a Mission Street rumble had earned him four stitches. And when she pulled him close to her, Apeman licked the tips of her breasts. "Ain't nobody messing with you," Rochelle told him. "Ain't nobody messing with you, Franklin."

He grunted. "Best keep it that way, Shell. Don't nobody mess with me. Dig it? They call me Apeman. They know I don't got to hide from nobody. Ask any Blood. What I say be the gospel."

Rochelle nodded, but she thought: *"Who am I supposed to ask? Cho-Cho? Snitch? Big Tony? Polo?"*

She was in love, but she was no fool. There wasn't a soul in the Projects who would stop that low-life to ask the time of day. Rochelle had watched Apeman's cut-buddies swoop across the compound, the backs of their leather jackets billowing in the wind as if they were about to inflate and rise to the sky like crows. They even acted like crows, talking loud and scattering folks too slow to move out of their way. "Hey Miz Thing!" they yelled if they saw Rochelle without Apeman to protect her. She knew she could defend herself against the social workers better than she could against that bunch. And when they came calling, whistling: "o-bop-shee-bam," all she could do was watch Apeman hit the floor, running.

"You done made your bed, you best lie in it," Apeman's mother told her. "What else you gone do? "

Rochelle bounced the baby on one hip, a bag of groceries on the other, and watched several women struggling with their own balancing act. While Apeman's mother counted her food stamps, Rochelle surveyed the scene. She didn't need anyone to tell her it was check day. All the ADC mothers from the Projects were trying to make the best of their welfare allotments with Feinstein's measly supply of meat. Although Feinstein had stocked his counter high with chicken backs, pork kidneys, and sausage that morning, the case was nearly empty, with the exception of a few neck bones. And those were made even less appetizing by the smudged handprints left by kids barely tall enough to reach the glass case. Their mothers, some pregnant and some balancing babies on one hip like Rochelle, had bought Feinstein's stock, and now they waddled to the door, children clinging to their coattails as they plunged into the chilly air and trekked toward the Clayton-DeWitt. Rochelle stood in Feinstein's doorway and turned her head in the other direction.

"What you got on your mind?" Apeman's mother asked. "You think you can step between him and tomorrow?"

"If I got to," Rochelle said.

Somehow, she made Apeman promise her three nights a week. Those other four, he claimed for the street. On the three nights she had been granted, she serenaded Apeman with stories as old as Aesop's fables. "Ain't but the three of us," she told him. "We could go somewhere new."

"Out there is where it's at," Apeman said. He nodded toward the window and the street below. "Ain't no reason to be blowing your soul for chump change. When I get up from this chair and go out there, everything best be on the up and up." He smiled and ran his thumb along the edge of one of her sharpest kitchen knives,

For a second, Rochelle watched him concentrate on the knife's tip, then she stood behind him and pressed her face against his head, marvelling, once again, at how smooth it was, hairless and black as if he had come from some other world. In a way, she was right. The Apeman belonged in another world, one that would allow him to breathe without forcing him to prick his skin, as if a drop of blood on a knife's blade could chase the anger that filled him. But the Clayton-DeWitt was the world that held Apeman, and as he reached for her body, Rochelle sucked the blood from his fingertip and tried to soothe him with stories.

"Got a cousin in Cleveland," she told him. "He say ain't no trouble finding work. Good jobs. Or we could go up by Duluth. They got the shipyards up near there."

Rochelle tuned her voice low and let her breathing match his. And when the night went on without him, the Apeman held her in the crook of his arm and pulled the bedcovers over her bare shoulders, smoothing the wrinkles his body had left in the tattered sheets. Outside, the winter wind screamed and beat against the windows like a lost bird. While Rochelle slept, Apeman dreamed of the ocean.

And sometimes, when those dreams were strong, Apeman swore he had been talking in his sleep. "Got me a cousin in Pasadena," Rochelle told him. "He say out there the ocean be warm all year round."

For a time Apeman listened, at least to the point where he could remember what she'd said from one day to the next, but while Rochelle's talk was built on dreams, he saw the street as straight on and up front. Then one night, word reached them that the Shads from crosstown had wasted two of the Bloods. And when his buddies whistled him out of the apartment, nothing Rochelle said could keep the street from claiming the Apeman.

"Baby, I got to split. It's blood for Blood and the dudes be waiting for me. When the deal goes down, the Apeman's around. Dig it?"

"Franklin, don't go. I told your mama you wasn't into that scene no more. What I'm gone say if you don't come back?" Apeman laughed. "You gone say: 'No better for him with his unlucky self.'" But when he saw the tears gather in her eyes, he kissed her and added, "I be back, Shell. Apeman ain't gone be leaving his baby."

Now and then, she went to the window, half expecting to see him strolling across the compound. Instead, she saw old men leaving for factory night shifts, young girls slipping into the darkness to meet boys, and a few boys, some almost as large as Apeman, slipping into their broke-down street walks almost before they left their mothers' doorways.

When they stepped free of the shadows of buildings, everyone was etched in moonlight for a moment, and in that moment, no one could be mistaken for the Apeman.

For two nights, Rochelle listened to the grapevine. "The street be hot," they said. "Dudes running every-which-way."

"The fuzz hanging out double shifts. The Man be sticking to the DeWitt like white on rice," they said.

"The Bloods playing for hard times. Like the deal gonna go double-d down. You dig it?"

By Saturday night, the moon was so large, Rochelle shrank from its light. Then Rochelle decided she couldn't wait any longer. At 11:50, she left the baby with Apeman's mother and went to search for him.

It had been several years since she'd walked at night that string of blocks leading from the DeWitt to Mission Street. Rochelle found nothing had changed. Only the moon left the street looking less ragged than it seemed during the day. She paced her walk: scanning the crowds, checking out doorways, even the open door of the Sanctified Church where she could see two or three women already leaning into the spirit, their cheeks rouged as brightly as some of the women she saw in the bars. Every few blocks she chose a place for five minutes of warmth: up one side and down the other, three blocks and pause at B&C Records, another three blocks and stop at Rosie's Bar-B-Q, two blocks later and Frickie's Tavern, two more and Cinnamon Ivory's Bar or Doc's Pool Hall. She bought half a bowl of Chinese noodles with soy sauce at Wu Fong's, feeling guilty about not sharing the food with Apeman. The jook joints kept their doors cracked to let in air, cold weather or not. In exchange, the smell of fried pork rinds and beer permeated the street along with the raucous beat of juke boxes that seemed stuck on one or two songs from their dozen or so selections. By the time Rochelle left B&C at 12:45, the street was jumping with sound of the top five songs of the season. And on those stretches of road where the storefronts were locked tight, the radios of passing cars took up the slack. Rochelle ignored the cars, especially those sporting whitewalls and two-tone paint jobs, some driver's grinning face accented by the cut-out of a pine tree dangling from the rearview mirror. Cars were for uptown dudes. She knew Apeman was on foot, so she kept her eyes trained on the narrow doorways and clusters of people hugging the circles of neon lights.

The Strip extended down the length of the street all the way to Cottage Grove before the night life slipped out of the boundaries of the Clayton-DeWitt. By 1:30, Rochelle was moving with its rhythms. At Rosie's, she spotted a woman she knew slightly, an ADC mother who once shared the same social worker. But she was in no mood for chatter.

"Stuck up heifer," the woman called out when Rochelle left without speaking. After being inside, the air seemed colder, but she ducked her head into her coat collar and kept walking. There were only a few people on the street, all of them bowed into the chilly gusts of wind. Even the girls who usually worked the block had taken their trade indoors. They were the ones perched on the bar stools nearest the exit, ready to leave in case they spotted the familiar car of an old customer circling the block. Some of those drivers, thinking she had braved the cold just for them, slowed down when they saw Rochelle. She ignored both them and the women who eyed her when she entered the taverns dotting the strip. She wasn't about the business of cutting in on anyone's territory, and her search had nothing to do with cars. "Pimp-mobiles," Apeman had called them. He had never learned to drive and hated cars, so when she passed Jimmy B.'s garage around 2:30, she ignored the dim yellow light in the back room that told her a few stragglers were shooting dice.

A drink here, a drink there, and it was well past three o'clock when she found herself doubling back toward the DeWitt. The air promised another drop in temperature before morning. Rochelle considered how long it would take her to warm her feet once she crawled into her cold bed. "I need my man tonight," she mumbled. Despite the few drinks she'd managed to buy, her arms were cold, and she rubbed them under the thin wool of her coat sleeves. As she passed an alley, she spotted a group of boys. *"Li'l crumb snatchers,"* she told herself, and didn't bother to turn away from their whistles. They were adorning a wall with curses, and judging by the strong smell of fresh paint, she figured they were more interested in finishing whatever plans they had for cursing the wall than they were in hassling her. She'd already walked past them when she heard the sound of paint cans exploding against the pavement. Then shouts, and running footsteps. Most of the words were muffled, but she thought she heard someone yell, "Apeman!" Rochelle turned back.

The alley was one of those narrow pathways that offered minimal access to the buildings on either side. A latticework of fire escapes lay against the backs of buildings like spines, and under these outcroppings, garbage bins were butted against backdoors of stores and abandoned warehouses. City planners had used the closure of four or five such alleys for arguments favoring plans to build the DeWitt. "A removal of the atmosphere that breeds crime," they had said, and erected a chainlink fence separating the Projects from the alleys. Later, gangs cut holes in the mesh, or cleared the fence like pole vaulters. Anyone who needed an escape route or a dumping ground had free use of the alleys.

The shadows were so thick, Rochelle knew there might be a dozen or so people hiding there. She narrowed her eyes, trying to force shapes out of the mottled forms. A cat howled and someone scuffled against a garbage can. Rochelle whispered, "Franklin?" and her answer was the clatter of cans tumbling against each other. She was considering whether to move closer when a car turned onto the street behind her. Even without the warning lights, Rochelle knew it was the cops. She could see the pale white faces of the driver and his partner. Between one breath and the next, she plunged into the alley, the patrol car's spotlight licking at her heels.

A moment later, a cop yelled, "Stop! Who's there?" as if he expected an answer. Rochelle began to run. The sound of her running was mimicked by footsteps ahead of her. Behind her, the cops fell into step.

She forced herself to concentrate on the center of the alley where light was reflected off a trickle of stagnant water. The smell oozing from it was sharp and pricked the inside of her nostrils. The entire alley reeked with smells, some of them as strong as a festering wound, others oddly dry. Rochelle stayed just to the left of the center strip of water, not close enough to be completely visible to the cops behind her, but far enough from the buildings to avoid plowing into the garbage bins and debris piled at the edges. If she followed that light, she could keep up with whoever was running ahead of her. The light was like a string leading her home, or at least, leading her back to the Projects where everyone, including the cops, seemed to be heading. Rochelle blocked out the sound of her own footfalls and tried to listen for any changes in direction the others took. At one point, she thought she heard someone duck into a building. She only stopped for a second, but that slowed down the cops as well. Instinct told those in front of her to stop. Rochelle inched closer to a wall. A door rocked on its hinges: squeaking shut, then open, then shut. A rock hit the wall ahead of her, and a cat streaked across the line of thin light and slid under a dumpster. Rochelle exhaled.

"This is the police. Stand clear and identify yourself now."

No one wasted any time answering them. The alley echoed with footsteps and heavy-throated voices. Rochelle yelled, "Franklin!" and the name wound itself around the wrought-iron fire escapes like a thin wire. Immediately, she wished it back, but it was too late. She heard Apeman call to her, then someone fired a gun. The shots were not aimed at them, but the cops returned the fire anyway. Rochelle flattened herself against a wall, but the gunshots had alarmed the rats and one brushed against her ankle as the pack scurried away from the piles of trash and darted into safer niches along the alley. She screeched and propelled herself off the wall. If she had not spotted the DeWitt's fence ahead of her, she would have been on a blind run. Usually, the separation between fence and post was barely noticeable, but by the time Rochelle reached it, the others had left the jagged hole bellowed out like a parachute. She hit the fence running, her bony legs flying, her arms spread as if she were about to take flight.

They were turning the corner near the incinerators when Rochelle gained enough ground to get close to them. Bloods and Shads—both groups running in one direction, away from the Man. As they slipped in and around buildings, apartment lights flicked on until the DeWitt seemed to rise from its sleep and announce itself open for business. But as soon as everyone saw who was doing the running and who was doing the chasing, the lights clicked off leaving them all in the dark. Even the moon had abandoned them, slipping finally over the edge of a world on the other side of the DeWitt. The only light left was the dull red glow from the incinerator. But Rochelle was close enough to see which ones were Shads and which ones Bloods. Close enough to see Apeman needed two dudes to keep him moving. He was hanging between them like an old tree trunk, his arms draped over their shoulders and his head thrown forward, his scalp an ebony glow in the flickering lights. She had to call him twice before he heard her. Only for her would he have made the others stop and turn toward her, the pain on his face slowly replaced by a lopsided grin. Only for her would he have pushed aside his cut-buddies and stood, for a moment, with his arms raised as if she'd caught him sneaking out of the house.

Rochelle covered the ground in half the time the gangs had needed. The cops needed even less time. Squad cars had pulled onto the main road of the DeWitt, and uniformed men were heading toward the buildings, fanning out in formation as if they were about the business of fighting a war. The newspapers would call it a confrontation, but reporters covering the story would not be asked to count the number of rifles and pistols trained on the two gangs. Only one newspaper would mention the woman who had thrown herself in front of one of the young hoodlums, falling into his arms as if the sheer presence of her body would keep him from harm. And in the photograph, the two of them lay in a heap among the ashes and debris of the trash fire.

Ruby–Ruby

ONE SUMMER during a sweet July evening of 1955, the same summer the city planned to celebrate the ground-breaking decade of the Clayton-DeWitt Projects by cleaning up the area, Eustacia Lucille Portugal took it upon herself to do a little housecleaning of her own. At first, there wasn't much of a connection between the two events. In fact, Eustacia's house was uptown from the DeWitt Projects, and while she attacked her house from top to bottom with all the available cleaning and scouring potions at her disposal—an act that caused her husband, Percy, to mutter, "Merde! Mah woman, she like somebody got thees personal war on dirt."—the city just half-heartedly repainted playground equipment and replaced a few loose bricks in the DeWitt courtyards. To cap the celebration, a fresh billboard dedicating the Projects was erected:

CLAYTON-DEWITT URBAN RENEWAL—A CITY PROJECT
PLANNED WITH AN INTEREST IN PEOPLE

Anyone could have told the city planners that most of the black folks who had been relocated into the DeWitt's rabbit-warren units weren't really fooled by that fancy billboard. Black folks knew the difference between removal and renewal. They knew the old folks, those who had lived in the Clayton District in the 1940s before the bulldozers razed the area, definitely had been removed and were never earmarked to return. "Cleaning out the slums is what them whites is interested in," folks complained. "Didn't even ask none of us if we wanted to be renewed. Just told us who could move in and who best move on." And for those black folks outside of the Projects, those who lived farther out near Indian Hills, or north near Kingshighway, the DeWitt towered at the edge of their neighborhoods in a line-up of eight-story brick structures that threw their two-story houses, bungalows and brownstones into almost constant shadows—shadows that were cast by rust-brown high-rises sucking the sun into dry canyons between buildings, and shaping a wind that warned folks in the old neighborhoods of a similiar fate should the wrecking balls and bulldozers turn in their direction.

For the first few years of the DeWitt's existence, those who lived uptown sympathized with the Projects. The socializing between the two neighborhoods was as regular as the teenagers' sock hops in the DeWitt's community center, or the older folks' Saturday night fish frys and bar-b-que picnics at Forest Grove Park. Seeing the Projects made folks living on the other side of Clayton spend a little more time tending their postage-stamp lawns and whitewashing their porch stoops. "Don't seem right, making folks live stacked one atop another like sardines in a can," they said, and queried DeWitt folks about Project living. "How can you be standing all them cooking smells commingling up and down the hallways? Be worser than Noo Yawk City after a while, I spect."

But Eustacia Portugal paid no more than lip service to her neighbors' casual remarks about the DeWitt, the comments they passed over garden fences, or whispered on the downtown trolley as it roared down Hodiman tracks past the Projects. To her, the DeWitt was just news stories about hoodlum gangs, raggedy Project kids, and welfare mothers. And it would have stayed that way if one evening she hadn't found herself, once again, sitting with her neighbors on the porch swing under the overhang of the hickory tree, while behind her in the darkened living room, the record player blasted out R-and-B love songs, and in front of her, three half-grown girl children, her sisters' daughters, gazed at the horizon where smoke from burning trash marked the location of the Projects—where, more than likely, her husband, Purcell Purcia Portugal, could be found.

Over the course of a year, Eustacia had inherited the girls, none of them from the same mama and all of them dangerously close, give or take a year, to their fifteenth birthday. She loved her nieces as if they were her own children, but that evening in 1955, watching those girls lean toward the shadows of the Projects made Eustacia Portugal come to her senses and realize that the presence of the girls seemed all too conveniently agreed upon by her husband. Most any man would have been impatient with a wife who took in her relatives' offspring the way some women take in strays, but Percy Portugal had taken it all in stride. Stacia complained that he was too generous, spoiling the girls with ice cream treats from Velvet Freeze, Chinese food from Wu Fong's, and bags of ten-cent hamburgers from White Castle's.

"Baby, thees girls can not stay in the house up under you all the time," Percy had told her. "Mahn, they got ta go. Let them have some fun."

Whatever he suggested was "righteous and cool" with the girls but when he piled them into his Thunderbird, Stacia still worried that Percy would turn loose-limbed and easy, the way he'd been when she met him, before her nieces had come to the house, before he'd become a family man. Looking back, the girls seemed to have arrived at the house with the same ease Percy had used to stay away.

Maresa, her sister Zenobia's daughter, had been the first arrival, coming in on a Saturday morning about two years after Stacia and Percy were married, coming first to spend the night, then staying the whole week and months of weeks afterwards. The next summer Stacia's sister, Lil'June, had brought all of Portia June's clothes to the house instead of "killing this heifer with my own hands," she'd snarled as she shoved her daughter into the living room and walked out the front door, slamming it behind her without so much as "Good-bye." Fed up with her mother, Lulu Mae had followed her cousins to their Aunt Stacia's before the school year began. In Lulu's case, Bernice, Stacia's other sister, would not even acknowledge her daughter's whereabouts—"a missing person," she'd mumbled.

Because they saw themselves as orphans, the girls stuck together, and Stacia, watching them, envied their closeness and missed her own sisters. In a way, having the girls there made it seem as if Stacia had gathered her sisters home. They ran their mouths as much as her sisters ever had, and like her sisters, they were moody—pouting one minute, laughing the next. Eustacia and her sisters had shouldered many problems by banding together to present a solid front to neighbors, and now, after having been evicted from their separate houses for real or imagined infractions of rules, her nieces banded together in a similiar way: them against the world. They were a cluster of complexions, brown, tan, and pale yellow, dressed in identical A-line skirts, short-sleeved sweaters, knee socks, and penny loafers.

"Vernida had her babies like stair steps," Dee Streeter gossiped, "but Stacia got herself a mish-mash. Some of everything, honey."

"Ain't none of them fit for nothing, cept Lulu," Corella Holmes said. "Lulu is sweet as she can be."

"You best take off them blinders," Dee told her. "Lulu peers sneaky to me. Too quiet and you know, still water runs deep. I likes Pepper. She comes right out and tells you what she talking bout."

Corella nodded. "Un-huh. Still, you ain't never seen nothing as pretty brown as when Lulu smile. And Maresa's skin just as smooth. Look like somebody been polishing that chile to put her up on a mantelpiece."

"Humph. The only place they done put that chile is up in Stacia's house. Now poor Stacia's stuck there with them girls."

And that was exactly how Eustacia felt as she sat in the raspberry-scented midwestern night watching fireflies flash their cold yellow light among the fat hedgerows near the walkway, and children, breathless with discovery, scream out their games of hide-and-seek. But it wasn't as if she had a plan when the thought first crossed her mind that something was wrong. That evening, Eustacia let the feeling of trouble enter her body and take hold in little corners where it rested for several weeks before she gave voice to it. That evening, she merely listened as her neighbor, Corella Holmes, related yet another story about the DeWitt.

"They ain't got no grass in amongst them buildings," Corella said. "Just some bricks and old scraggly trees what ain't had no more than five leaves on them the whole time them Projects been there."

"Um-hum. Spozed to be giving them people some decent housing," Dee Streeter grumbled in a hoarse voice that held all her years of whiskey drinking and smoking. As usual, she had a cheroot in her mouth. "Don't look decent to me one little bit," she added.

As Dee took a drag off her cheroot, Corella interrupted. "Ain't even no place where you can sit down for a spell come evening."

"Yeah, it is," Lulu said. She had just put a new stack of records on the phonograph, and was on her way to the end of the steps to join her cousins who were already popping their fingers to the records Lulu had picked, songs that were the favorites at the DeWitt sock hops. "They got sit-down places," Lulu said. "Benches. Got 'em bolted down to the ground so can't nobody steal 'em."

"How you know so much, Miz Lulu Mae?" Dee challenged the girl. "I ain't seen bench one when I go past there." The grunt that followed was caught in a rattle of spit laced with tobacco, but Dee had made her point and knew it.

Caught in the tattletale trap, Lulu narrowed her eyes and for a moment, Stacia was reminded so much of being at home with her sisters, she automatically stifled the impulse to laugh. But her sisters had taught her a hard lesson on laughing against someone—Stacia still had a scar near her hairline to prove it—so instead of laughing, she sucked her teeth and watched Lulu trying to get out of her trap.

"Can't nobody see nothing from no trolley," Lulu said. "You can't see nothing if you ain't been in the DeWitt."

"And since when you been allowed in the DeWitt?" Stacia asked.

The other two girls stopped their finger-popping. A cicada buzzed against the screen door, then stunned, looped-the-loop into the night while Little Richard shouted the last *"bop-lop-a-doo-wop"* verse of "Tutti-Frutti." As the phonograph whirred a Fats Domino 45 into position, Eustacia cleared her throat. The cousins picked up on the signal immediately, their treatises of commentary held inside mutterings of "un-un," "un-huh," and "un-un-un"—that inherited language passed down from slavery to generations of black women who learned to speak volumes without ever saying a word.

Then Portia, living up to her nickname of Pepper, added spice to the mess and verbalized Stacia's suspicions. "Shoo-oot! Somebody had they mouth talking when they should be walking." Maresa grunted her agreement.

"Lulu, just how you know what's what in them Projects?" Eustacia repeated. The girls on the front stoop jabbed each other with bony elbows and giggled, but the older women were patient, allowing Lulu the opportunity to squirm under their studied gazes.

Then, in an effort to cover her nervousness, Lulu pushed her glasses up on her nose, and drew herself up as tall as her fifteen and a half years would allow. "Uncle Percy, he told me.", she announced.

On cue, Fats crooned, *"Ain't that a shame . . ."* and all the women, except Eustacia, agreed.

More than once, folks had said it was a shame Eustacia had not done any better than Purcell Purcia Portugal. Before Percy came along, folks had wondered if Eustacia, with her straight-on looks and buxom shape, would ever get married at all. Stacia, at twenty-six, had been ensconced in the same house that had weathered her family since her grandfather brought his wife and children up from Alabama on the Jim Crow section of the train. The whole family had died of one city-bred disease or another, leaving behind Eustacia's mother, Vernida June Garrison, a woman so sanctified, so bent on raising her daughters to be God-fearing in accordance with her own fears of God, most folks figured Eustacia never would find a husband.

"Lord knows, ain't no man knocking down Stacia's door," her sister, Lil'June, would say. Then along came Percy Portugal, and the day she'd learned her sister had set her mind on marrying him, Lil'June had told her husband, "Stacia musta gone clean outta her mind, chasing behind Purcell Portugal. I tell you, if Big Mama was here, she'd put an end to that business right now. You see that man? He ain't but a little bit of a thing. Call himself from one of them Islands with his funny talking self. And big as Stacia is, if she hug him too tight, he ain't even gone be that little bit."

Eddie Mason laughed. "You said that right."

Lil'June looked at her husband, and for a second, shuddered as she eyed the thick black rim of grease and dirt edging his fingernails. Lil'June was Vernida June's oldest child and Eddie Mason's wife, while Eddie, Lil'June's second husband, was Purcell Purcia's cousin on his mother's side—"twice removed on account of them being from the Islands," as Eddie loudly proclaimed to anyone who questioned the connection. Not that anyone would. Neither Percy nor Eddie really seemed locked in place. Eddie's life was made up of bits and pieces of things—barrels of crankcase oil, stacks of corroded batteries, old sprockets, and a mess of grease-thick debris that filled every nook and cranny of Jimmy B.'s garage—while Percy, who claimed he had been on his way from Tampa to Chicago the summer he met Eustacia, sometimes still talked about the roadmaps tucked in the glove compartment of his car and referred to the Islands as "home." And even after they heard Purcell Purcia had found a job working evenings at the post office, some folks still expected him to pick up and move on. No one expected Eustacia to tame him. In fact, before Percy came along, Eustacia had seemed destined to be the only daughter hamstrung by Vernida June's sanctified ways.

"She was my mama, but I swear, all that religion had her acting nuttier than a pecan tree what ain't seen no squirrels all year," Lil'June would say carefully, lest someone accuse her of speaking ill of the dead, or worse yet, being disrespectful of her own mother. Lil'June had no such reservations about talking against anyone else in the family. "You know, Stacia and Bernice was the onliest ones who went to church with Big Mama. But Stacia was the one took care of her when she got real sick and started seeing the Lord everywhere, even up in the hickory tree. In one way of looking at it, I can understand why Big Mama left everything to Stacia."

But when Lil'June's daughter, Pepper, started sassing and giving her headaches, Lil'June sent the girl to Stacia's, because, as she said, "My sister got some Catholic sitting up in my mama's house, so it ain't but fair she take care of Pepper, seeing as how she done dumped everything else Big Mama taught her."

What with Stacia's house full of loud-mouth girls, all of whom were only half-related, and Stacia acting as if she herself had just dropped into the neighborhood by accident, saying, "How-do" and "Fine I'm sure," polite like everyone was a stranger, some saw it as fitting that Vernida Garrison's daughter had hooked up with a French speaking fool from the Islands, a slick customer who carried the improbable name of Purcell Purcia Portugal in a neighborhood where names ran the gauntlet from the Bible to the insane. And as Corella Theda Holmes would say, "With them Garrisons, you never know if you got somebody talking crazy or speaking in tongues."

"I swear, Big Mama just left Stacia set for some trifling fool like Percy," Lil'June told her husband. "That's why me and my sisters left that house soon as we could."

"You trying to tell me y'all left your mama cause of Percy?" Eddie asked his wife.

"You know what I'm trying to tell you, Eddie Mason. Don't be acting dumb." Then Lil'June shook her head. "The way Big Mama fussed at Stacia, it's no wonder she took up with Percy. That's how come I sent Pepper over to Stacia's. I said to myself: Better get her outta my house fore I start picking at her like my mama did with us."

"Un-huh. You got that right," Eddie muttered.

Lil'June eyed her husband sideways but once more, decided to let him slide. "What I'm trying to say is Big Mama didn't give Stacia no rest. Always snatching at her. Yanking on her clothes and pulling at her hair and all. Like Stacia was at fault cause Daddy went off and got himself killed in World War II. I tell you, Big Mama used to pluck at that chile like she was a chicken."

"Baby, Stacia ain't been a chile for some years," Eddie said. "and she sho is one big chicken. She weigh 170, 180 pounds if she weigh an ounce. She surely done been past plucking. Um-um. Plucking won't help none. Ol' Percy could pinch a bit here an there, but plucking won't get him nowhere. No-siree."

This time, Lil'June snapped at him. "Don't be making fun of my sister. All us Garrison women is big-boned. Runs in the family. And don't be suggesting no devilment for Purcell Portugal neither. I'm here to tell you I member who made it easy for Mr. Percy to come sniffing round Eustacia. You understand me, Eddie Mason?"

Eddie didn't answer, though he had it in his mind to give an answer, because Eustacia had met Purcell Portugal at the repair shop where Eddie worked. When Stacia first saw Percy, he was leaning against the door of a ruby-red Thunderbird, both the pomade on his hair and the wax on his car whistle-slick and winking in the dim light of the garage. Even without the car, it would have been hard for Stacia to miss him. He was railbird thin and moved like a dancer, like water rolling over rocks. And when he smiled, slow and deliberate as if he'd just traced his finger along the side of a woman's face, or settled in for the evening instead of following the flash of streetlights sparkling against the polished surface of that T-Bird, more than one woman had forgotten she had a life waiting for her come morning. Introducing Stacia to Percy had been as accidental as Eddie marrying Lil'June, yet his marriage had turned out all right, so Eddie figured he was free and clear where Percy was concerned. And when Stacia and Percy were getting along just fine, it seemed like a lame excuse to declare himself innocent in the whole affair. Later, it just seemed stupid.

Not everybody blamed Eddie Mason. Some folks said Percy had turned soft and easy the very day he watched Stacia float into the middle of that oil-pit of a shop, watched her seemingly materialize in the doorway, her body filling the garage's entry ramp as the sun caught the pattern of her flower-print skirt, and multiplied it even larger than Stacia's already ample hips.

"Mahn, when I see her," Percy said later, "I say ta myself: 'Qu'est que moi t'ape jongler? Who thees Angel Chile comin for ta carry me home?'"

If Purcell Purcia had been a book-reading man, if he had been caught up in any of the omens of Vernida Garrison's superstitions or those of his Island heritage, he might have been struck by a better name for what seemed to be unfolding before him. What did strike Percy that day was how Eustacia had stepped into the muggy shadows of Jimmy B.'s shop, and how suddenly he had felt he'd forgotten something, some nameless thing he had mislaid somewhere between the city and that Caribbean island of his birth.

"Mahn, you know I kept trying ta make some picture outto mah mind what it was thees ting I lose," Percy had said. "Still I don see nothing but mah Eustacia."

Folks said after that, Percy Portugal's nose was open so wide, he was ready to spend the rest of his days hanging around the edge of Eustacia's smile, just hovering there the way mourning cloak butterflies and buckeyes spent the whole of a summer's afternoon flickering in and around the blossoms of hockberry and thistle that grew near the backyard fences where everyone liked to gossip. But some said Stacia never did tame Purcell Portugal. They said he was just too wild and pretty, paper bag brown with slicked-back hair and a fancy car, always dressed up and ready to go wherever the night lights took him. Like those luna moths or what the old ladies called sweet-heads, the kind that fluttered around sassafras and cherry bark trees when the early night sky was losing its last tinge of twilight blue and trapped the moon against it, the way a spot of light could burn against the smooth blue glass of a bottle of Evening in Paris perfume, that cheap stuff old ladies claimed only hussies wore—not like the scent those girls in Eustacia's house snitched from her dressing table when her back was turned.

And those who said Eustacia hadn't changed Percy one bit laid the blame on those three girls Eustacia had living in her house—teenagers, a time all the neighborhood women remembered as the years when they were wild and love was nothing but the making. Those women would not give Stacia credit for being the only one of Vernida June's four daughters who would put up with the nonsense of three teenage girls and a husband as handsome as Purcell—"handsome as midnight on the river," Corella had said when she first saw him.

Until he met Eustacia, mornings had never been Percy's concern. He claimed morning was for folks who were afraid of the dark, and that was the one thing he had never feared. He'd say, "There be more troubles when the sun it is up in the sky, mahn." So Stacia, who thrived on sunlight, tried to keep the house quiet until Percy was ready to rise from his bed. The girls knew that if Eustacia was likely to find something wrong with the world, she was likely to find it in the morning. Hiding out until noon suited them just fine. In fact, they also preferred the night, that forbidden time children believed all adults coveted—"Else why would they be calling us home soon as it gets dark?" kids whispered. The girls shared two bedrooms connected by a small balcony, a widow's walk that jutted away from the house and was embraced by the overhang of the hickory tree. The branches of that tree also leaned against the wall where Eustacia's bedroom was, and some nights when the rustle of leaves cooled the humid night air enough for Stacia to sleep soundly, the girls crept from balcony to tree and shinnied to ground. Then the night was theirs. But the mornings were always Eustacia's.

Corella accused Eustacia of knowing all along that the girls used that tree for their escape route. "Elsewise she'da kicked that man out of her house the minute she heard he took them childrun into the Projects. Was bad enough when Vernida June had that house full of girls. Now Eustacia done filled her house with girl childrun again."

Dee Streeter's gravelly comment was, "Honey, I done always had my suppositions as to why Stacia got all them girls in that house. Don't look regular to me."

"Ain't nothing bout it regular," Corella sniffed. "I said that the day she brought that West Indies man to the house."

"And did you see the look on her face when Lulu told her what that man's been up to?" Dee laughed.

Corella laughed too. "I thought she was gonna bust something trying to look all nonchalant. I knew she was fit to be tied."

But Stacia held onto that look for several weeks. It took that long for her to gather enough anger from all the little things she saw as ways Percy and the girls tried to "pull the wool over her eyes," as her mother would have said. By the time she really was "fit to be tied," Stacia decided to clean up her house.

"She cleaning, but she ain't cleaning out the right things," Corella remarked.

"I hear you," Dee said, and squinted into the morning sun in an effort to get a clearer view of Stacia's bedroom window.

Eustacia was standing a bit away from the window so Dee could only see her profile as she leaned toward Purcell, but he was centered in Dee's line of vision. He was dressed in white boxer shorts, the rest of his body a shade darker than the bark of the hickory tree near the window, and in the morning's sweep of humidity, he was already oily with the promise of the day's perspiration. Stacia was waving a work shirt under Percy's nose. "Um-um. Done caught him, I spect," Dee Streeter snickered. But not even the vengeful God of Vernida June's nightmares would have made events that easy. Stacia was simply using the work shirt to nail herself to the cross of martyrdom as she complained of turning her life upside down to accommodate Percy. That morning, she had counted his work days, mentally adding the number of hours he was away from home against the federal code of sick leave and holidays postal workers had threatened to strike for that year.

"That's the trouble wit gov'ment jobs," Percy said. "Put your business all in the street, mahn."

"The street is what I'm talking bout," Stacia told him. "How come you got to work every night this week? Decent folks is halfway through with their day this time of morning."

Percy blinked and tried rubbing the sleep from his body. His chest was smooth and hairless. A gold crucifix lay against the dark backdrop of his skin. Stacia watched his hands pass over his body, wiping away moisture and pressing his body into a shape that was so familiar to her, she already knew the next curve of muscle and hardness of bone before his hands found those places.

But that morning, Stacia did not want to allow herself to succumb to the sweet musk of Purcell Portugal. She clenched the work shirt and shook it again. "Seems to me you been working too many nights lately. Decent folks pay attention to what's what," she added as her husband yawned. "Less'n you think folks in this house done come to live like that trash over in the DeWitt," she said slowly.

Even in his sleep-struck state, Percy didn't have to be told that remark was pointed. "Woman, what's the matter for you? What you saying wit thees DeWitt, huh?"

"I'm saying I want to know if you been spending time in the DeWitt. I'm saying I want to know how come the first thing Lulu say is: 'Uncle-Percy,' right after she say: 'De-Witt'?"

Percy reached for his wife, but she dodged his hands, and for a moment, they circled each other, Percy's long arms grappling to catch Stacia, and hers jabbing the air in quick darts as she flicked his work shirt at him. In the space of the bedroom window, their dance seemed to center around the flutter of that pale blue cloth Stacia was using to bat Percy away from her. But even to the critical eyes of Dee and Corella, this was more of a mating dance than a fight. The two women clicked their tongues disapprovingly as Stacia and her husband moved away from the window.

Percy dropped his arms and stepped back to get a full-length look at Stacia. Her eyes held the light of anger, but he ignored that. "Woman, you take the cake," he laughed. "You know I come home for mah loving, so why you talking bout DeWitt?"

"I don't know what you do at night," she said. "I don't know what goes on in the dark when I'm home sleeping."

"Baby, what ting got you so scared in the dark? I got no reason for ta be scared in the dark. Not like some thees church folk I hear bout. No, mahn, not me. Got no sins biting on mah heels like some snake come a-calling," he said, and with his eyes full of mischief and a wicked grin, he pulled Stacia onto the bed beside him. As she let Percy caress her, even as she began to respond to the urgency of his body, Stacia made a mental note of how deftly her husband had turned the conversation from the DeWitt to her mother. Even though Percy had never laid eyes on Vernida June, Stacia knew his remarks about sinning were a way of referring to her mother. As always, she was surprised at how Vernida's spirit drifted through the house, how it chewed at the edges of her marriage and left her feeling ragged and limp. Stacia had no doubt that her mother would not have approved of Percy. More than likely, Vernida June Garrison's second objection to Percy Portugal, after she finished ranting about his being Catholic, would have been the color of his eyes.

In a way, eyes are important to understanding what went on between Eustacia and Purcell Purcia because that was their first attraction to each other. Where Percy's eyes seemed to hold little pinpoints of light that glittered like laughter or the flicker of candles on a dusky evening, Stacia's seemed to be searching the distance for answers to some mystery. Some said Purcell Purcia's eyes made him too pretty on account of they were beige, like the speckled eggs of guinea hens and that, coupled with the Island lilt in his speech, made folks think of his looks as secretive and full of myth—"like the evil eye," Vernida would have said if she'd met him. But before Purcell came along, no one thought much about Eustacia's eyes, except for that small patch in the white section of her left eye, a dot like a mole or bruise caught under the iris and as deep brown as her pupils, a mark Vernida Garrison had referred to as her daughter's inner eye. That birthmark had hypnotized Percy, had kept him staring at Eustacia until he had had to move to relieve the itching at the base of his skull, an itching he felt only when he was embarrassed or lying—"But mahn, there I was, stuck to the spot by thees ting what is in mah woman's eyes," he'd said. He had stared, and when Stacia stared back, she'd realized nothing had prepared her for the hook Purcell Purcia baited with his beige eyes and lopsided grin.

So when Percy pulled her to the bed, she closed her eyes rather than face his smile. He simply resorted to a kiss that raised the hair on her arms, and left her curled up in the cocoon of herself. If Eustacia had allowed her high-school English teacher to fill her head with all those sonnets and romantic verses, she would have placed this moment inside those poems. But Mrs. Crutcher, for all her purple hair, had not been able to explain to a mottledly class of noisy black kids why some dead Englishman's notion of love could change what was happening to them in the middle of the twentieth century, in a city where the color line of demarcation cut black and white cleaner than any words on a page. Besides, what Eustacia felt would not have fit those stiff poems. So she built her own poetry out of how Percy held her, lazy and wandering above the bed until she took flight—erratic, zigzagging, opening and closing, fluttering higher until all she felt was how he danced inside her. But this time, she did not come gliding toward ground. This time, Stacia's eyes were cloudy with irritation.

After Eustacia closed the bedroom door that morning, after Percy had returned to the sweetness of sleep, she whispered, "Percy Portugal, that's the last time you gone pull the wool over my eyes."

That afternoon, Stacia let everyone go about their business as usual. She even sat on the bed as Percy dressed for work—"making ready for thees day," he said—and when he left the house, she stood in the doorway and waved until the Thunderbird turned the corner. The girls might have been momentarily unnerved by the narrow-eyed look she gave them once Percy was out of sight. In fact, the girls had been set for an explosion since Lulu had blabbed about the DeWitt. It seemed logical to expect some sort of fight for breaking the rules. Hadn't they fled houses where women were set for battle? But Stacia put them at ease, and after they finished supper, she let them clean the kitchen and retired to her room. "I'm just too tired to sit on that porch tonight," she said.

"Don't you worry none, Aunt Stacia. We can take care of the house," Maresa told her. The other girls nodded their agreement.

Stacia said, "I just know you will," and closed her bedroom door.

She undressed and stretched out full length across sheets that still held Purcell's scent. Beside the bed, in a straight-back chair, the girls had placed a pitcher of ice water and a dish of lemon slices. Stacia left it untouched, and buried her face into the bedclothes, her arms wrapped about her head. The radio, frozen on the city's one black station, slipped from Ruth Brown screaming about "Wild Wild Young Men" to Johnny Ace crooning "Cross My Heart." Eustacia listened to the radio slide from song to song and chalked up the probability that something wild was brewing in all the whispers she heard coming from the girls. Their muted voices mingled with the swish of limbs from the hickory tree bone-rattling against the balcony, its leaves gathering the shouts of children playing the night's first game of 24 Robbers: *"Last night the night before—24 robbers at my door—ALL Hid."* Stacia thought about how wonderful it was to get caught when everything was still a game.

"Ain't gone be no easy pickings out there," her mother had warned.

"I never said Percy was easy," Stacia answered, and in the gathering coolness of her bedroom, while crickets made their first tentative night calls and gnats buzzed street lamps, Eustacia half-dreamed and half-remembered those early days when Purcell Portugal could do no wrong.

Although she had no intention of falling asleep, she must have, because she awoke to an odd silence. Listening to the street, she knew the children had been called home from their games, and old folks, walking off their evening meals, had returned to their houses. Even her house seemed already settled into its night rhythms, but there was a buzzing in her head, part of it from an ache pulsing behind her eyes, and part of it, she realized, noise that originated somewhere else. She lifted her head, fighting against a heaviness that, like a large hand, threatened to hold her down. She was turning her head ever so slowly when she saw the hickory branches begin to shake as if a windstorm were sweeping the tree. Then she knew the buzzing she heard was caused by twigs scraping against the side of the house—that, and the girls hissing warnings to each other as they scrambled from house to tree. Stacia watched Lulu's legs swing past the window, and heard a thump as the girl dropped to the ground. A few seconds later, Maresa followed. By the time Stacia raised herself to her elbow, the three girls were at the end of the yard, and by the time she reached the window, they were racing across the street, skittering like leaves down the block. The bureau clock read: 9:30.

By 10:30, Stacia was heading for the DeWitt. She had phoned Lil'June, and ordered her to "get your butt on the Clayton-DeWitt line by 11:00 or take Pepper home this very night." Before she stepped from the Hodiman trolley, Stacia saw Lil'June's bulky frame standing under the dedication billboard. Lil'June's mouth clicked into gear the moment she saw her sister. As Eddie would have said, her mouth almost got in the way of her good sense.

"I wouldn'ta thought you'd do this to me!" Lil'June yelled. "I wouldn'ta thought you'd let my chile run wild in the streets."

"If you don't like what she do in my house," Stacia said, "you can always come get her."

Silenced by those niceties out of the way, Lil'June fell into step next to her sister. Eustacia boldly walked past the first set of buildings, but the shadowed doorways of the Projects seemed to challenge her every step. Instead of "How do, Miz So-and-so," rough voices called out, "Hey Mama," and "Baby, you sho know how to shake that thing."

"Who they talking to?" Stacia asked.

Lil'June grinned and said, "They just funning."

Stacia walked faster. "Not with me they ain't," she said.

Half a block from the trolley stop, they turned a corner and walked toward the center of the Projects. From that point on, everything changed. The smell of night flowers and wet grass was replaced by the odors of garbage pits and dusty sidewalks. The streetlights were huge chrome-yellow bulbs placed so high on the tops of skinny steel poles, they offered no relief from the light slamming against sharp angles and corners of buildings. Even with all the walkways, folks seemed to cling to the walls where the light was not as harsh. What surprised Stacia was the amount of space between buildings, too stingy for a lawn but wide enough for two-lane roads if it weren't for the high curbs and constant obstructions of concrete blocks, planted like tree stumps, and restricting the access for cars to only four side streets leading to Mission or Kingshighway. Everywhere else, walkways criss-crossed, seemingly going nowhere in that maze of buildings numbered and lettered in the code of some madman's equation. Eustacia walked as if she instinctively, knew where she was going, but Lil'June did not. She stopped, dead center, in one of the crosswalks.

"I ain't going another further till you tell me what we looking for," Lil'June said.

"I don't know yet," Stacia said. "I just know it's out here somewhere."

Lil'June spread her hands to the heavens and for the flash of a second, Stacia remembered her mother's gestures. But Lil'June wasn't calling on dead. She said, "Shee-it! You brought me out in these Projects in the middle of the night and don't know what you looking for? Is you crazy?"

Stacia didn't answer. She turned her face to the wind, a rare cool breeze that carried the scent of gardens outside the DeWitt's confines. Stacia closed her eyes and prayed for help. When it came, she almost didn't recognize it, but slowly, as if she were picking out the notes from memory, she heard the echoes of music on a loudspeaker. Lil'June started to speak again, but Stacia shushed her and turned to catch a clearer sound. The buildings muffled the noise, and in their sameness, their solidness of denied entry, made it seem as if the music could have come from all directions at once—or from no direction at all. Then her ears rewarded her. "That way," she told Lil'June, and pointed to a hump on the landscape, a slight hillside etched in blue lights and framed by buildings that fanned away from it in a V shape.

"That's where we going," Eustacia said, and left without waiting for Lil'June to follow her.

As soon as they cleared the crest of the hill, the music was right upon them. While the area they'd left was barren and lonely, this part of the Projects was filled with people, most of them crammed into a one-story blockhouse at the bottom of the slope, some just milling around the outside. Lil'June said, "I be damn!" and was ready to head for the doorway, but Stacia skirted the rim of the slope until she saw the parking lot. It was several days later before she bothered to tell her sister she'd spotted Percy's red T-bird parked there. Percy, on the other hand, was destined to know by morning that Stacia had spotted him. Inside, the room was so filled with bodies, Stacia felt as if she'd pulled a blanket over her head, then tried to breathe. This was how the rumors had described the DeWitt: folks almost stepping on one another and smells commingling in a small noisy space. But the music was a slow drag, so Stacia had time to sort out faces. Lil'June was too occupied with men who thought "Baby" and "Mama" were common names for all women, but Stacia scanned the crowd until she saw Percy belly-rubbing to "Saving My Love for You," his long arms wrapped around a twig of a girl who was so small, she seemed to melt into his body. Then the record changed to a mambo, and folks started booty-shaking and grinding their hips like they could sandpaper the grainy light until it was smooth. The temperature of the room rose at least ten degrees. Stacia pursed her lips and turned away just as Percy fell into a fancy two-step that got lost somewhere between a tango and a limbo bend almost as deep as Pedro Aguilar's.

She grabbed Lil'June. "Let's get out of here, less'n you want to pick up your daughter. I spect she in here somewhere."

"I couldn't do nothing with her when she was at my house," Lil'June said. "What I'm gone do with her now?"

Stacia sniffed. "Bout the same thing you think I'm gone do, Miz June." Then she walked out the door before Lil'June could protest.

That next morning, Stacia swept through the house looking for a bit of trouble to gnaw on. She decided to let Percy take his own good time waking up to that brand new day—*"I'm gone see how smooth Mr. Smooth can be,"* she told herself—but the girls were a different matter. She didn't know whether to deal with the DeWitt direct or take it up later. As usual, they made the decision easy for her. They were scattered around the rec room like loose assortments of arms, legs, and old rags draped over the grungy sleep-sofa and floor cushions, but so quiet, Stacia had reached the door before she recognized the record on the phonograph was *The Honey Dripper."* She surveyed the scene from the doorway. Percy had made the bar from part of an old telephone pole he'd sawed in half and bolted together, smooth sides up, before coating it with a translucent varnish to seal the soft wood. Two low tables were really giant spools the telephone company had once used for cable wire, and the bookcases were packing crates stuck end to end. In fact, most of the rec room furniture was make-do that Percy had converted from freight yard rubbish. "We make thees good as new," he'd told Stacia. "On the Island, they take the cans for oil ta make drums. And pipes. One cut and you got the roof tiles. Every ting got some place it can go."

That extra reminder that the girls had nowhere to go made Stacia invade the room like a one-woman wrecking crew. Once inside the door, she caught a whiff of cigarette smoke. She reached for the phonograph first. The needle shrieked across the record as *The Honey Dripper* died. Bodies tried to assume normal postures, but Stacia snatched them to their feet. Pepper yelled, "Oh shit!" and scrambled to fan smoke away from her as if she'd suddenly been attacked by bees. And it was Pepper who made the ultimate mistake. With no place to hide her cigarette, she dropped it to the floor, and in a frantic attempt to grind it out, kicked it under the partition that separated the rec room from the furnace area. Smoke from the burning cigarette changed from the faint odor of Pall Malls to the waxy stench of burning cloth. In one move, Stacia clawed her way into the wall and ripped it open. Even though the girls knew the partition was only plywood with burlap tacked to it, it was as if their aunt had turned into Superman, or Wonder Woman laying out criminals with a magic lasso. In that single, straight-arm move, Stacia bared their secret and left them standing on the brink of disaster.

Usually from late April to early September, no one bothered with the furnace. That area, with its moldy pipes and gargantuan stoker's oven, was gratefully ignored until the winds gathered brume and forced everyone to think of central heating. If Pepper's panic had not sent a burning cigarette under the partition, the furnace would have kept its silent vigilance over spiders, mice, dust balls, and in the case of that particular summer, wads of dirty clothes the girls knew they could never clean to Eustacia's satisfaction. This was especially true of Lulu, who was forever borrowing her cousins' clothes and not bothering to tell them about it until she'd ruined whatever she'd borrowed. "Even if them clothes do get clean, don't nobody want to wear 'em no more," Lulu had said when the others had caught her stuffing gummy socks and stolen underwear under the partition. That had happened in June, and by the time Pepper almost set the hiding place on fire, all of the girls had taken to stuffing dirty socks and gritty drawers into every nook and cranny the basement offered. By that time, they had gone beyond socks and added to the piles of truant laundry, skirts that needed to be ironed and shirts that had been scorched in episodes of bad ironing.

Stacia dangled the scorched sock from her fingers. "What is this?" she asked.

The girls inspected the floor, and from behind her horn-rimmed glasses, Lulu answered. "A burnt sock?"

Stacia wagged her head, imitating the girl. A burnt sock, huh? What kinda ol' answer is that?" This time, all three were quiet. Stacia nudged the cigarette butt with her foot. "This what you do when Percy take you to the DeWitt?"

In unison, the girls said, "No ma'am."

"You mean he don't take you?" Stacia asked.

Lulu Mae said, "No ma'am. I mean, Yes ma'am," while Maresa sputtered, "Sometimes," and Lulu added, "If we see him . . ." Pepper just threw up her hands and said, "Shit!"

"Shit, huh? Well, you got that right," Stacia said. "Um-um-um. Smoking and dancing. Now, you spoze this here sock got some friends in this house?" she asked. The girls shrugged.

Taking that as an affirmative, Eustacia held the sock away from her like a divining rod, and began to search the house. She kept the girls behind her, in case one of them tried to remove evidence before she could discover it. It is doubtful whether the girls had planned to leave their grimy bundles hidden indefinitely, but certainly those first months of languid summer days and DeWitt dances had made real work seem unlikely. No one needed to tell them those days had come to an end. Stacia moved through the house like the bulldozers had moved through the heart of Clayton: Upending overstuffed chairs, pulling bookcases away from walls, checking the dark corners of closets and pantry shelves, poking under beds with broom handles, and generally leaving the house itself trembling in her wake. Finally, she accomplished what she'd set herself to do in the first place—her noise pulled Purcell Portugal from his bed.

After Percy gave up on what little sleep he'd hoped for, and got dressed, he found his wife sitting on the basement steps by the laundry area, a broomstick in her hand as she beat out a work rhythm for her nieces, the three of them lined up like a nineteenth-century daguerreotype photo of children in a sweatshop: Pepper stood at the steaming washtub, and Lulu Mae, her glasses fogged up, at the bleach tub, while Maresa was in front of the mangle and rinse tub.

Stacia's broomstick was there for effect more than force. She only had had to stop one fight, and that was when a wasp had stung Pepper, causing the girl to swat the pest with a soapy wad of clothes. Unfortunately, she flap-slapped Lulu across the face with that same wad of clothes. Her glasses completely coated, Lulu pulled her broomstick out of the bleach tub, and blindly slung it this way and that, flinging bitter water the length of the basement and into all four corners. When the moisture sizzled against Maresa's iron, she slammed the thing against the wall. By that time, both Maresa and Pepper were throwing wet laundry at Lulu.

"If you don't stop," Stacia had screamed, "I'm gonna make you wash everything in this house, even if I got to pull the curtains from the windows!" So by the time Percy appeared, the girls were working at a steady pace.

"You tink I can have some little peace in the morning?" he asked. But looking at the scene, he had the feeling he'd entered the seventh ring of hell. Mist from the hot water melted the soot coating the rough basement walls, and the thick steamy air was filled with a buzz of flies coming in through the open screen door.

He waved his hand to clear away some of the steam. "Mahn, thees place look like ol' Badessy done took it over," he laughed. "Look like we got a bunch of hoodoo mambos in here."

Stacia trapped him inside that false eye of hers. Behind her, Lulu's broomstick punctuated her remarks. "Ain't no hoodoo Badessy put these childrun here, Percy Portugal. You put them here."

The splash and swish of clothes and water stopped as Stacia's logic gathered in the steamy air. "What you talking bout, woman?" Percy asked. "I don't make no chile work down here in thees hot weather. No, mahn, not me. Ca m'enquiquine!"

"Speaking French ain't gone help you now, Purcell Portugal. I'm talking bout the DeWitt. That's what I'm talking bout," Stacia told him.

Even with sudsy vapors clouding their vision, the girls could see Percy's good humor leaving his face. He squinted through the mist at each of them. Pepper and Maresa stared back at him, but Lulu bent her head over the tubs again. Percy said, "What thees you say bout DeWitt? Who see me there?" his voice as low as the hiss of water escaping from the mangle's rollers when Maresa cranked cloth through it. A June bug skimmed the top of the bleach vat, then drunkenly fell against the side of the tub. Lulu scooped it out and flung it against the wall while it was still buzzing. When she turned away from the tub, her uncle caught her pleading glance. Percy looked from Lulu's face to Stacia's.

"Woman, you gone believe your ears or you gone believe me?" Percy asked her. "I don't know what it is thees ting you hearing, but less you see what I been doing your own self, don't let your mouth come ta ruling your head."

"You want to know what I been seeing, Mr. Percy? You come on outside. I show you what I been seeing." Stacia threw down her broomstick and stomped up the stairs. The girls clustered behind Percy, waiting for him to make his move because they knew he was, as they said, "get-down cool." But Percy stayed near the house, more uncertain about himslf than about what Eustacia might have in mind.

Outside, Corella and Dee were hanging across the ragged edge of the garden fence where the three backyards converged in a mutual square of ground. In that position, the women seemed to be caught in a children's game of "Simon Says," their bodies in an attitude of frozen postures, and moving only occasionally to brush away insects that swooped toward the baskets of vegetables they had propped on the garden rail. As soon as they saw Eustacia marching across the lawn, they turned their attention on her. Stacia flapped her way through the sheets and towels fluttering on the clothesline, and walked around the side of the house toward the curb. Percy's bright red T-bird rested there, waiting.

Behind her, both the girls and Percy made little grunting sounds, but Stacia took her time. She inspected the car, walking its length as if she were checking the chrome trim for damages. Once, she even reached toward it, gently as if she were about to stroke it. Percy yelled, "Woman!" but she turned on him with such a scathing look, he swallowed whatever he was about to say. Stacia circled the car, and the deliberateness of her pacing gained the attention of several other neighbors. For their benefit, she pulled herself onto the fender of the car, crossing her legs like a movie star posing for a photographer.

Neighbors clucked, and the girls muttered, "Um-um" and "Oo-wee." Percy yelled, "Woman, what you doing? Thees car ain't no easy chair."

Eustacia smiled and leaned back onto the hood. Her dress rippled against the fender until the rose pattern design looked like a flower bouquet caught in the tangle of a summer's breeze. She called out, "Percy . . . Percy, I want me some music. Throw me them keys so's I can turn on the radio."

"Mahn, I ain't throwing thees keys. You gone crazy. I swear must be ol' Badessy got you. So you listen now, woman. I say thees one time—

take your body off mah car. La chanterelle va casser."

Stacia laughed. "You better play me some music, Percy. I know how you like to dance."

"I'm coming over there. You hear me, woman? I'm coming over and drag you from off that car."

Stacia sat up straight. "Drag? You gone drag me somewhere, Purcell Portugal?" As she laughed, the weight of her body jiggled the front end of the T-bird, and Stacia said, "Don't worry bout no keys, Mr. Percy. I can dance without no music." Then she threw back her head and let out a laugh that rumbled up from her stomach to her throat—a laugh with just enough anger to cool down the madness. A laugh that reminded Dee and Corella of Vernida's holy-roller laugher.

In one movement, Eustacia hoisted herself upright onto that Thunderbird. Then Percy noticed she was wearing heels, thin spikes which, as the fashion dictated, elongated her plump legs into shapely, albeit hefty, calves. He said, "Sacre bleu! Woman, what you doin?"

What Eustacia was doing was lifting her skirt daintly between forefinger and thumb as if she were about to curtsey. This movement exposed a good inch of brown velvet skin above her knees as she began a sweet little tap dance across the hood of the car, her skirt spread like the silken wings of a swallowtail butterfly. Both Stacia and the T-bird's heaving body seemed exceptionally graceful. With each step, her shoes kissed the red metal with a little "ping," leaving a round print, like a dot, a mark that after two or three downbeats took on a pattern. Percy rushed to the curb, but by some trick of fate and balance, Stacia leaped to the roof of the car before he could reach her. This was too much for Dee Streeter. She applauded and tried to cheer. Even though she collapsed into a spasm of coughing that rattled phlegm around in the back of her throat like marbles caught in a drainpipe, the other neighbors picked up her sentiment, and soon, Stacia had all the music she wanted as old men hand-clapped, and a mess of little bullet-headed boys ham-boned: *"I got a girl and Ruby is her name . . ."* And Stacia's shimmy left patterns of metal marks criss-crossing the T-bird's glistening roof.

The old boys of the neighborhood shouted encouragement as Percy scrambled onto the hood of the car, but there wasn't much he could do with a crowd around, and Stacia, the 180 or so pounds of her precariously balanced on killer heels, would have fallen on top of him if she had not acted quickly. Like a can-can dancer, she kicked off her shoes and sort of slid into Percy's arms. There were still some folks who believed he'd hurt something trying to catch that woman, but everyone agreed that Eustacia Portugal's dance could have won her a starring role in any production of *Porgy and Bess* "Could go on stage at the Club

Riveria or the Apollo," the old-timers said. "Ain't seen nothing like it since Ida Berry and Snake Hips Tucker over at Small's Paradise in Noo Yawk City."

But no matter what their reference, gossips told of how Eustacia had finally done away with the neighborhood's image of Vernida's holiness. Even those who knew Stacia did not speak in tongues said, "She can outdance and outshout her mama any day of the week."

"I'll carry to my grave the sight of Stacia up there tap dancing cross the top of Percy P.'s car," Dee laughed. "It was a sight."

And finally, after he'd cooled down, even Percy agreed that when Eustacia got the spirit, "Ain't mahn nor woman can shout that way like mah Stacia." But that day, he also announced he couldn't "stay round thees house less Badessy allow some sense ta come back ta that woman's head." And he drove off to Eddie Mason's house. The girls held their breaths while the Thunderbird roared to life.

"Don't you got some work to do?" Eustacia asked them when the T-bird finally whipped around the corner. All three ducked back into the house and returned to the business of laundry.

The other neighbors, seeing the end of the floor show, returned to their houses also. As the commotion died down, Corella Holmes took a fruit jar of her best Shadberry wine from the pantry shelf and brought it to Eustacia. Stacia looked at the Shadberry, the unspoken question of why Vernida June's daughter would dare to drink country wine just about to leave the tip of her tongue, then she grabbed the bottle from Corella. Stacia watched the angle of sunlight fractured inside the amber liquid as she tipped the fruit jar. Drinking wine from anything other than a proper glass was something Vernida June would never have tolerated either, but then there were many things about her life these days that her mother would not have tolerated. Purcell Purcia with his Catholic crucifix, his red T-Bird, and eyes like the moon when it was full of itself surely would have rested at the top of her mother's list. So on that sweet July afternoon, Eustacia Portugal sipped Shadberry wine with her neighbors and listened to Lulu Mae trying to cheer up her cousins by singing yet another off-key chorus of "Moody's Mood for Love." By now, the girls collectively realized how their salvation from their mothers' houses had been to purgatory and back.

Soon, Dee and Corella returned to their gardening. Stacia's own garden was full of monarchs and spangled mourning cloaks flittering among the wilting plants. That year, the cabbages and tomatoes looked ragged and limp. Only the onions seemed to have taken root. Stacia watched Dee pull chickweed, thistle, and prairie smoke free of her onion beds and tomato plants growing near the fence—"Everything's got its place," Dee said. Corella, who was gathering mustard and dandelion for supper, clicked her tongue at the waste of good edible plants when Dee tossed the chickweed onto the mulch pile, but Corella made no comment. She continued to check the undersides of leafy plants, moving quickly, her judgments swift and irreversible. Stacia knew the routine: Pinch the crickets and bean beetles with a thumbnail but leave the ladybugs and mantises to do their share of keeping the garden clean. On Stacia's side of the fence, an errant breeze blew the bleached white sheets like lazy clouds, and even with rivulets of sweat staining their faces, her nieces laughed as they fought the billows of cloth. A few minutes later, Dee offered Stacia a basket of squash blossoms and roots for supper. "They come fresh out the ground," Dee said. And Corella added, "Yellow like the sun done spoke right to them. Root stuff is good for what ails you," she laughed.

Stacia heard Lulu's sad song wafting across the yard: " . . . *my soul's on fire, come on and take me, I'll be what you make me, my darling, my sweet* . . ."

"I done already made good for some of what ails me," Stacia said, and walked into the house—the bottle of Shadberry in one hand, and Dee's basket in the other.

Driving Under the Cardboard Pines

FOR MORE THAN TWENTY YEARS, Blind Birdie sold newspapers, shoelaces, and pine-scented air fresheners on the corner of Newhope and Cottage Grove. "Got me a little something for them what's walking and them what's riding," Birdie would say. "If they going somewhere, they got to pass this way." At least two generations had passed by Blind Birdie before that summer in the early sixties when anger bloomed into riots and the world Birdie knew began to pass out of existence.

Birdie was a neighborhood fixture in a neighborhood that was no more than a notch in the heart of the Black Belt. On the city council's planning map, the district bordered the DeWitt Housing Projects then zigzagged through a quagmire of streets, where two-story family houses were nested between hulking brownstones and vacant lots, where the only things blooming were stinkweed and puddles of oily water attracting clouds of sulfur-yellow butterflies and gnats. With each change of hands, from carriage trade to Irish to Jewish to Black, the neighborhood had grown into a patchwork of houses turned into storefronts which, in turn, became houses divided into flats, and flats into rooms. Even Birdie's stand had changed hands, shifting in ownership from an Italian fruit vendor to an Irish bootblack to Blind Birdie, who had had the stand permanently installed in a recess between Abe Feinstein's Market and Cinnamon Ivory's Bar, the walls on either side of the stand emblazoned with graffiti: THE CHAMP CAN DO IT, BIG ROSIE, and APEMAN LIVES. There, Birdie had the advantage of monitoring the comings and goings of the folks who were about the business of changing the face of Newhope and Cottage Grove. The smart ones followed Birdie's lead. When the riots came, when the neighborhood went through its final upheaval, like Birdie, they listened to the promises of politicians with one ear, and the counter movements of the National Guard and Black Nationalists with the other.

As far back as 1943, folks remembered seeing Birdie's three-sided stand on that corner. Those who first took notice said he just appeared one morning, the lean-to fixed in place, its decoration of pine tree cutouts dangling like Christmas ornaments above the stacks of newspapers and bundles of shoelaces Blind Birdie offered to passersby. In those days, Birdie was a young man, or so they say. In truth, Birdie did not change much in appearance from one year to the next, his dark brown head tilted back to catch the drift of sounds floating past him. And for Birdie, inside his well of never-ending darkness, those noises told him all he knew about age and change. "I seen it all," he'd say, his voice holding the quiet laughter of a blind man's joke.

Birdie shaped the neighborhood from the clacking of scissors and hum of razors floating out of Pearl Brown's Barber Shop, the clatter of billiard balls in Doc's Pool Hall, the ripeness of odors from Feinstein's Market, the numbers runners and the number of folks entering and leaving Cinnamon's Bar, or the number of shouts from the Holiness Sanctified Temple competing with the choir at the good Reverend Blankenship's AME Methodist Church, where Birdie always knew the ladies were heading by listening to the crackle of starch in their dresses. Their children brought him chips of coal in the winter for his camp stove, or read him comics on early summer evenings when the fireflies had just begun to buzz along the scrawny hedgerows and mulberry trees clinging to the walkways bordering the brownstones. Birdie knew when the widow, Thelma Wooten, was coming home from her job by the faint odor of bleach and scouring powders staining her hands, and he recognized her daughter, Doris Jean, by the heel drag of her left foot, while the sound of ragged tennis shoes slapping the pavement like a loose board caught in the wind told him when Frederick Douglass—Clinton Fredericks' youngest boy, the one everyone called Fred-Fred—was running away from home, or while he was still pretending he'd been in school all day, rushing to get home before his father discovered the truth.

Sometimes Birdie only needed the smallest sound as a clue. He claimed he knew when T-John Granger was chalking his cue to run the table at Doc's, and that he knew the age of a woman by the hiss of nylon brushing against nylon when she passed by, especially church women like Sister Bernice Roper, whose ample thighs and hips could cushion his bulky frame. For them, he'd cock his head and pull himself up tall, grinning in the direction of that secret sound. This talent did not set well with all the women in the neighborhood.

"Girl, that blind man's too nosy for me," LuRaye Turner told Pearl Brown. "I don't trust no man what don't see nothing, but is always looking up under your skirts."

"Now just what you think a blind man's gone find up under your skirts, Miss Lady?" Pearl would say. "You complaining or wishing?"

And they would both laugh as LuRaye elbowed Pearl. "Girl, you oughta stop," she'd say.

But on that same day, Pearl was likely to look through the window of her barber shop and spot LuRaye bringing a piece of fried buffalo fish or a dish of corn pudding for Birdie's supper, then walking him home "just to make sure he eats proper," so she'd say. And in the mornings, when Pearl went across the street for her paper, Birdie always greeted her with, "How do, Miz Pearl?" and handed her the *Post Tribune* folded and ready before she could open her mouth to speak. Likewise, he had the racing forms ready for Cinnamon Ivory, the *African Defender* for T-John Granger, and promptly every Thursday, the good Reverend Blankenship's weekly copy of the *Methodist Christian*.

"Don't need these here newspapers to tell me what's what," he'd say. "Them white folks writing this paper don't know what's going on down here. I'm the one in the know. Y'all just stop a minute and ask me."

Most folks accepted Birdie's invitation. Even Abe Feinstein checked in regularly. "Birdie boy, when you gonna get yourself a good job and stop bootlegging this junk in front of my store?"

Birdie would laugh that tight throat laughter blind folks unravel when they throw their heads back as if they are searching for a hidden eye underneath their useless ones. Then he'd say, "I spect I'm gone get me a good job bout the same time you stop selling colored folks that bad smelling meat, Mistah Feinstein."

Then Feinstein would laugh, a narrow twisted sound that sent Birdie back to his youth and his sighted years in Georgia when the noise of foxes made him sit up in bed and search the night for some sign of movement. While Feinstein let the joke sink in, Birdie would pass his thick hands back and forth over the newsprint until Feinstein and some of the other regulars could almost swear Birdie was able to read what was there, braille or no.

Birdie would say, "What do you think about this stuff, Mistah Feinstein?" Then he'd hand the newspaper to Feinstein. "Ain't it something?" Birdie would add. "Seems to be no end to it."

Feinstein would read the headlines and shake his head. "Oy vey. More taxes," he'd mutter. "And cutting back on the city budget, too."

"Naw, I don't mean that stuff," Birdie would chuckle. "This city ain't had no decent budget since Franklin D. Roo-sevelt. I mean, look at the politicians you got there now. Ain't much them news folks can say in their favor on this day, Lord knows."

And Feinstein would grunt, unfurl the paper, and within a matter of minutes, Birdie would know all there was to know about the day's events in city politics. Or international business. Or sports. It all depended on his victim's interests. Birdie hit Feinstein for local politics but with high school coach Woody Crenshaw, it was sports. When Jimmy B. Turner crawled out from under one of the busted cars in his mechanic's shop, Birdie tricked him into reading the results of the horse races and the hopes of the want ads. He even targeted a few of the Methodist Auxiliary ladies to open the paper midsection and reveal the latest happening in the big cathedral downtown. And when Sister Bernice Roper wasn't too busy meeting with the other ladies of the Sanctified Church, she'd spend a few minutes with Birdie reading a few scriptures from the Bible. The only ones hip to his games were the children. Birdie had to just flat out ask them to read him the comics, but most did not mind the chore, even though Birdie pushed them to the limits of their reading level. They sat on stacks of newspapers under the tarp canopy with its hanging decorations of pine tree cut-outs, and for a penny or two, they'd read aloud the adventures of Dagwood, Mopsy, Li'l Abner, and Terry and the Pirates. As they got older, their prices went up, and so did Birdie's requests. Teenagers made Birdie fork over as much as a quarter for reading editorials, and in the summers, Doris Jean Wooten sometimes included a cardboard pine in her fee, while Fred-Fred would pinch a dozen of them to sell for twice what Birdie charged.

There were those in the neighborhood who used their few cents worth of attention just to humor Birdie, and there were those who knew Blind Birdie heard more in the ebb and flow of things than any sighted man could discover. The first sign of Birdie was the clatter of his cane against the sides of the stand, and the hatch squeaking open at 6:00 A.M. These noises were wake-up calls for folks who lived above the store fronts near Newhope and Cottage Grove. Some, like Doris Jean, whose mother rented the flat above Cinnamon's Bar, were awakened half an hour earlier by the thud of papers hitting the sidewalk with a fresh delivery of the day's news—the *Post Tribune* from the city plant downtown at 5:30, the *African Defender* from the Urban League office at 7:30, the racing forms at 6:00, and on Thursdays, the *Methodist Christian Weekly*. In the winter, Birdie's early deliveries woke Doris Jean with plenty of time to dress, eat breakfast, and walk the fourteen blocks to the segregated high school instead of draining her mother's meager budget for trolley fare. Summers, she used those early morning hours to clean the flat and help with the bar clean-up before the midwestern heat sucked all of the air out of the rooms. That was how she spent most of her days that summer before riots brought the winds of change to the Black Belt. In the summer, when the late afternoon light was beginning to fade, and the flutter of copper and spotted butterflies was about to give way to the evening's moths and fireflies, passersby might see Doris Jean perched on a stack of papers, the day's edition open to the editorials and not more than two inches from her nose as she painstakingly moved from word to word of what had lately commanded everyone's attention—the Civil Rights Movement and Dr. Martin Luther King, Jr. Anyone walking past might be caught by the silence of folks standing near Birdie's newsstand as he listened to Doris Jean, the automatic movement of his hands as he folded and stacked his discards for the night pickup seemingly unconnected to his sightless stare. But even if they did not bother to turn in that direction, even if they did not bother to glance at the blind man tying up bundles of unsold papers, or the young girl in her faded print dress, shapeless and loose to cushion the humid inner-city air, they were still drawn to the corner by the strangely sweet but distinctly fake scent of pine. Blind Birdie claimed his trees closed out the odors of rooming-house kitchens and communal toilets, back alley garbage and smoke-filled parlors. Anyone ever trapped with the scent of those cardboard trees never forgot the smell, or its promise to make the air fresh as new—even for the second-, third-, and fourth-hand cars owned by most of the men in the neighborhood.

"When you finish fixing up they cars in that garage of yours, you just send them to me," Birdie told Jimmy B. "These here trees is gua-ran-teed to make any auto-mobile fresh as new. Don't matter what kind they got. Ford or Rolls Roy or one of them funeral parlor limousines from down the street. It don't matter. These here trees make folks forget they troubles. Just take yourself a deep breath and let your mind to rest," he'd say, and release one of the pines from its tightly sealed cellophane package.

The aroma exploded the moment it was exposed to air. It was a cloying scent—as unforgettable as cheap perfume from Woolworth's five-and-dime, the heavy fragrance of a door-to-door salesman's toilet water, or mothballs lingering in the back of a musty closet. That smell traced its way through the air in a single line, a pungent odor suddenly knifing through the stench of stale beer from Cinnamon's and the aroma of rotten meat from Feinstein's. Those pine trees, greener than any of the real trees still managing to grow in the leached soil of the area, always won, however temporarily, that battle of odors. And although they did not remind folks of being back home in the Georgia pines, as Blind Birdie promised, the scent did take them outside of the world of train yards, cattle pens, breweries, and laundries where they worked if they were "lucky enough to hit them hard licks," as the old men said. But young men, like T-John Granger, out of work since his discharge from the military, answered, "Ain't gone be no luck on a white man's dead-end job," reminding everyone of how many black veterans on welfare had been to Korea, and how many had yet to return from Vietnam.

For all of them, working or not, Birdie's cardboard pines offered the smells of a world that didn't reek of hand-me-downs, handouts, or back alleys. For all of their cheapness, those pines closed out the smell of a world that had sold them cheap. The old men, who held their daily debates on Roosevelt, Truman, and Kennedy politics, bought their trees as regular as clockwork, and the young men, drifting from the Army to unemployment, had Birdie's pines hanging in the front windows of their cars. Young boys bought them because they didn't consider a car really theirs until they had adorned it with a pine, while the fancy men, the neighborhood gamblers and pimps, bought theirs curb service when they pulled up to Birdie's stand for the evening's edition of the racing forms. Not that anyone mistook Blind Birdie's pines for magic, but there was something about them that made a difference, that little touch that said the owner knew there was a better life than what the city offered. Most of the neighborhood cars sported a scented pine—the sportier the car, the fresher the pine—and the sight of that cut-out hanging from the rearview mirror was a signal that said its owner was ready to party.

"Ready to sporty-otee," as Jimmy B. and his cronies would say.

"Don't you be thinking what I think you thinking," LuRaye warned her husband if she caught him replacing a faded pine cut-out with a fresh one. "This here car ain't for no fancy women," she said, as if she could not remember that spring night following her senior prom when she and Jimmy B. had parked on the bluff by Cobbler's Creek and she had lost her virginity while watching one of Birdie's cut-outs swing gently in the moonlight.

And LuRaye wasn't the only woman in the neighborhood who associated that sweet pine fragrance with late night parties and some radio disc jockey pitching just the right record to turn the inside of a Dodge or Oldsmobile steamy with heavy breathing and the husky voice of some singer. LuRaye's downfall had been to the tune of the Platters singing "Only You," while the good Reverend Blankenship's daughter, her eyes fixed on a pine cut-out twisting like a whirligig above the dashboard of the choirmaster's car, had fallen under the spell of Arthur Prysock crooning, "You're My Everything."

"It's something about that car," the girl had said. "Makes me feel like I'm in one of them silver roadsters from the movies. And the smell . . . ooh-wee . . . honey, that smell's all over that car."

No one was willing to tell her that movie stars didn't have fake pine trees stinking up their cars, and their cars weren't painted rattletraps that sounded like the clatter of oven doors or jailhouse cages. Like most women, the Reverend's daughter came to expect a cardboard pine, hanging dead center in the windshield, would block her view of screen action at the drive-in movies, or road signs of dark country lanes near the fairgrounds. Only a few, like Thelma Wooten, voiced any objections.

"That stink reminds me of some of that cleaning stuff I got to use in that white woman's toilets out in Belmont. I don't need to be smelling that stuff all night after I done smelled it all day," she'd say, and banish the trees from her house.

But after Thelma retired for the night, after she fell into bed, her swollen feet propped on an extra pillow, Doris Jean would take her vigil in a window, one of Birdie's pines tied to the window shade's cord and swinging slowly in the glow of the neon sign that blinked: CINNAMON'S—a three second flash of red light every five seconds. The smell of pine softened the smell of tobacco smoke drifting up from the curb where men gathered in bunches and bragged about their women, or cursed the absence of jobs. Doris Jean could put recognizable faces to voices without straining to see beyond the red glare of the neon sign, and some evenings, when Fred-Fred whistled her away from the window with a doo-wah downbeat signal, she tiptoed past her mother's room, down Cinnamon's back stairs, and joined him.

When Birdie heard her halting footsteps, he'd pull a final edition of the day's paper from the stack, and tease her into reading the headline story. "Sho got a lot of news here today," he'd say, and Doris Jean would answer in that polite way the neighborhood women instilled in their children, "We got news every day, Mr. Birdie."

This was the act that brought Birdie's day to a close—a simple ritual that included Doris Jean's nearsighted stammering from one word to the next, embellished by a running commentary from Jimmy B., T-John, or the Reverned Blankenship sauntering toward the AME chapel for evening prayer services. Through it all, Fred-Fred slumped against the side of Birdie's stand where the scent of pine was strongest. Some nights that aroma set Fred-Fred's teeth on edge while he watched fishtail Cadillacs and chrome-sided Thunderbirds stop by Birdie's for a copy of the day's racing forms. Fred-Fred's idea of what went on in those cars began with the image of a pine tree swinging above the dashboard, and under the arc of its scent, a woman wearing a shiny dress, and silver earrings, her head thrown back and her eyes full of laughter.

"If I had my druthers," he'd say, "I'd get me a Buick semi-automatic with fluid drive." Then he'd dream of sporting Doris Jean, his hand on her thigh as he cruised to some lonesome spot where he would find *"Oh Baby, a little taste of heaven,"* as the song said. Of course, the picture wasn't complete without a sleek mustache and diamond rings on his fingers. Meanwhile, he stroked his hairless face and dutifully waited for Doris Jean.

Birdie had already made his final sale of the day when Doris Jean began reading the latest news of freedom marches, sit-ins, and voter registration drives. She commanded Birdie's attention while he automatically counted his stacks of unsold *Post Tribunes* and *African Defenders*, then tied them in separate bundles before collecting the string of cardboard trees hanging along the rim of the stand. Usually, he paused as he placed the air fresheners in a paper bag, allowing the scent of pine to momentarily close out the smell of night-blooming jasmine, sour beer, and the smoke from trash fires in the DeWitt Projects. Under the smell of pine tree cut-outs, Birdie and his neighbors listened as Doris Jean read accounts of Dr. King and the Civil Rights demonstrations.

"It's God's work," the good Reverend Blankenship rejoiced.

"If it is, God be the onliest one working," T-John muttered, and complained of his routine of want ads and pool games at Doc's. "Don't see me letting somebody go upside my head just so's I can eat at Woolworth's or go to some big-time school for some de-gree that ain't gonna buy beans. I need me some action right now."

"Your problem is too much action," Jimmy B. grumbled, and for a moment, Jimmy B. and T-John looked as if they were about to square off against each other.

Birdie listened to the quickening of their breathing, and swayed the way blind men do when they become uneasy with the space around them. He wasn't the only man uneasy in the space of a world around Newhope and Cottage Grove. For weeks, T-John and Jimmy B. had been edgy. Birdie first noticed the difference after the Reverend told him Jimmy B. was among the volunteers staging the weekly sit-ins at the mayor's office. And when LuRaye asked for signatures on a petition for the Reverend's committee, T-John had filled in the first twenty lines with names of dead men who had been drafted right out of high school and killed in action. "Blasphemy," the good Reverend shouted, but T-John said, "Some black folks got to be dead to be counted," and rounded up another dozen veterans to add more names to the list. That's when T-John turned militant, his handshake an elaborate series of signals that left Birdie exhausted trying to remember the sequence. Birdie's newsstand became the neutral zone, with T-John and his buddies clicking in combat boots at one end, and at the other, Jimmy B. and the Reverend's coalition members, stacks of handbills and petitions fluttering against their clipboards. And that line of cardboard pines separated them as they debated the pros and cons between passive resistance and war.

"We can't have brothers fighting brothers," the Reverend said.

"I hear that," Fred-Fred laughed, and although he was only seventeen, he slapped hands with the older men and winked at Doris Jean to let her know he'd already entered his manhood. Doris Jean wasn't quite sure what to do with all that winking. That summer, she wasn't yet convinced her life would be any different than the lives of the older women. She had yet to tell her mother she had decided to go to the state college, to "get in that school even if I got to do like Reverned King say, and sit at the door till they let me in." That summer, she had Fred-Fred, and as long as that held true, she followed him as soon as she finished reading for Birdie. After his brother Clint, Jr., was killed by a cop his first day home on furlough, Fred-Fred quit school and everyone said he was headed for no good end, running the streets and taking Doris Jean with him. But in the evening, it was Doris Jean and Fred-Fred who helped Birdie tidy up his stand and lock it before he dropped into Cinnamon's for his evening drink. And that summer, it was Fred-Fred who first drew Birdie's attention across the street to the young Muslim hawking *Muhammad Speaks*.

When the Muslim had first appeared, Birdie had confused his street corner rhetoric with Pots, the Doomsday-ragman who preached the end of the world while he scoured the trash bins and gutters along the street. But Birdie always smelled Pots' rancid odor before he heard his rantings, and Pots always confused the Bible with the Blues, which caused his lamentations on sins of the flesh to take a wistful turn. The Muslim smelled of Castile soap, and though his laments condemned the same sins as those Pots spouted, Birdie also heard repeated references to Elijah and Allah evoked in the name of black people around the world. With the appearance of the Muslim, Seku Ahmadu, they called him, Fred-Fred waited until Doris Jean had finished reading the day's account of Freedom marches before he dragged her away from Birdie's stand to perform the same task across the street with a copy of *Muhammad Speaks*.

"Who be them black folks?" Birdie asked. "And who he be, calling on them with that all commotion?"

"He say he be descending direct from Al-Hajj Umar from Africa," Doris Jean told Birdie after the old man pressed her for answers. "He say Sena-gal."

"What gal?" LuRaye snapped. "I don't know nobody by that name."

"Some of these girls be following behind the first man they see,"

Sister Bernice Roper said, remembering how just that month, her daughter, Lulu Mae, had run off with a boy from the West Indies.

"Ain't no woman," Doris Jean said. "Sena-gal. It be some place in Africa." Both LuRaye and Pearl grunted their rejections of that notion. "No, it be a real place," Doris Jean added. "Tell 'em, Mr. Birdie. You member. The newspaper say they was talking bout that place up at the United Nations."

Birdie smoothed down a stack of papers, his thumbs thick as hammer heads, pulling the cord tight as he tied the bundle. Each movement fell into place automatically, but when Birdie searched his memory for Senegal, he only managed to capture dim fragments of stories. And one afternoon, when Doris Jean introduced the Muslim, Birdie extended his right hand. Seku Ahmadu grasped it as if to complete an ordinary handshake. Instead, he placed his other hand on top to close the grip, and Birdie's hand was encircled by both of the Muslim's. There was a slickness to his skin, and even with the smell of pine as the man's arms rustled the trees when he reached toward Birdie, there was the smell of oil, heavy as incense, heavy as the odors of the medicine sachets Birdie remembered old country women using in Georgia.

If Birdie could have seen Seku Ahmadu, if, in some other life, he had visited the great kingdoms of the Senegalese, he would have immediately seen the similarities between that street corner Muslim and those warriors of the Sudan. Draped in his broadcloth desert robe, Seku Ahmadu stood taller than any of the neighborhood men, a fact that did not go unnoticed by the women, or the old men, who shook their heads in confusion over his dress and admiration of his style. The younger men said, "Check it out," and diddy-bopped past him, bragging of their street smarts with their hip-slouch walk. "Nothing to it," the fancy men said, then grinned and called him "Brother" when they caught a flicker of the Muslim's gold tooth as he hawked his newspapers and his politics.

But that gold remnant was the only visible link Seku Ahmadu had with his gambling days. Now, instead of stingy brim hats and Hickey-Freeman shoes, he wore sensible oxfords and wrapped his head in three rings of cloth shaped like a flattened fez, his hair hanging below this crown in thin braids, like those of the little girls attending Sunday School at the Reverend Blankenship's AME Methodist, but scented with the same pungent fragrance as the prayer oils Sister Bernice Roper used at the Holiness Sanctified Temple. There was an exaggerated cleanness about this look, a deliberateness that suggested the purpose and history, captured in his face, with its wide forehead and elongated chin framing large features so carefully defined, they seemed to be chiseled from those sunstruck rocks still mined in the quarries of southern Africa. And while his smile revealed the gold tooth from his days in the life of the streets, his chin was bearded at the point like a Babylonian's. Or a Jew's.

"He talks against my shop," Abe Feinstein complained. "He tells the people I sell them poison. The devil's meat he calls my pork. How am I to make a living, I ask you?"

Birdie tilted back his head, his sightless eyes aimed at Feinstein. "I recollect you telling me your people don't eat no pigmeat theyself, Mistah Feinstein. Same with the Muslims."

"You done made enough living off us," T-John added.

And the Muslim declared, "Let Allah take into his arms all those who rightly claim this life. Our great leader, the honorable Muhammad, calls on all peoples of the Black Nations to let their voices be heard." And Doris Jean read how Martin Luther King, Jr., said, "Let your voices sound the trumpets of freedom."

As the weeks passed and the hub of voices grew louder, Birdie heard less and less from Abe Feinstein. What he heard was an increase in sirens as patrol cars howled through the neighborhood like cats stuck on one note of a mating cry. Someone told him Hesselman's Ice Cream Parlor had been firebombed, and someone else said Oscar Flowers had sold his dry goods store after thirty years in the same building. After they torched the junkyard, oily smoke from burning tires hung in the air for days. Only Wu Fong's Eatery went untouched, and even so, wrought-iron grating was nailed over the windows and doors. By August, Birdie was not surprised when Pearl told him Seku Ahmadu had another Muslim working beside him. What surprised him was how familiar the voice seemed to be. Even from across the street, he knew it was Fred-Fred proclaiming the teachings of the Prophet Elijah.

"That's Clint's boy going round calling himself by the name of Nysase," Pearl said.

And Doris Jean added, "He ain't so bent out of shape no more, Mr. Birdie. That's how come he call himself Nysase."

"Well, you got that right," LuRaye said. "That boy's always been nasty."

Yet Pearl's description of Fred-Fred was anything but nasty, and although Birdie would not have expected Fred-Fred to start wearing desert robes, he wasn't prepared for the black suits and ties Pearl claimed he now wore. If T-John had been the one to don a uniform, his conversion might have been explained by his stint in the military where he'd been forced to button up, but after all those years of recognizing Fred-Fred's approach by the slap of his loose canvas shoes, the notion of Clinton Fredericks' youngest boy wearing a tie was more than Blind Birdie could imagine.

When he asked what kind of tie, Pearl replied, "Square knot. And his hair's cut, too. Looks like the bad end of a stovepipe. Just right up close on the sides and mowed flat at the top of his head. Razor-edged like a preacher's. No offense, Reverned Blankenship, but what with everybody wearing them bushy Afros, them Muslims bout the only customers I got anymore. Can't keep up with these young ones. Don't seem to want to sit still for nobody," Pearl added, then told them how Doris Jean, always dependable, now hesitated to answer even when her own mother called her name.

Sister Bernice Roper patted the beads of sweat kinking up the edges of her hair, and said, "I seen her hanging round them women come over from Mission Street with that dude Seku Ahmadu. You ought to see them women. Dressed up like one of them Cath-olics, all in white like they done took to the vows. Them Muslims take the chillun same as the Cath-olics do." Then she fanned the air with her handkerchief as if waving away the memory of how her own daughter had given up the Holiness Temple, run off to the West Indies, and married a Catholic.

"Them Muslims take what folks they can get," LuRaye said. "I sho hope Doris Jean ain't falling for that baloney. Thelma have herself a fit if that chile goes Muslim."

"Thelma gone lose that chile for sure," Sister Roper agreed, her white handkerchief fluttering like a distress signal.

"The Lord works in mysterious ways," the good Reverend said, and the others mumbled, "Amen," as if the Reverend had had a sudden revelation.

"Ain't nothing mysterious bout the mess I hear coming," LuRaye muttered. And though Birdie said, "I seen them coming and going. Ain't no different," he had to admit he heard it, too. All the signs pointed to a difference.

For Birdie, that difference was finally brought home in late August when he heard the quiet steps of Feinstein turning into his store instead of stopping by the newsstand for his usual chat. Several weeks later, Feinstein closed his doors for good. Then Birdie noticed the absence of laughter from Pearl's shop, and that she spent less time cutting hair and more time listening to the radio soaps with LuRaye. Already, some of the folks had moved uptown, taking with them the women who saved him dishes of collard greens and pig's feet stew from their suppers. As his sales of *Post Tribune*s fell, so did the run on the day's racing sheet, and those cars that did stop had their car radios tuned to credos from the Last Poets instead of funky R-and-B.

"Mr. Birdie, Brother Seku wants to trade some space with you for *Muhammad Speaks*," Fred-Fred announced in his best Nysase voice.

Birdie shook his head. "I hardly got room for myself," he said.

Seku Ahmadu interrupted. "Them white folks been calling you Birdie all your life, blind man?" But he had to swallow his words when the good Reverend said, "Watch your mouth, boy."

"You show Birdie some manners," Pearl told him.

Birdie took a deep breath and rubbed his head. That movement, so slow and deliberate, drew Doris Jean's attention and she noticed the slight stubble of thick gray hairs that, more and more, Birdie missed in his daily shaves, a duty LuRaye used to perform when she was of a mind to let Birdie lay his head in her lap. LuRaye hadn't been of that mind for some months, and now, Doris Jean watched Birdie turn his face toward the sound of the Muslim's voice as if the change in angle would give him a better sense of who was speaking. Whatever view he got didn't seem to set well with him. "Just cause I'm blind don't mean I can't tell what's what," he said, and quickly began folding papers, a useless activity in view of the already neatly folded piles of dailies.

It was one of those humid August evenings before twilight when most of Birdie's friends were gathered around the newsstand. Those who weren't sat on their front stoops, or like Thelma Wooten, stationed themselves in an open window and leaned into what little breeze the evening offered. The doors to Cinnamon's and Doc's were open, and Birdie could hear the noisy talk of evening starting up at the bar and the pool tables. A few cars cruised by, radios blasting and barely drowning the noise of sirens, which seemed to be growing louder a few blocks away. Everyone was aware of the metallic smell of smoldering debris from the DeWitt Projects that filled the air, but for the first time in Birdie's memory, not even his pine trees covered the stench. He opened a package and draped a fresh one across a nail behind the overhang.

"I got enough trouble moving the stuff I got," he said. "Maybe you boys can help me out."

"Take more than these here trees to cover up this stink round here," T-John said. "Making it smell better don't make it no better."

"We don't need to be covering it up," Jimmy B. added, and slapped the row of cut-outs as if he were shooting at a line of ducks in a carnival game.

The tips of the trees whacking against the brittle wood of the lean-to sounded like the pop of a child's BB gun. The sound seemed to echo down the street. In the beginning, that's all there was. A series of small explosions, then the scramble of feet, and the Muslim falling against the newsstand before he scurried away and Doris Jean screamed. Or was it LuRaye? Or Pearl? Or Sister Roper? In the confusion, all of them may have made a noise that sounded like a scream. The street was alive with screams, and the rush of folks running away from and toward the source. For a moment, they seemed to forget the blind man. Birdie hung onto his papers, his hands automatically counting a stack he'd counted only seconds before. That's what he was doing when the first wave of demonstrators from the DeWitt Projects rounded the corner. Those in front, looking more like gang members ready for a rumble than political agitators, rushed down Cottage Grove and collided with the police racing into the intersection off Newhope. The air was filled with shouts and everyone seemed to be throwing something—curses, bullets, homemade bombs, a load of garbage that smacked a GIONIO FOR MAYOR poster dead center. About that time, Jimmy B. turned back, T-John close at his heels.

The lean-to was already burning when they reached it, thick smoke caught in the red glow of Cinnamon's neon sign. Birdie's line of pine tree cut-outs dripped green and purple liquid fire like wax from a candle, each drop igniting the stack of papers with a puff of black smoke. T-John yelled something that sounded like a military command, and pulled away the side of the stand with his bare hands, but it was Fred-Fred who crawled over the smoldering papers and shoved Birdie clear of the tinderbox before it collapsed. "It's over," Birdie mumbled, as T-John grabbed him, and with Jimmy B.'s help, dragged him into the vestibule of a nearby building. Doris Jean stumbled in behind them. That's when Pearl caught up with them. She had tried calling to LuRaye, but Jimmy B.'s wife was halfway down the block—Sister Roper right behind her, her arms flapping like any sanctified sinner who had gotten the calling—and neither one of the women had any intention of turning back. To this day, no one knows where the good Reverend hid, or why Doris Jean saved the box of cardboard pines Birdie kept under the counter of his stand.

While Pearl and Jimmy B. tried to make the old man comfortable, Blind Birdie muttered something about Georgia none of them could understand. Soon, his breathing was so quiet, no one could hear it above the noise of the mob. "Tell him I got some of his stuff," Doris Jean said. They all turned to look at her. "Tell him," she repeated, and held up a pine tree still wrapped in cellophane. Fred-Fred dipped his hand into the box and let the trees fall from his fingers like tinsel. Where the cellophane had loosened, the sharp smell of pine wafted into the hallway.

Pearl whispered, "Chile," then shook her head. What could she say when they were kneeling in a hallway in front of a box of cardboard trees while a whole street full of crazy folks rushed past like fools trapped in some wartime newsreel? "I never did like the smell of them things," Pearl said.

"Me neither," T-John agreed.

How I Came to Dance with Queen Esther and the Dardanelles

IT MIGHT NEVER HAVE HAPPENED except that one day in the autumn of my senior year in high school, my Aunt Stacia sent my cousin Lulu Mae to the corner store for a loaf of bread. That heifer came home two years later with a baby, and no bread. Lulu Mae had never been known to keep time too well. In fact, she was known for bad timing, and her sudden appearance at our front door, a baby in her arms and a suitcase by her feet, was no more than we could expect from a person who, two years before, had announced that she had every intention of changing her name to Queen Esther so she could go on the stage with the Dardanelles. Those boys just took that name because they'd read about that place, and got it fixed in their heads the place had something to do with Hannibal getting all those elephants out of Africa. They thought using the name could be the hook that would get them out of the Projects. What they knew about Africa you could lose inside a crocker sack, but that didn't matter because those Dardenelles were dancing fools, and next to my Uncle Percy, who was from the Islands, there wasn't anyone for miles who could outdance Jock and Ferro Maitland. The three of us—my cousins Pepper, Lulu Mae, and I—didn't care what they called themselves. The minute we saw the Dardanelles, we wanted to dance with them so bad, we were willing to maim each other for unspecified lengths of time just to get a clear shot at the chance. We might have been cousins, but blood was never thicker than a good cha-cha partner. And Lulu Mae standing in the doorway, that baby in her arms, on what otherwise might have been a dull Saturday morning in autumn, proved at least one of us had chosen the cha-cha over cousins.

"Lord today," Aunt Stacia said when she saw Lulu on the porch with that baby. "Lord, Lord, look at you."

At first, nobody moved to open the screen door. Lulu Mae was on one side of the screen, grinning and jiggling that baby up and down like she had herself a bottle of Dairy Fresh and was trying to mix the milk at the bottom with the cream on the top. Aunt Stacia stood on the other side of the screen with me and Pepper. There we were, three females who were known to have more mouth than they had sense, struck dumb by a woman-child and her baby. I just kept blinking my eyes, thinking somehow the wire mesh was playing a trick on me. But Lulu Mae and that squirming mess of fat fingers and drooling mouth did not go away.

"Com'on in here," Aunt Stacia said. "Open that door, Maresa, and let that chile in here. Don't leave her standing out there. Folks be talking bout us if they see her standing out there like that."

I opened the door, not because of what folks might be saying, but because it just didn't seem right for us to be standing there gawking at each other. Maybe Aunt Stacia had forgotten how many times folks had gossiped about us already. What with Grandma Vernida, who used to get the sanctified holiness and scare all the neighbors, and Aunt Stacia with a houseful of girls who were not her daughters, we had given folks more than enough gossip, even if they didn't count my two uncles, Eddie and Percy—especially Uncle Percy, who was handsome and came from the Islands and could speak French, which folks around here thought was really strange for a black person to do. By their notion, all black folks were supposed to have been pulled out of the same colored bag. It's like Grandma Vernida once told my mother, "There's more colored folks in this world than them what's slaving down in Dixie. They got some of us everywhere." And since we seemed to have family just about everywhere, I figured we'd given folks plenty to gossip about already, so Lulu's sudden appearance at the door wouldn't change their habits. But I opened the screen door anyway, and while Aunt Stacia snatched her into the house, I got her suitcase. Once inside, that baby took one look at my aunt and held out its arms.

"Lord, how come they all gotta come home to me?" Aunt Stacia said, but we could see how happy she was holding that baby. I leaned over to take myself a good look at the baby. I wanted to know right away whether or not I could figure out just which one of those Dardanelles might be its daddy, and what kind of baby it was. Aunt Stacia cleared up the mystery for me.

"Lulu, is it a boy or a girl?" she asked.

Lulu Mae grinned. "He's a boy. My little man. Me and Ferro calls him D.P. I bet you can't guess what them initials mean."

Aunt Stacia frowned. "What you saying, chile?"

"You know," Lulu answered. "Like his daddy's name stands for the T. in Booker T. Washington. D. P. stands for something, too."

"Oh, now we got to play a game," Pepper butted in.

She had been standing off to the side, watching Aunt Stacia and me make baby noises. Her tone of voice told us Lulu's return hadn't exactly thrilled her. It was as if all the old arguments were right back in place. At any age, a grudge could be a lifetime cause, except at eighteen, time was a relative thing and grudges could be dropped as fast as they were adopted. I saw I had underestimated Pepper's staying power. Her eyes were full of accusations against Lulu for running off with Ferro Maitland, a boy Pepper had picked for herself.

Pepper grunted. "Miz Lulu's back and we gone play let-me-guess. OK, I'll do it. Don't tell me . . ." She closed her eyes and put one hand on her forehead like she was trying to conjure up something.

Aunt Stacia said, "You behave yourself," but Pepper waved away that caution.

"Don't stop me, Aunt Stacia. I see it." Pepper opened her eyes wide. "Yeah. I know what them initials mean. Lulu Mae named that baby . . ." She paused and hummed the "Dragnet" tune: "Dumb-de-dumb-dumb." Then she grinned and said, "She named him DAR-DA-NELLE! Wonder how I knew that. I oughta go on 'The $64,000 Question,'" she laughed.

Aunt Stacia said, "Portia June, that is not funny."

But come to think of it, it was kind of funny—funny in the way some people can look so pleased with themselves when nobody's laughing at their joke but them. Lulu wasn't laughing one little bit. She gave Pepper a tight-mouthed look like she smelled something bad but couldn't quite figure out the direction of the odor. I knew it wasn't that baby. I couldn't smell any diaper smells even though I was standing close enough for the child to grab my nose, my ears, whatever its chubby little fingers could clutch.

"Lulu, what does the D. really stand for?" I asked.

Pepper started to say, "Maresa, ain't nobody asked you nothing," but Lulu interrupted. "Pepper's right. It's Dardanelle," she said.

"See," Pepper sneered. "And it ain't even a real name. It's the name of some old island in the middle of the ocean."

"It's my baby's name now," Lulu told her, and plucked the baby from Aunt Stacia's arms. "Everybody knows the Dardanelles. We the best dancers on the whole circuit, and the onliest reason we come back to this town is cause we're booked at the Club. Everybody's gone come to see the Dardanelles. Ain't that right, D.P.?" She cooed to the baby, then she shoved her glasses up on her nose with her middle finger, and strutted into the kitchen as if to say to Pepper, "Eat that, Miz Thang."

I said, "Oh-oh...Ohhh," signifying without putting words to it.

Aunt Stacia shook her head. The problem wasn't what the Dardanelles called themselves. The problem was my family didn't want any of us falling under some white folks' notion that all black folks could do was sing and dance, or if we had been boys, no matter how great Sugar Ray Robinson was, become boxers. We didn't have to worry about the boxing part. By the time I was born, the only family children near my age were my cousins Pepper and Lulu. It was as if male children had looked at our family and said, "No way, man," then moved on down the street to the Nelsons, who already had three boys, or to the Pritchards, or over to the Projects with the Maitlands, who had given us Taliàferro and Joaquim—otherwise known as the Dardanelles. Lulu Mae ran off with both of those Dardanelles, and when she returned with the first boy-child the family had produced in two generations, part of the family was torn between wanting to exact punishment for her disappearance, and at the same time, wanting to kidnap that fat brown angel-cherub of a baby to see who could spoil it first. For the rest of us—that is, for me and Pepper—the flak over Lulu Mae's return only meant we had to deal with just how the fallout would affect us, because somehow, the family was sure to connect the consequences of Lulu's behavior with us. And it was the family's brand of rules and retribution that had driven us away from our own mothers and into Aunt Stacia's house in the first place.

Aunt Stacia had inherited all of us when we were about fifteen. We had descended on her after our own mothers, Aunt Stacia's sisters, had thrown up their hands—or as in the case of my mother, when I'd moved out before Mama could throw me out. In less than a year, my aunt had gone from being childless to being a mother of three teenage girls, all born within a year of each other. The spring Lulu Mae came home, Pepper had had her eighteenth birthday a couple of months earlier, while I was looking forward to mine right after the school year began. And Lulu Mae? Well, a week after her eighteenth, Lulu Mae was standing in our doorway, wide-eyed behind her horn-rimmed glasses as if she'd simply returned from a two-year walk and had to ring the doorbell because she'd forgotten her key. We sort of figured that after her trip to the store, she'd bypassed that nonsense about celebrating birthdays. It wasn't that we weren't ready to wish her a happy birthday, but after showing up with a baby, following two years and no word from her or the Dardanelles, it didn't seem fitting to say, "Oh, by the way—happy birthday, Lulu Mae."

Pepper and I would have let the whole thing slide, but later that week, after we had all gotten used to Lulu's return, Aunt Stacia made us wish her a happy eighteenth. Unfortunately, Pepper was in charge of dessert that day, and while she'd come to terms with the notion of Lulu actually running off with Taliàferro Maitland, she just didn't think Lulu should get away with it scot-free. So Pepper made tapioca pudding, stuck a big old church candle right in the middle of Lulu Mae's tapioca, then handed her the matches so she could light it herself.

It's a good thing Pepper hadn't done that on the first day of Lulu's return. On the first day, it was clear that everyone needed a period of readjusting to Lulu Mae again. There were too many things to remember and too many things to forget. Most certainly, we had to forget that Lulu had simply left town two years before, presumably with that loaf of bread still tucked under her arm, and not bothered to look back. At the time, Aunt Stacia had merely made a few phone calls to satisfy herself regarding Lulu Mae's whereabouts without notifying the police. But for me and Pepper, Cousin Lulu's disappearance was like having some part of us ripped away, and the wound had never quite healed over. Now that she was back, we set about the task of recovering from her departure, but I don't think Pepper or I quite understood how Lulu could have just turned us off and gone on about her business the way somebody turns off a leaky faucet and leaves the house, the door unlocked and wide open.

"Bernice done taught that chile to act like she don't see nothing she don't like," Aunt Stacia used to say. "Lulu ain't just wearing them glasses cause she half-blind. After living with her mama, that chile need some help just to see some of what the rest of us been looking at."

When Lulu first came to live with us, I thought Aunt Stacia was exaggerating because she and her sister Bernice used to fight so much when they were young—"Went at each other like cats," my mother used to tell me—but after Lulu Mae had lived there for a while, I understood what Aunt Stacia meant. Lulu had a habit of borrowing things without bothering to tell the owner. One day, something that had been lost would just turn up near her: a favorite pair of somebody else's blue jeans hugging Lulu Mae's narrow ass, a book stuck up under her pillow—the pages all bent—a hair clip lost until it was spotted on Lulu's head, or in the case of Pepper, a boyfriend whisked away as quietly as Lulu used to swish the dustmop across the parquet tiles in Aunt Stacia's living room. In fact, the last time Pepper had confronted Lulu about taking something that didn't belong to her was the last time all three of us had cleaned Aunt Stacia's house. It had happened a few days after Pepper's birthday, the year we were sixteen, the year Lulu had run away.

I had been on my way to the garbage can with the trash from the upstairs bathroom when I'd spotted Pepper standing in the living room doorway watching Lulu, who was doing her usual hit-miss-and-a-promise dusting of the two front rooms downstairs. Pepper had that look of "I'm gonna get this heifer" in her eyes, and I knew she was still seething from the way Lulu had flounced onto the dance floor with Taliàferro Maitland the weekend before. To make matters worse, on that night Lulu had been wearing something of mine: a sweater with mother-of-pearl flowers all down the front of it that my father, who was in the Merchant Marines, had bought in Hong Kong. I didn't care one way or another about that sweater, actually. If the truth be known, all those gifts had been the reason I'd moved to Aunt Stacia's in the first place. Mama had started accusing me of being ungrateful because I was always complaining about Daddy not being at home. So I'd moved out. Living with Aunt Stacia meant I didn't have to care what my father bought for me, when he was going to be at home, or how long he stayed. Mama said it was like cutting off my nose to spite my face, but at least I didn't have to hear all that crap about not being grateful. Like Pepper, I just plain didn't want to listen to my mother's yapping about "Maresa Hayes, you do this." And "Maresa Hayes, you do that." Still, a gift was a gift, and if Pepper couldn't complain about Lulu stealing Ferro from her, she certainly could complain about her lifting my daddy's gift. So on my way back from emptying the trash, I took a detour to the living room to watch the fight I figured was brewing. What I found was Lulu backed into a corner, the telephone in her hand, and Pepper standing in front of her, her hands on her hips.

"So call her. I dare you," Pepper said.

"What's happening?" I asked.

Pepper answered me without once taking her eyes off Lulu. "This heifer claims her mama gave her one of them pearl sweaters last year. I told her she better prove it. Go on," she said to Lulu. "Call your mama and ask her when she give you that sweater."

Lulu was shaking, but she dialed the number anyway. I couldn't figure out why Lulu would even try to call her mother. Aunt Bernice had made it clear that she didn't expect to hear from her daughter. But Lulu could be as dense about what folks told her to do as my Aunt Bernice could be about telling folks what to do. According to Aunt Bernice, Lulu had fallen from grace when she'd stopped going to church. Moving in with Aunt Stacia only showed how far she'd fallen. Lulu had as much chance of talking to her mother on the telephone as her mother did in trying to make Lulu go back to the Holiness Temple. Sure enough, Lulu Mae no sooner had her mother on the phone when Aunt Bernice hung up on her. Two days later, Lulu was gone. For weeks after that, Pepper had moped around feeling guilty about making Lulu call her mother.

More than once, we'd heard the women discussing Aunt Bernice's behavior—how Aunt Stacia had been the one left to tend Grandma Vernida after she got sick and took to shouting even when she wasn't in church, but Aunt Bernice had been the one who had had the religion rub off on her. The holiness religion had left Lulu Mae's mother unforgiving and stubborn. My mother would say, "She'll come outta it," and Aunt Stacia would add, "Yeah, we all did and look at us." My cousins and I would look and shake our heads. To us, they didn't seem to have come very far at all, and more than that, they weren't about to let us get very far. While we were living in Aunt Stacia's house, our mothers checked up on us to see how we were doing every Saturday. Moving was supposed to have helped us get away from our mothers, but come Saturday, we could count on Aunt Stacia dragging our mothers to the house. And when they came in, it was inspection time.

I remembered what had happened the time Pepper had jumped so bad behind those boys at the dances, she'd started walking and talking like she was from Spanish Harlem, saying "ting" and "mahn" like she was some kind of Island girl. Imitating the way Uncle Percy talked was one thing, but when she started wearing a crucifix in front of the family, instead of slipping it on just before we left for the dance, we all got into trouble. Of course, when Lulu came home with that baby hanging around her neck same as that crucifix stuck up under her blouse, it was different, but back then, wearing a cross could get us all into deep trouble. You have to understand, there were two sure-fire ways of upsetting the women in my family: one was to make fun of Grandma Vernida's Holiness Sanctified Temple, and the other was to tell those women they didn't know what they were talking about. It didn't matter that they themselves talked bad about the H.S., as Aunt Stacia called Grandma's church, and it didn't matter that half the time, they were running their mouths just to hear themselves think—rules were rules, and if we broke too many, we had to find some place else to live. Or as my mama would say, "If you gonna stay here, you gotta walk the chalk line, sister." Living with Aunt Stacia hadn't removed the line, just its location. So when Pepper had jumped bad at sixteen, and started flaunting a bright gold crucifix on a chain around her neck, we figured she was ready to step off the line.

On Saturdays, our mothers breezed into the house on clouds of talcum powder and kitchen odors, their faces full of "Hello, chile" and "Girl, let me look at you," and their arms filled with packages of this and that meant to sustain us during our unlimited stay at Aunt Stacia's. As usual, Lulu's mother was conspicuously absent, but on Saturdays, Lulu helped the rest of us get ready. On Saturdays, the house would smell like cinammon toast and mango-flavored tea, and the Motorola would be set with a stack of records that ranged from Sister Rosetta Tharpe's gospel songs to Ray Charles' honky-tonk. "Can't never tell what them women gone want," Aunt Stacia would say, "but I'm gone give them a little bit of Grandma Vernida's music just so's they feel at home." Then she'd throw back her head and laugh in what we called her "holy-roller laugh"—the one that made Uncle Percy get real jumpy and claim he didn't know what Aunt Stacia had on her mind. The only thing on Aunt Stacia's mind come Saturday was her bossy sisters. And they certainly were on the minds of my cousins and me. With our mothers present, we had to make sure we did everything Aunt Stacia asked of us, even those things we'd avoided during the week. Of course, the threat of being asked to return home made discipline easier for Aunt Stacia, but that threat made it harder for us to understand why Pepper took it upon herself to wear a crucifix when she knew our mothers were coming to visit.

Listening to my mother and her sisters talk and eat was like watching hungry folks trying to dance and all the while, grab food from the buffet table. They didn't miss a step. Uncle Percy told a dance story about where folks had been and where they were going. Sometimes the women in my family told the same story, splitting hairs six ways from the part, taking two steps forward and three steps backward. Sometimes they took far too many steps, and other times, none at all.

We had no sooner sat down to lunch when my Aunt Lil'June spotted Pepper's crucifix. With one breath, she stared at it, and in the next, asked, "Eustacia, just where in the world would any of these childrun be getting some kinda Catholic-type neckpiece?"

Aunt Lil'June searched our faces for an answer, but nobody spoke up for the longest time. Finally, she got to Lulu, and Lulu, with her blabbermouth, came across like a champ. "From them Island boys," she said.

Pepper reached behind Lulu's chair and gave her a big pinch. I said, "Shee-it." But I don't know why we were so bent out of shape. We had always made it a habit never to tell Lulu anything we wanted to keep secret. Lulu could keep a secret about as well as Pepper's mama, Aunt Lil'June—which was not at all. Uncle Percy called Aunt Lil'June's mouth "the black dispatch." He'd say, "You got someting you want put on the grapevine, then you go tell Lil'June. Mahn, she send out the news better than Paul Harvey on the radio."

Now Aunt Lil'June said, "Well, Eustacia, I see Percy Portugal done made you go Island all the way, huh? My husband might be Island same as Percy, but I made sure Eddie wasn't gone give that chile no Catholic upbringing in my house. Big Mama would roll over in her grave if she knew you was raising my chile to be Catholic."

Aunt Stacia grunted. "Why don't you go out to the cemetery and tell her about it, Miz Motor-Mouth? I'm sure your big mouth can reach past the grave."

"Stacia, ain't no needa getting mad with Lil'June," my mother said. "You gone get mad at somebody, get mad at me cause I want to know what that chile's doing with that cross, too. Seems to me like you and Lil'June both done turned Island with your husbands. I ain't saying it's wrong, mind you. When you get yourself hooked up with a strange man, you gotta make some adjustments to what's foreign. And even Big Mama musta knowed something bout foreign stuff. That's why she named me Zenobia. You know, like in the ancient times? It means Bathsheba." My mother sniffed. "It's a pretty name, if I must say so myself."

"Can we stop you from saying it?" Aunt Lil'June asked. "If you don't say it, nobody else will."

Aunt Stacia interrupted before Mama could argue with Aunt Lil'June. "Zenobia, stop it. And Lil'June, you listen too. Ain't no childrun round here gone Catholic."

Aunt Lil'June said, "Bet not. Big Mama didn't take kindly to them Catholic folks and all that missionary stuff they did in Africa."

And my mother waved her fork to get Aunt Stacia's attention. "It don't matter what Big Mama thought, honey. She dead now. But if Bernice finds out you letting these girls turn Catholic, she gone have a shit-fit and little babies. You know she think Lulu's leading a sinful life as it is. Lulu, I hope you ain't thinking bout turning Catholic. Lord help us if you are. I sho wish Bernice was here to see bout this."

The women nodded their "Amen" to that, but Lulu just sat there looking down at her plate with her glasses hanging on the end of her nose, looking all sweet like butter wouldn't melt in her mouth. That was the way she usually acted when our mothers came calling, speaking up at the wrong time and silent the rest of the time, and everybody thinking she was so good, being mistreated by her churchifed mama and all while Pepper and I took the flak, so busy watching Lulu that when Aunt Lil'June slammed her hand on the table, we jumped.

"How come we can't never stay on the subject? How come y'all can't stop this jawing and tell me why mah chile done took it upon herself to put that thing round her neck?"

"What thing you talking bout?" Pepper asked her mother. "It's the same cross what's on the altar at the H.S. with the same white man hanging on it."

Aunt Lil'June said, "Ohh, Lord today," and my mother added, "Have mercy, Jesus! Lil'June, you let Pepper talk to you like that? You hear what that chile's saying? I wouldn't let Maresa say them things to me," my mother laughed. "That chile's gone have her grandmama's spirit eating up this house. Um-um. Calling that church *H.S.!*"

"That's what you call it," I told her.

"Don't you be sassing me, Maresa Hayes. Don't you be mouthing off. You best watch yourself, Maresa Hayes," my mama said.

"Zenobia, you hush," Aunt Stacia said. "You talk about somebody mouthing off and when you was growing up, you was sassing Big Mama all the time. And everybody else, too. So just hush, both of you. Long as you sitting round my mama's dining room table, you can just stop your fussing. Don't matter whether you talking Catholic or H.S. The only difference is which slave master give it to us. Now, pass me some of that buffalo fish. And Lulu, you go change them records on the phonograph. Put on something by Reverned Staples' choir."

The sound of Lulu's chair scraping across the floor almost drowned Aunt Lil'June's complaints. "Humph! She talking bout *my* mama like the rest of us didn't have no mama a'tall. Better stop with that *my* mama stuff. Just cause Big Mama left everything to you don't mean she wasn't my mama too."

"Just pass the fish, Lil'June. We ain't here to be talking bout who inherited what."

Aunt Lil'June handed Aunt Stacia the platter, but she gave her a look that said she clearly wanted to discuss why Aunt Stacia had been the one to inherit all of Grandma Vernida's belongings.

"Eustacia, you still ain't told us what Pepper's doing round some Island boys," my mother said. "I thought the only Island boy was in this house."

Aunt Stacia stabbed a piece of fish. "Ain't no boys in this house, Zenobia. And you know it."

"So where they be?" my mother asked, all sweet-like.

For a minute, there was only the sound of chewing. Then Lulu looked up. Everyone was staring at her.

"What you looking at me for? Always think I'm gone be snitching on somebody. You see me with some cross? I ain't got no cross. Don't nobody in them Projects be asking me to dance."

Pepper rolled her eyes to the ceiling, and I giggled. Lulu had come through again. I caught Pepper's eye, and mouthed the word: BINGO!, while the women started having little hissy-fits.

"The Projects!" they yelled in a chorus of soprano voices that would have gained Reverned Staples' attention, if he'd been in the room instead of leading his choir on the gospel record that was just beginning to play. "What y'all doing at them Projects?"

Aunt Lil'June looked sideways at Aunt Stacia and smirked. "If I remember correctly, somebody told me there wasn't gonna be no more doings in them Projects after all that business with they husband going there."

Aunt Stacia shrugged. "That's old news, Lil'June."

My mother interrupted. "I don't care if it's old nor new, nor whose husband been there, I bet not catch Maresa in them Projects."

And Aunt Lil'June chimed in with, "Pepper, I know you ain't gone tell me you been fooling round in them Projects, girl. I told you before not to go there. Ain't you got no better sense than that? No telling what kinda people be in them Projects. Um-um. That's the last straw. I can't have that. I ain't gone have you taking your butt down to them Projects. No, sir." With each word, she got herself more and more worked up, until finally, she had to wipe her mouth with a napkin.

"Hold it!" Aunt Stacia yelled. "Just make up your mind. You more upset about them Projects or about this chile turning Catholic?"

"You know how we all feel bout them Projects, Eustacia."

"Lil'June, all I know is them Projects is here to stay, and don't matter what folks be saying, they give them people some place to live. And I don't know why anybody in this room is so down on the Projects. This house woulda been IN the Projects if the city hadn'ta run outta money fore they got this far. If Papa had bought a house on the other side of Cottage Grove, we'd be Projects sure as I'm sitting here."

"Well, we ain't," my mother said. "And the Projects ain't sitting here. And ain't no chile of mine gone be in them Projects either, not long as she be a chile. Since I ain't heard different bout no childrun sitting in this room turned grown-up all of a sudden, if somebody tell me Maresa's been in them Projects, she ain't gone be sitting here no longer."

Aunt Lil'June nodded her agreement, and my cousins and I saw Aunt Stacia's eyes fill with disappointment over our behavior.

So we'd tried to straighten up. We'd heard the verdict implicit in my mother's threat: no Project dances or home to Mama until we were old enough to find homes of our own. But like Uncle Percy said, we had smarts. We'd changed to Plan B: the Club Riveria and the Dardanelles, music by a real-live steel band straight from the Islands. If my mother had known that her ultimatum would've caused us to abandon the Project dances for the supper clubs and throw us, headlong, into the path of Jock and Ferro Maitland, she might have relented. On the other hand, if she'd known that meeting the Dardanelles would've caused Lulu Mae to run away from home, she might have called for a stiffer punishment. And I suppose if anyone had predicted which one of us seemed likely to run off with one of those boys we met at the dances, the choice would have been Pepper, not Lulu Mae. But like old lady Holmes next door said when the weather messed with her garden, "Well, that's water under the bridge." A lot of water had passed under the bridge by the time Lulu returned, but most of it had passed a little slower for us than it had for Lulu.

The morning she came home, I watched her waltz into the house and sit down at the kitchen table, comfortable like no time at all had been spent since she'd last sat there. Aunt Stacia and I followed her, but Pepper stayed where she was in the hallway. Still, as soon as she heard us playing with the baby and asking all kinds of questions about the pictures Lulu had brought with her, Pepper came to the kitchen door, looking all down in the mouth and close to tears. And Lulu, as usual, let her forgetfulness cancel out what had just passed between them.

"Pepper, looka here. Here's a picture we took on the beach before we got on the ship for the Islands. I'm wearing that blouse you give me."

I giggled. I knew full well Portia June Mason had never in her life willingly given Lulu Mae Roper anything. For a minute, Pepper looked like she was going to jump salty all over again, but she shook it off and came to the table to take a look at the picture. As she sat down next to Lulu, the baby grabbed a hank of hair and sort of swung himself from his mother's arms to Pepper's lap, spraying her face with a raspberry of spit as he made baby noises on his way to his destination. Pepper had no choice but to hold him. We all tried to help her, but if there was one thing little Dardanelle could do, it was hold onto something once it was in his grasp. From the way Pepper was looking at that picture, I figured she wished the same could be said for the baby's father.

"See, Pepper. The boys got on them straw hats you always liked. Y'all member them hats?" Lulu asked me and Pepper.

And we said we remembered, pretending we were looking at Lulu's face in the photo, pretending we were only glancing at the boys dressed as the Dardanelles in midriff shirts, the fronts tied in knots just above their navels, the sleeves layered in ruffles like accordions, and their chests as smooth as if skin color had been painted on silk. We pretended not to be interested in Lulu, who was dressed as Queen Esther, Carmen Miranda style, a big flower in her hair, a fluted skirt hanging on the dangerous end of her hip bones and exposing miles of pale brown thigh. It was too close to the memory of us sitting at the back table in the Club Riviera—Sister Vernida June Garrison's granddaughters as far away from the holiness religion as they could possibly get: their legs brazenly crossed at the knees, cardigans opened two buttons too low past the cleavage they hoped for, and red candlelight painting their lips even redder than the slick coats of Coty they'd layered on. At the Club, King

Midas used to sing: "*On the Island you find a man. The sun give him such a permanent tan. All the women they think he is grand. So they follow this Island man.*" Too bad King Midas hadn't told me and Pepper that Lulu would be the one to follow this Island man, and we'd be the ones left with souvenir photos.

"Ferro looks like he scared of the camera," Pepper said, still trying to untangle the baby's hands from her hair.

Lulu reached over to help her. "Naw, Ferro was tired, that's all. We just finished three shows at the Palm Tree, and all of us was sick off some bad food we'd had the night before. You member how Ferro useta like Chinese food? We was always stopping by Wu Fong's. Y'all member?" she asked us.

And we nodded "yes," and tried to signal that we also remembered Aunt Stacia didn't want us eating at Wu Fong's. Every time we'd brought her an ice cream box full of roast duck and soft noodles, the soy sauce leaking through the cardboard like blood, Aunt Stacia would scrape the stuff into a bowl and pick through it to make sure it was just duck and noodles. And we always had to eat a little bit with her, although we were stuffed full after helping Ferro and Jock eat about five boxes of the stuff before we got home. Ferro always ate more than Jock, even though he was skinnier, and we always knew he'd had enough when his eyes started to swell up and turn glassy. That's how he looked on that picture Lulu brought back from Atlantic City: a bug-eyed dark-skin boy grinning on one side of Lulu, his brother, on the other side, laughing straight into the camera's eye.

They were both long-legged and bony, their shirts open to expose gold crucifixes, like the one clearly outlined under Lulu's blouse. It didn't matter that the pictures were in that funny shade of brown like the old-timey ones Aunt Stacia had of Grandma Vernida, I knew those crucifixes were gold as surely as I knew those boys smelled of wintergreen cologne and skin turned hot with the sweat of muscles moving like oil. I have to say, I'd always thought Jock was the handsome one. Jock had a sweet look about him, a teacup full of laughter always playing at the corners of his mouth, and his face was rounder than Ferro's. Ferro looked like his name, kind of weasel-like with too many teeth and a pointy chin. And he could be moody, like Lulu. But both of the boys had the most beautiful eyes anyone could imagine, eyes that would make you move one step closer to the water or climb a rung higher on the ladder, even when you knew you couldn't swim and were afraid of heights. Their eyes were full of devilment, like Uncle Percy's, except Uncle Percy's eyes were beige—"des yeux gouères," he called them—while the boys' eyes were brown and full of dark lines that circled in a pattern, the way the straw did in those reed baskets old lady Holmes used when she was gathering vegetables out of her garden next door. That straw was so dark and those vegetables so bright, it was if someone had taken a photograph called: "Basket with Flowers," or if it had been music, the sound you'd hear when you listened to a flute on a hot sunny day. Those boys' eyes were full of that music. When I danced with Ferro or Jock, I couldn't look in their eyes. That would make me forget to tell my feet what to do, and if I wasn't careful, I'd look right into that pretty brown laughter and find it pulling me back from a wild spin at the last minute, as if the earth had taken over the spin and gravity had snatched me home.

I was lucky Uncle Percy had taught us how to do Island dances, like the rhumba, mambo, merengue, and cha-cha-cha. I could do them all with my eyes close. Still, the sweet whisper in the eyes of some Island boy could make me lose track of the steps. Even now, with the pictures, we were losing track of where we were.

"You can just put them pictures away," Aunt Stacia said. "We might as well get this table cleaned off so's we can eat something and you can feed that baby."

She was talking normal enough, but I noticed her hands were fidgeting with the photos. So I said, "Aunt Stacia, don't you think them boys kinda look like Uncle Percy when he gets dressed up to go to his lodge meeting with Uncle Eddie?" I figured a question about Uncle Percy and Uncle Eddie, who were cousins, would help Pepper cool down about Lulu and Ferro. What I didn't know was that I was playing into Lulu Mae's hand.

She laughed. "Y'all forgot to ask me what the other part of the baby's name was. He do have two names, you know," she said.

"What you mean?" I said. "We already know his name."

"You just know the first name," Lulu answered. She waited. We gave her blank looks. "Member, me and Ferro calls him D.P." she added.

"De Pee-Pee," Pepper said, and gingerly handed the baby back to his mother.

Lulu felt his bottom, then smelled her hand. "Aw, he's just wet," she said. "You just wet, ain't you, Dardanelle Purcia? We gone have to change your diaper fore your Uncle Percy gets a look at you."

Surprised, all of us, even the baby, turned to stare at Aunt Stacia. It had never occurred to us that Lulu Mae would call her baby by our Uncle Percy's real name. Aunt Stacia frowned, then scooted her chair back from the table and started gathering the photos. "That name sho is a mouthful for one little bitty baby," she said. "Let's hope he got better sense with it than his uncle. Even if he is as cute as Purcia," she added. And we all laughed.

Before Lulu Mae went off to Oz for a loaf of bread, the three of us could coax our Uncle Percy into doing just about anything we wanted him to do. Part of it was bribery. Part of it was because our uncle was a pushover, pure and simple, so even if we had some dirt on him—which was fairly easy considering how handsome he was and how the women were always flocking to him—we only relied on bribery when we were in a real bind. We had used bribery twice: once to make Uncle Percy take us to the Project dances, and then to make him teach us how to drive his Thunderbird. But we never really needed bribery when it came to dancing. Before Lulu Mae ran away from home, a day didn't go by without us rolling back the living room rug and turning the Motorola up to full volume. When we first came to live with Aunt Stacia, we only listened to rock-and-roll. "Why you always got ta turn on thees loud R-and-B stuff?" Uncle Percy would ask. And we'd remind him that the white disc jockeys only played soupy music that didn't have anything to do with black folks. "They don't know diddly bout songs like like "Dancing in the Street," "Stand by Me," or "In the Still of the Night," we'd say. Not that we had to convince Uncle Percy about the differences in the music white people and black people listened to. Those were the days before crossover records, the days when the black disc jockeys on all-night party stations were the only ones playing R-and-B, when Dick Clark's "American Bandstand" didn't have everyday black folks on it any more than the crowd scenes in movies and on television did. And when my cousins and I danced the Hully-gully, we didn't look like we'd just caught a bad case of the St. Vitus disease, the way those folks did on Dick Clark.

"This is what all the kids at school are doing," we'd say to Uncle Percy, then fall into something like the Slop or the Stroll.

"If you want to do someting all the black people do, then let me teach you how they dance in the Islands," Uncle Percy said.

And that's how we came to learn the Island dances. Now that I think about it, watching us learn the intricacies of Island dance must have been painful for Uncle Percy.

"Mahn, don be switchin yourself round like you tryin ta find some place ta sit on the toilet," Uncle Percy would say as steel drums slammed out a rhythm on some bootleg recording of "El Cata." "Sway on the beat, mahn. Move the hips smooth. C'est non se débattre. Move like you writin on the wall and thees ting you write make you feel good."

And we'd sway and sway until our stomachs ached from tightening muscles to make those movements just right. Except Lulu Mae never got it quite right. Lulu Mae always moved too slow, with her eyes half-closed and her face wrinkled up more than old lady Streeter's neck, and I'm here to tell you, Miz Streeter's neck looked like she'd folded it up every night and forgot to iron out the wrinkles in the morning. And when Lulu was trying to remember something complicated, like the Cuban mambo STEP-STEP HIP-TO-HIP BRUSH-BRUSH-SLIDE, her eyes would bug out behind those thick glasses like the headlights on a Chevy. Uncle Percy would stare at her and shake his head.

"Lulu, sweet chile, why you look like somebody who got stuck wit some frog they tryin ta catch for the jumpin contest? And the frog jerkin its head ever-which-a-way and makin some frog-leg moves like it's gone ta wrench the backside from its po head." But Uncle Percy could see Lulu Mae got mad when he picked on her, so he'd laugh and tell us all to "study up on the meanin of thees rhythm what you movin your body for. Ain't you got no sense of why you got ta make the body go thees way and that?"

One day Uncle Percy just plain got tired of looking at us half-step as Lord Invader sang the beauty of *"goin-down-Rockaway,"* with a chorus of steel drums sounding like sea shells tumbling across a coral beach. Uncle Percy groaned as we did something that was a cross between a diddy-bop walk and a boogie break. "Mahn, you doin too much rock-and-roll stuff," he said. "Some kinda la ripopée. You tryin ta dance like you in a back-up group wit Ray Charles or somebody?"

We shook our heads: No. We'd already tried Doo-wah. Who in the neighborhood hadn't? Everyone had recordings of Mary Wells, the Marvelettes, the Shirelles, and the Chantels. Project kids were as faithful at practicing some kind of routine as any choir member practicing gospel songs. Except for Doo-wah groups, singing came second to the routine and a special outfit: sequined dresses, pointy-toed shoes, beehive hairdos, six coats of lipstick, and eyelashes a mile long. We had to be at least as cool as the Chantels, or the Shirelles. We practiced all the time. At school, we diddy-bopped in front of the lockers, and in the summertime, we used the hedgerows and sidewalks as a stage for our practice of synchronized back-up lyrics, while fireflies added their flickers of light. My cousins and I had our routine down pat by the time we were thirteen. We wore identical cardigan sweaters—buttoned up the back—three layers of stiff crinolines under our skirts, high-high pink satin heels, and matching pink gloves—because a good doo-wah was as much hands as feet.

Our special routine was a Doo-Wah-Shoop: DOUBLE FIST-TURN-STEP-STEP—SLIDE-KICK . . . CLAP-CLAP-CLAP-AIRPLANE-WINDMILL . . . doo-ooh-wee-ahh. It was so cool, we added bubble gum to a step-clap-clap beat, timing the bubbles so they popped out right on the musical cue. It was better than those dumb hoola hoops the Greenlee girls had, but I have to admit, after all those doo-wahs, our Island dancing looked more like crabs scuttling sideways than sweet calypso.

Uncle Percy said, "Lord Invader don be asking for no mop for you ta scrub the floor, mahn. Thees music it comes from Afreeka through the Islands. It is how we go back from here ta the old country where the people have the Afreekan way." Then he pulled out a big piece of butcher paper he'd brought home from the post office where he worked at night, and drew circles that were supposed to show us how the steel drums were hammered into patterns for musical notes. But seeing our ignorance, Uncle Percy's lesson on steel drums shifted to a lesson on how slave trade routes moved from Africa to the Islands to America.

"It is all in the music," he told us. "The drums tell you how thees ting goes. On the steel drum you got some notes round the circle and one note always in the middle. You got only five notes wit the bass pan, but how many you got wit the ping-pong pan, huh?" We giggled. Uncle Percy stared at us.

I guess he started with me because I just couldn't stop giggling. "Maresa, why you tink it so funny when I say ping-pong pan?" he asked. I shrugged and tried to swallow my laughter, so he moved on. "And you, Miz Lulu . . . you tink thees music is funny? Maybe you, Pepper? Thees is funny to you too, huh?" His face didn't say funny at all.

"No, we don't think it's funny," we told him, sobering up like good little chickens. "Un-un." "No way." "No, not us."

Our protests did not fool Uncle Percy. "You see, thaat is the problem wit childrun today. You make a joke for everyting. Thees music is serious. On thees drums we have the history of the black people. All the notes here . . . Movin in and out like our people been movin when they took the slaves outto Afreeka." He pulled his finger around the rim of a circle. "The music is from Afreeka. When you hit the drum here—it goes, cleep . . ." He patted the edge of the circle. " . . . you get the big notes. Then you go round ta get a different sound. Dink . . ." He moved from the outer rim to a smaller circle drawn nearer the center. "One sound here . . . and one sound there. But no matter where you hit the drum, you tell about when the Mahn take us outto Afreeka and the ships move cross the big ocean. All that we know is here in the drum." Uncle Percy ran his finger around the rim of the circle. "It is the old country and many centuries of the black people. The song and the dance. But when thees ships move ta the Islands, we maybe loss some tings." His hand traced the circle again. "Then the Mahn he bring us here in thees country." Uncle Percy pulled his hand dead center of the circle. "Here the Mahn take everyting. No song. No dance. No place where we can go. You see, it is very far away from Afreeka. They tink we forget, mahn. But we remember."

"Percy, how come you acting like you know so much?" Aunt Stacia asked him. "The way you tell it, none of us know nothing less'n we from the Islands. Why you always got to be syndicating bout them Islands? We was all slaves out there in them fields, Aye-lands or no Aye-lands."

"Woman, you listen up ta what I been sayin. I know the Mahn have us all in slavery. But I tell thees childrun bout the Islands cause many great mahn come from thaat place. That is where the great Marcus Garvey come from. And the poets like Countee Cullen and Nicolàs Guillèn. And even thees boy, thees Harry Belafonte, who come over here singin thaat day-o calypso stuff with his shirt open down ta the navel. Thay all come from the Islands, mahn."

Aunt Stacia grunted, "Humph... If they so great, how come they always got to be coming FROM them Aye-lands? And how come you ain't got no women come from them great Aye-lands?"

"What I want to know bout some Island woman? I got mah woman right here... eh, mon 'e chou?" he'd laugh, teasing Aunt Stacia with his best cat-eyed look. "I just tell thees childrun what I know bout the Island music and how ta look for why it comes ta be played thaat way. They got ta know what the music can do for the black people."

"I ain't worried bout what the music do for black people," Aunt Stacia said. "I'm worried bout what them players gone do to these girl childrun."

Aunt Stacia had good reason to be worried. I never figured out exactly why Aunt Stacia put up with our foolishness. At the time, I thought she did it because she'd had no children of her own. Later, I decided she was either crazy or a saint. Certainly the three of us gave her enough reasons to achieve sainthood, sneaking out of the house on Saturday night to go to the Project dances when we didn't have permission. "Why don't y'all go to some of them high school dances," Aunt Stacia said when she finally found out where we were going, but by that time, it was too late. We had already met boys named Eduardo, Tiño, Henri, and Rafael. And of course, Taliàferro and Joaquim. All of them from the Projects.

The Projects were called the War Zone, and kids who went to the vocational high school, right next door to the Projects, were known as the Warriors and the Bloods. Most of them came from families that had moved from the South or the Islands during the war, when factory work was available. Aunt Stacia said Grandma Vernida used to tell her what it was like before the city tore down the tarpaper shacks in the flatlands and built the Projects. She said Grandma Vernida had even seen black folks jumping off the trains down in the flatlands, folks who had set up housekeeping almost on the same spot where they'd jumped from the train. When the war was over and the city put up the Projects, some of those folks got stuck there. My cousins and I went dancing in the Projcts, but we were always happy we had some place else to go when the dancing was over.

But those Project boys didn't mess around when it came to dancing. Those boys were hip even though the dances were nothing more than sock hops. The three of us had ruined many a pair of socks until one summer when Aunt Stacia caught us hiding our dirty clothes in the basement, and made us wash everything until the Project dirt was out of them. After that, we wore dancer's slippers with clunky heels and soft leather soles, and the boys thought we were uptown Puerto Ricans moved in from Spanish Harlem. They were the ones most likely to have come from Spanish Harlem, but uptown they were not. Project boys were different from the ones in our neighborhood. The boys we grew up with were stuck-up and thought they were cute because they belonged to the right clubs and the right church, because they went to camp in the summer, wore letter sweaters, and played basketball at the Y in the winter. Project boys hung out on the street corner and wore leather jackets. They usually went to the vocational high, and their families were the ones left without jobs when the war ended, and the factories and railroad yard cut back on workers. If those boys had jobs after school, they were likely to be cleaning up at the gym where the white boxers trained, running numbers for the local gamblers, or helping their mothers clean houses out in the ritzy Belmont District. When Ferro and Jock got their first gig dancing at the Club Riviera, everybody in the Projects said they'd gone big-time, and crowded around them when they dropped by the Project dances for old times sake. The one thing you could count on in the Projects was some cool dancing partners on Saturday night.

No matter what those boys looked like in school with their ratty clothes and chewed-up pencils, when they hit the dance floor, they turned into Belafonte, Piro, and Cuban Pete, all rolled into one. Out there on the dance floor, with the rhythms of a steel band singing like palm trees kissing each other at the edge of an ocean, those boys were hot, their open shirts framing chests so hard and muscular, they seemed carved from stone. In the seventh grade, a museum trip to see marble statues had given me and my cousins a first-time look at a man's naked body, all long-limbed with muscles stretched flat across broad chests, and penises, like budding flowers, cradled in the nests of thighs. There, we were wide-eyed, little black girls staring at sights our church-going mothers absolutely had forbidden us to see. We were giggly, shoving and elbowing each other, afraid to touch the smooth marble, the outthrust hip so inviting our fingers itched to press against it. We didn't know much more by the time we started going to the Project dances, but we pushed against those boys and imagined the statues. On the dance floor, their skin glistened with beads of sweat that winked like jewels in the dim light, and we were like little kids learning what the word "hot" really meant—sticking out our hands just to see if the touch really would burn our fingers. Let me tell you, it did. And that was all the more reason to go back for more.

Dancing with the Dardanelles was like stepping onto concrete in the summer in bare feet. It was so hot, we had to move. When those boys danced, they grabbed us and hung on until the last note. Some of the little kids playing in the street near Aunt Stacia's house had Gumby dolls that kept whatever shape they were bent into. That's how we acted when the Project boys grabbed us, especially Ferro and Jock. Like the other boys from the Projects, they wore their hair glued down by Brylcreme and water. They were boys with no shoulders and biceps as big as Popeye's. Boys with hard chests, and tight pants covering an ass like a fist. Boys with bean breath and eyes like liquid. Boys who slid by and asked us to dance like they were snitching something off a rack while looking the other way, looking cool. They used their hands like they were driving stock cars: one hand clutching a chunk of some girl's butt, the other low down at her side to shove her in gear. The phonograph's blast of the drummer's first beat was the flag to tell them they were off and running. Jock could move his hips so I'd forget to listen for the sound of the congas. And Jock loved to dip. Ferro did too, but Ferro would bend my body down from the small of my back, and at the same time, pump me onto my toes and off center until one hip was brought up to meet his oncoming hip. And that was just a mambo spin. But don't get me wrong, the Project boys weren't into belly-rubbing grope-and-grind like at the high school dances where church boys waited until the lights were low, and copped a feel in the middle of the Huckle-buck.

All of the Project boys were smooth, completely Island like Destinè and Prado. The floor was always packed tight with bodies, and when some boy locked you in a dance, your very bones picked up the Latin heat of drums until, like the air in the room, nothing moved before the drummer moved. The problem was that sometimes, at the end of the dance, the very same boy who had moved his hips like you were the last uncharted continent he wanted to march into, would turn on his heels and walk away—no word, just a glimpse of him trucking toward some other unexplored territory. So we learned to do that too—dance all close with them, then turn it off as soon as the music ended. Lulu had learned that lesson too well. She had walked out of our lives, past that grocery store, and into unknown territory with the Dardanelles.

We were sitting on the porch, and Aunt Stacia was singing to Lulu's baby, who was fretting for a nap: "*Go tell Aunt Rosie . . . Go tell Aunt Ro-oh-sie . . . Go tell Aunt Rosie, the old gray goose is dead. The one she's been saving to make a feather bed.*"

She was sitting beside Lulu Mae, the baby between them on a pallet in the porch swing. We had finished up the breakfast dishes, and had come outside to wait for Uncle Percy to wake up. It was one of the last few days of good weather when the wind still carried enough summer heat to make being outdoors tolerable. The shadows of leaves from the hickory tree dappled the baby's bare back with patterns, like the birds and flowers on the crib blanket Aunt Stacia had dug out of the attic and given to Lulu—"In honor of Grandma Vernida's first great-grandbaby," she'd said. But Aunt Stacia hadn't invited our neighbors, Dee Streeter and Corella Holmes, onto the porch to see the baby. Those old ladies had been sniffing around the edges of the yard since we'd come outside. I saw them watching and nudged Pepper.

She laughed. "I guess they want to meet Pee-pee."

"I told you me and Ferro calls him D.P.," Lulu said, and brushed a fly away from her child's head.

"How come you didn't bring that baby's daddy over here with you?" Aunt Stacia asked Lulu.

Lulu didn't answer, so I said, "I think Danny P. sounds better than P.P. Don't you, Aunt Stacia?"

"Lulu Mae, I asked you a question," Aunt Stacia said. "How come you didn't bring that chile's daddy home with you?"

"He's coming," Lulu told her.

"When?" Aunt Stacia asked.

Lulu let the whisper of leaves in the hickory tree answer Aunt Stacia's question. For a moment, she was the old Lulu again and the three of us were sixteen, sitting on Aunt Stacia's front porch waiting for evening when we could sneak out of the house. Lulu had her eyes half-closed so we could see more of the rim of her glasses than her face. Pepper was sitting beside me on the steps, a stalk of sweetgrass stuck in the gap between her front teeth, and I was chewing on a flower petal I had pinched from a bloom in the clump of marsh poppies growing near the porch. The flower was one of those big cheesy ones that we had liked to eat when we were kids. Except we were no longer kids, and Aunt Stacia was still waiting for Lulu to tell her where Ferro Maitland was.

"What's that baby's last name?" Aunt Stacia asked Lulu.

We knew she was asking if Lulu and Ferro were married, but Lulu evaded the question. "Ferro says it don't matter what we call him long as he ain't got no family but us. I went off to the Projects and met Ferro's folks yesterday fore I come here."

The sheer boldness of her actions stunned me and Pepper. Lulu had always been one with the downcast eyes and whispers, waiting on someone to tell her she was doing right. But not anymore.

"What's that got to do with the price of potatoes?" Aunt Stacia asked her. "We family, too."

"Ferro ain't met Mama yet," Lulu answered. The porch swing creaked as gently as her breathing. "I ain't gone ask him to come here till he can do that."

Aunt Stacia sort of moaned and sighed, "Oh chile . . ."

"That's how come I waited till Saturday," Lulu continued. "I figured you could call Mama. Everybody still come over on Saturday, don't they?" She didn't pause long enough for anyone to answer her. "If my mama's gonna be here at all, it's gone be on Saturday. You go on and call her, Aunt Stacia. I'll wait."

Pepper snapped off her sprig of sweetgrass, and I snatched the last petal from the poppy I was holding. My cousin and I looked from Lulu to Aunt Stacia to Lulu again. For the first time, I saw Aunt Stacia wasn't doing so well in this stand-off. Lulu was staring straight at Aunt Stacia, who was looking down at her lap where her hands rested, curled up like the leaves get when the first chilly rains of autumn hit them. And here it wasn't even October yet. None of that seemed to faze Lulu. She just rocked that porch swing like she had all the time in the world, and at that point, I saw the new Lulu as she was. It occurred to me that I'd been missing something about her all morning. Unlike the Lulu Mae of two years ago, this Lulu never hesitated to demand answers. This Lulu took charge and didn't wait for anyone to ask her opinion. This Lulu had maps of towns in her head that we had not learned the names of yet. And she had done something the women in my family had yet to do—she had left home and returned. She no longer needed their version of the world and its sins. But there was no way the Lulu we saw would pass our mothers' inspection. Even without that baby, the crucifix she had hanging around her neck would raise their hackles. That alone would surely make Aunt Bernice rant about Lulu's fall from grace.

In the past, Aunt Stacia had tried all sorts of tactics with Aunt Bernice. If any of her other sisters didn't show up one week, by the next week, Aunt Stacia would force them to visit on the pretext of helping her bake a cake for the ladies social club, or finish sewing one of us a dress she was perfectly capable of finishing herself in an afternoon, if left alone. And when they did show up, Aunt Stacia would nag us to clean our rooms so our mothers could see how well-behaved we'd become once we'd left their houses. But it was a kind of conspiracy that had worked out fine for me and Pepper, who wanted our mothers to see us having a wonderful time away from home. And it had worked for Aunt Stacia, who had never quite forgiven her older sisters for abandoning her to take care of their mother, my Grandma Vernida. In fact, the conspiracy of guilt had worked with everyone but Aunt Bernice. She had had fifty dozen reasons for not coming by, and fifty different ways of juggling those reasons to make it seem like she really was unable to make the trip. So when Lulu Mae sat on that porch defying Aunt Stacia to call her mother, it was as if she'd forgotten all the times Aunt Stacia had tried to get her sister to visit like everyone else. Lulu sat there looking like she'd carved a whole new set of rules to live by, and one by one, she was telling us what they were. So we were grateful when Uncle Percy interrupted.

"Why you all come outside thees morning?" he asked. "I come down for some coffee and mahn, I don't find nobody in the kitchen."

He was still standing inside the house, so he hadn't seen Lulu. Although he was half-hidden by the screen door, I could tell his face was rumpled with sleep. It may have been past noon, but for Uncle Percy, who worked the graveyard shift at the post office, it was early morning. And in Uncle Percy's mind, walking out of the house meant you were on your way somewhere. Like Aunt Stacia sometimes said, "Purcia was on his way out of this town when I met him, and he still think you don't step out the house less you gone travel." The idea of sitting on the porch on any morning made no sense to Uncle Percy, and that morning, my uncle didn't yet know that Lulu Mae had ended her travels on his porch.

Uncle Percy shoved open the door and asked, "Stacia, why you got ta be sittin wit thees girls? Don't you know my stomach is cryin for some food when I get outto the bed?" That's when he saw Lulu. "Sacre bleu! Is it a ghost? What it is the cat drag here? Is thees Lulu Mae I'm seein? Maybe my old eyes trickin me. C'est bon comme la vie. Com'on, chile, ta your Uncle Percy."

Watching Lulu rush into Uncle Percy's arms really wicked off Pepper. "She oughta sit herself down," Pepper muttered as Lulu jumped out of the swing so fast, she woke up the baby. Hearing D.P.'s cry sent Uncle Percy into another round of: "What it is I see here?"

He pulled himself away from Lulu and picked up the baby. "What it is here? Mahn, what is thees?"

"You know what it is," Aunt Stacia told him. "Somebody think you be wanting a baby round here the way you carrying on." She was looking more at the old women next door than she was Uncle Percy. When they saw Aunt Stacia eyeing them, they grinned and waved, but it did them no good. Aunt Stacia was having too many problems with family to add Corella Holmes and Dee Streeter to her list.

"Put that baby down, Percy. You holding him up like he's some kinda trophy you done won."

"Oh, he is a champ alright," Uncle Percy laughed. And D.P. came through like a champ. He burped a dollop of sour milk and gurgled at his uncle. "Stacia, give me someting for ta wipe thees babee. He is so happy ta see his Uncle Percy, it make his stomach dance."

Pepper said, "That does it," and stomped into the house. I was going to follow her, but Aunt Stacia asked me to help get stuff for the baby. So I stayed there while Lulu rummaged around in her diaper bag. But I still had it on my mind to get away from that porch as soon as possible. That is, until Uncle Percy said, "Well now, Lulu, you tell me all you been doin." Hearing that, I thought I'd stick around for a bit.

"They tell me you goin on the stage now," Uncle Percy added. "It ain't so good ta be movin about when you got a babee."

Lulu said, "We don't move that much, Uncle Percy. Before the baby, we was in New York and Tampa. And we was over round Maryland and Virginia some too. But that was before we went to the Islands."

"You been over in them Islands?" Aunt Stacia asked.

Lulu laughed. "Of course we have. I told you that, Aunt Stacia. Member them pictures we took on the beach? That was the Islands. You member, Maresa?"

I shrugged. "Yeah . . . I remember . . . Some . . ."

"Too many things to be remembering," Aunt Stacia said. She was watching Uncle Percy play with Danny P. like he'd never seen a baby before. "I got enough trouble keeping up with things going from day to day," she added.

"Lulu, when you go ta the Islands, you go ta the French or the British?" Uncle Percy asked.

"Naw, we didn't get to where you was born, Uncle Percy. There was too many Maitlands for me to meet, so we only went to one place. And when the baby come, all of them wanted to see me all over again. I musta met a hundred Maitlands out on that Island."

"Well, now thees baby got ta meet the Portugals and the Garrisons and the Masons and the Hayes and the Ropers."

Uncle Percy bounced D.P. every time he called out a family name. But we noticed he'd left Lulu's until the last.

"I bet your mama got a big smile on her face seein her fine grandbabee, eh Lulu?" The baby cooed, eyes big as his mother's.

Aunt Stacia tried to hush Uncle Percy, but Lulu answered in a loud voice, "I don't know what Mama got on her face. I ain't seen Mama for more'n two years and Mama ain't seen this baby a'tall, Uncle Percy. You member the last time she was over here."

I watched Uncle Percy stop jiggling the baby and turn to Lulu. He frowned at her and I could see he actually was trying to remember the last time Aunt Bernice had visited. I thought: *"He should be remembering the last time Lulu Mae ended her visit.* But I wasn't going to say anything. I'd had enough "you member" to last me longer than that day.

Uncle Percy said, "What you be tellin me, chile? You better take thees babee ta see his grandmama."

"Not if she don't want to see me," Lulu said.

"Percy, Bernice won't talk to the chile."

And Lulu added, "When I called her, she said: 'The voice sound familiar but I just can't place you.'"

Uncle Percy handed D.P. to his mother. "I don understand your people, Stacia. What is the matter wit thaat woman? This be her flesh and blood." Aunt Stacia shrugged. "I don know bout your sisters, Stacia. I don know why they be actin so funny." He stood up. "But I don like it. I don mind when the childrun come here, but mahn, it ain't right ta be leavin them like don nobody care."

This time, Aunt Stacia managed to signal Uncle Percy to be quiet. He saw it, but it didn't really stop his train of thought.

"Ahh . . . what it is I say? Your sisters make me boil, Eustacia. Sometime I come ta be fairly disgusted wit them women," he said. "Bernice gone ta bring herself here for ta see her grandbabee or my name ain't never been Purcia Por-tugal."

"Percy, you stay out of it," Aunt Stacia called as my uncle walked down the stairs. "Percy, you hear me?" she repeated. The old ladies next door stopped looking at us out of the corners of their eyes, and turned to face our house straight-on. So Aunt Stacia waved at them. "Damn," she whispered. "Now I got to talk to them old biddies." Then she called out, "Percy . . ."

"Je vais lui foutre un galop," Uncle Percy answered, knowing how he frustrated the neighbors when he spoke French—"Like the Island."

"Percy, you don't need to bring nobody here. Stay out of it," Aunt Stacia repeated, but Uncle Percy was already at his car. "Lulu, you coulda handled this some other way," Aunt Stacia told my cousin.

Lulu smiled. At least, that is the way it looked from one angle. From the other angle, without her glasses clouding the view, it was more of a smirk than a smile. Lulu kept that half-smile in place until Aunt Stacia turned to greet her neighbors, waving "Hello" as if she had just that moment recognized the two of them.

Then Lulu said to me, "Com'on. Let's go see what Pepper's doing upstairs."

While Aunt Stacia walked to the gate to deal with old lady Streeter and Holmes, I followed Lulu into the house. Even with that baby in her arms, she walked with her back straight and her rear-end swaying as if she had done nothing all her life except dance with the Dardanelles. In a way, she seemed to have taken on some of Ferro's characteristics, the chameleon look he had when one minute, he was the youngest partner in the Dardanelles, and the next, he was upstaging Jock with every move. That's the look I'd been seeing in Lulu all morning. Pepper used to say that, glasses or no, Lulu looked like she was trying to see through water and fight her way clear of it. Now it occurred to me that the real Lulu had floated to the surface and shed the cover of water the way trees shed their leaves for winter. Maybe she wasn't as twig-thin as she'd been before she'd had the baby, but she seemed to have turned as hard-edged as tree limbs did in winter. Even her walk suggested the sway of trees in the wind. It made me feel like I was sixteen and silly all over again. It was as if I had stayed in one place while Lulu had moved on without me. I didn't like that feeling. I wanted the old Lulu back, the one who'd snuck out of the house on Saturday nights, and acted as dumb as me and Pepper.

Nobody had told us dumb was only a look, so we had taken it on as serious business. We wore satin skirts, the material from Woolworth's and the pattern from Butterick, slinky-straight and extra tight. Pepper wore hers with a side slit cut clear up to her thigh. And I'm here to tell you, Pepper had some thighs on her—"thunder thighs," we called them. Me? I added three layers of flounce to the bottom of my skirt, and every time I tripped across the floor, I looked like I was going to audition for a part in some movie about flying off to Rio de Janeiro, or some place. And I looked like I was ready to fly all by my lonesome. But in those days, Lulu was the one who seemed to be only half there. She'd take off her glasses, and without them, she was so nearsighted, her eyes were wide with the strain of seeing past anything that wasn't right in front of her nose.

We'd always tried to time our arrival at the Club Riviera to coincide with the last part of the R-and-B set. The Riviera was part bar, part club, with live music nights on Fridays and Saturdays when the R-and-B dance band traded off sets with the steel band. In those days, some white folks might have known about the Ink Spots and Nat King Cole, but none of them could have identifed King Creole's Calypso Band, Perez Prado, or Lord Invader. At the Riviera, the R-and-B warmed up folks for some righteous steel drum Latin beats. That music transformed the Riviera into Club Havana straight out of Cuba, or the Folies Bergère, where everyone knew Josephine Baker could rhumba meaner than anything seen outside of the Islands. I say this because for us, that place was magic and we were unbelievably shy, shy the way black girls could be when they had bought into that racist crap about how being black made them automatically cool and in the know about sex and all that goes with it—and that, in turn, made them run a bluff they couldn't put down for fear of finding out just how little ground was under their feet. In those days, we ran that bluff by sitting at a back table at the Club Riviera. Both of the Riviera bands were hot, and by the time they really started cooking, with the crowd clapping their hands, and screaming "aRRRiba!" in an ear-splitting trill of *R*'s jitterbugging out of everybody's mouth, King Midas would yell: "Ladies and Gents, and all those who ain't—It's SHOW TIME at the Club Riviera." And then we'd get the Dardanelles. To us, they never seemed to stand still, partly an illusion of the chandelier ball spinning above their heads, and partly because we knew they were going to come over and pick one of us for a dance. My cousins and I would scream louder than anyone else. By the time that band turned up the heat on those steel drums, timbales, and congas, they were glistening with sweat and so were we. And all the time, we swore we were cool, shaking our hips like we could wear out a dress from the inside.

"Looking sixteen and going on thirty ain't too bad." That's what Bruno had said the first time he served us. Bruno was the bartender, and he called out the names of drinks as if they were words in a scat-man's song: *"gin-mill-double-fizz, Johnnie Walker Red-and-milk, C.C.-coming-up-on-seven"*—whatever the traffic would bear. The traffic at the Riviera would bear most anything, and Bruno presided over this menagerie of bottles, bar stools, and plate-sized tables—their candles trapped in tiny red-lacquered cages—while a revolving ball coated in slivers of glass sprinkled pinpoints of light over the miniature stage and dance floor. At first, we let Pepper order for us. "A Manhattan, straight-up," she'd purred, her voice pitched real low trying to imitate movie stars in films where men were Belafonte-cool and danced with women, like Dorothy Dandridge, who always had husky voices. Pepper had practiced smoking, so she'd tried her Bette Davis trick of blowing out a match without taking the cigarette from her mouth. At home, Lulu and I had applauded when she finally had learned to kill the match without showering us with sparks from the cigarette. But Bruno hadn't been impressed one little bit.

"You got a choice," he'd told us. "Canada Dry with or without the cherry."

It wasn't the kind of statement that invited a challenge, so we went for broke. All of us had said, "Cherry," except Lulu. She'd said, "No cherry, thank you," in a small voice, and all the time looking down in her lap.

I saw Bruno smile. "Take your glasses off, kid," he'd told Lulu.

She'd grabbed her specs as if she thought Bruno would snatch them away from her. "I can't see without my glasses," she'd mumbled.

Bruno had grunted. "In here, you ain't missing much. Besides, some cats like thinking a chick can't move less they got the lead. Get it?" He'd grinned. Lulu had grinned back, but all of us got it.

From that point on, Bruno served our Virgin Marys in tall glasses, cherries on top, while Lulu got hers in a champagne glass, a half-slice of lime clinging to the side. From that point on, whenever she was in the Riviera, Lulu took off her glasses and left one eye shadowed by a flower she'd pinned in her hair. But you can't go from playing Dorothy Dandridge out of Porgy and Bess to actually being Dorothy Dandridge, and it seemed to me that Lulu Mae had drifted home from the Dardanelles thinking she really was somebody's idea of Dorothy Dandridge. The problem was that nothing had changed except what was in her head. While Lulu Mae had been busy forgetting the way home, all we had was a memory of her. That's why she didn't need to keep getting on everyone's nerves by saying: "You member?" What we remembered was already enough to get on our nerves.

I found Pepper sitting up in her bed when I got to the room. She had left my bed untouched, but Lulu's bed, the one we'd been using to hold our dirty clothes, was piled high with clothes, books, shoes, and whatever else Pepper could find to cover it.

"Where's that heifer?" she asked. Then she punched the pillow like it was a catcher's mitt. "Where's Miz Thang?"

"Down the hall putting the baby to sleep in Aunt Stacia's bed."

"I'm sick of her," Pepper said. "Coming in here like she knows everything and we don't know nothing. Talking bout: member this? Member that? What she think I am? The Encyclopedia?"

"Just let it rest," I said. "Let it rest." Then I plopped down on my bed and tried to clear my head of everything that went with thinking about Lulu and her baby. That was difficult. I realized life had been a lot easier before 7:00 A.M. when Lulu had rung that doorbell. "What are we gonna do?" I asked Pepper.

She stopped filing her nails long enough to glare at me. "Why do WE have to do anything? WE didn't run off nowhere. You didn't see me slipping outta here and getting myself preg-nut, did you?" The angle of her nail file was directly in line with the light filtered past the hickory tree. I shook my head, No, meaning none of us could slip out of the house. The tree limb we'd used had been cut clean down to the trunk by Uncle Percy the year Lulu ran away. There was a scar on the cross-section of trunk where the limb had been was sealed with tar, and the center glowed yellow-brown, like skin in the sunlight.

"WE ain't gone do diddly-squat," Pepper said.

I said, "I guess not," and closed my eyes, trying to take my own advice about resting. It still wasn't easy. The very air betrayed me. The room smelled like me and Pepper: her Bluegrass cologne and the Chanel No. 5 my father sent me every Christmas. There was still a faint aroma of Bergamot Hair Oil, Noxzema, and Pepper's ever-present bottle of Witch Hazel for her pimples. But underneath it all, I picked up the scent of Lulu's Cuticura Ointment and Avon Magnolia Blossoms, although we'd packed away Lulu's stuff long ago. Even the extra desk was sitting in the hallway, and her bed, under the mass of stuff Pepper had put on it, was made up like a sofa. But despite our clean-up, Lulu had never left that room. We'd just been faking it, and we would have kept faking it, even with her return, if she hadn't walked into the room and pretended to ignore all the stuff Pepper had piled on her bed.

Lulu sat herself on that pile without even bothering to look at what might be under her. "I wish I coulda brought my Queen Esther dress for you to see," she said, "cept it's too big to fit in that little old suitcase. I ate so much, I put on a little weight after the baby, you know." She showed us her dimpled knees. "Couldn't seem to stop eating. But what I really missed was them bags of caramel corn we useta get from Sears. Girl, sometimes I swear I could member just how that stuff smells when you first get off the elevator. You know, right there by the shoe department. I can't wait to pick up a bag. I know the stuff's fattening, but Ferro likes me a little on the plump side though. What you think? You member how I was always trying to keep from putting on too much weight, an . . ."

Without opening my eyes, I interrupted. "Lulu Mae, if you ask us to remember one more thing, I'm gone wring your neck."

"Girl, you ain't changed a bit," she said. "You was always running off at the mouth."

"You know, she don't even listen to her ownself," Pepper said.

"You can't listen when your lips be flapping," I muttered.

"And I still have trouble membering all the words to songs," Lulu said. "It's the same as when we useta go to the Club Riviera. Even before that. Y'all remember how I useta sing: *'granite Jesus if you please?'* I thought Jesus was made outta some kinda stone."

The bed creaked as Pepper stood up in it. When I opened my eyes, she was poised to throw the pillow at Lulu's head. I yelled, "Pepper, don't you do that! Let me!"

Lulu sort of half-covered her head. "This is just like old times," she giggled.

I groaned. Pepper let the pillow fly and yelled, "Will you shut up with the old times, for Cris'sake?"

The pillow knocked Lulu's glasses cockeyed across her nose, but her hurt look was not about her glasses. "I thought y'all would be glad to see me come home." Pepper grunted and fell back onto the bed. I plopped down again too. We were about to be had. Lulu had put on her chameleon look—the "what-about-li'l-old-me? expression. That was the look she'd used when the Dardanelles bounced onto the floor after King Midas warmed up the crowd with a couple of easy pieces, like "Stardust Mambo," or "Goza Cha-cha-cha." It was the look that got Ferro's attention when the boys were ready to pick partners from the audience for their demonstation number. Pepper would say, "He just talked to her cause she was sitting there looking like she just been sucking her thumb." It had worked with Ferro. Now Lulu was trying it on us. Why not? It was what she remembered, and we'd done nothing to set her straight on how we'd changed.

"You didn't even write," I said.

Lulu settled her glasses back onto her nose and whispered, "I guess I just forgot."

Pepper sat up in the bed "Ohh mahn, leesten ta thees girl, eh? Thaat boy screw her so good she forget how ta read and write."

"Naw, we was busy," Lulu said. "It's like I told Uncle Percy, we played clubs from here to the Islands and back. It didn't have nothing to do with sex. Besides, y'all had boyfriends. I mean, I know y'all ain't still virgins."

I looked at Pepper. We both knew that was a question, but it wasn't one we were about to answer. "What makes you think we'd tell you about it, Miz Rusty Butt?" Pepper snapped.

"I was always talking bout y'all," Lulu whimpered. "Ferro didn't like it that I was talking bout y'all so much. He said . . ."

"Lulu, has it ever occurred to you that we don't give one diddly-damn about what Ferro likes and don't like anymore? We ain't been to the Projects since the riots. We don't even go to the Riviera. We listen to jazz now."

Teary-eyed, she stared at Pepper. "But you useta . . ."

I sat up so abruptly, she stopped mid-sentence. "Lulu Mae Roper, you can't just waltz in here and expect to take up where you left off like we just been waiting for you to come home so's we can finish the next sentence. And it won't do you one bit of good to be telling us to remember stuff all the time. I spect we remember better than you do anyway. But that don't matter. We just ain't the same folks as when you left. Like Pepper said, we listen to jazz now, and go over to the Y to go swimming. And Aunt Stacia was sick all last winter. And my mama had an operation." Lulu opened her mouth as if to say something, but I held up my hand to stop her. "What I'm trying to say to you, Lulu Mae, is we been living while you been Lord-knows-where. You didn't tell us where you was going, even though we were supposed to be telling each other everything. So now that you back, don't be trying to play catch-up."

Lulu was really crying by that time. "I don't know what to do."

"You can start by saying: 'I'm sorry,'" I told her.

"Then you can get your butt up off my clothes," Pepper said.

We let her cry for a while—there was no reason to let Lulu think it only took few tears to turn us around—then we listened as she told us stories about the Islands, and clubs where she and the boys had danced. Before long, she was teaching us a few new dance steps—"the paz," she said, her French just as bad as it had always been—and we found out Lulu had learned to let herself go loose, arms and legs moving against the rhythm of her body until she looked like cloth falling away from the bolts of material Aunt Stacia unfolded when she was ready to lay out a pattern for a dress. Pepper and I tried to follow her when she told us how folks danced "more the Afreekan way" in Jamaica, Bermuda, the Bahamas, and all those Islands laying south off the Florida Keys. And Pepper and I welcomed the old Lulu home while asking the new one, Queen Esther herself, how we could get to those places, seeing as how by the end of the year, we would have outgrown Aunt Stacia and everything else in our hometown. But whenever Lulu got too big-headed about being the first one out the door, we pulled her up short. We might have been having trouble forgiving her for abandoning us for a life that had made her grow up faster than we had, but as long as she was in that room, she was still the same old Lulu, and the three of us were still subject to the same failures, the same rules and regulations that had brought us all to Aunt Stacia's house.

A noise in the hall made us remember that's where we still were. Aunt Stacia was standing in the doorway, holding the baby. Danny P. was only half awake, rubbing his eyes with the backs of his hands, his mouth open in that oval shape babies get when they know somebody's going to take care of them even if they can't speak for themselves.

"Lulu Mae, what was this baby doing by his lonesome?"

Pepper and I grinned and gave each other the high-five sign. Once again, Lulu's forgetfulness was catching up with her.

"I made him a pallet," she told Aunt Stacia. "He was alright when I left."

Aunt Stacia grunted. "This baby ain't like a package you can wrap up. He ain't on loan, and you can't be walking off and leaving this chile like you done forgot a bundle of laundry somewhere. Don't you be leaving this baby by himself like that."

Lulu looked down at the floor. "Yes ma'am," she said.

Aunt Stacia saw me and Pepper grinning like Cheshire cats. "Everything alright in here?" she asked.

"Yes ma'am," we said in chorus. "Everything's fine."

"Well, you might as well get on downstairs. We gone be having company. Your mama's on her way here, Lulu Mae."

Even though she was still standing up, I could see Lulu slump a little. Pepper and I moved closer to her. Not touching. Just there.

"I don't know how Percy did it," Aunt Stacia said. She was looking more at Danny P. than at us. The baby stuck his head in the soft crook of Aunt Stacia's neck. "He's bringing her over soon as he stop by for Zenobia and Lil'June."

"Aunt Bernice is coming here?" I asked.

Aunt Stacia nodded her head. "That's what I said. And maybe you best call the baby's daddy, Lulu. Ain't no reason to put it off, I guess. I don't even know if we got enough food for everybody."

"I can run down to the store and pick up something," Lulu Mae offered.

In chorus, all of us, including Aunt Stacia, yelled, "NO!"

The baby yelped, and Lulu's eyes grew wide. Then we all realized what we'd been thinking and began to laugh. Little Danny P. clapped his hands with delight at the noise we made.

The Haunting of Cashew Fenney

BERNADETTE WHITCOMB SWEARS she can not remember when her daughter, Arjula, first saw the movements in the hallway, or when Arjula talked Fran and Willie Mae into helping her with the conjure. What Nettie is sure of is that once the girls set their mind to do something about whatever it was that kept messing with the house, everything changed. But it wasn't Arjula who first saw something moving in the hallway. It was her cat. Miz Cat, she was called—partly because the cat wouldn't answer to any other name, and partly because Arjula would forget by morning whatever name she'd chosen for the cat the night before. Having a cat made Arjula feel different. Fran and Willie Mae had dogs. In fact, the neighborhood was filled with dogs. But Arjula relished the difference. Her mother did not.

Nettie had no choice. Cashew Fenney had brought the cat home the day he moved Nettie and her daughter into the house. Nettie hadn't much liked the house. It was too much of an add-on, the back section hooked at an abrupt right angle to the end of the hallway. She liked the cat even less.

"Storeroom cat had a litter right on top of a box of Johnnie Walker Red," Cashew had told Nettie. "Couldn't keep them in the bar, so I gave them all away cept this one."

Nettie had stared at him and was grateful tending bar had not made him a drinking man. But looking at his sweet face also made Nettie aware, once more, of the seven years' difference in their ages, how willing he was to try anything, how suspicious she was of everything. "Ain't nothing to it," he'd said, and had been the one who insisted they live together, telling her, "Don't make sense for me to be sneaking in and out of the house when Jula knows I'm in here all the time anyway." During the day, before Cashew left for work, he always found some time for Arjula. *"If the truth be known, he's more like her daddy than her real daddy was,"* Nettie had said to herself as she watched both of them grin foolishly at her while she decided what to do about the cat.

There, under the brim of the gambler's hat, man and cat had waited for Bernadette Whitcomb to welcome them. "Can we keep it, Momma?" Arjula had begged. "Can we keep it? Can we?"

In her eagerness to get her mother's approval, Arjula fairly danced from one leg to the other. Nettie touched her shoulder to calm her down. Since Arjula had turned thirteen, Nettie seemed to spend a lot of time trying to keep her daughter calm. That was why she didn't mind the almost constant presence of Fran and Willie Mae. Even when she heard the three girls making a mess in Arjula's room, some nonsense about a Ouija board Fran's grandmother had given her, Nettie knew that was better than watching Arjula slump around the house, impatient to get past thirteen and on to being a woman. She didn't have the heart to tell her daughter no one year would give her that magical step, the event Nettie secretly dreaded—Arjula's final change from girl to woman. Because if Arjula grew up, where would that leave Nettie? And most of all, where would it leave Cashew?

But finally, Nettie had leaned back into her sense of patience—and onto Cashew's broad chest—and made room for her daughter, her lover, and that damned cat.

Because Nettie instinctively cringed at the sight of the kitten, Cashew tried to offer the cat to Arjula instead.

Arjula had squealed with delight. "Thank you, Momma. Oh, thank you. Thank you."

Even then, the cat, whose fur was only a shade darker than Cashew Fenney's skin, had seemed reluctant to leave its perch on Cashew's shoulder. Arjula had to pluck the kitten from his shoulder and take it down the street to show off for Fran and Willie Mae. Nettie was pleased to see her so happy, but still, that cat was a lot to ask of a woman in a neighborhood full of women with an aversion to cats.

"I'm scared of cats," they'd say. "Looking at you all spooky like they know something you don't know."

"Cats don't like colored folks. And that's the God's truth," they'd say.

Even when Nettie pointed out how the cat washed itself every morning, and after every meal, they'd say, "Trifling. Just like the man what brought it here."

"Stay out all night and don't care bout nobody else. Ain't nobody I know let no cats hang round their house. Nasty buggahs."

Nettie ignored the women's cracks about Cashew's habits, but she did confide her uneasiness about Miz Cat to her best friend, Opal Barker. "It ain't that it's nasty," she said, "but I do get sick of watching that thing licking its butt all the time."

"Girl, I won't have one round my house. Them things eat rats. Remind me of those ol' white women out in Webster Grove. Chewing all dainty and just as dirty as they can be. Then looking at you like you bet not say nothing." Opal glanced across the room at Cashew Fenney, who was cleaning his already immaculate nails with a pocketknife.

Cashew smiled, but it was the kind of smile a sleeping baby might have, just a faint upturn of the lips, either from a dream or slight indigestion. Cashew had that kind of face. Innocent, if you didn't look at the light dancing in his eyes. He could fix you with his eyes, make you stare at him until you shook yourself awake and realized that, like the cat, he was looking straight through you. In the two years since they'd been living together, Nettie had yet to shake herself awake.

So it was natural that when Miz Cat first started to bristle and hiss at something Nettie Whitcomb could not see, she kept quiet about it. At first she blamed it on the cat's diet—canned pet food gone bad, worms, or those dead mice Nettie used to find in the corners of the basement when she hung the wash indoors on rainy days. But she hadn't found mice in the cellar for months, not since that first evening when she saw the cat stiffen and dart away from the back stairs. So she told herself the animal was dumb, skitterish, frightened by the shadows of the apple tree prancing across the faded leaf pattern of the wallpaper. Except any shadows from the backyard would have had to bend around the corner to catch the light in the hallway. She blamed it on squirrels scampering across the roof, cockroaches scurrying into cracks in the floorboards, noises made by old houses with badly hung doors and plywood walls. She blamed it on long nights when she had to wait, alone, for Cashew's return home.

"Baby, ain't nothing but your imagination. You ought to be more friendly to the cat," Cashew told her. "Something to keep you company. She good company, ain't she, Jula?"

Arjula had nodded, but Arjula agreed with anything Cashew said. When Arjula came home from school, she looked for the cat, Cashew, and her mother, in that order. If even one of them were missing, she claimed her day had been ruined. "Arjula, you go fix that cat a box down in the basement. Let it sleep down there, then maybe I can get some rest."

Arjula screeched. "In the basement! Even Fran's big ol' dog don't stay in the basement."

"I can't stand that thing underfoot," Nettie said. "I'm liable to step on it."

"Ought to play with it some," Cashew said. "Miz Cat be on her toes and knows how the wind blows. Ain't that right, Miz Cat?" He winked at the cat and it seemed to wink back. Then he put on his gambler's hat, gave his shoes one more lick with his handkerchief, and left the house. Arjula went to the dining room window, and Miz Cat leapt onto the ledge to watch him disappear over the crest of the hill toward the river and the fading rays of the sun.

The neighbors watched him, too. "Trifling," they said. "Just plain trifling."

Of all those who watched Cashew Fenney leave the house, Nettie was always the first to turn away. Each night, his departure seemed to signal a need to get the house in order. Her routine involved a frenzy of cleaning: table cleared and dishes washed, pots scrubbed spotless, floors swept and doormats shaken. There always seemed to be some odd corner somewhere that needed dusting.

Opal would laugh. "Girl, you can clean all you want, but you still gone be mad and horny as a goat till Cashew brings his butt back here."

Nettie knew Opal was right, but she wasn't about to admit that. Even admitting it to herself made her scrub or polish something twice. Arjula and Miz Cat learned to stay out of Nettie's way, so that by the time Nettie crawled into bed, by the time Arjula was asleep and the house smelled of wood soap and bath talc, the frightened cat stalking the hallway shadows always surprised Nettie.

"Cash, something's scaring the piss outta that cat," Nettie whispered one night when he finally made it home around 4:00 A.M. Since Cashew had started coming home later and later, Nettie had had plenty of opportunity to watch Miz Cat backing off from whatever it was that lurked in the hallway.

Cashew rolled Nettie onto his chest and smiled up at her. This time, the devil in his smile matched the light dancing in his eyes. "Baby, ain't nobody here but us chickens," he laughed and stroked her back.

Usually the movement of his hands soothed her until she stretched the full length of his body, but this time, Nettie forced herself to concentrate on what she had to say to him. "I ain't playing, Cash. Something's making that cat act funny. And with you gone half the night, any fool off the street can walk in here."

Cashew's hands stopped at the small of her back. He sighed. "I got to work. I can't be here and down at the bar, too."

Without thinking, Nettie's real complaint began. "That bar closes at two o'clock. Don't take you to four to get home."

Cashew pushed her back onto the bed. "I got to do more than just lock the door. You know that well as I do."

For a moment, Nettie lay on her back and stared at the strange shapes watermarks had left on the bedroom ceiling. Then she said, "What you got to do that takes you till four in the morning, Cash? You answer me that."

He rolled onto his side, away from her, before he said, "Don't start on me, Nettie." Then he turned out the light.

Neither of them knew the cat was huddled at the top of the basement stairs, its ears pricked up to sounds only it could hear. And neither of them saw the light go out in Arjula's room. That night they slept at opposite ends of the bed. And for the next three nights that week, Cashew slipped through the front door just as the sun cleared the horizon.

"How long you gone sit in this house every night waiting on that man to come home?" Opal asked. "All you do is clean and sit by the window waiting for him."

"I ain't never stepped out on Cashew," Nettie said. "I did enough of that with Arjula's daddy. See where it got me?"

"Cleaning house," Opal grunted.

"Who's cleaning? I'm just straightening up."

Opal shook her head as Nettie sponged another section of wallpaper. Then Nettie stopped and tapped the wall, her ear against it as if she were listening to something. "Girl, what you doing?" Opal asked.

Nettie leaned away from the gaudy old flower-print pattern and stared at the spot that had held her attention. It seemed to be like the rest of the wall, but under the movements of the sponge, it seemed lighter to her touch. "I'm just looking for a stud," Nettie muttered.

Opal laughed. "I'da thought you already had one of them," she said.

By the next week, Opal had embarrassed Nettie enough to get her out of the house. They avoided the bar where Cashew worked, and though she laughed and danced, especially when the jukebox selection was Smokey Robinson, Nettie refused to encourage any of the men who came to their table. When the neighbors saw Opal and Nettie, dressed to the nines in tight skirts and killer high heels, the old women, who still thought it was good luck for a pregnant woman to eat starch and bad luck to leave a hat on the bed, pulled back the corners of their crocheted curtains to watch Nettie and her friend.

"Look at that," they said. "Won't settle down to save they souls."

After Nettie left, Arjula let the cat out of the basement so it could sleep in her room. For a long time, the house was quiet. Arjula was fast asleep, but Miz Cat's hissing caused the girl to sit bolt upright in bed.

When Nettie returned about an hour or two later, she found her daughter standing in the middle of the living room. Arjula was holding the cat. At least, she was trying to hold it. Miz Cat was stretched like a broad jumper caught midflight above the crossbar.

"Momma, you think something's wrong with this cat?" Arjula asked.

Nettie stared at the cat. It stared back, its eyes wild with apprehension. "Ain't nothing wrong with that thing," she said, and snatched it from her daughter's arms. The cat didn't struggle until Nettie reached the basement door. Then it clawed and yowled, and when she released it at the top of the stairwell, seemed to forget all of its surefootedness and fling itself into the blackness at the bottom of the stairs. It was still screeching when Nettie slammed the door. Arjula's eyes accused her mother of cruelty.

Nettie put her arms around her daughter and led her toward the back of the house. "Com'on baby. Let's get some sleep. That cat can take care of itself better than you can."

Except that night, Nettie dreamed the cat was trapped in a box and clawing for air. She was still trembling from the nightmare when Cashew returned at dawn and pulled her into his arms.

The next day, she found herself trying to coax that damned cat out of a tree. "Com'on Miz Cat. Com'on down, please. Cashew and Arjula gone be coming home. That movie's gone let out any minute. They gone think I chased you up there." Instead of moving toward Nettie, the cat moved toward the end of a branch, then froze when the tree started to sway.

Nettie yelled, "Cat, you get your butt out of that tree right now, you heah?"

The old woman across the street, the one who claimed she could read tea leaves, sucked on one of the ragged teeth in the back of her mouth. "Cats ain't good for nothing but crossing you up," she said.

"Know too much for me," another one whispered.

"Get you killed trying to drag them home."

As Nettie paced back and forth, the cat followed her movements. "I got no time for this," she muttered. "Too old to be chasing some damn cat. I don't even like the thing anyway," she said, and shook her fist at the animal.

That's when she noticed the outline of a window on the outside of the dining room wall where, Nettie knew for sure, there was no window. She was still standing there trying to puzzle out how the window might have been overlooked, the cat clinging to a limb in the tree above her, when Cashew came home with Arjula, Fran, and Willie Mae trailing behind him. Fran and Willie Mae giggled when they saw Arjula's mother standing, barefoot, in the middle of the sidewalk.

"Lots of folks lived in this house, baby. Somebody just must've figured the place already had enough windows. Can't hardly say as I miss one more peephole where them nosy ol' broads can be staring at us." When he looked across the street, a curtain trembled shut. The girls giggled at how fast the old lady's claw hand snatched at the curtains.

"How can there be a window on the outside and not on the inside? And Cash, you know that window wasn't there when we moved in. You didn't see no window there, did you, Arjula?"

Her daughter shrugged. "I don't know, Momma." Willie Mae and Fran giggled again. Arjula glared at them, then clicked her tongue the way her *Book of Cats* had said she was supposed to do, and waited as Miz Cat scampered down the trunk of the tree and jumped into her arms. Nettie gave the cat the meanest look she could muster. It fixed its eyes on Nettie while Arjula cooed to it like a baby.

Arjula said, "Miz Cat, have you been a bad girl? Bad kitty." Fran and Willie Mae dutifully followed Arjula and Miz Cat into the house. When Arjula passed Cashew, the cat extended one paw and batted the air as if it wanted to shake hands. The girls laughed and skipped up the porch stairs. *"Look at them. Like they got no bones,"* Nettie thought.

"Take that cat on inside," Nettie said, as if Arjula wasn't already halfway in the house. When Cashew turned to go, she stopped him. "Cash, I'm not through talking to you."

"Baby, I don't know what you want me to say. The house just got painted fore we moved in. I spoze they painted over it."

"It takes more than paint to hide a window, Cashew Fenney."

"Nettie, I don't see how it matters if the window was there or no," he said.

"Well it does," Nettie told him. "It matters just as much as it matters that I'm standing here right this minute."

Cashew smiled his half-smile. "Well baby, I sure enough see you standing there. But how come you ain't got no shoes on?"

Nettie wiggled her toes against the warm pavement. The heat felt good spreading across her instep. "My feet been hurting," she said. "I ain't had time to find no comfortable shoes."

"Looks like you didn't hardly have no time to step out of the ones you had on last night. I almost tripped over them getting to bed. What time you get home anyway? Your clothes was all over the living room floor."

Nettie didn't say he had nerve asking her what time she got in, when the only reason she went out was because he never came home. Instead, she raised her face to the sun.

"I don't need to splain my comings and goings," Nettie huffed.

"What I need is for somebody to splain that window." Then she turned on her heel and marched, flat-footed, back to the house.

"Thick as thieves till they fall out," the neighbors said.

"Gone let that man drive her crazy."

"She already half crazy trying to keep up with that man."

That night, Nettie didn't wait for Cashew to settle into bed before she pulled him to her. That night, while Nettie rocked gently in Cashew's arms, she pretended not to hear the cat scrambling away from the basement door. But Arjula heard it, and for the first time, Arjula saw the shape of the thing that frightened the cat. Wisely, she waited until morning to let her mother know what she had seen.

Nettie turned away from a griddle full of buttermilk pancakes and made her daughter repeat the story. "Momma, it was just a shape," Arjula said. "Like somebody come out of the dining room and walked down the hall."

"Toward the bedroom?" Nettie asked. "Toward our room?"

Arjula nodded.

"Was it a man or a woman?"

"What difference is that gonna make?" Cashew laughed.

Nettie glared at him, then asked again. "Was it a man or a woman, Arjula?"

"Sorta both, Momma. Not very tall. And dressed in a white dress, like a long underslip, or something. Aww, I don't know."

"Was it a white somebody or a colored somebody?"

"Momma! I could see right through it. How could I tell what color it was?"

"Don't sound like nobody we know," Cashew grunted.

Nettie pointed the spatula at him and shook it. "How you gone splain that?" she asked. "You gone splain that like you splained that business with the window?"

Cashew calmly wiped drops of pancake batter off his shirt, but for a second, he looked worried. Then he laughed. "Jula, you been reading too many of them books you bring home from the library. You get folks all worried doing that. Ain't nothing to worry bout, baby. Ain't nothing to it," he told Nettie.

As any of the old women could have told him: Saying don't make doing. Whatever Arjula saw had something to it. At first, she only saw it when Miz Cat began to hiss. But each night the shape became more distinct, and soon, Arjula knew it was there almost before the cat did. Even though Nettie stayed home nights to keep vigil with her daughter, she never saw whatever showed itself to Arjula and the cat.

After a while, Opal got tired of being put off by Nettie's abrupt phone calls. "You can't hardly get into trouble with just one night out," she said, and took herself over to Nettie's to see just what the problem was.

She found Nettie sitting in a straight-backed chair facing the dining room wall, which was checkered with half-peeled strips of wallpaper. The rest of the furniture had been shoved into one corner of the room, except for one chair by the door. Arjula was sitting in that one. The cat was sitting on the floor beside Nettie's chair.

"Don't tell me," Opal laughed. "Cashew found out you been a bad girl and made you sit in the corner."

"Opal, there's a window on the outside that ain't on the inside."

"Excuse me, girlfriend. But what you say?"

"I know it's there." Nettie leaned forward. "I know you there, you hear me? Miz Cat sees you. Arjula sees you. And I'm gone find you, too." The shredded wallpaper quivered slightly.

"Honey, don't be talking to them walls," Opal said. "I liked it better when all you did was clean them up, not talk to them."

"Momma's thinking bout tearing them down," Arjula said.

"Un-un. No you don't, Nettie Whitcomb. If that white man finds out you been rearranging his house, he gone raise the rent. Then kick you out."

"If I do rearrange it, I won't be the first one. Somebody's already done something to it."

"Well, I can't stand you talking to no walls," Opal said.

"I tried talking to Cash. But he thinks there ain't nothing wrong. Who else am I gonna talk to? The cat?"

"You could talk to me," Opal thought. She looked down at the cat. Miz Cat stared back at her, then casually lifted its leg and started washing its crotch. Opal made a face. "Ugh. Look at that. And my mama always told me not to wash my feet in the same pot I cook in."

"I can't even twist my neck down that far," Arjula said. She lifted her leg and tried doubling over.

"Arjula, you sit yourself straight in that chair." Nettie threw up her hands. "See Opal? See what I mean? Bad influence."

Opal looked around the room. "I hate to tell you this, girl, but the cat didn't move all this furniture. You did."

"I know that," Nettie said.

"If you knowed it, how come you waited till it was time for us to go out fore you started your redecorating? What you doing, anyway? Making more work for yourself so you can stay at home and clean it up? I didn't know Cashew had you that scared bout leaving the house."

That made Nettie so mad, she didn't even want to talk to Opal. Instead, she rose from her chair and began pounding her fist against the wall, sending a shiver through the ribbons of paper hanging in the air. She didn't respond when Opal told her to "call if the walls start to answer," and by the time Opal reached the door, Nettie had Arjula helping her take soundings. The only sounds they heard were the flat thumps of plasterboard, the swish of shredded paper, or dull thuds whenever she hit a two-by-four. Outside, the neighbors watched Opal pace back and forth in front of the walkway as if she didn't know whether she was coming or going. Finally Opal called to Nettie. When Arjula opened the door, Opal squinted into the doorway through the orange-red light of the late afternoon sun. At first, she didn't see Nettie. Then Miz Cat wriggled between Arjula's legs and hopped onto the porch rail. The girl walked to the end of the porch and began stroking the cat. Each time she rubbed the length of its back, it humped against her hand like a Halloween cut-out. Finally Opal noticed Nettie standing in the open doorway.

Opal shaded her eyes and took a deep breath. "Nettie... Girl, I didn't mean to get you mad. If you still want to go out..." She waited, but Nettie only looked at her. It was one of the many times in her life when Opal wished she could say just the right thing to her friend. But like too many other times, what she had to say had just the opposite effect of right. "Nettie, you don't have to make up something for me just cause you think Cashew don't want you going out."

Nettie grunted, leaned forward, and without moving from where she stood, grabbed the door with one hand and slammed it shut the way baseball pitchers hurl a fastball. The sound of the door caused Arjula to jump and made the cat leap from the porch rail. Opal swore and kicked the gate for want of something better to do. She swore again, because it was a shame to be pissed off and hurting at the same time. As she rubbed the pain in her foot, she yelled to Nettie.

"You just stay in there and talk to them walls, Nettie Whitcomb. But if they talk back, you best be careful, girl. We coming up on a full moon most any night now." Then she waved to Arjula and limped up the street.

"Um-um," the neighbors said. "Haints. Some restless soul."

"Ain't no telling who it is."

"Some folks can't get shed of them."

Arjula stood at the gate and watched Opal march up the street. A dog barked and the cat screamed an answer, but Arjula knew Miz Cat could outrun any dog in the neighborhood, so she didn't even turn around. She saw Fran and Willie Mae turn the corner. When they passed Opal, they said, "Hello, Miz Barker." "How do, Miz Barker." But Opal didn't respond.

"She surely got her jaws tight," Willie Mae said when the girls reached the house.

"Got her lips poked out too," Fran added.

"Momma got her hopping mad," Arjula told them. "Momma's in there tearing up the house talking bout ghosts."

"Ghosts!" Willie Mae bucked her eyes. "You got ghosts?"

"You seen them?" Fran asked.

Arjula nodded. "At night," she said. "They wake me up. Miz Cat too. Momma thinks its got something to do with that window. The one you can see on the outside but can't find inside the house."

Arjula and the girls walked to the side of the house and climbed onto the fence that separated it from the neighboring house. There they examined the rectangular shape etched in the cracked paint. Fran said, "My mama says ain't but one thing to do if you got haints. Get rid of them."

"She say how?" Arjula asked. Fran shook her head. "Must be some way we can do something," Arjula said.

As if on cue, the old lady next door drifted out of her house and shook a dust rag full of bread crumbs in the air. Miz Cat, scrunched down in the bushes, let out a howl of protest. The old lady yelled, "Skeedeerump! Don't be tracting my attention," and the cat scampered back to her perch on the porch rail where she hissed at the old woman, who grunted, folded her dusting cloth, and smiled at the three girls.

"How you doing?" she said. The girls nodded hello. "Is that your mama making all that racket next door, Jula?" Arjula nodded. The old woman shook her head. "Um-um. Seems to me your mama got some troubles, honey."

"Some," Arjula said.

"She seeing ghosts," Willie Mae said.

Arjula punched her. "Momma ain't seeing nothing, girl." She stopped. "I wish she would see something," Arjula added.

The old lady said, "If you can't see it outta one eye, look out the other. You take care of your mama, chile," she added, then went back into her house. Across the street, the crocheted curtains fluttered shut.

"What you spoze she means?" Fran asked.

Arjula shrugged and reached down to pet the cat who was twining itself around her legs. "I don't know," she said. When she picked up the cat, it purred against her chest. "You know," Arjula told Fran and Willie Mae, "if we can't help Momma, I bet Miz Cat can do it."

The three girls looked into the cat's eyes. What was there was quizzical and laughing. "Yeah," Fran said. "Sure won't hurt to try," Willie Mae added.

That night, Cashew Fenney didn't know quite what was in store for him, but as soon as he entered the darkened house, he knew something was wrong. The first thing he smelled was chalky plaster from the section of dining room wall that had been stripped of paper. With the wallpaper stripped, the dining room looked almost empty. Cashew groaned and thought about the work he'd have to do to repaper the wall. When he went down the hall, the cat peeked out of the doorway of Arjula's room, but would not come to him. Cashew shook his head and muttered, "Women!" but he felt there was something else wrong about the house. Then he noticed the condition of the doorway.

He went from room to room, examining spaces where doors used to be. In the whole house, only the front and back doors had been left on their hinges, but in each doorway there was a thin, neat line of salt. Cashew walked back to Arjula's room. She and Nettie were sitting, cross-legged, on the floor. Between them was Fran's Ouija board. And the cat, its purring sounding like rocks in a rain gutter. The only light was from Arjula's bedside lamp, which had a thin cloth thrown over it for shadows. Neither Arjula nor Nettie looked up when Cashew came to the door, and for some reason, he couldn't quite bring himself to step across the salt line to reach them.

As he rubbed the excess grains from his fingertips, he made little spitting sounds in an attempt to get the taste out of his mouth. That noise got Nettie's attention. "Cash. What's the matter? You sick?"

Cashew blinked. "What? What you say, woman?" He rubbed his mouth with the back of his hand. The salt grated against his skin. "You asking me if *I'M* sick! Now correct me if I'm wrong, but which one of us sitting on the floor like some . . . some . . . What the hell is that headrag you got tied around you? And who the hell put all that salt on the floor?"

Nettie tightened the knot in her scarf. "How you know it's salt, Cash?"

Arjula squealed, and both Cashew and Nettie flinched. Miz Cat even twitched her ears. "MOM! He touched it. He broke the spell!"

"Jula, don't scream like that. Cash didn't mean no harm."

"What old harm? What you talking bout . . . spell?" He took a half step forward but the line of salt stopped him, so he leaned into the room and shook his fist. "I want to know what's going on here. You hear me, Nettie? I want to know RIGHT NOW!" No one had ever heard Cashew raise his voice, and for a moment, the room was quiet. Then the cat looked up at him and meowed in that confusing, blunt language of all cats. Arjula giggled. "What's so damn funny?" Cashew sputtered.

Nettie passed her hand over the Ouija board as if she were smoothing sand on a beach. "This ain't funny, Cashew. We as serious as a headache."

"Somebody's gone have themselves a headache if I don't get me some answers. What you doing with that thing? Working up some kind of conjure?"

Arjula grinned. "In a way of speaking," Nettie said calmly.

Cashew said, "Well, I be damn," and rubbed his chin, regretting the movement as soon as the salt on his fingers scraped his skin. "Is that what you been doing in here?" he asked Arjula. "Fooling round with ju-ju stuff?" He gestured to a gourd doll, wooden mask, and goatskin drum Arjula had placed on a shelf next to her rosary beads and crucifix. Over it all loomed a map of Africa.

"Now Cashew, don't be like them white folks and think just cause it's African, it's voodoo. That's our history you messing with."

Cash kicked at the ridge of salt across the doorway. "And you messing with my sleep."

Arjula jumped up. "Don't! Cashew, don't! MOM . . . He's making a mess. It'll take us all night to put it back."

"Cash, don't . . ."

"Nettie, how I'm spozed to get some sleep? You in here going woogie-woogie, and ain't no doors nowhere in the house."

"The bed's still there, Cash. You can still get in bed."

"I can't sleep. I can't sleep if everything's all wide open. And where the hell you put them doors?" Nettie kept her eyes on the Ouija board. "You gone answer me, woman?" He raised his foot to kick again. "Where them damn doors?"

"In the basement," Arjula said quickly.

Cashew said, "The basement! We gone see bout that," and stomped down the hallway. The house shook with his footsteps.

Arjula yelled, "MOM, stop him!" But Nettie did not move.

"That man sure is bent out of shape," she thought as her daughter leaned over the doorsill. In that moment, Miz Cat took advantage of the space Cashew had kicked into the salt, and slid between Arjula's legs. By the time Arjula recovered, the cat was already in front of Cashew, and skidding around the right-hand turn at the end of the hall, her belly flattened against the floor, and her body curved and boneless. "MIZ CAT, NO! Momma! Momma! Make them stop!"

The girl hopped up and down, beating her fists against her thighs in frustration. Nettie stared at her daughter. *"How can this woman-child change from gypsy to baby girl like it ain't nothing to it?"* She asked herself. She was about to ask why she, being full grown and of sane mind, had become a party to her daughter's spirit tricks, when she saw the Ouija board begin to move. A cold breeze seemed to blow through the room and the light flickered. Then, almost simultaneously, they heard Cashew scream and Miz Cat howl. Both Arjula and Nettie jumped over the doorsill as if they were clearing a fence instead of a ragged line of salt.

The cat was standing, frozen, at the top of the stairs where Cashew had tripped over it. Cash lay in a heap on the landing where the stairs crooked from the newer section of the house into the old section that held the basement. Nettie yelled, "Cash! Cash!" and Arjula whispered, "Momma, is he alright?" Cashew groaned an answer.

Nettie started down the steps. When her foot touched the first step, one of the doors stacked against the wall crashed to the cement floor. The noise resounded throughout the house. Arjula screamed, the cat screeched and bristled its fur. Nettie landed on the second stair. Another door lumbered into the first one. This time, the staircase shook. Cashew moaned. Nettie stopped for a moment. She let her foot approach the next step. There was the slow sound of wood creaking against wood. While Nettie balanced over that third step, Arjula yelled, "Momma, don't!" The whole stack of doors thundered to the floor and the entire house seemed to shake.

"Shee-it," Cashew moaned. "Woman, ain't you got no better sense than to stack them doors smack-dab on top of one another like they was tent poles?"

He was sitting upright by the time Nettie reached him. "Cash, you alright? You alright, honey?"

He said, "Yeah, baby," but to be sure, Nettie kissed his neck, his ears, his eyes, lips, and chin. "Baby, you best slow down or we gone be in some serious trouble right here on these stairs," he told her. While Nettie muttered, "Scared me to death," and checked him for broken bones, Cashew looked up at Arjula. "Why don't you get your momma some water or something to calm her down?"

"Did you see it?" Arjula asked. "Did you see it, Cashew? Went right down the hall and down the steps. Went right out them doors, bam-bam-bam. Now it can't get back in cause can't no ghost cross over salt. Did you see it? Did you see it?"

Cashew tried peeling Nettie away from him long enough to look at the pile of doors splintered on the basement floor. He discovered getting rid of a weeping woman was not easy. And with Nettie pressed against him, he really didn't want to make it easy.

"Nettie," he whispered, "I been thinking lately I ought to change my shift to Happy Hour stead of night. Folks be getting too rowdy at night. Keep you from worrying so much too. And now . . ." He nodded toward the broken doors. "I don't spect it be a good thing to leave you and Jula by your lonesome after dark."

Nettie cried, "Oh Cash," and held him closer. Arjula stepped over the salt line and came to the landing with a glass of water. As she sat on the stairs, waiting for her mother to reach for the glass, she looked back at Miz Cat. The cat peered at them, and though she meowed and swished her tail contendedly, she refused to move even when Cashew called her. At that moment, while Arjula and Miz Cat watched Cashew and Nettie, rocking gently in each others arms, the house seemed to settle peacefully on its timbers.

The old woman next door finally turned off her light. "Gone tear up that house," she muttered.

"Fighting all night. Can't nobody sleep," her neighbors added.

"Enough noise to wake the dead," they said.

The Blooming of Asphodels

After he made men, Kalumba realized
that Life and Death were coming down
the road to meet them. So he ordered
Dog and Goat to guard the way. Only
Dog thought he could stay awake long
enough to stop Death, so he made a
watch-fire while Goat went away for a
while. But Death crept past the sleeping
Dog and when Goat returned, he arrested
Life that was just coming down the road.
"How Death Came to Man"—Zaire

FOR MINUTES, THE MAN BARELY MOVED. He was still alive, but the only indication was the slight rise and fall of one strap from his bib overalls stretched across his bare black shoulder like a dirty Band-aid. Occasionally his breathing was ragged, causing him to strain every muscle of his body in order to drag in air. When that happened, his hand, almost, casually extended over the edge of the stairs, would clench and the movement always caught the attention of the face peering up at him from the bottom of the stairs.

That face belonged to Marvin Poole, and at that moment, Marvin Poole was wishing the man would rise up and play ball, crack a joke, or dance a turkey-trot, a cakewalk, or jitterbug, anything that moved him from the top of those stairs. Marvin Poole desperately wanted that massive body on the move. He wanted it to take back the night that had brought them to that stairwell and its horrors. Marvin Poole stirred as if he were about to leave, but the man whispered, "Do it. End it. Com'on," and Poole was stuck to the spot.

Marvin Poole shuddered with each raspy word. His hands rubbed against each other in a motion like washing, dry skin flaking off in a sandpapery noise that seemed to be in rhythm with the wheezing sounds drifting down the staircase. Poole looked around. Nothing had changed. Behind him, the dark tubular hallway was quiet. Through the cracked fan-light window over the door, half-cast shadows from the street blended into dirty gray paint—the ash of decay that covered all of the buildings near the wharf. Marvin Poole, in his sports coat of oatmeal tweed and polyester brown slacks, seemed crisply pleated even after the night's events, but he felt like those bums he'd seen standing near the courthouse—not those who bore no traces of a past life other than the street, but the ones who seemed to be wearing their last good suit, their last links with another life that would allow the street to be simply a path crossed on the way home. Poole wiped the back of his neck with a handkerchief and grimaced at the traces of grime caught in the fine cotton cloth.

"Pain," the man whispered. "Pain." The sounds floated down the stairs and lodged themselves in Marvin Poole's ears. "I can taste it, man. Blood. Sweet... tastes sweet... I can smell it. Blood behind the eyes. You can smell it. Fills up the head."

Now Marvin Poole really began to weep, a soft purring sound that seemed to fit the texture of his clothing. He listened to the man's murmurs but did not answer. Yesterday Poole had known what the world was by definition of his life in it. Today, in the gray light of a Thursday morning, the world had grown distant. He tried conjuring up what he had believed to be normal: how on Wednesday he'd pulled the stocking cap from his woolly head and set about the task of bringing order to the mass of thick-cropped hair covering his perfectly round skull. He had moved from his hair to his bath to his early morning exercises, and finally, with a certainty of purpose, to the responsibility that tied him in with the rhythms of the Great Continental Insurance Company. "A good job," as his father would say.

That was Wednesday. Now it was Thursday, and Marvin Poole had no need to worry about the rhythms of the Great Continental. It was Thursday, and nothing other than the sounds from the top of the stairs seemed worth the worry. Poole's shoes were still soft crafted leather under the coat of dust that had collected on them since Wednesday, his tie, Italian knit, was folded neatly in his jacket pocket, his pants were still creased despite a wine spot here, a beer stain there—but Marvin Poole's body had ceased to be his own, and whoever he had become refused to leave the building. He was trapped in a scene as surreal as a movie, or an abstract painting in which a man's huge black arm was draped over the risers of the stairs like the melting face of a clock, its digits turned to thick fingers that threatened to grasp Marvin Poole's neck. Nothing in Poole's life had prepared him for this moment.

No one had ever referred to him as anything but Marvin Poole, never Marvin, or when he'd finally secured the job at Great Continental, as Mr. Poole, but always Marvin Poole, or just plain Poole, the word spit like an unwanted fruit pit from their lips. It was "Welcome to our firm, Marvin Poole," and "Hello, Marvin Poole." "Would you like a cup of coffee, Poole?" "I can't marry you, Marvin Poole, but of course I'm fond of you." And finally on that fateful Wednesday, "Poole, I'm afraid we'll have to let you go, but surely a man with your qualifications . . ."

And so it was that Wednesday had marked the last day of Marvin Poole's responsibility to the Great Continental Insurance Company. He had been put out. In one fell swoop, he had been tossed into the maelstrom of the great unemployed. But Marvin Poole did not feel like one of those folks. After all, he was twenty-seven years old, an East Coast educated, post-Kennedy graduate of sobriety and direction. He had an MBA and only last year, had paid the government more in income tax than his father had earned in two full years of employment as a Red Cap at the airline terminal—a steady union job. Poole had sniffed the political winds and transferred west on the coattails of the Great Continental's push to hire blacks. Their enthusiasm for hiring was matched only by their eagerness to fire, and that Wednesday, he'd jammed his body in the revolving door in the company's marbelized lobby one last time. It hadn't seemed worth the transit fare to go home, so he'd joined the after-lunch crowds milling through the center of town, and before the night was over, Marvin Poole had found himself huddling over a drink in the Post and Pike Bar. Or to phrase it better, the man in the bib overalls had found Marvin Poole.

The bar was no different from any of the others along the waterfront—different perhaps than the uptown hotel lounges Poole usually had frequented—but here, along the wharf, it was one of many. The bar had welcomed Marvin Poole the way it welcomed everyone, from hustlers and waterfront drunks to cleaning ladies with arms sturdy as mop handles. They came in with the wind, popping through the door like yo-yos on loose strings, bouncing first into the heat, noise, and compact air of the room, then recoiling, momentarily, back to the doorway where the sea air lingered but did not enter. Some strolled toward a table, claiming with great formality an empty seat still warm from its last occupant, while others circled the room, eyeing the clumps of people huddled over their drinks. They waited like actors without stage directions, the horseshoe-shaped wooden bar in front of them, and behind them, a wall covered with black-and-white photographs which had hung there so long, they'd faded like old Polaroids

Poole had chosen a close-fitting space at the bar. From this vantage point, he could see the entrance. Whenever the front doors were rudely shoved forward, he could see figures linger there for a moment, clinging to that last second of fishy smells, salt water, spices and rotting vegetables in the Farmers' Market. Then the doors closed, sucking them into the stale air of the room. But for that moment, they were still different, still as distinct in this montage of the unusual as new coins in a church collection box. Marvin Poole had kept that shiny, untouched look about him long after he'd entered the bar. Perhaps that's why the man in the bib overalls had picked him out of the crowd.

Poole had seen the man enter, but lost him when he moved to the left side of the room. In that split second when all newcomers were still fresh, Poole had been amazed at the man's shoulders, their massiveness exaggerated by the absence of a shirt and the contrast of that single overall strap cutting across the oily blackness of his skin. When the man gained a seat at the bar next to him, Marvin Poole had once more been surprised by the sheer exposure of so much skin, so much blackness and body musk clinging to one man. The man in bib overalls had eased his weight onto the bar stool, and Marvin Poole had winced at the sudden contact of leg against leg, or more important, the heavy metal of what was unmistakably a gun, its menancing outline crushing into Poole's Manhattan-creased slacks.

"How you doing, fella?" the man had asked.

Marvin Poole had turned back toward the bar.

"They all out here tonight, huh fella? The whole lot of them. Look at me, no see me, no look at me. The lookee-loos. They got nothing better to do."

Marvin Poole had not answered.

"I like moving around in the streets," the man had said. "That's where you see it, out here, moving around. They come out every night. I watch. That's what I do when I don't know what it is I'm doing."

There was no answer.

"You got to be moving around out here to see it. All day you can't see it, but out here at night, that's where it's at. They're keening for the dead, you know. Every night they keen for the dead, not the daytime dead, but the real ones. Folks who don't know day from night. Listen fella, you can hear them."

Marvin Poole had listened. Noise clouded the room, rumbling like thunder, invading any efforts at speech. The ceiling was as low as a rain-heavy sky, and noise filled the recesses of the room, twisting around and over the clusters of people as if building toward some final torrential relief. The bartender swore constantly, flinging drinks to his customers like a reckless newspaper boy, his delivery broken from time to time by a drunk who objected to having his drink spilled before it reached his own unsure hands. Marvin Poole had closed his eyes and searched for the safety of the Great Continental Insurance Company. But the man's bulk continued to wedge him against the wall at the end of the bar. To push against the man meant leaning into his body odor. That odor was the smell Poole remembered from the Hall of Records, the sub-sub-basement labyrinth where all that was important was filed by number and letter on paper trying vainly to return to its natural state of mulch. But the man's skin seemed honed like fine wood, its blackness so smooth and shiny, Marvin Poole's impulse was to touch it, to brush its surface, if for no other reason than to feel its sleekness. And then the talk, the flood of words that oozed from the man as smoothly as his body odors permeated the air. On Thursday, Marvin Poole would be reminded of how stupid it had been to listen, how incredible it had been to want to touch that man and his madness.

But when the man had seated himself at the bar, Marvin Poole had thought escape was as easy as walking away. He had sensed the man's bulk without turning his head. At that moment, if someone had asked, Marvin Poole could have described the man, defined him muscle by muscle as if the man's flesh were his own. There had been so much of him—so big, so black. But the notion of being trapped was yet to come.

"Dry," the man mumbled, and Marvin Poole jumped. The word, so sudden and crisp after a long spell of silence, jarred him back to the stairwell. "Dry," the man repeated. "So dry . . . so tired."

Poole got up enough nerve to walk slowly to the top of the stairs. Four steps up and the gun greeted him with the same shiny impertinence it had had the night before. Poole hesitated, then stepped over it, his eyes closed and the muscles in his neck tensed. He misjudged the distance and stumbled. The man called to him.

"Brother man, that you? You coming up? I'm hurting, Bro. Pain. I smell it . . . blood . . ."

Poole climbed the final group of stairs. The man's wound had begun to crust over, but he still had not shifted the position of his legs. Marvin Poole thought of his survival training class, of the emergency rescue plans he'd so carefully memorized, but the idea of touching that body, that hulk of blackness bulging inside the faded bib overalls, dispelled any notions of where to begin.

"I can get you some water . . . from the toilet," Marvin Poole said.

The man laughed, a harsh, phlegmatic hack that seemed to strip his throat. "Fitting," he cackled. "Fitting. Marvin Poole suggests a drink of septic essence. You think that's gone make me feel better? Perk me up a little?" More coughing.

"Why me?" Poole asked him. "Why did you pick me?"

"I picked you? Who said?" The man wheezed into a pocket of breath. "Seems to me it's the other way around. Seems I saw you out there looking. You know, visual-lizing. Ain't that what you uptown cats do? Visual-lize with the crystals? So you visualized yourself a ME. I'm here. You needed me and I'm here." He would have laughed, but his body begged for air.

"Who are you?" Poole asked.

"Jack, you're full of questions. Don't you have any answers? What about all that stuff you put on those ledgers? The stuff you tuck away on microfiche? All that alphabetizing of health certificates and bad grades? Pick a name. You got plenty of them. Adams to Sarabloom. Smith to Winchelblatt." His voice echoed down the hallway like vague warnings from ghosts Marvin Poole had packed away in beige cartons full of insurance folders.

"You've got a name," Poole insisted. "What is it? Tell me."

"What do you want it to be?" the man asked. "We all got names. Ones picked for coming into this life and ones for a life we won't know until we close our eyes on this world. Maybe I'm Charlie or Willie. Maybe I'm Legba. Better yet, Kalumba. Yeah, Kalumba. Maybe I'm Kalumba bringing Life and Death down the same road laughing hand in hand. And you? You're Goat. You got to make a choice, Jack. Life or Death? You take down one, the other passes through. Which one you ready to take down, Mr. Goat?" He threw back his head, but his laughter was soundless. The wound at his side blushed with fresh blood under its crust.

For a moment, Marvin Poole imagined himself watching the man, the stairs, but not a part of what was happening. "I'll get something to fix you up," he told the man. "There's a store. The market . . . about a block away. I'll get you something. I got money." He groped in his pocket and pulled out a handful of change and a wallet. Maybe it was the sight of the bills, or the weight of the coins, but somehow, Marvin Poole felt he'd just opened an escape route.

"They sell inflatable surgeons?" the man laughed, and then caught in the waves of his laughter, began coughing.

"Just wait," Marvin Poole said. "I'll be back. I swear, man. I promise. I'll be back."

"Finish it, fella," the man whispered. "It's easy. Just finish it. Then you don't have to come back."

Poole backed against the wall, his foot edging toward the step. He almost slipped again, then he turned and raced down the stairs, skipping the step that held the gun. The man yelled, "Shit. Poole, you can't do nothing right," but he was already at the door.

Poole was a bit surprised that he remembered the intricate system for getting in and out of the building without disturbing the look of vacancy needed to keep the curious away, but within a matter of minutes, he was walking toward the end of the block, the stark sunlight of midmorning burning against his eyelids. He had reached a bus stop for the crosstown before he realized his mistake. He was heading for the Great Continental. More than that, he was heading for safety, for a hole in the curtain that had pulled him into the nightmare of the man in bib overalls. Poole stood there and pleaded with the sky. It looked exceptionally calm and promising, but offered him no answers. The choice was his: home or something to help the man lying at the top of the stairs.

For the second time that morning, Marvin Poole made a snap decision. He boarded the crosstown bus and rode as far as a block away from the Great Continental. When the bus let him off within the shadow of the insurance building, he was breathing heavily. He stood on the sidewalk across the street from the company and tried to draw from the structure that hint of security he'd always felt when he'd entered it. But the Great Continental no longer offered security. He bought a donut and coffee from the vendor at the corner of the block. One bite and he spit out the sugary mess. The steam told him enough about the watery packaged coffee and waxed container, so he threw it in the trash along with the donut. His mouth still held the taste of liquor and Italian red hots from the sausage stand near the wharf. Reality had become the man in the bib overalls, the gun three steps down from the second floor hallway, and a day without the endless sheets of green columns, red lines, and blue numbers of actuarial charts and premiums. Poole turned and waited for the next bus that would take him back to the pier. Going in circles and going nowhere, that's what the man had accused him of.

Half a block away, Marvin Poole filled a bag with meager supplies from the quick-stop grocery and dragged himself back to the building at the end of the pier. He no sooner climbed the stairs and began pulling items from the bag when the man threw him back into the world of the absurd.

"Sing me a song," the man asked him.

"You're fucking crazy," Marvin Poole replied, and poured them both a glass of Smirnoff's.

"Sing for me," the man repeated. "Sing me a sweet song, brother man."

"Drink," Marvin Poole commanded.

He tilted the glass to the man's mouth and watched him down it in one gulp. The alcohol convulsed his body, and the wound leaked a litmus pink smear of blood, petal-shaped like an asphodel. Marvin Poole had somehow managed to pull the man upright. Propped against the wall, he seemed ready to take whatever Marvin Poole offered, but he refused to allow Poole to touch his wound, a small hole that entered through his side and exited from his back where it blossomed into a fleshy red smear just above the socket of his right hip. The man allowed Poole to feed him until he began to cough. Then the talking started again.

"I want the last rites. Man deserves the last rites. Sing me a song. Sing a song for the death of all men."

Marvin Poole brushed an empty bottle of Smirnoff's down the stairs, and reached for a fresh one. Just to shut the man up, he began to sing: *"Hambone, Hambone where you been . . . Round the world and I'm going again . . . Hambone, Hambone where'd you stay—got my ass in the alley cause crime don't pay . . . Ham-bone . . ."*

Remembering that song surprised Poole more than it did the man in bib overalls. Poole hadn't thought of the song in years, and then it had been in connection with his father's late night hours. "Boozing it up," his mother would say, and make her son swear he'd never indulge. Marvin Poole had thought he'd put the song behind him with that oath. He remembered the sulking groups of hard-faced boys with patent leather names and bags of cheap wine, how they'd moved in packs and early in high school, turned from students to truants slapping hambone rhymes under the schoolhouse windows just to taunt the teachers. He had been drawn to them, afraid of them and their bottles of tokay red. Now he'd met one of them, grown up and dressed in bib overalls.

Poole started again: *"Hambone, Hambone where'd you go . . . Right straight up to Miz Lucy's door . . .* And the man joined him: *I asked Miz Lucy if she'd marry me . . . She say make yourself some money baby—then we'll see . . . Ohh-wee . . ."* And they laughed together. For the first time since they'd met, they were in harmony. Poole was even relaxed as he poured the man another drink. *"Like last night,"* Poole thought.

"You look like a dude squeezing himself out of a little bag," the man had told Marvin Poole after the bartender had served him.

Poole had said nothing.

"You must be from Noo Yawk or something," the man had continued, surveying Marvin Poole's tie and clean-edged haircut. "You look like a man who's got a head full of information."

Marvin Poole remembered the percentages of black policy-holders and the thin line graphs of full-term policies that never seemed to match the mortality ratios. Too many heart failures, job failures, too many life failures for black folks even in a town that once had been the gateway to the Gold Rush.

The man raised his glass of whiskey to his lips, then said, "You the kind who fits uptown, huh? Got just what the Man needs to sit up front and make folks think he's a liberal? You the kind knows what the Man is looking for, huh fella?"

"I don't know. Maybe." Marvin Poole loudly swallowed his drink. He was beginning to feel less and less comfortable, his head pulsing with too many drinks and the knowledge that somehow he had failed—that all of his maps to success had collapsed inward, imploding as if indeed the world was flat and he was trapped in its endless horizon.

"Hey, fella," the man had nudged him. "That suit got you zipped up or you just drinking tight cause you don't know no better? Best be careful. You get a hernia all choked up like that," he'd laughed.

Marvin Poole felt trapped against the rim of the bar. He concentrated on the wall in front of him, the years of accumulated dust that had outlined a rectangular space about the size of a large oil painting above the row of fly-specked glasses in back of the bar. Eight or nine bullet like holes were visible in the upper right-hand corner of the space, and posted slightly off-center to the left was a NO MINORS sign.

"Next one's on you, fella," the man had said. "I like a man who knows how to listen."

It took Marvin Poole a few minutes to get the joke, then he'd tried thinking of a response, but none of them seemed right. He'd always shunned men who took the world too lightly, always believed them less capable of understanding him and what he knew. But that night, he took a chance. He'd laughed at the man's joke and said, "Sure. Sure, on me. Sure, I'll sport you for a second."

The man had slapped him on the back. "That's right. Loosen up. Look at them." He'd waved toward the crowd. "They too busy running a game to hear anybody. Man, ol' prophet Nate could walk through that door and they'd just offer him a drink and keep right on playing and laughing. Keep on high-timing it."

Marvin Poole had followed the sweep of the man's arm. Five or six people had crowded into the space near the end of the bar and were laughing and pointing, seemingly at nothing. By the door, a stocky Indian, citified in his Pancho Villa sideburns, wide hat, and heavy turquoise jewelry, began to laugh hysterically, his sounds echoed by a couple at the front table and a loosely dressed blonde waddling flat-footed toward the restrooms. The blonde turned and screamed, "No, damn it. I said, NO!" then continued her walk out of Marvin Poole's line of vision. No one even looked at her except the Indian, who raised his glass and said, "Good thinking, babe."

The man nudged Marvin Poole sharply and without smiling. "Move! Come on, fella. It's a big world. Reach out and touch somebody." He held up an imaginary telephone. "Just reach out, fella. Reach out and touch . . . you know—bing, bing . . . all them little buttons light up."

The man laughed again, his head thrust forward, his face almost against the bar—black skin against ebony wood, heavy shoulders drawn up and hiding half of his thick neck. Then he'd turned and studied Poole, his laughter disappearing somewhere in the bulk of his throat.

"There ain't nothing new, Jack. That's the sum total of it all, nothing new. You looking for something new all hooked up in that suit of yours? What are you anyway? Some kind of social worker?"

"Accountant," Marvin Poole had answered. "Insurance accountant."

"Yeah, same thing," the man had remarked. "A man who feeds on pain and death. Accountant, social worker . . . same thing. Order. You want things in order when there ain't no order. You ever read Dumas? Pushkin? Heidegger? Dos Passos? Heavy-duty, Jack. Up there with the best. And you know what they found?" the man had laughed. "Ain't no order. That's what they found. Out here, out there. Same thing. Dig it fella? Same old same old. Ain't nothing between us but air."

The man had leaned toward Marvin Poole, grinning and reeking of well-worn clothes and sleepless nights. He'd stuck out one finger and jammed it against the lapel pocket of Marvin Poole's Wednesday sports coat, turning it slowly and forcing it deep into the material until Poole could feel the blunt end of the finger grinding against his ribs. Marvin Poole had held his breath.

"Pain, that's what's new," the man had continued. "Ever notice that, fella? We can't move until we feel pain. Especially black folks. Give 'em some old-time religion and lots of pain, and they'll shout: Hallelujah! from here to Cincinnati." He'd twisted his finger in the opposite direction. "You show me any man who's done something without pain. Philosopher or pimp. Marcus Garvey, Malcolm, King, and er . . . what's that other dude's name? Don't matter. Nothing moves without pain. Love or money. It hurts to get it, keep it, or lose it."

Then, as abruptly as he had started, the man had withdrawn his finger and turned back to his drink. For a moment, Marvin Poole felt as if someone had played a trick on him, as if some magician had suddenly transformed the beefy man into a revolutionary, a preacher, a philosopher. But in the murky air of the bar, a man could become preacher and hustler at the same time. Poole watched the man's thick hand engulf the glass and raise it to his lips. The man sneered, barely showing his upper teeth, then slammed the glass on the counter, grinning and beckoning for another drink. Marvin Poole had automatically paid for the next round, but he had never imagined spending the night with this smelly hulk of flesh, much less tending him in whatever limited way the man allowed himself to be tended.

Poole had been trying to hold a conversation with the man in bib overalls when the fight had started. The bartender had tried to heave himself over the bar, swearing at a drunk with a game leg who was repeatedly slapping the counter with his cane. The drunk leaned at an angle just outside the bartender's reach, but close enough to flail the bar on either side of him at regular intervals. The staccato slap of wood against wood held everyone's attention until the drunk, a tall angular wheat-colored man with an uneven line of crooked, rotten teeth, lost his balance and fell into one of the front tables. The laughter that followed relieved the tension in the room, and the bartender immediately resumed his routine duties when the drunk was hauled upright and shoved toward the door.

Although he appeared to be a relatively young man, no more than mid-thirties, the drunk moved with the unnerving slow-motion pace of other wharfside derelicts. He hobbled between the tables for a few seconds, his cane no more than a third unsure leg, then he headed for the bar again. Just as he reached the bar, he stumbled into a knot of people. Although Marvin Poole could not see it happen, the laughter had led him to assume the drunk had been assisted in his fall. When the man reappeared, his confusion and anger were obvious. He began to quarrel with a redheaded young man seated at the bar, a man, as Marvin Poole had observed earlier, with one leg in a cast.

The young man shook his long hair, pulled at a few burrs caught on the ends, then reached over to scratch the knee of his cast-bound leg. He was leaning back, pulling at his bright red beard, when the drunk took a swipe at him with his cane. The redhead jabbed once.

During that second his arm was extended, the redhead's expression remained unchanged. Then there was a scramble and this time, the bartender cleared the bar with one hurdle. He slammed the drunk backwards against the counter and brought his fist down on the man's head like a mallet. In the scuffle that followed, the drunk was shoved down the bar. He fell, righted himself and fell again, bouncing along the line of customers like a pinball. Finally he collided into Marvin Poole's neighbor, and the man in the bib overalls, laughing louder than anyone else, shoved the drunk back toward the redhead. This started a second chain reaction. The line of men began to sway. The heavyset blonde screamed her usual song of protest, "No, dammit! Not now!" The Indian toasted the fight, the customers, the drinks and ashtrays tumbling to the floor. Marvin Poole was wrenched from his seat, his eyes round and white as marbles. He tried to stop his descent by grabbing for the bar rail, the air, anything; then he felt the brunt of his neighbor's head as the man rammed into his stomach.

Marvin Poole was surprised at how familiar the smell of blood was to him. For a moment, after the shock of being punched, his body was bent in a perfect U, then he struck the side of the counter and snapped back, the top of his head hitting the floor before his neck could fully relax. He moaned as hot drops of blood filled his throat, then somehow, he was outside and the man in the bib overalls held him as he spit blood onto the bricks of the courtyard near the entrance to the pier.

"Never had a chance," the man had sneered. "Trying to fight what already was. Trying for balance. Let it out, fella. Just spit it out."

Marvin Poole heard the backwash of muddy water lapping the pilings below the pier. None of this should have happened to him, yet he was here—and he had nowhere else to go.

"That's right, fella," the man had said. "Bloodletting. There's got to be bloodletting before you're free. When I was a kid, I watched this other kid swallow a string. Had it in his mouth and the damn thing kept disappearing. He'd open wide, maybe to scream or something, I don't know which. Then he'd clamp shut again and that string would be one inch shorter. I tried grabbing it a couple of times but the kid's eyes got so big and watery, I just let go. He was crying, I guess. Couldn't tell. Every time he swallowed, a little bit at a time, that string just kept going. Some folks just can't let go of nothing. Spit it out, fella."

"I'm not a complete fool," Marvin Poole had said. "Nobody would swallow a string."

The man had looked up at the thickly clouded sky. "Just goes to show you," he'd laughed, and Marvin Poole, watching that same sky, had followed the man in bib overalls; the man who said he had a name but wouldn't give it; the man who said he had no country except the geography lodged inside his head.

They both woke up around midnight, but the man still wouldn't let Marvin Poole touch his wound. "Shit, this hurts," the man yelled.

"What can I do?" Poole asked.

The man laughed, this time coughing as each convulsion travelled to the wound bulging from his right hip. "Fella, if I knew what to do, I'd flip myself over the edge into the sea and let the slippery waves set my soul free." His laughter brought up a mucus-filled ball of fresh blood.

Poole handed him some napkins. "Ain't nothing but one thing for you to do," the man added. "You got no choice."

"Oh Jesus," Marvin Poole moaned. He tried thinking of yesterday. Of all his yesterdays with no tomorrows. He tried to trap himself in yesterdays. But not even his own apartment, dimly remembered by the key resting in his pants pocket, could free him from the man's awful presence.

"Tell you what, brother man. Why don't you go get Betsy?" the man teased. "Betsy make you feel good like a real man should. Go get Betsy. Lay down on them big titties and stop thinking."

"I don't need no woman," Marvin Poole told him, yet somewhere in his memory, there was Wednesday night and Betsy, coal black and beautiful.

"A stone fox," the man had said. Betsy with a laugh that invited Marvin Poole to try whatever he dared, whatever he'd dreamed of. Betsy of the Pike and Post Bar and the neon street around it, a street the man had called home.

"Go find Betsy," the man insisted. "She's a good ticket. Course ain't nothing wrong or right about a woman who's warm and willing. Ain't that so, Jack?"

Marvin Poole refused to answer him.

"Go on, man. Less you want to watch me check out, go find Betsy. She can make you forget the sun's gonna rise."

"Why?" Marvin Poole asked. "Why me?"

The man inhaled, and the sound rattled in his throat like the scuffling of rats in a hole. He did not answer for a second, then said, "I ain't doing nothing for you, Jack. All of this is for me. Dig it? Find Betsy and make her moan them sweet, sweet words she knows. Tell her How-do for me."

Marvin Poole had waited for a moment, but the man seemed to drift into unconsciousness or sleep, so he moved toward the door. He pulled back the boards just so, the way the man had told him, and stepped into the courtyard. The street held alternating slots of neon lights and figures flickering past them like images of silent movies. In a few hours, it would be Friday. Two days, three days. Numbers didn't matter. Marvin Poole blinked at that thought. He had been in the building all day. He had propped the man against the wall, mopped up the blood, opened cans of peaches and chili con carne, cut slices of fresh market tomatoes and oranges, and helped the man to the bathroom at least twice. Together they'd finished off two bottles of Smirnoff's—but Poole hadn't remembered the hours passing, or the sun melting into evening.

"He's still up there, huh?" a woman asked him, and turning, he reconized Caitlin, the one who could "take you apart and put you back together again . . . Old witch-eyes," the man had called her. The man had warned Poole of Caitlin's mean mouth. "She snarls before she strikes, just like a snake," the man had laughed.

Poole said, "Yeah. He's, uh . . . sick. I can't get him to leave."

"He'll leave when he wants to," Caitlin sniffed. "Looking for somebody in particular?" she asked.

Marvin Poole looked away, tracing the moldy path of underbrush that patterned the cracked bricks and flagstones of the courtyard.

"What you hanging around here for?" Caitlin demanded. Her tan skin glowed yellow with the sheen of too many drinks. "You let that fool get to you," she motioned toward the building where the man lay sleeping, "and you ain't never gone be right in the head again."

"I'm looking for Betsy," Marvin Poole muttered.

Caitlin laughed, her beige eyes turning amber in the shadows of the courtyard. "He tell you to go for Betsy? Figures . . . she been after him for months and he won't give up nothing. She's gonna give it to him free, and he cross his legs like he was in Sunday school. You think maybe he don't like women?" Marvin Poole shrugged. "Well, you one helluva stand-in," Caitlin laughed and groped him. "Chump-bait," she said, cupping his balls.

The smell of rotting fish and rotting wood gathered inside Marvin Poole's nostrils until it seemed that only by consciously breathing could he stop the odors from clogging his throat. Women like Caitlin had always been too pretty to be real with their oil-and-water hair, and skin like desert sand. "Hoo-joo women," his mama had called them. "High yellas." He turned away from the sharp gaze of Caitlin's beige eyes. "It's not for me," he muttered. "I just thought . . ." He hoped those green-flecked eyes wouldn't cut him too deeply.

Caitlin stared for a moment, then shrugged. "Well, don't give it another second, chump. Betsy got somebody hustling for her and if she want that big ugly dude, she can find him any ol' night." Caitlin narrowed her eyes and snorted. "No skin off my nose," she added. "If anybody knows where Betsy's hanging out, it's liable to be the Topper." She shook herself as if casting off Marvin Poole's presence, then walked toward the full light of the street that marked the rim of the waterfront tavern area.

Marvin Poole followed. He was amazed at how much he'd remembered from the night before, but pulling himself tall as a preacher, he followed Caitlin into the street's neon glow. After a few hours, he'd found the patterns of the street to be as methodical as those at Great Continental.

Caitlin led him to the Topper who had set up his usual post by the newsstand, his stump resting on a wooden board, the brakes set so he wouldn't roll down the slope of the sidewalk. Topper always had one hand clutching his curved metal crutches as if to reassure himself they'd always be there. The way he was sitting, with his top-heavy body at an odd angle to the ground and at no particular angle to his head, Topper gave the impression of having been tossed lifeless into the corner where he kept watch. But Topper knew everyone on the street, and even with his eyes closed, could tell if someone was drunk or sober no matter how carefully they maneuvered around his body. When Marvin Poole asked the whereabouts of Betsy, Topper showed the tips of his undersized teeth and hissed, but he steered Marvin Poole to a baby-faced white girl called Speedy. "Betsy's on the move tonight," Topper said. "The moon. Gets her. Calls her to water, tell me. She's moving. Sure as this night's turning over, she's turning too." Topper laughed. "But turning's what she do when she got nothing better to do. Speedy can find her. Speedy's out there moving around with them that can't do nothing but move around every night. Every night . . ." Topper stroked the steel shaft of his cane, chanting as Marvin Poole went in search of Speedy.

He'd met her the night before as well, and he suspected she was no more than about fifteen years old. A white girl dropping away from money because being white was not enough. She used her guilt to lure black men into her bed, that is, as long as they didn't mind the freak-night hairdo she wore. But Speedy was young enough to be frozen inside of whatever amphetamine dream that kept her living from one day to the next. Speedy didn't talk much so the next few hours were easy for Marvin Poole. After Speedy shared sweet wine and a speckled pill, he made no attempt to map his steps, and sometime before morning, before his lungs begged for gill slits and his eyes dilated in the predawn light, he found Betsy.

He hadn't realized how big she was. So much and so black. No wonder the man in bib overalls dreamed of her. They were a matched set, except Betsy was encased in an exaggerated fantasy of ebony silk, while the man was all meat and sweat and the madness of conversation. Marvin Poole tried to imagine defining Betsy's body. The roundness of each hip almost more than he could hold. She pulled him to her, muscle by muscle, but laughed, teasing him with her body as easily as Caitlin had teased him with her eyes. Although there was light in the shabby room Betsy called hers, he could not see her, knew he dared not look at her. So much, so much settling around him. She was there to be tasted and fed upon. And finally, when he broke free of all the booze and Speedy's pill, Betsy set up a humming in her throat where the soft pocket of flesh nestled at the triangle of collarbones, a humming that did not even stop when she whispered, "Let it out."

She'd held him close, and when she released him, she'd somehow been as sober as she was when he'd found her. On the other hand, Marvin Poole had to hold each bill up to the light, announcing the numbers before he paid Betsy.

He had to beg her to lead him back to the courtyard. When they arrived, she asked, "What you doing with him?" and nodded toward the building.

Poole had tried to grin. "Yeah, well, uh . . . You know, we friends."

Now Betsy really laughed. "Don't let that dude do you, man. Get out of this. You get caught up with that fool and you gone, Jack. He got a Jones nobody can cure." Then she'd left.

Briefly, he'd wondered how she would have looked waiting for him outside the Great Continental, then he'd turned to the building and methodically removed the loose boards that would allow him entrance. In less than three days, he could work his way through the debris as if it had always been his home. His first thought was to stumble up the stairs to the second floor toilet, "the one that works if you jiggle it right," the man had told him. But at the bottom of the stairs, he'd stopped. Poole could distinguish the shape of the man leaning against the wall. The man did not seem real but more like a piece of driftwood washed in from the muddy waters below the wharf. Poole could detect no signs of breathing, still he hesitated. Maybe it was the sour taste of booze in his mouth, or the smell of Betsy's perfume clinging to his clothes, or her warning. "Don't let that fool do you," she'd said. But whatever had blocked those last hours of Wednesday night's events from his memory eased away, and as he stood, once again at the bottom of the stairs, Marvin Poole let the scene come back to him. This time, he left nothing out.

They had cruised all the bars along the waterfront when Marvin Poole had told the man he was tired and needed to go home.

"You need to get loose, Marvin Poole," the man had chided. "Find yourself a game. Set yourself free like the Great Emancipator wanted us to be. You need to get something to keep you level. I tried games. Two years of college. They told me I needed discipline. Did a year in the joint. They tried to teach me discipline. Even did a couple of years in the state boogie pen where you got to pretend you got discipline if you want to come out looking at your feet and not your ass. Thirteens. I was playing thirteens and they called it para-noi-ah. Names. Just names, brother man."

The man had pulled a gun from his pocket. "This keeps me going," he'd said, smiling as Marvin Poole blinked at the bright metal. "This keeps me on top. This is my game to end all games." Then he'd shoved, no—tossed the gun into Marvin Poole's hands, and Poole, somehow, had caught it the way a player catches a ball passed under the basket. "Take it," the man had said. "Com'on. Take it. Power! Feel the weight? You're on top now, Marvin Poole."

Marvin Poole had tried to shove the gun back toward the man. "I don't need this," he'd declared.

"Listen to him," the man had laughed. "Marvin Poole, Marvin Poole—the white man's burden, the woman's fool. Don't need it. Got his suit and don't need no piece. Watch yourself grow, Marvin Poole. Let it fit your palm. It's smooth. Cold. Warm it up and it's yours, Marvin Poole, Take your piece. Can you grow, brother man?"

He'd tried backing away from the man. "No. I don't need nothing like this." But the gun was still in his hand.

And the man had roared with laughter. "Don't need it, you say. You think some cop's gonna stop a bullet from coming your way cause you got a de-gree? Un-un. They don't see nothing but color. And the women ... Think they gonna break down your door to hear Mo-zart on that mess of speakers you built all by your lonesome? What kinda woman you got in mind anyway, Marvin Poole? Black is black and you is you. Come on, Jack. Be yourself."

"I am myself," Marvin Poole had whispered, but even the light was not convinced. "I am ME," he announced loudly, "not some fool walking around spouting philosophy and stinking up the air at the same time."

"But man, that's what we philosophers do," he'd laughed. And as Poole had rubbed the gun against his pant leg, the man had begun to smile. "Come on, Marvin Poole. Don't hold it down. Arms up. Com'on. Hup, boy. Jump when the Man tells you."

He'd pulled Marvin Poole toward him, hugging and leading him through a dance, whispering trash in his ear until Marvin Poole had no choice but to squeeze the trigger. The man had crumpled, pirouetting against the impact of the bullet, grunting like a rhino and crashing to the floor. So much of him to fall. And the wound like a red carnation pinned at the waistline of his overalls. So large and raw. And the man smiling or seeming to. He had narrowly missed tumbling down the stairs, his legs folded beneath him, twisted away from his body and still in flight. His head turned toward the wall and his right arm trailing down the steps.

Marvin Poole knew he should have left, that he had nothing in his experience of book learning to cover large men who invited death. But he'd stayed, and Friday morning, after a night with Caitlin and Betsy and Speedy, he willed himself to move up the stairs, to try to forget he had lived with the memory of the man's dance of death for two days. He picked up the gun from the corner of the third step. The man seemed not to be breathing, and Marvin Poole exhaled, ready to consider the next stage should he find the man had died during the night. Then the man whispered, "Not yet," his voice rasping against Marvin Poole's weary brain.

Poole leaned toward the man, kneeling and balancing with his empty hand, almost unaware of the gun hanging from his other hand.

"We gonna play games?" the man wheezed.

"Nothing. I won't do nothing. I don't have to."

"You're ready," the man interrupted.

"I don't have to do a thing," Marvin Poole said triumphantly. "You gonna die anyway."

The man tried to laugh, his heaves forcing the strap deeper into his shoulder. "Die?" His voice sounded like crusts being scraped from the bottom of a burnt pan. "You think that's the whole point? We all die, Jack. They dump you in a body bag and . . ." The man worked his way through a cough. Marvin Poole could see where fresh blood had soaked his pant leg. Each cough robbed the man of more words. "Can't change death," the man gasped. "Just change how life ends."

Poole watched him struggle to continue. He could see him try for that grin, the irritating, knowing sneer that barely exposed the edges of his upper teeth and stretched his mouth the way it had been when he'd tossed the gun into Marvin Poole's hands. Now his breathing was as wet and bubbly as a skin diver's under a loose face mask. Blood formed at the corners of his mouth, and his breath was rancid with the odor of blood. Marvin Poole leaned closer, his mouth against the man's ear.

"Can you hear me?" he asked carefully. "You can't make me do anything anymore. I don't have to play your game anymore. I can get a job." Marvin Poole slammed into the uncertainty of his future. "I can . . . I can . . ."

The man puckered his lips into a kiss, and before Marvin Poole could avoid it, a spurt of spit and blood hit his face. He moaned as the wetness and fetid smell enveloped him. And he remembered how the man had danced in the dim light of that Thursday morning, leading him through his steps until he'd had no choice but to pull the trigger. And he remembered how Betsy's face had stayed calm in the yeasty light of dawn, how all she wanted to know was why the man in the bib overalls had sent him to her. "A helluva stand-in," Caitlin had said.

The man had told him that death was a role, like slavery or war. "You say your lines and when the end comes, you're the only one applauding," he'd grunted, his breath already turning rank. That stench now filled the hallway.

Marvin Poole realized he was crying. His tears fell onto the man's shoulders as he raised the gun, aimed it first for the throat—the center of that raspy voice—then the chest. He heard the noise, saw the red circles blossom like poppies in loamy black soil. He smelled the acrid burp of powder as the bullets left the gun, but he could not connect himself with the scene. There was a loud gravelly sound as breath was released in one burst from the man's lungs. When Marvin Poole looked at the face, the death mask was already there—the man's eyes narrowed to a slit and his mouth pulled into a grin. A death mask on a clown's face, on a face with no name, and behind the body, a wall with one blood-stained word scrawled on it: MARVIN.

Poole headed toward the warehouse end of the pier. Later, if they asked him, he would tell them how he'd found the man. He would explain the gun, explain the average life span of a man with no dreams and how the man was smiling when he left. He'd tell them how the name meant nothing. Nothing at all. An uptown bus went past him but he did not turn around. Behind him on a billboard, the handsome black face of a poised young man, outlined by a jungle background, beckoned the world to taste the best whiskey money could buy. On the next billboard, a young white man in a suit beckoned that same world to be careful of their investments. Marvin Poole slipped into the crowd of people heading toward the market where hawkers had already begun to line up rows of dull-eyed fish and pyramids of fresh produce. "There's a world out there," the man had said. "A future." Marvin Poole was looking for order, for patterns of linear growth. A world where children stumbled into his dreams with happy endings to stories, common events he could translate into numbers.

The Edge of Night

THE FIRST TIME I SAW PHILADELPHIA SUTTON, she was pedalling across the top of a hill, the sun behind her, her tie-dyed skirt fluttering away from her legs like a flag, and making that pucka-pucka sound wheels make when kids stick playing cards in the spokes. I didn't know her name back then, and wouldn't know it until two years later when both Philly and I were miles away from where I'd first seen her. But on the day she appeared in my life, I knew she was one of those Civil Rights workers who'd come to the Projects to help folks register to vote. Not that I cared. I was seventeen, living in the Clayton-DeWitt, and no doubt heading for trouble. In those days, I didn't care much about anything. The day I saw Philly, my sister Evelyn and I were doing our usual thing: hanging out near the playground until someone else showed up, usually some boy heading for Mission Street or Cottage Grove. Although I didn't know it at the time, seeing Philadelphia Sutton would put an end to that, and in another two years, she'd be a part of what would put end to a lot of things I'd come to expect out of life.

I only caught a glimpse of Philadelphia that day, and if it hadn't been for Evelyn, I would have missed ever seeing Philly again. Without Evelyn, I might have stayed in the Clayton-DeWitt, waiting for another sight as wonderful as that of Philadelphia riding her bike. But because of Evelyn, I moved to the Coast and began to study art. Studying art wasn't a big jump for me. Back home, I was always messing up something, as my mother would call it when she found my doodles on the walls, the newspaper, the tablecloth, and one time, smack-dab in the middle of the toilet seat. I always had an itch to draw whatever I saw. I even wanted to draw Philly the first time I saw her, but all I could do was watch her ride out of sight while I stood there, wishing for a canvas and a paintbrush in my hand. Luck was with me. Soon after that, Evelyn began bringing home a bunch of brochures the school counselor had given her about going to college. Mama and I just shook our heads. Going to college was something big-time folks with money did, and Lord knows, we had no money. But Evelyn finally got me to go to that counselor, and he told us all about our civil rights, and how we could use it to get to college.

So the next thing I knew, Mama was putting us on the Westbound Limited, and crying about how the Lord had found a way to help her girls. Even though it was in my mind that Philadelphia Sutton was the one who'd helped us, I didn't say anything. Of course, if you ask her now, Philly will tell you she can't quite remember seeing me and Evelyn that day in October when the sky was gray-white with winter, and the Projects looked all washed-out and deserted, trash piled up everywhere as if someone had had a great picnic and sent folks home without cleaning up the rubbish. But I'd like to think that my sister and I, sitting on the wheel-rim of the carousel, were somehow changed by seeing, for the very first time, a black woman so enjoying the act of riding a bicycle, that when Philadelphia Sutton sailed past us, she was laughing. That scene would mark the beginning for me and Philly. I secreted it in a corner of my mind where it still remains.

But if you can imagine how I was totally unready to see a grown woman like Philadelphia riding a bike down the middle of the Clayton-DeWitt, then you can just begin to imagine how bummed out I was by what Evelyn and I saw when we moved to the Coast. As soon as I stepped off that train, I lost all sense of what ordinary life was supposed to be. My mama could just as well have sent me into space, the way the Russians had done with those men they put in that satellite the newspapers had made such a fuss about. For the first six months, the whole world was different, and I just didn't fit. Not that I really had fit into the scene back home. Folks always thought I was kind of odd, not just because I took to sketching them if they sat still for more than five minutes, but because I acted kind of mannish, which is the way Evelyn put it. In every way possible, Evelyn and I were opposites—sisters, but not sisters at all. Evelyn was angular and boy-crazy, ready to whip her way into the world the way Mama whipped a froth out of eggwhites when she made pies to take to the white women out in Belmont. It always surprised me that the women who bought the pies Mama made in our kitchen were the same ones who said kids from the Projects were too dirty to go to school with their children. But that was another way in which I was different from Evelyn. Evelyn could turn her back on folks who acted two-faced, while I was more likely to get a muscle spasm from trying to see around the side of everything. I knew there was another story to most people, because Lord knows, there was another story to me. And Evelyn was the one who finally brought that story out in the open. One day, when she was screaming because I'd picked a fight with another boy she'd set up for me to date, she'd just stopped, mid-sentence, and stared at me.

"I know what's wrong with you," she'd said. "You just mad cause you're after the same thing he's after." I'd walked away without answering her, but from then on, Evelyn never bothered me about dating boys again. In fact, she didn't mention it until we started talking to that counselor about going to college. "Let's pick a school out West," she told me. "They got some different folks out there, you know what I mean?"

I knew what she meant. Like everyone else, I'd heard about the flower children hugging and kissing and carrying on—"the blacks with the whites and the dykes with the queers all out in the streets," Miz Washington had said after she went to visit her oldest daughter in Oakland. My mother got worried about sending us out West when she heard that, but other folks in our building knew Sadie Washington hadn't been any farther from the Projects than the Belmont District before she went to see her daughter, so they discounted much of what she said. Maybe if I'd listened a bit more to Sadie Washington, I would have been prepared for what I found. As it was, the Coast hit me—BLIP—right in the face. What I found was a conglomerate of whites, blacks, Asians, and Jews, with a few American Indians sprinkled in as if every group had to have one for luck. What I found was folks caught somewhere between that 1950s dream of Ozzie and Harriet, and the dawning of something called Aquarius. And let me tell you, those folks put me through some heavy-duty changes. Of course, living in a brownstone was better than living in the Projects any day of the week, but the folks in the brownstones didn't hang out together. They were some cold-ass folks, and the Pacific breezes didn't even leave them smiling. On good days, I sniffed the salty ocean air, but on bad days, most days, I fought the throat-clenching smells of greasy food and talcum sweet perfume oozing out of restaurant doorways, bars, and crowded hotels. Most days I turned away from the blinding flash of the latest horror story splattered on the front pages of the dozen or more newspapers that had been hung like soiled diapers across the front of sidewalk newsstands. If it weren't for Evelyn, I'd have boarded the next train home.

"All you want to do is sit on your butt and draw pictures," Evelyn told me. "Well, I got bigger fish to fry, and I'm not stepping another farther till I do it."

She should have stepped somewhere, because those folks out on the Coast almost fried her butt, and she wound up with the scars to prove it. But that happened much later. What was important when we first arrived was that I stayed with Evelyn, which wasn't an easy task, but then, nothing about Evelyn was easy. She was always on the move, spending more time in the streets than in class. "Them profs are rinky-dink," she'd say, and hit the door running. As much as I could, I tried to keep up with her. Mostly all I could do was watch her throw herself in the center of things, her life turning inside out and around between one step and the next, the way a river can change its direction when the ground shifts and the sandy bottom sinks or rises as the water fights to keep some kind of course. That was me and Evelyn. She was changing, and I was floundering around, half-way fighting while my life took just any old course.

"What you gone do?" Evelyn asked. "Sit out the revolution?"

And to make her point, she joined a campus coalition, and changed her name to Erzulie. "Girl, you got to get rid of your slave name," she told me. "Evelyn was just some old name Mama picked up from the white folks. So don't you be using that name with me no more. From now on, I'm Erzulie. In Haiti, Erzulie means the woman of love, flowers, jewels, and dancing, you know."

I said, "All that, huh?" and she got so mad, she started talking about how there was no need to try explaining anything to somebody who didn't have enough sense to drop their plantation mentality.

I assumed she meant I was still acting like I was in the Projects, so from that point on, I pretended I was hip, and took to wearing paint-spattered coveralls or full-length dashikis. I even let my hair go au naturel, and although I never wore a big Afro, beads, or geles turbaned around my head the way some folks did, I could pass for one of the in-crowd. Everything was "in" in those days. We had sit-ins, be-ins, love-ins, and you were either in it and hip, or outside and totally square. Our stomping ground was Kalava Park—the Beehive, we called it. We hit that park day and night. At night, sea mist drifted right above the ground, and things seemed to happen in slow motion as if we were all dreaming the same dream at once. The fast pace came during the day, after the sun had burned off the smell of the sea. Mostly we milled around, listened to speeches, got high, and sang a lot. There, it was possible to see everybody and everything from music and bad poetry to anarchists and the next governor. And it was there that I finally saw Philadelphia Sutton once more. But like the princess says in the Gay Fairy Tale, I had to put up with a lot of toads to get to that point.

"We liberate the liberals and negotiate with bigots," a dude named

Bukwa told me. "Listen, it ain't strictly a revolution, but it gets the young dudes off the streets."

Before the first year was up, Bukwa, a sculptor of questionable talents, had almost become a permanent fixture in our two room apartment. He was nice enough, especially after I sat on his chest and told him that if he ever grabbed my butt again, I'd make him walk funny and speak in a high voice. Bukwa became our hook to the in-crowd. Evelyn, turned Erzulie, let me know that he used to be called Clifford Morton, "before he got hip and made me his main squeeze." I didn't think his turning hip and her being a squeeze were equal terms, but I listened when Bukwa talked about getting the kids off the streets. I knew about the streets. You couldn't be raised in the Projects without knowing about the streets, and it made sense to plan ways to keep kids from falling into the cracks. So I listened and let Bukwa become my first character study in what I would call my "revolutionary phase." Picasso might have had his "blue period," Duke Ellington his "big band era," and Archibald Motley his "Paris phase," but I had the Coast, and if I sat long enough in Kalava Park, I could sketch every revolutionary who was getting ready for the next the revolution. The problem with selecting a revolution wasn't about the lack of conviction, but the fact that so many systems needed to be overturned, it was hard for a real revolutionary to know where to start. And as it was with any revolution, some folks weren't for real. They were just in the right place for all the wrong reasons.

"Man, there's six brothers to every ten pseudo-liberals. You can't tell the real players when you ain't got no cards," Bukwa would say. Then he'd walk around and see if he could sniff out any FBI informants. And Erzulie would walk around behind him seeing if she could sniff out any broads trying to make time with her man. Usually she found more offenders than he did. But then, like Bukwa said, it was hard to tell the real players from those who were just playing.

I'd like to think some of my sketches cut close to the bone, and enabled folks to see who was for real. Even if I didn't quite capture every expression, I certainly filled a mess of sketchbooks. I carried my books in a fringed leather pouch, and as soon as there was a gathering, which was all the time, I could whip out any of those books and put a face in its proper place. I numbered the books one, two, and three—with one being the in-crowd, and three being so far away from the center, names didn't matter. At the center, names mattered a lot, and just in case the FBI stumbled onto my books, I ran a little code that would tell me what somebody's birth-name had been. Lots of folks changed their names. Shirley Jefferson became Koji, Emmanuel Seaton was Ultra Blue, Lisa McQuaid was Sen-sen. The list could go on, with names taken dead serious, or as the spirit moved the namer. I was not moved. No matter how much my sister protested, I insisted on keeping my name.

"Lorraine was good enough for Mama to put on my baptismal records," I told her, "so it's good enough for me. I was born Lorraine, so I guess I can die Lorraine."

Those were highfalutin words for a woman who had not yet met her match to be saying, but as long as I was the only one I had to answer to, I could say them with conviction, and not bother to add that I was already different enough without having to change my name. That would come later. Then, I just watched that city turn my sister into someone who called herself Erzulie and spent too much time hanging out with dudes like Ultra Blue, or Clifford Morton, who really did believe he was a Detroit-born African named Bukwa. Once I let Bukwa run down the African roots of his newly acquired moniker for my edification, but with people like Sen-sen—a pale little blonde who looked as if she were recovering from some disease—I suspected they had taken their names off the back of a matchbook cover. I know that when my sister saw Sen-sen looking all silly and swallowing every word Bukwa uttered, Erzulie was ready to strike a match off that white woman.

Coming West was the first time my sister and I had had more than a passing contact with white people, especially those whose conversations centered on color. On the Coast, they were the folks always asking me if I knew some colored person who lived in some city back East that I'd never visited. I'd tell them there were folks in my own family I'd never met. Then they'd try to describe this person I was supposed to know, as if somehow that would help. It never did. Sometimes they could tell me about height and weight, but that was it. Mostly, all they knew was color, and then only one: black. I mean to tell you, that one little old color couldn't be used to describe the different types of my people living on the same street, much less those living in some other town. But color was all some folks seemed to know.

"Oh, you look so nice," they'd say when I showed up in baggy coveralls, or tie-dyed dashikis, shapeless as muu-muus. "Those colors do wonders for you," they'd say. "But then you folks wear colors so well. You make reds come alive and give purples and greens a rich glow. Does being colored ever get you down? I mean, when it comes to clothes, it's such an advantage. You have so many choices with basic black, if you know what I mean. I'm so limited in what I can choose, but I'll bet you never have to think twice, do you?"

I'd look at them and wonder what fool question they wanted me to answer first. Those were the times when the revolution seemed distant, when I'd try to get Erzulie to tell me just what the hell we were supposed to be doing. I had to catch her before she boogied out the door to meet Bukwa, or Ultra Blue, or some other dude who had drifted into Kalava Park where most of the demonstrations were held. And even if I did slow her down enough to stop for a minute, she was likely to front me off.

"Chill out," she'd say. "Ain't but a little thing."

Well, one little thing led to another. Conversations went from color to questions about curing a bad sex life. Cure? There I was: five foot seven, and one hundred sixty pounds of post-acned brown sludge. What kind of possible cure could I have had? But minutes after an introduction, between the mystic tea and the artichoke dip, or during a quick hand wash in the ladies' room, a shared joint, and "Are you leaving?" I'd get the lowdown of intimate details about the bedroom, the psyche, the psycho. I don't mean to say those folks singled me out. Usually they made the rounds, from one woman of color to the next. Koji, Lily Stonebird, and Norma Littlejohn had the same complaints I had. We'd watch the white girls wearing the same tribal junk their folks used to make fun of our folks for having. Now all those bones and turquoise beads were hip.

"A Wanna-be-Navajo in a blonde Jew-fro," Littlejohn laughed.

"White folks won't let us have nothing," I grunted.

"This place is as American as Campbell's soup," Stonebird said. "You know, we're the exotics. Like the letters in the soup. Just there to make that weak shit look good. You need a quick fix, get a bowl, and your sex life is back on course."

"Have you had your soup today?" Koji winked.

Then we'd all laugh and watch Koji walk over and hassle some dude, usually some little white boy with his hair still cut short. Before the day was over, she'd have him eating out of her hand, never knowing that she wasn't about to put out for him or any other white man. "It's a game," she'd say, and I'd say, "Right On." Then Stonebird, Littlejohn, and I would give her the peace sign.

If Erzulie went off with some dude, I'd hang out with Stonebird and Littlejohn when they'd let me. When they didn't want me around, they'd saunter over to some other Indian girls and stand around talking about the Rez. When they talked to each other, there was so much left in the spaces of their words, I couldn't follow them, and if I tried, they seemed to grow distant, so it didn't matter what I thought I'd heard them say. One time I tried to tell them how the Projects were as bad as the Reservation, but I guess I didn't put it right or something, because they gave me that look they usually kept for the white girls. That was the day my sister saw me watching them share a joint, their bodies loose inside their jeans and their eyes full of something I couldn't read.

Erzulie left the man she was with long enough to see how I was doing.

"What do you think about those Indian girls?" she asked.

"Woo . . . Scare me!" I said, and laughed.

But I didn't tell her how much time I'd spent watching them hang out in the quad or downtown by the coffeehouse. I guess now I can say that if I'd ever been in love, aside from what I felt that first time I saw Philadelphia, the feeling had something to do with what kept me watching Lily Stonebird and Norma Littlejohn. Some kind of vibes passed between me and Stonebird, and no matter how you slice it, if Lily Stonebird hadn't been standing behind me the day Philly appeared in Kalava Park, I definitely would have lost my cool.

Philly showed up on one of those days when the park was filled with poets and politicians, not a bad combination when most of the crowd was high on weed and not listening anyway. Stonebird, Koji, and I had arrived late and were heading for the center of the park, where I assumed we'd find Erzulie and the rest of the coalition. Every demonstration was divided into self-assigned subsections, with each political faction finding its place on a first-come-first-serve basis. And if I knew my sister, she had herded Bukwa and the others as close to the speaker's platform as she could get. The day before, Sen-sen told us a big-shot Muslim named Seku Ahmadu was going to speak. Erzulie and I remembered that name from back home when the riots had burned out half the Clayton District—"outside agitator," they'd called him—and even though we had been too young to take part in the riots, we'd heard folks talking about Seku Ahmadu. I'd never laid eyes on him, but I knew he was a bad dude who meant business.

When we arrived, the first part of the talks were already underway, so we took our time getting to the speaker's platform. Still, we could hear the Right Reverend William Puce, of the Christ-in-God Methodist Church, intoning his usual rap in his usual semiliterate style, his facts as scrambled as his pronunciation. If he were Pope, he would have been called Puce the Pompous, but his church was a cornerstone of the black community, a dependable sanctuary if any of us got busted by the cops, and the sisters in his flock gave generously to the cause. The Rev's voice was replaced at the mike by Big Jim Cummings'. Cummings was a district politician who thought his profile was Shakespearean, and used it to emphasize whatever lukewarm point he was making. His main function was to pour oil on troubled waters in the form of old-style rhetoric, and he was a pro. He could discuss any problem with the ease of a chameleon, provided his audience understood the problem, according to his logic, was a black one. Having him speak first was an obvious set-up to give Seku Ahmadu more power, and from the murmurs of those few who were listening to Big Jim, Ahmadu couldn't come to the mike soon enough. But most of the crowd were filling themselves with smoke, or dancing to flutes and finger harps on ground that had already begun to grow spongy under their weight. That combination—wet grass and smoke—tripped me up. The first time Philly got a look at me, my butt was stuck in the mud.

It happened when Koji, Stonebird, and I were shoving our way through a particularly pungent group of long-haired chanters. I slipped, and my only thought was to save my sketchbooks. In my efforts, I did a little dance that probably hadn't been done in Kalava Park since the Indians. I landed—SPLAT—in a puddle of what I hoped was 3.2 beer, my dashiki stuck so tightly to my legs, I looked like I'd been swaddled in African print in preparation for mummification. At least, that's what Stonebird said when she could stop laughing long enough to talk. I didn't need her to tell me about the mummified part. Stumbling in the middle of that crowd was like taking a slide down the inside of a waterpipe when the good genie was still dragging on a toke of pure Egyptian weed. By the time I took two deep breaths and turned around twice, I was high before I hit the ground. That's when I looked up at the hillside where a dirt path separated Kalava Park grounds from the zoo. That's when I saw Philadelphia.

Actually, what I saw was the outline of a woman on a bike, her skirt fluttering in the breeze. It was as if she'd floated out of my memory of the Projects to Kalava Park. I thought to myself: *"These folks sure been smoking some heavy-duty ganja."* So I blinked to clear away the illusion. But when I opened my eyes, she was still there, coal-black and beautiful, the same vision I'd seen back in the Projects, except now, her hair was ringed in buttercups and pansies, and a French horn was strapped to her back. This time the background was as perfect as those paintings I studied for Art History, something with a title like, "Black Girl Biking on an Afternoon in the Park." The textbook painting would have been signed by some bourgeois French Impressionist, and designated for a museum where it would be displayed on occasion. I had the real thing. One look, and despite all the bad poetry I heard in those days, I remembered the wonderful lines from an Anne Spencer poem: *Lady, Lady, I saw your face / Dark as night withholding a star . . . And altared there in its darksome place / Were the tongues of flames the ancients knew / Where the good God sits to spangle through.*

There I was, sitting in the dirt of a political demonstration, thinking poetry, while Philly was poised on the horizon, the sunlight tinted violet on her black skin, bits of light playing in her Afro and the flowers circling her head. That light burned against the golden glow of the French horn riding easy on her back. That's what caught Koji's eye when she turned to look at what had set me staring.

"Hey, it's Philadelphia Sutton!" Koji screamed. "Philly's back in town!"

And Stonebird yelled, "Philly! Hey, Philly, down here!"

I said, "You know her?"

"Yeah, everybody knows Philly," Stonebird answered in a matter-of-fact way that told me I'd asked a dumb question.

Everybody knows her but me, I thought, as I watched folks waving Philadelphia down the hillside. Philly coasted down that hill in a straight line as if someone had laid out a path for her. And it didn't even pass my mind that I should try to get up. I just sat there, waiting like some kind of mantelpiece ornament, the wet grass soaking through the bottom of my dashiki. That's how Philadelphia found me: sitting in that muddy grass, my leather pouch held over my head as if I were trying to bring some tribute to the gods. When she propped her bike against a tree and walked over to us, all I could do was look up at her and laugh. Of course, my laughter was part embarrassment and part contact high, but once I started, I couldn't stop.

Everyone laughed with me, including Philadelphia. Then Stonebird announced it was time to haul my ass out of the mud. With Koji and a couple of other people helping, Stonebird pulled me upright, and I stood in front of Philly, trying my best to control the shit-eating grin I had on my face. It was one of the few times I was happy to be able to hide my blush. If my skin had been a few shades lighter, I would have been red from my hairline to my chin, instead of just having a real dark rim around my ears and mouth as if some child had drawn an outline of my features in black crayon. Philadelphia was grinning back at me, but that didn't help. I giggled in little hiccoughs, and I didn't quite know what to do with my hands. They were sweating, but I certainly couldn't wipe them on my dress. That was covered with mud, and in a crowd full of folks wearing enough tribal robes, beads, head wraps, and shawls to lay claim to at least five different continents all at once, I looked like a rag-picker. I had no beads, no feathers, no Afro. And until then, I was still stumbling around under the name Lorraine.

I finally managed to control my laughter and stretch out my hand. I started to say, "Hi, I'm, uh . . ."

Philly interrupted me. "Kicheka," she said.

I said, "Huh?" It was the dumbest sound I'd ever heard come out of my mouth.

Philly didn't seem to notice. "Laughter," she said. "That's what they'd call you on the Gold Coast. Kicheka is laughter."

"You coulda fooled me," Stonebird said. "Every time I see this heifer, she's looking down in the mouth."

"You're not looking right," Philly told her. And I felt that kid's crayon mark grow wider.

"I kinda like it," Koji said. "What'd you call her, Philly?"

"Kicheka," Philly repeated, and put her ring of flowers in my hair.

And Koji said, "Yeah, it's about time somebody cheered up ol' monkey face." Then, taking my hand, she led me dancing through the center of the group, toward the speaker's stand, Philly and Stonebird trailing behind us like children caught in the act of flying under a golden sky.

But of my mother's two daughters, I was the only one laughing that day. When Koji and the rest of us broke into the clearing by the far side of the speaker's platform, Erzulie copped an attitude, and just out and out pouted. I don't know if it was the sight of me, mud-splattered, and bedraggled as an old mop with that ring of flowers in my hair, or if it was Philly, dropped out of some dreamer's sky in her gauzy white blouse and Indian print skirt. I watched Philadelphia moving in and out of the crowd. She seemed to know everyone from Bukwa, Sen-sen, and Ultra Blue to Toni and Loni, twins from San Bernardino who were hoping to cut a record with Motown. She told everyone about being in the picket lines in Montgomery, how many police dogs she'd seen in Jackson, and how it was in Chattanooga when the fuzz used cattle prods. When she held up her foot, we could see that she had the scars on her ankles to show for it.

"I came back here to cool out," she said. "To play me a little music before I jumped back in that mess."

Then she and Ultra Blue played a duet of some tune I didn't know the name of—"Classical," Blue told me later—and I watched Philly's gauze blouse float around her in a ripple like a leaf tumbling around the bark of a tree. As she swayed to the notes, her skirt wavered in the breeze of her legs, that flash of smooth skin winking with the promise of something else I wanted to put a name to. We all applauded when they finished, all of us, that is, except Erzulie.

My sister told me, "Close your mouth. You look stupid."

"That's the woman we saw back home," I said. "You know, riding a bike."

"Big fucking deal," Erzulie sneered. "She ain't pulled my string."

"Well, she surely pulled your sister's," Stonebird laughed.

And Koji added, "Yeah, somebody's warm for that form."

Erzulie stared at me. I stared at Philadelphia. She was like a character come alive from a novel, a combination created by mixing generous portions of Harriet Tubman with Cleopatra and Marie Laveau, while I was some recently freed slave come to ask for her benevolence.

What I was thinking took up all the room on my face, and made Blue change his guitar tune. He fell into a square's rendition of Dionne Warwick singing: *"Wishing—and hoping—and dreaming—each night of her charms, won't get you into her arms. . ."* We all laughed. Blue, with his big fat self, was nobody's version of Dionne Warwick, but he could sure sing, and he definitely knew how to read my face. So did Philly.

While Blue was singing, she looked at me and smiled. I smiled back. "What do you think about a name like Kicheka?" I asked Erzulie.

My sister said, "What?"

"Kicheka," I said. "That's what Philly called me. It's a Gold Coast name. You know, African."

Erzulie grunted. "Humph . . . How come you didn't take one I gave you? How come you got to wait for some skinny heifer to be telling you what to do? Wouldn't even talk about names when I asked you."

"That's cause it's got nothing to do with you," I told her.

And that set the tone that would lie between us for the next few months. Just as I was determined to hook up with Philadelphia, Erzulie was determined to not see what was going on between me and Philly. There wasn't much I could do about a sister who had suddenly gone dumb and blind, except be there when the spell wore off. As usual, Erzulie didn't make it easy for me.

"Don't be coming in here taking over," she snapped when Philadelphia came to visit us.

I have to give Philly credit. She tried hard with Erzulie, even to the point of making jokes about stuff that was as serious as a headache. To tell you the truth, I had never heard anyone talk like Philadelphia did.

"I'm a throwback," she'd say. "An aberration. It's been that way since ought-ten, the year I was born . . . or was it forty-eight? No matter, cause that was the year my daddy took one look at his third daughter by his second wife and decided to spend the rest of his life reading books on reincarnation. No lie. I had broken his perfect record of coffee-colored Creole offspring. My old mammy bore up quite well. She simply refused to look upon my face if she could help it. Sent me to boarding schools, she did. How do you think I know so much about 'coloured society'? Don't ever let them tell you money improves black folks. They act as silly as rich white folks ever did. Dig it? I was engaged to a colored doctor, an obstetrician who actually believed he had to use light-skinned folks for his hired help. My only complaint is that Mu'dear made the unfortunate decision of giving birth in this country. When I went to Brazil, I almost became a blood-sister in the Candomblé just to stay away from here. But the rituals were too exhausting. Wore me out, girl. Still, if

I'd had my druthers, I'd get my black ass away from this country."

With that bit of information, she'd leaned back against the worn chenille of our one comfortable chair, and offered her laughter to the sun. I didn't have the heart to ask what a Candomblé was. I knew if I waited around long enough, Philadelphia would tell me. She knew so much, it made me curse that pitiful excuse for an education I'd received back in the Projects. If being with Philadelphia didn't mean I knew what course my life was taking, at least, it meant I knew how far I'd come from where I'd started.

None of it fazed Erzulie. She still spent a lot of time trying to get the best of Philly. A waste of time, if you ask me, because Philly was ready for anything my sister threw at her. Like the day Erzulie wanted to know why Philly was called Philadelphia.

Without missing a step, Philly answered, "Cause Pittsburgh's a boy's name."

That was one time I didn't dare laugh, and live up to my new name, Kicheka. Not when the joke was on my own sister. But it didn't matter. Erzulie seemed to reach her limit with Philadelphia at that point.

"Miz Boarding School," she called her. "Dump your doctor and come slumming."

Philadelphia got right up in her face. "Let me tell you something," she said. "Ain't nothing slick about where I been but the wax on the floor. As long as my behind is black, folks see me and you as one thing. Get it?"

"So how come I ain't got no doctor-friend, Miz Thing?"

"You want to know about doctors? I'll tell you about doctors. This one was the local knife. He could pull two, maybe three babies in that back room and never miss a course at the dinner table. Sometimes I'd hear him telling some woman to relax. He'd say: 'Breathe from the stomach.' Then ten minutes later, he was at the table cutting up his meat. It was always for a good cause. Always cause some-man-had-done-her-wrong. I figured it was better than a coat hanger, and I guess I could have lived with that. I don't know. See, I'd been bred to be a proper girl. A good wife. But there was this dog. A big standard poodle, three feet tall, at least. He was supposed to be chained up in the back, kept there to keep the junkies from breaking into the pharmacy. You know how you can dream and still be fully awake? Well, one morning, I woke up and stared right into that thing's eyes, and I knew it had been sniffing me. That wet nose was still twitching, and it was licking its chops. Waiting for a meal or just finished? I was afraid to ask. I left that morning."

Erzulie said, "Your choice, baby," and flounced out of the door. After that, she came home even less. There was always some excuse about crashing at someone else's pad. I found myself doing fewer sketches of Erzulie, and dozens of Philadelphia, who would sit for a pose as my sister never would have. It took me a while to get used to being with Philly, especially when she'd sprawl on the sofa, her arms flung wide and her legs apart, not caring how the light fell onto her skin or who was watching. I'd try not to stare at the clump of hair saddling the space between her thighs, or watch how shadows wrinkled with the rise and fall of her stomach as she breathed. It was then I'd notice I was holding my own breath, and Philly, laughing, would cup her breasts and present them as gifts for my patience. It was a while before I could sketch her and concentrate on what the charcoal was doing, not what was going on in my head.

Finally, when Philadelphia moved in with me, my sister stayed away altogether. Sometimes the two of us would see Erzulie at Kalava, or in one of the coffeehouses when Philly sat in with a jazz group. But mostly Erzulie avoided me.

"She can't handle it," Stonebird said. "You being with Philly just blows her mind."

"How come?" I asked. "I put up with all those dudes she was dragging home."

Littlejohn laughed. "You know it ain't the same."

"I'm the same as I've ever been," I said. "This place is the same. Same old people, and same old B.S. about revolution."

Philadelphia shook her head. "Un-un. Revolution is never the same across the board. Don't think that whatever you're doing out here playing hippie-in-the-sun has a thing to do with black folks living hand-to-mouth on sharecropper's wages. What you're doing is playing."

"Just leaving the Projects and coming out here was revolution enough for me," I said. "I didn't know nothing about playing in the sun before I came here. Just living was too hard. But if anybody's playing, Erzulie's the one doing it. I don't plan to ever go back to them Projects."

Philly smiled. "I hear you," she said. "But the skinny is: You're both playing. Me too. All of us who don't have to stay out there in the People's Battlefield. We're playing. Only difference is which version is more dangerous."

I didn't quite know what she meant until about a month later when we went to a Pan-African rally at Kalava. Once again, a coalition had flown in Seku Ahmadu for a speech. Philly saw him and said, "This ought to be something else." There were certainly more black folks in the crowd than I'd ever seen at Kalava. They were singing gospels and clapping their hands in rhythms I hadn't heard since home and church with Mama on Sundays. Philadelphia seemed to know as many folks in this crowd as she did in the usual bunch hanging out in Kalava. But this was a different kind of crowd. Where I'd usually overheard white hippies talking about their last plane trip to see the latest guru, folks talked about how many had been killed in what demonstration, and which ghetto was said to be burning. There was the smell of ganja in the air, but most of it was covered up by odors of talcum powder and stale tobacco. Some folks were older—family men and people with hard-looking hands, their faces lined like maps of anger. Or dudes in silk suits, cruising.

Watching those cats in their tight-ass suits made me look around for Erzulie. There were knots of people I knew. Stonebird and Littlejohn were with three big dudes who might have played Indians in Western movies, if Hollywood had ever been honest enough to use real Indians who were as mean as they looked. I saw the twins over by the bandstand where a church choir was gathering. Then Blue and Sen-sen.

"What it is," Blue said when I tapped him on the shoulder.

"You got it," I told him. Sen-sen looked like she'd been dipped in the ocean, rode hard, and put to bed wet. I wondered where Bukwa was. But I was more curious about my sister than I was about Bukwa.

When I asked him if he'd seen Erzulie, Blue said, "Hey, well, you know... We don't dig the same vibes no more. That chick's giving out some bad vibes."

Sen-sen looked at me and giggled.

"What's the matter with this one?" I asked Blue. "Can't she speak words no more?"

He shrugged. "Hey, you know how white broads are..."

"Un-un. You the one who knows that, brother-man. So tell me."

"She strung out," Blue said. "Stoned to the gills."

"Like your sister," Sen-sen laughed.

Blue grabbed her arm. "Sometimes you talk too much," he told her. "I'ma get me a new woman if you don't keep your trap shut."

They turned and walked away. "Where's my sister?" I called, but they slid into a hole in the crowd without ever looking back.

I wasn't sure what to do. In my head, I carried a picture of Erzulie when she was still Evelyn, and we were still sisters, blood kin who looked out for each other. Now she was lost out there. "I've got to find her," I told Philly.

She put her arm around me and nuzzled my ear. But that didn't cheer me up, not even when I saw her give the finger to some uptight churchgoers clicking their tongues over seeing the two of us hug. I wanted to cry.

"Hey, Cheka. It's cool... OK? Erzulie's a big girl. And if she's strung out, we can't get her off the stuff in a day. And we can't go looking for her now. We'll find her."

"Promise?" I whispered.

"Promise," Philly said, then put both arms around my waist.

So we stood there, listening to speeches, and I pretended all of me was still in that park, while somewhere, Erzulie played out whatever bad dream she was trapped in.

The speeches started off in high gear. Preachers followed politicians, and sometimes, one person served as a combination of the two. Then a dude from Chicago, imitating the style of Dr. Martin Luther King, Jr., chanted "Raise-Your-Conscious" to the point where I began to think the whole park would levitate. But that got everyone ready for Seku Ahmadu. That man came on like thunder. He was as close to looking like someone from the kingdom of Timbuktu as anyone I'd ever seen. He had a way of moving the crowd from hymns to chants that made a lot of black people cry, including me and Philly. But I could see that some of the white folks were a little uneasy. I didn't know just how uneasy they were until Ahmadu began talking about the treacherous dogs enslaving all the peoples of the African nations, including the ones in America. Then two things happened all at once: It began to rain, and folks began to riot.

The sky had been dark most of the day, but when the storm broke, it was without warning. "Brothers and Sisters, Allah has blessed us with a taste of His precious rain," Seku Ahmadu shouted. "Let it wash away the white man's evil smell. Rejoice in its peace. Stand your ground."

But the sky just opened up and turned the park into a swamp with about four hundred people pushing and shoving until the mud was silt, threatening to cover us like prehistoric beasts. Those folks forgot about Allah, Jesus Christ, or any other messenger of God.

"Damn," a woman behind me shouted. "I just been to the beauty shop this morning." Then she slipped and fell headfirst into a patch of mud-soaked grass.

Another brother tried to dash for the safety of a tree in order to protect his white-on-white shirt and silk suit, but his top grain leather shoes slid in the muck. "Unless them Pan-Afric cats got a dry cleaning business, somebody better lay some coins on ME!" he yelled.

About that time, four young punks, white boys high on wine and whatever else, slammed into a knot of people and tried to lunge up on the platform after Seku Ahmadu. Someone screamed, and the cops, who'd been waiting at the edges of the park, started to move forward. Philly snatched at my arm so fast, the momentum of my body almost caught us both off balance. We were thrown against several other people, all of us falling and sliding on the soft ground. Somehow I managed to keep my pouch of sketchbooks with me. I don't know how. I had never run so fast in my life. I wanted to run straight, but Philadelphia knew what to expect with cops, so she pulled me on a zigzag course that took us through the zoo. As we whipped past the cages, animals shrieked and stomped around in their cells as if they were trying to remember what running was. I heard gunshots, and for the first time, I was glad Blue had told me Erzulie was not in the park. Stoned or not, she wouldn't get caught on that day.

But a whole bunch of folks did. Even before she opened the newspaper, I knew that riot had started pulling Philadelphia back to the battlefield. I sat at her feet while she read me the story. The text wasn't much different from that of any other demonstration gone sour. Just the names were changed. Erzulie's was not among them.

"I've got to find her," I told Philly. "What would happen if they throw her in the slammers and find out she's got a habit?"

Philadelphia sighed. "Same as what happens to anybody else who's black, on dope, and in jail. You see where they let Sen-sen out on bail, but kept Blue. That's what will happen."

"I've got to find her," I said.

Philly looked at me. "We all do what we got to do. Right now, I've got to get out of here. Don't look at me that way. You knew it was coming from the start. I can't be out here playing pretty-in-the-sun while folks are getting beat up just trying to live one day to the next. That's what I'm about, Kicheka. Making changes. I told you that. I told you I just came home to rest."

"I can't leave without finding her," I said.

Philly's voice was flat. "I have to go, Kicheka. Before long, I'll have to go."

We went around like that for several weeks. There was another riot. The papers gave some account of what happened to the people who got arrested, but Erzulie wasn't on that list either. I couldn't find Bukwa, and as far as I knew, Blue was still in jail. I was beginning to think I'd be left there, looking for Erzulie by myself, while Philly went off to the next People's Battlefield. Then one day, the two of us were actually across the street from Erzulie. She was down by the Petra Tunnel, and if the traffic hadn't been so heavy, I could have reached her.

Philadelphia said, "Be cool. Don't scare her."

My sister didn't see us, but while we waited for the light to change, we had a clear view of her. It didn't take much to put words to what I saw. At first, she stood near the curb. She wasn't actually thumbing, but anyone could tell she was selling. One car slowed, and she leaned over. Seconds later, the driver gunned his motor and Erzulie had to jump back onto the curb. Folks two blocks away could lip-read what she called him. Then the light changed, but before Philly and I could cross the street, Erzulie skittered to the opposite corner. I saw her approach an old white woman who was dressed as if she'd just been picked off some tailor's cutting room floor. Erzulie had her hand out. The woman walked faster.

Erzulie screamed, "Well, how's about something for coffee?"

The old woman was almost trotting.

"How's about a dime?" Erzulie yelled. "A quarter? I been to college. How's about a quarter for a college girl?"

By this time, the old woman was close enough for us to hear her. "The university's just down the block," she told Erzulie. "Walk."

My sister screamed, "Bitch! Do I look like I want to walk to that uptight place?" Then she saw me and Philly. I yelled, "Evelyn!" but she was running before the light finished turning in our favor.

I figured if I spotted her once, I could do it again. I started hanging out downtown, but Philadelphia only came with me a couple of times. Every day, I could see she was getting closer to leaving. Then, one rain-soaked night, my sister just showed up at my door. I woke up feeling Philadelphia's hand rubbing my forehead.

"Your sister's here," she whispered. Then she moved aside so I could get out of bed.

All I could do was hug Erzulie. I guess that in those first few minutes, my sister and I were as close to being kids again as we ever would be. I was so glad to see her that, for a while, I didn't notice she bore no resemblance to the child I'd grown up with. She was wearing jeans and something African, at least the material was African print, but the shirt itself was tattered into a pattern of rips and cigarette burns, bits of thread trailing from the sleeveless armholes as wispy as the fog that drifts inland from the ocean. Her Afro looked like it had been chewed by a storm at sea, and her face had that splotchy look junkies get.

"Where you been?" I asked.

She pulled away and went though a two-handed, shaky routine of lighting a cigarette. "I'm pregnant," she said.

I looked from Erzulie to Philly, who was standing in the doorway, her arms folded across her chest.

"Sure beats the hell out of: Hey, what's happening?" Philly grinned. Erzulie glared at her. I opened my mouth to speak, thought better of it, closed it and opened it again. "Well, I suppose one of us needs to say it," Philadelphia added. "So here goes: Hello, Lil' Mama."

Erzulie finished a long drag off her cigarette. "Just because I'm straight, don't mean I'm maternal."

"Just because I'm gay, don't mean I'm not," Philly snapped.

It would have been like old times if it weren't for the little bomb Erzulie had just dropped in the middle of the room.

"So what you gone do?" Erzulie asked me.

"Yeah, what you gone do, Miz Fix-it?" Philadelphia echoed. I looked at her like she'd grown fangs. She leaned against the doorjamb. "You could opt for adoption. White folks are ready." We groaned. "OK, what we can do is theorize about the demise of the Western world. Ruminate on the impending disaster created by the Man and supported by the sordid masses. And you, Lil' Mama, you can add your version from the feminine perspective on how a country break turns into a city whipping."

"Philly, your humor leaves much to be desired," I said.

"I didn't mean for it to be funny," she said.

"What about that doctor friend of yours?" Erzulie asked her. "Can't you get *your man* to help me?

Philly grunted. "Girl, there was more than one reason for me to leave him, and only one of them had to do with him being a man. Ask your sister about it sometime." She paused. I did not offer her a way out. "I've got no reason . . ." Philly began.

"Screw your reasons," Erzulie snapped. "I need help."

Philadelphia shrugged. "Don't say I didn't warn you."

"Is it safe?" I asked.

"As long as it's in a back room, it's never safe. But what choice does a woman have?"

"That is the problem, isn't it?" Erzulie sneered. "Choice? You with your boarding schools, and me with VocTech High."

Philly said, "I don't think I need to hear this. I'll be in the bedroom when you want me."

As the bedroom door slammed shut, Erzulie opened her mouth to say something, but I shut her up. For the first time, I made her listen to me. At first, she looked everywhere but at me. But you can only look but so long at faded wallpaper, and sagging furniture. Slowly, I made her tell me the details of what she'd been doing, until the whole sordid mess was hanging around her like those threads trailing from her blouse. At first, Erzulie got edgy whenever she mentioned drugs. She talked about where she'd been as if she were reciting lines from a play. It was as if I were being taken for a ride, except some crazy person was at the wheel. Everything was on automatic pilot, moving on overdrive until each little piece was an accident more reckless than the last. And none of it was her fault. That's what I really noticed, but I let her go on until the subject of drugs was no better or worse than sex or all the other crap she'd piled on her head. Especially anything concerning Bukwa. When I asked her if it was his baby, she just went to the window and stared out at the rain. The sky above Kalava Park was leaning into the gray light of morning, and both of us were bleary-eyed and half drunk from the lack of sleep. The park looked innocent in the first hours of dawn, and it was quiet. *"Even the zoo animals sleep,"* I told myself.

"What's Mama gone say if you come home with some baby and don't even know who the daddy is?" I asked Erzulie.

"You saying I got to have this baby?" she asked me.

"You know what I'm saying," I told her. "We ain't in the Projects no more . . ."

Before I could finish, she said, "And I ain't stepping back in that trap neither." She was quiet for a while, then she finally muttered, "What difference does it make whose baby it is? I don't want to have no baby while I'm on the stuff."

I looked out the window. The park might still be blurred by morning mist, but I was just beginning to see my sister clearly. Somewhere along the line, I had supposed I was the one hiding from her, keeping a part of me close, even when Erzulie recognized that part. Somewhere, I had decided my secret was greater than anything she felt. Now I began to understand that ninety percent of the time, all my signals were right out front, but like the dismal clouds hanging over the city, I'd only been able to see the gloss Erzulie had painted around her. This last year had scraped off that gloss. I watched her standing in front of the window, nodding out, swaying a little, like a cobra caught in the hypnosis of its own reflection. Inside, I wept.

"How's about some breakfast? Waffles . . . I think I got some eggs. You like eggs. And bacon?"

Erzulie turned around. "I don't want to eat until this is over," she answered.

"Just give her some coffee," Philadelphia said. "She'll be sick soon enough." I hadn't heard her come to the doorway, but when she brushed past me, she touched my arm and smiled. It was no big deal, that touch. Just enough to let me know she was there. Philly took a seat at the kitchen table. "You two been up all night?" she asked.

I nodded. In one window, morning light was just beginning to crack at the edge of the skyline, while across the room, in another window, darkness still hung, blanket-heavy, above the ocean. In a way, I wished the night was still there. The day that was dawning was not going to be pleasant. I began to make the coffee, and Erzulie slumped into a chair. I sat across from her and turned on the television, hoping to catch the early morning news show. What we got was an ad from one of the soap operas. The three of us watched it, dumbly waiting for the commercial's punch line while the coffee brewed. And I thought of how much easier it was to watch the soap's troubles than to think of our own.

The Losers

DARDANELLE WATCHED A LEAF DANCING onto the hood of the jeep, winds juggling it across the shiny gun-metal surface, then leaving it hanging near the edge. The leaf fluttered and twitched like the ears of the doe Hammond had sighted in the cross hairs of his .22, the doe Hammond had aimed for and missed. A bad miss, wide and low. A miss that finally brought them to the top of Mesa Flats to follow some wild scheme Hammond had for getting them clear of the law. *"That's what I get for messing around with a Mex,"* Dardanelle told himself. *"This desert's colder than the Hawk blowing across Chicago. I don't care if this is supposed to be the West, it's a cold mother out here."* He tucked the springy mass of his kinky beard under his upturned collar, and snuggled lower into the warmth of the sheepskin jacket. With his nose jutting from the thick lining like the tip of a sandblown rock, Dardanelle was no more than another part of the weathered landscape. The wind changed course, lifted the leaf for a second, then let it slide from sight over the hump of the jeep's hood and into the darkness. The wind also brought a full whiff of the acrid smell of Hammond's cigar to his nostrils.

"Kill that cigar, Hammond."

"Screw you, Dardanelle."

"Man, don't call me Dardanelle. Darnell, man. Darnell. I don't know why I even bother with you, Jack. Goddamn Mex," Darnell snorted.

"Tu culo."

"Man, I told you . . . I don't speak that shit. So knock it off with the Spanish, OK?"

"Then how come you brag about being born in the Islands fore you turned city?" Hammond said.

Darnell spit over the side of the jeep. "I can be born where I damn well please and it still don't mean I speak that shit." He was settling back into his slump when something caught his eye. "What's that, Hammond? Over there? That light . . . there?"

"Cars, Darnell. Cars on the road. Can't you see nothing, man?"

"Naw, I can't. I'm a city boy, remember? I'm not a hotshot, sharpshooting nature boy raised picking peas. I can spot the fuzz, and whatever I shoot at moves on two legs, not four. And if I'm shooting, they best keep moving, Jack. I don't miss."

"I told you what happened with that deer," Hammond interrupted.

"Yeah, Jack. Yeah, I know. The ghost of Christmas past. Ooiiee—Ooee!" He pulled his hands out of his coat sleeves long enough to wiggle his fingers.

Hammond crawled back in the jeep and snapped at him. "Shut up, Darnell. Just shut up, man."

Then they both hunkered down in the seat and sulked. The air was thick with the moss-wet hint of rain. Under the cloudy half-moon sky, the shadowy outlines of the men, their hats, and the jeep were barely visible. But their vision was better than that of anyone coming toward them, which was why Hammond had picked that spot. From there, they could see the rim of the mountain range on the other side of the scrub brush valley. Occasionally, the bright lights of a car outlined the road that wound along the jagged contours of the mountains. But the valley, a natural trench for the high winds rolling off the mesa toward the mountains, was nearly invisible. From their vantage point, that valley floor was so heavily blanketed in darkness, it made them uneasy, and they anxiously watched the mountain range where signal towers flashed red warnings in timed intervals. Each pulse of light made Hammond conscious of the minutes creeping past. He imagined the light sending out the coded message: "day-after-week-after-month-after-year." It was the same message he'd imagined in his cell, a message coded by the leaky water faucet.

The lights sometimes confused both men, but Hammond would never admit it. He let Darnell bear the brunt of the confusion. It was an old game with them. One that allowed them to let time use itself. That's what the tower light was doing now. Eating time.

Hammond flipped his cigar over the side of the jeep, stretched both arms and yawned loudly. "Think I'll take a walk," he said. "You gonna sit here?"

"Yeah. Why not? I can't fly."

Hammond grunted and hoisted himself out of the jeep. Darnell watched him swing clear of the vehicle, his six-and-a-half-foot frame unfolding with the agility of a dancer. *"Reminds me of my old man,"* Darnell thought. *"All he's missing is them steel drums."* Then he spit again, this time in memory of his father. Darnell was aware of how the bulk of his own weight was tucked clumsily into the seat. In the city, he was tough, a badass. Out here, he had no choice but to rely on Hammond.

"Stupid," he muttered as he remembered what his Uncle Percy once told him: "Sometimes a mahn is lost in thees dust he make of his own raising," his uncle had said. "And we're sure as shit lost right now," Darnell mumbled. A capricious gust of wind shifted suddenly, and slammed into his face like a back-handed slap. Darnell grunted. Everything seemed after him: the jeep breaking down every ten miles, the sun burning a hole in his skull, the nights made colder by the wind. "And all that damn sand," he grumbled. No, this definitely was not his idea of God's country. Hammond could have it. Darnell was willing to give him the whole mess, sand and all, as soon as they crossed the border. *"Anything to get shed of this place."* he thought. Out here, it was hard to remember that he'd taught Hammond what to do in the city. Darnell could not see Hammond's eyes under the brim of the black gambler's hat, but he imagined them to be narrowed as usual. He watched Hammond stretching and tried to remember the noise of a city street. "Too damn quiet," he muttered.

Hammond hooked his thumbs into his belt, and walked away from the jeep, rolling out on his heels like a sailor. Darnell pulled his own hat, a brown suede wide-brim, over his eyes and nuzzled deeper into the seat. He had only been asleep for a few minutes when Hammond returned, his voice so close, Darnell sat bolt upright in the jeep, knocking the hat brim into position above his forehead and reaching under the dash in two synchronized moves. Then he realized it was Hammond.

Despite their agreement, Darnell shouted. "Damn, you got to always sneak around like that, Jack?" The echo came back with exacting intonation.

"Great. Now they know we're here for two counties."

"Man, they knew we was here before we arrived."

"Maybe we ought to go looking for them," Hammond said. He pulled down on the corners of his mustache, a habit that usually irritated Darnell. But this time, Hammond got no response. "Maybe we ought to go looking for them," he repeated.

"OK, you go. You can track 'em down. Use that Indian part you always talking bout, Big Chief."

"If they was eating chitterlin's and wearing coon skins, you could track 'em, Boy."

"I'm laughing. See my teeth? I'm laughing real hard."

Hammond squinted at the sky. Nothing had changed. The stars were still bright, and seemed to be hanging right over the edge of the next ridge of mountains. That's what he'd missed in the city. The absence of stars and clear air. He took a deep breath, and looked up. Then he asked, "Hey Darnell, que hora?" He got an answer, but knowing the exact hour and minutes did not make him feel better. "Where the hell are they?"

"How the hell am I supposed to know?" Darnell complained. "I told you, you got the Indian in your blood. You track 'em. Besides, this ain't my show. I just come here to see if you really do fall for this shit, man. You know all this spirit crap sounds like something made for TV. I'm auditioning for the lead. Mr. Maitland, they'll call me. Yeah, this is quick shot video, and I'm here for the ride."

"Keep this up and you gone walk, man."

"Just track 'em. You Navajo, ain't you?"

"I got as much Navajo in me as you got Island in you."

"Jack, you must be the big-cheese Navajo then."

"Que te jodas. I'm Aztec."

"Last week, you was Cherokee."

"That too."

"You know, Jack, it don't matter what you call yourself. If the Man catches up with you, he's gone shoot you and me, and call it even. He sure won't divide up them bullets. One for one color. One for the other. Dig it? To the Man, you ain't . . ."

Hammond shouted, "Can it Dardanelle!" Then he drew the side of his hand across his throat in a slicing motion. The last finger on his hand was stiff and oddly bent as if he were mimicking society ladies holding teacups. That finger had been poorly set after a bad fall from a horse. Hammond had hated horses ever since. He leaned against the hood of the jeep, stroking and pulling his mustache down on each side of his mouth, and thinking about how much he didn't like horses.

"Man, you know what you look like when you do that?" Darnell asked. "You look like you been doing something smelly with that muff-duster. Stop licking your hair like that, man."

Hammond grinned, and stuck his hands in his pocket. He felt something crinkle, and pulled out a sheet of paper. "Hey, Darnell, turn the lights on. Low."

"You read that damn thing fifty times already."

"Turn the lights on, man!"

Darnell sighed and pulled himself up, groaning as he reached for the light switch. The headlights came on bright, then dimmed when Darnell lowered them. The jeep creaked once on its shock absorbers as Hammond moved forward into the direct flow of headlights.

Darnell settled back in the seat and pulled his hat brim over his eyes, muttering to himself, and wondering half-aloud what he was doing there with a crazy Mexican who was waiting for a bunch of crazier Indians to come riding out of no-man's land. *Comes from making friends in the joint,* he thought. It was like his mother told him: No good could come out of going to jail. "So what else is new?" he muttered. He rubbed his cheekbones and tried to remember when he'd last shaved. Having a beard made him feel unwashed, and now he had a four-day growth stubbling his chin. That was tough for a man who used his looks to close out the world.

"Hey, Jack, how long we gotta wait?" Darnell snorted.

"I don't know. Not long," Hammond answered.

"Un-huh. You really want to do this?"

After a moment's hesitation, Hammond said, "No."

"Say what? Then why'd we come all the way out here to this damn desert? We could be halfway to San Francisco by now."

"Yeah, I know."

"You know! You know! Jack, you don't know shit. You don't know why we out here; you don't know what to do when they get here. You out here playing Zapata meets Cochise, and I'm the one freezing my ass off. I got better things to do."

"Like what? What you got to do?"

"Hey, I got some deals going down . . ." Darnell began.

Hammond grunted. "Man, you lying through your teeth."

"If I'm lying, I'm flying. And out here, I might as well be flying. Man, I got to get to a city where I can see some folks. All we been seeing is white people. Like that honky back in Concrete who looked me right in the eye and said: 'A nigger in a white pick-up means it's gonna rain.' Said it like he couldn't see I was black."

"Just small town shit, Darnell."

"Small! That's what I mean. The last town we was in was some little one-horse-spit named Eunice. Who the hell would name a town Eunice?" Darnell spit as if to illustrate his point.

Hammond shook his head. "You said the same thing when we went through Paradox."

"Paradox! That's another one. And Trinidad. Yeah, Trinidad, and Cortez and Peru. And ain't none of them seen Islands nor ocean. All of them stuck in the middle of the country where there ain't no water for miles, cept some little trickle with a name as funny as the town they got near it. You can't trust nothing out here, Jack. They got names that make you think you lost even when you got a map. Give me some place I know, like St. Louis, St. Joe, St. Kitts."

"Don't sound like you want to go to town. Sound like you want to go to somebody's church."

"Hey, ain't nothing wrong with church. They got some righteous foxes sitting up in church."

Hammond watched Darnell grin in that slow, easy movement that had lured more than one woman too close to him. "Give me a break, OK, Darnell? And Jack, I don't care what town we're going through. I'm tired of running, that's all. Everywhere I look, I see his face. Man, I got to get it over with, once and for all. It was him, that kid's face, that's what I saw when I was aiming for that deer this morning. He's showing up all the time now, man. I've got to put an end to it, Darnell. Gotta tell them what happened."

"Jesus shit, you could have sent them a letter and saved everybody a hell of a lot of trouble."

"I've sent letters. Dozens! But it gets worse, and they say the same thing: 'We'll wait for you here at such-and-such-a-time.' Every letter gets me the same answer. 'We'll meet you here.' So now, I'm here. I'm waiting. They'll come tonight. The old man, the last of the stargazers, and maybe the kid's brother."

"His brother? Man, Eddie Longman is dead. That dude crapped out before we went on strike up in Kodiak. Froze to death, I heard. Didn't you talk to them Filipino brothers?"

"They'll be here tonight, Darnell. Eddie Longman and maybe a few others. I'll settle it. Eddie will let the old man do the talking. That's why our plan's got to work. It better work. Ol' Eddie will watch, see if the stargazer can settle it, and if he can't, Eddie will finish it. You know, that dude could break a wolf's neck? Man, tonight it's settled. Eddie won't give me a second chance."

Darnell muttered, "Crazy. You been reading too much sci-fi stuff. Stargazer. What's the hell's that? Some movie title?"

Suddenly, a sliver of lightning traced its way across the mountain ridge, licking the ground near the signal tower. In the flash of light, Darnell's beige eyes, with their black center-points, winked like stars trapped in polished sapphires. He took a swig of water from the thermos, and scrunched even lower into the seat. "Shit! Now it's gonna rain. I'm gone be tired, cold, and wet too."

Hammond didn't respond. He folded the paper and returned it to his pocket. Then he flexed his legs, and jammed his thumbs in his belt.

Darnell was muttering again, but there was really no need for Hammond to ask him what he'd said. Hammond had heard Darnell's views a dozen times since they'd started for Mesa Flats. Actually, he had no way of deciding when he'd actually started the trip. Perhaps he'd never really left this mesa. Perhaps his spirit had stayed here, tied to the sand hills, the skinny bushes of the valley, the winter towns where migrant workers camped until picking season. Half of his family was still living somewhere in those towns.

Darnell interrupted Hammond's thoughts. "You really don't believe in all that spirit shit, do you?" Darnell asked in a loud voice.

Hammond sighed. "I thought I did. But this is the only way to find out, ain't it?"

"What if it don't work?"

"I don't know."

"Hey, do better than that, Jack. You don't know? You don't know? Well, I know! I'm leaving!"

Darnell sat up and began fumbling with the ignition switch. Hammond stepped away from the jeep as Darnell gunned the engine and put the jeep in reverse. The car moved back up a few feet, then stopped. Hammond had not moved at all. Darnell gripped the steering wheel with both hands, and moaned through clenched teeth. He slapped the wheel with his palms, cursing between slaps. Then he missed the wheel and struck the base of the steering column. The turn signal flashed on, and the yellow light buzzed against Hammond in regular intervals, deepening the shadows of his cheeks and pasting a waxy glow on his nose and chin. Hammond's face looked like a skull with a wire mustache. But in this angle of light, Darnell could see his eyes.

Darnell muttered a string of oaths, then said, "OK, Jack, five minutes. I'll stay with you for five more minutes. But no more, no more." He put the jeep into neutral and let it coast to within a foot of its former position. Slapping the flat of his hand against the leather seat, he began to whistle through the space between his upper front teeth. To Hammond, the slap of flesh against leather seemed to fill the valley with sound. He leaned against the jeep's fender, and reached for another cigar, but thought better of it. He'd learned to regret all those half-finished cigars he'd discarded. So he lit a cigarette instead, attempting to relax by inhaling and holding his breath twice the length of each puff. He had never been able to relax in the city, even Darnell could not help him do that, but here in the shadow of mountains flung like an old necklace across the flatlands, he was at home. Here, he was a part of the land, a part of whatever he had been before the Army and regular paychecks from fishing the Bering Strait. The rain was getting closer, and streaks of lightning touched tip to tail in their impatience to reach the mountains. Hammond narrowed his eyes, squinting into the smoke of his cigarette as if he were an eagle tracking his quarry through a haze of lazy circles. Darnell saw him clenching his jaw muscles.

"Hammond, it ain't gonna be no easier later, so relax."

Hammond wheeled around and leaned his palms flat against the hood. "Do you remember everything your aunt told you, Darnell?"

"She ain't really my aunt, man. She's my cousin. On my mother's side, if Ma would stay home long enough to have cousins."

"OK. But all I have to do is repeat the stuff on that paper, right? You remember your part?"

"Yeah, Hammond, I remember. But I'm not sure it'll work. I've never really tried it myself. That's my cousin Maresa's bag, and she got it from Ma, who got it by way of Greatgranny on the Islands. That stuff's been watered down six times fore I hear it."

"Just tell me again what they said, man."

"Them old women say a lot, Jack. I heard it from day one. They say: Sprinkle powder and scrub your steps white every morning." When Hammond sucked his teeth impatiently, Darnell added, "Let me see..." Then his voice grew high-pitched as he imitated his relatives. "Boy, you liable to get your wish if you member how to say my name. Speak it three times fore you turn, but don't you go raisin no umbrellas in thees house," Darnell laughed.

"OK, OK, but you know what the stuff's supposed to do?"

"Whatever it does, Hammond, it ain't gonna bring back that kid."

"Look, I didn't mean to leave him out there. I knew he was young, but he begged me to let him go along when we went to town. It was raining, man. Like tonight. The air was thick, heavy. I couldn't keep my eyes open. I loved him, Darnell, loved that stupid kid. He followed me around all the time, but I loved him, man. We got lost. Lost! It was cold and dark, and I was floating ten feet off the ground. Then, I heard the wolves, heard them as plain as my grandmother said she'd heard them when they was really out here on the mesa. When my folks come back from picking peas up by the Canadian border, and the valley would be waiting for them. The wolves calling them. I closed those wolves up in my sleep, man. Forgot that kid. He probably watched me for a while before he fell asleep. His big hero come back from the war, sleeping, snoring. I should've built a fire. A Boy Scout knows how to build a fire."

"The kid was Indian. How come he couldn't build a fire?"

"He was a kid, man. He was raised on gas stoves and heaters just like the rest of us. I should've tried to find the road again, but I dreamed wolves and slept. He was so stiff when I woke up. I wanted to give him my blood, make him warm again, but I was scared. So I ran, left him here, sprawled out like some city kid sleeping by the garbage cans. We got lost, that's all."

"Hammond, you was high, not lost."

"Bad luck! And that's what I've had ever since Nam. First the job, then the fight, then prison. Shit."

"Hey, man. I told you. We was all shit-out-of-luck the minute we went to Nam. Then came home and no jobs. But you killed a white boy. Don't never kill no honky, Jack. Stupid, walking into that bar, picking a fight with the first redneck you saw. Just stupid. It's all right to kill an Indian, even a young one. You can kill a Brother, or a Mex. But never, never kill a honky. Kill a honky and you go to jail. Do not pass Go, do not collect—"

"I didn't think I could make it, Darnell. Thought I'd go crazy cooped up in there. It was worse than when the V.C. got us in Nam."

"Yeah, tell me about it, like I don't know. But jail ain't Nam and the Army. Uniform's all different," he laughed dryly. "Jail's simple, Jack. You kill and you do your time."

"He was drunk."

"YOU wasn't white. Why you think the slammer's filled with folks like us? Half them cells chock-full of Brothers doing time."

"Then I kept seeing that kid's face the whole time. In bars, in court, in jail."

"Uh-huhh. Never could talk to you when you start seeing things. I member when you started that shit in-country. Even scared the V.C. Damn, I hope . . ."

Before Darnell could finish, Hammond banged his fist against the hood of the jeep. Darnell watched him walk in circles between the jeep and the edge of the mesa. His steps were careful and fluid, but his hands were jammed into his pockets and his shoulders hunched up. The rain was closer. Lightning fell short of the mountains. He nodded his head each time a bolt hissed toward the ground. "ZAP!" he muttered to himself. "Sho glad the cops ain't got that kinda firepower. We'd all be dead, Jack." The signal towers kept a steady beat of red light pulsing against the flashes of lightning. Darnell muttered to himself, discussing nothing in particular. Then he was silent, grunting only now and then when a large streak of lightning popped across the ridge.

Hammond intently followed his own circles, toeing in as he navigated the curves. Then he also stopped and watched the ridge. "You know, I never imagined I'd know fear out here before that night with the kid. But I feel it now, man. Strong as I felt it then. I don't think it ever left me since that time."

"Look, you killed that honky fair and square, but that Indian, that kid, he just died. You got high on some shit and the kid died. Whatever you afraid of is in your mind. What you need to be afraid of is the Man. After you kill one of them, they *all* come after you."

"Darnell, the kid was there this morning, man. When I went after that deer, I could see him, his face, not the deer, his face dead center in my sights. I knew I had to come back. The stargazer, he was right.

"OK, Hammond, you saw him. His face, OK? And our ass if we don't get out of this state. Three more years, they'll add on. We cruising low, Jack. Like the song says: *We're running on empty. Parking on overtime.* We gotta move, man. Big idea you had: Head for the border—they won't find us—live off the land. What happened to all that, Jack? Now you got me calling my cousin Maresa in the dead of night, and them folks back home see more spirits than you do. I tried to leave all that spirit shit back there. I felt stupid asking her them questions, Jack. You know how crazy my folks act. Put me in a trick bag, man."

"Lay off, Darnell. We wouldn't be running away from three years if you didn't want to whup every honky you saw."

"I'm just trying to catch up with you, Jack. Add some more notches to my belt. Besides, we wouldn't be *here* if you didn't see dead Indians around every corner."

Hammond opened his mouth to answer, then stopped as he heard a sharp noise. Darnell reached for the dashboard, but never made it. A flash of pain whipped through his left shoulder, traced the ridge of his spine, and left him buzzing in a wake of shock. As he tumbled out of the jeep, his knee banged against the door. He almost regained his balance, but his hold on the hair and wrist of whoever was lifting him could not stop his fall. His chin took the brunt of the landing. He tried again to regain his balance, and was up on one knee when his head felt as if it had exploded. He bit his tongue, and blood filled his mouth. Then he felt nothing until he regained consciousness.

Somewhere in his dreams, he was seventeen again and tumbling from a V.C.'s tiger cage through the flat blue plate of an in-country sky lying across a shelf of hills where rice brown grass grew thick as mud. Clumps of bushes, clothed in orange spangles, waited like dancers at the rim of the valley floor. Darnell knew all the names without knowing what it was he knew: Eunice, Muong May, Paradox, Dong Hoi, Valencia, Thai Binh—all strung together and dancing on the mesa. And him with his father, pleated sleeves rippling like prairie grass, drumming the earth into movement. But the place remained flat, dry, sandy, even with a river runnning across instead of through it as all rivers must. A true paradox where the wind rose, and wove light into a tapestry of red wings, blue doves, and soft echoes, a Bell-jet's blades whizzing above him. He heard his father's steel drums and wept, his tears salty and thick.

And then Darnell awoke. He opened his eyes to ants scurrying around a clump of dirt in front of him. The first drops of rain had begun to fall. They plopped softly to the ground, sending little puffs of dust into his face. It took him a few minutes to remember how his mouth was supposed to feel. His head ached and his throat was raw from breathing. He gave his heartbeat a few seconds to fix onto a settled rhythm. Then he lifted himself on one elbow. Squatting a few feet away was the biggest dude he'd seen outside of prison. He remembered Hammond's description of Eddie Longman, and grunted. His ankles and feet were propped against the side of the jeep, so he eased his shoulders forward, turning his hips so that his legs would fall to the ground. Eddie walked toward him. For one awful moment, Darnell was certain he was going to die. He repeated the chant he'd used in Vietnam: "Baron Samade, find youself another boy." Eddie stopped a few feet from his head, and Darnell grunted as the moment of panic passed.

A white hot boom of thunder, followed a finger of lightning down the valley and startled both men. Then, Eddie extended a hand and Darnell pulled, letting himself be raised to a standing position without resisting. The rain was gradually increasing, and he swallowed the damp air as he tried to clear his head. He stood, hunched forward, his shoulders tucked around his neck. Even using the jeep as extra balance, he swayed like a bowling pin before gravity decided it should fall. The mountains seemed to be ten miles away, a foot above the horizon and papery, but his vision was clear now. Once again, he saw the three signal towers with their synchronized lights.

Darnell hoped he would be able to leave the mesa with the same number of ribs he'd had on the way in, but the pain made it impossible to determine the damage to any particular part of his body. His knees folded suddenly and he slid to the ground. When Eddie helped him up again, Darnell smiled weakly, letting his swollen tongue rest between his open teeth. He tried spitting to clear his throat, but the pain forced him to swallow. He looked at Eddie's hands. They certainly weren't the hands of a dead man. Either those Filipinos had deliberately lied, or they'd been too scared to tell the truth. Darnell figured Eddie could land a punch that would break a man's skull. His own thick hair had helped cushion the blow he'd received.

Aloud, he said, "You Eddie Longman?"

"Yeah."

"Where's Hammond?" Darnell grimaced as the pain peaked again.

"Gone," Eddie grunted.

"Gone where?" Eddie stared at him. *"A man of few words,"* Darnell thought. "Gone where?" Darnell asked again.

"Don't matter."

"The hell it don't." Darnell began to cough. Each hacking discharge split the back of his head and his eyes let him see a black sky full of red stars. The coughing stopped and the stars disappeared from the sky exploding in his head. After he wiped the blood and spit from his beard, he leaned into the jeep and took his hat from the floor. As his hand left the floor, he dropped the hat under the dash—then in one move, brought out both the hat and the snub-nose.

"OK, let's go find Hammond," Darnell said, hefting the comfortable weight of the gun in his hand.

Eddie shrugged, and without looking back at Darnell, headed for a clump of trees on the other side of the dirt road behind the jeep. As they stumbled through the brush, the place began to smell moldy like in-country, and Darnell's head really began to ache. Fifty yards away from the jeep, he pulled a vial from his pocket and yanked out the cork with his teeth. He sprinkled a little of the vial's contents on the ground, hoping both his head and the vial would hold out until he reached Hammond. Eddie never looked around to see if Darnell was still following him. After another hundred yards, they reached an open area.

Hammond was kneeling in front of two other men, one an older man with a full head of long gray hair. Darnell flashed on Thai Binh interrogations, and blinked to clear the vision as Eddie walked over and stood behind the men, both of whom were wearing suits–pin-stripes, if Darnell could believe what he saw. "Be damned. Uptown stargazers," he muttered. He could hear the old man saying, "If I had wanted to answer you . . .," but neither of the men had looked up when he and Eddie entered the clearing.

It was good that they had not looked at him. If they had, they would have seen he was having trouble concentrating on those last few steps that would bring him closer to Hammond. Darnell pocketed the gun, and found the matches in his left breast pocket. Then he unwound the thick string twisted around the neck of the vial until the string hung free. As he lit the match, he hoped he had released at least an inch of free string. The flame caught with a sputter of blue and red fizz. Darnell dropped the vial, and the sputter licked up the length of string, turning it black. The vial exploded when it touched the ground, a bright flash of yellow igniting another clump of powder before fizzing backward toward yet another. Darnell lost control over his pain before the third clump added more yellow and smoke to the clearing.

When he awoke the second time, the mountains were partially

hidden behind a curtain of rain, and Hammond was swinging the jeep toward the road. Darnell finally managed to separate the dull roar in his head into three distinct sounds: his pain, the loudest, closely followed by the jeep's motor, and thunder rolling down the valley.

"I didn't do it right, Jack. I tried."

Hammond laughed. "It worked, man. It worked! I remembered the whole thing, everything your cousin said to do. Soon as the powder went off, I started chanting. The old man, the stargazer, he believed it, man. He just walked away. Teke's spirit is released!"

"Aw, shit, Hammond. That's a bunch of crock. Cousin Maresa just cooked up that stuff to make me feel better cause my mama run off again and nobody can find her. She just told me something so I wouldn't keep calling home and bugging her. I should never have said nothing to you, Jack. You can't believe in that spirit shit. Teke, Samade . . . Man, it was a bunch of firecrackers, that's all. Ain't nothing magic. They just gave up. Like you said: just walked away."

"It worked, man. I tell you, it worked. The kid's gone. Resting at last."

Darnell muttered, "Hi-Ho Silver. Can we shoot somebody else now?" He told himself to give up. What Hammond wanted to believe was what he would believe.

"It's cool, man. We did it. You shoulda seen it."

"Yeah, I shoulda. But I was sleeping at the time, remember?"

"That stuff went off . . . *Pow! Pow!* The old man's eyes got big. He left when I got to the end. The others too. And they looked scared."

Hammond stopped just as he completed turning the jeep toward the road. He grinned at Darnell, then threw his arms in the air and yelled, "I'm free! I'm free!" The rain hit his face.

Darnell muttered, "You ain't free till the Man says it's over, Jack. And even then, you ain't never free. Member when the V.C. let us go? The Man's got a price on your head. Slave tax. You ain't free, you can't win, and you can't even buy out of the game."

Hammond laughed and shoved the jeep into gear. The exhaust coughed and the jeep shot forward, carrying them away from the mesa—one man drunk with power, the other sober on his own sour and cynical air. Darnell turned to take one more look at the mountains. The signal lights seemed to swing in tired, sad circles, like an old movie where the film breaks and the light moves real slow. When he looked at the horizon, he saw a star winking in the first rays of the sun. Darnell touched the earring in his left ear for luck, then pulled the wide-brimmed hat down over his forehead, and pretended to sleep.

All This Wall and I Can't Read

THE CARS HAD BEGUN ARRIVING at three in the morning before there was any hint of light in the sky, their owners hoping to make it to the gas pumps before the hoses dribbled that last bit of petrol for the day. On the wall beneath the logo of the oil company, someone had scrawled: REVOLT AGAINST THE REVOLTING, and beside it, tagged by the artist's signature of three wavy lines, the graffiti had been molded into a life-sized clay figure of a girl, stuck half-in and half-out of the wall as if she were trying to pull free of it. Occupants of the cars only glanced at the graffiti. They were about the business of getting gas, petrol, the stuff of combustion engines. By presidential mandate: All refuel stops were moved outside the city's perimeter. The ghosts of Petrol Kings and OPEC denizens strutted the edges of those supply-and-demand lines of cars, those silent vigils rutted in place like the Old West wagon trains of more than a century ago. But this waiting involved neighbors who had not spoken to each other in ten or twenty years, neighbors who would have avoided each other ordinarily and, as in the case of Eric Van Ayns and Arjula Whitcomb, held no hope of changing their behavior in the foreseeable future.

Once a week, Eric and his wife checked their children's rooms, set the home service system computer for No Entry, and drove to the pump lines. A two car family, they arrived in tandem: Eric in front in the Solenoid System 500, and Arjula following in the Lakrits Thermodynamic 606. Once in line, they used the first few moments of being alone to reacquaint themselves with silence, a luxury they so rarely enjoyed in a world of constant noises from hovercraft, entertainment modules, aromatic discs, and electronic gadgetry. In the parallel lanes of the service station's waiting lines, they could tune out the quiet hum of air filter systems, and imagine the virtual soundlessness of natural order—a breeze gently rustling a spring blossom, a dog barking somewhere in the distance, a child singing a wordless tune. Periodically, that silence was shattered by the arrival of another car. Then they would rouse themselves back to the world at hand, back to the sad caravan thrown into intimate proximity by a common need: gas-gas-gas.

Those needing gas came in vehicles of all sorts: steel-bolted collector's items, vintage twentieth-century, or the newer laser-plated fiberglass bodies set with on-board computers, the six cylinders or eight cylinders, the oxygen fed, the fuel injected, and the last of the production-line models, with or without solenoids and conventional converters—and all dependent on gas-gas-gas. Those who watched the sky for the first hint of dawn, caught sight of the blue-red streak of booster flares from space probes leaving the planet from the launching station forty miles down the coast. Only a few of those viewers questioned the economy of how much fuel was needed on and around the launch pad, and of those, fewer still accepted the notion that they were not among those included in the government's selection of private citizens paid to venture into space. They simply took their places in line and waited.

They came alone, or with lovers, children, or mates. With coffee and its substitutes, the juices of fruit, fermented or not. They slept, they played, they bitched, they read. And all of them—the watchers, the sleepers, the readers—waited through those eternally long hours of predawn for the lights to blink on in the station owner's hut. Despite the convenience of their on-board computers, fax teleprompts, and modular libraries, waiting in line was a tedious chore. They looked down the hoods of piston-driven vehicles and watched the sky for signs of light. But the only lights were rocket-booster afterglows, or ground lights, like the amber nightlamps of the service station, the pale glow of a car's dash panel, or the thimble screens on lap-top computers lit up by a few who wanted an early start on the next day's work schedule. The early risers, like Arjula Whitcomb Van Ayns, divided their time between the boredom of waiting, and working. Arjula set about the business of reviewing the case history of a clinic patient scheduled for a settlement hearing later that day.

The medical jargon she read on her computer screen might have confirmed the thoughts of those suspicious enough to question the government's wisdom in handling the country's present state of unrest.

MARION X: CASE #77154 CLEARWATER ECO-BALANCE PROJECT: Optic damage, extensive membranous occlusion,

> muscular atrophy. DDI Rx: chemical exchange, corneal implant, micronic optic fusion. Initial contact: four days after reduction of traumatic insult. Patient narconic, hypoglycemic, sometimes hostile . . .

Arjula told the computer to stop. The screen buzzed in readiness for her next entry. *"What to write,"* she thought. Certainly not a random search of Marion's stream of consciousness. As if picking up Arjula's brain patterns, the screen clicked once, and asked if she wished to continue. That was the same question Arjula had asked of Marion six months before, when the girl told her she wanted to be called Willow.

> They call me Willow cause I'm stringy looking, cause I slip through the cracks and over the walls before the Eaters reach my section. But it don't matter. What you see inside your head belongs to nobody but you. You don't have to share. Inside your head tiny ribbons, light, all different shaded colors. Everybody breathing. You bend, stretch, make patterns. Things you see. Places you want to go. They ain't real. The places, I mean. Just maybe you've been near some place that looks almost the same. They tell us: Watch the lights. Watch the lights. But when the lights just blow up and stink, you got no place else to go. That's when . . . [pause] . . . what you really see and what you try to see don't make sense. Somewhere, a mass of light, ugly swirling nothing that was . . . [pause] Can't remember. I saw . . . [pause] Can't remember. And the pictures begin to pull shapes, you know . . . lines, angles, and stuff. Makes you scream words . . .

Arjula read it quickly, without giving the contents much thought, without correction. *"It's the training,"* she told herself. *"Don't think about the person. Think about the organism, as a life form."* As the screen blinked from page to page, Arjula was drawn farther into her office at the clinic, its only light source a glass wall separating the clinic from the atrium, the artificial forest put there to remind the clinic staff that by presidential mandate: All personnel will concentrate on every available means of rejuvenating the planet's natural resources. But the ozone rift in stratospheric layers widened, and the research was a race with time. Arjula's unit was one of three hundred global teams studying the issue, the patients she saw, a mere handful of the thousands drafted into the ecological projects. Her problem was seeing them simply as numbers, and when they became real, like Marion X, her problems increased.

Arjula was still with Marion or Willow or whatever the girl called herself, when suddenly there was the sound of sharp tapping, a clicking like Willow's fingernails impatiently striking the sides of a water glass, or the neurotic pecking of snipes and sandpipers against the atrium's glass dome. But it was only Eric tapping on the car window. Still Arjula reacted as if she'd stumbled into a restricted zone. The mistake had been in turning on the viewing screen and pulling herself toward the clinic and Willow. *"One more patient to bring home with me,"* Arjula thought as she dimmed the computer light and released the door catch. Eric was in the car, a kiss on her cheek, before the hydraulic wheeze stopped. Although the door had barely opened as he'd entered, threads of thick, moist air wormed their way into the car, and a few wisps of the night fog clung to his sleeve. The on-board sensory monitor signalled the presence of pollutants, and Arjula engaged the cleaning system. A faint scent of pine trees filled the air.

Eric was grinning, but Arjula was thinking of Willow, of the girl's acerbic comment when she'd seen Arjula's desk-sized hologram of Eric and the children. "A white man," she'd said. "Mas'suh, mas'suh, where you been?" the girl had sneered. Then she'd refused to talk to Arjula for almost an hour. Arjula sighed and tilted the computer screen toward the ceiling, but Eric turned it back to viewing position.

He nodded toward the screen. "Which one is that?"

"Marion X," Arjula answered. "Willow."

"Bring up the data on . . ." Eric began, but Arjula interrupted by saying, "Let me pull it off voice command."

She engaged the scanner and watched him read the entry. She supposed she should not have allowed it, but after all, Eric was cleared for security in the underground city and the VTS, so reading a patient's log wasn't a real breach of national defense. Silently, they stared at the screen as the minutes ticked closer to the hour when the station would open its pumps.

There were lineups like this all over the nation. Where once automobiles had been created and nurtured into perfection, now gas hogs were eating their way toward the eternity of junkyards and recycling depots. Their rotting metal corpses were beginning to present a series of new problems in ecological imbalance, and inventors who had had the foresight to consider the economic gains were thinking of ways to turn obsolete ignition devices into profit. That was Eric's job. Just as Arjula reviewed the breakdown in the pyschometry of human organisms, Eric examined alternatives to transportation systems. He could determine probablity quotients for a vehicle's trajectory and the degree of stress on the occupants within seconds of its actual onset, as long as the parameters were not significantly changed. The day before, he had set a two-hundred-thousand-mile trip pattern for five robotic units. Those parameters would remain stable, except for the one unit with a human driver where the variables would be significant.

Eric did not like to think about the variables of human interference. He settled himself in the Lakrits 606, and rubbed the front of his head where the hair plugs, still darker than the rest of his light brown hair, had remained as thick and blunt as the stunted forest growth along the Peninsula Road he and Arjula would take to get to their respective jobs. Eric did not like thinking about his hair, that road and the wall that bordered it.

The wall, a three-mile stretch of supposedly impervious concrete, surrounded his lab and Arjula's clinic. Nearly every morning, he and Arjula saw signs of the graffiti artists who left the wall plastered with life-size silhouettes of human figures, outlines like those of a running man that had appeared on city sidewalks in the 1980s, or further back, the solidified ashes of Hiroshima and Nagasaki victims frozen on the spot. And like those atomic bomb products, these new bits of graffiti ate their way into any material, impervious or not, and stayed there. When the graffiti sculptures began to appear, the authorities had issued a new mandate: Disfigurement of public property will be handled with extreme prejudice. Eric decided reading the computer screen could keep him from thinking about extreme prejudice. He was wrong, of course.

> MX: On break-time, we useta see how high we'd fly on a new cam disc. Me and Neva. We could levitate. It's Robo . . . get it? I made a quantum on one burst. Blew all the spores off the rock face. The sound . . . you can't hear it but it's there. They check us. Four, six, ten centimeter depths. That's all we're allowed, but I did a twenty on one burst. The only colors are floaters, the stuff the Eaters don't get. The Woebegones can't stand it. They got to cover everything, you know. [laughs] The Eaters munch through stuff till it's white like paper. That's why we cut in names and leave them so the Woebegones can't find them. I got my tag. In here I'm Willow. Out there I'm Marion. Three waves. The water sound. That's what the echoscopes pick up. Mar-i-on. Mar-i-on . . . Sounds like mel-a-nin, don't it? Really RAD . . .

"This one's a problem, eh?" Eric nodded toward the screen.

Arjula grunted. "They all are. But yeah . . . this one. I just wish they wouldn't pick them so young. I just wish I could find the jerk who started all that melanin research crap. I don't care if darker skin can handle the light stress, those kids are still in pubescence. Just pubbies, Eric. Babies."

Eric leaned back in the seat and breathed out as if he were pumping weights. "Famein's too young, but Cassie's almost old enough for testing."

"I won't have it," Arjula said. "Not my child."

"Somebody's got to do it."

"Not Cassie."

They fell silent. Eric thought about the last test results he'd pulled off the prompt—the frequency of decreasing human error versus mechanical failure when he used his wife's patient instead of a robot. Arjula set the computer for scroll lock, then leaned back and closed her eyes. Outside the opaque windscreens, dew rolled in like fog, silently threading its way over and around any obstacle, linking man to car, car to pump, pump to ground, like a water spider's trap. Each night, those beads of moisture drifted inland from the reef to coat windshields, clothing, skin, lungs—anything the air touched. Left in the open, unprotected in this night dew, a garment would look moth-eaten within a week, a man critically ill within a month. In those days, sunsets turned russet, a photographer's dream, a medical nightmare. *Life behind the orange curtain,* Arjula thought! By presidential mandate: No cars were allowed within certain parameters of the city. Clean air, they said, and pointed to L.A., New York, Bogota, Mexico City, Paris . . . The list was too long.

Viewed from the outside, the cities were bathed in the auburn afterglow of pollutants, and acted as backdrops for passengers aboard the VTS, the silent, core-powered vehicular-transport systems that cut through the muck in temperature-controlled cylinders on silver monorails. Not everyone favored a high-speed ride in those glass coffins, as they were called. Some, like Eric and Arjula Van Ayns, were stuck in lines of cars squirming like corteges into gas stations. Each city had its complement of medical facilities to study the ramifications of problems created by the removal of petrol as the life force of a mobile society. That was Arjula's job—recording the psychometric effects of what was called "a society in transition."

"My mother used to tell me about the days when folks would get out in the street and fight for integration. By the time I was born, they weren't burning black folks or beating them over the head with baseball bats, but they weren't exactly welcoming them either. It was supposed to be the dawning of Aquarius, but most of us lived in ghettos, like the Jews did in Europe."

"That's history," Eric said.

She grunted. "You think so? Mama said whole neighborhoods were turned upside down just because the government passed a law that the schools had to be integrated. Folks acted like they had the right to divide this planet up according to color. Now those same people are asking colored folks to bail all of us out. And not just folks. Kids. Pubescents the same ages as those the law once banned from certain schools. Kids told that working on this damn Project will get them an on-the-job education. Whole neighborhoods turned upside down because the government passed a law about it. One more law. One more neighborhood. History, eh?"

Eric saw how she was trembling and held her hand. "Baby, we do what we can, that's all. We just keep working. We save one, two maybe ... But that's one or two more than yesterday. If we can't change the law, at least we can fuck it up."

"What purpose am I really serving?" Arjula asked. "What good does it do to look at speech patterns when the whole planet's going to hell in a hand-basket? What will hesitations, ellisions, inversions of order tell us if they all point in the same direction, no matter how often we alter the sequence?"

"Stop talking riddles," he sighed. "You sound like those damn reports."

"Eric, it is not a riddle. The answer is right here." She pushed a button and Marion X's face appeared on the screen. The computer scanned the image, reading weight, height, the percentage count of melanin enzymes, the 5+ dopa measurement of tyrosine oxidation, the excess of chromoproteins within the colored prosthetic groups. In other words, the computer saw a pubescent, fifteen-year-old black girl, slightly built, of medium height with dark hair and dark eyes—eyeballs, palms, and nail bases also tinged by an abnormally altered concentration of melanin, a disorder usually found in older patients or those subject to certain phases of melanoma. The computer did not indicate how, in a society so advanced it catered to its young, those characteristics might have been enhanced or altered by the degree and length of contact with job-related toxins. Nor did it note that the cutting line, no matter what name she chose, or how much on-the-job training she received, was that Marion X could not read.

AVA: I want you to answer some questions.
MX: I've got nothing better to do. Right?
AVA: [no response]
MX: You put everybody through this?
AVA: Everybody.

MX: Even Buck?
AVA: Even Buck.
MX: Why? Buck didn't lay no solar whorls. Buck got his legs cut off underneath that mountain. Got run over by a Caterpillar. Wasn't like Neva. She worked next to me on the line. Neva can carve up wall so God wouldn't recognize it. I've seen her outride a cam-flare. Then one caught her. A circumflex. [pause] Sometimes I think about Neva and it feels like I can't breathe. You know? Ohh God, I be hurting . . . [pause] I be . . .
AVA: Why are you talking like that? You don't have to pretend to be uneducated?
MX: [laughs—high pitched, harsh, old] Better pretend something. Why not pretend. Do I look vacuumed? Besides, what's educated? I can decode a micro-pattern faster than anybody out there. And when I tag my name on a wall, it stays. Get it? They gone hafta blast that wall to move my ass. [pause] Besides, you don't hafta read to use no sensory-code printout.
AVA: But think of all that you're missing. All the great books. All the wonderful ideas.
MX: [laughs again] Shit-shit-shit-double-shit . . . [pause—leans forward] Triple-shit—miles and miles and miles of shit . . . and all of it nigger shit—straight out nigger shit . . . [holds up arm] Check the skin, Doc. Like yours. Like mine. Is reading gonna change that? [pause—begins to cry]

"That was all she said?" Eric asked.

"No. She also showed me a keloid and yelled: Damn and double-fuck!"

Eric groaned. "You know how I feel listening to that race shit? You'd think we were in the nineteenth century. Jula, when we were in school, in the eighties, I thought this country would grow up enough to leave that kind of talk behind. I thought maybe for our kids, you know, mixed bloods . . . Damn, I don't even like that term. I was hoping the world would grow past that racist shit—coloured, negro, black, third world, melanin positive—whatever euphemism's in current vogue."

Arjula laughed. "Yeah. Willow has some primo phrases to redline that subject too."

"I don't want to hear them," Eric sighed. "It's too much. I'll download. Makes my head hurt. Makes my heart hurt."

For a moment, Arjula ran her fingers through the thick crop of hair along the side of his head, amazed again at how the pattern of baldness had so selectively chosen the crown as first point of attack. "You know," she said, "it's virtually impossible for man to mechanically duplicate the speed at which impulses travel across the synapses and switches of our nervous system. The only thing we can measure is what comes out of our mouths."

"No shit," Eric grunted. He would have gone on, but Arjula didn't leave him enough time to continue.

She said, "Right. The eye scans and receives more information than the brain can ever hope to sort, classify, and identify. Yet a camera, that inaccurate illusionary device, can fix upon and transmit the visual image of interstellar phenomenon light-years away."

"Do I have to be light-years away to get close to you?" he asked. He stroked the angle of her jaw, the gentle slope near the hairline where her skin darkened—"Just an increase in dopa count," she would say if he let her. But, as it was, she was saying too much. His fingers played against her jawline, passing close enough to create patterns of static electricity as her sideburns rose in reponse to his skin. He loved the feel of her hair, the soft, downy texture of it, a tangled mass floating long on the sides and back of her head, but cut close at the crown, almost as if she were unconsciously duplicating the haircut nature had left him. "Buffle head," he whispered. She ignored him.

"How could we come this far and be reduced to this?" Arjula asked.

"We have seen the future and we are in it," he sneered. "Supply and demand. They want the money. We need the gas."

"No, I don't mean this gas line. Although that does have some connection. I mean, the screen . . ."

"I can solve that problem quick as a button." Eric laughed at his own weak joke.

Once the thimble screen was turned off, the dashboard light was barely bright enough to illuminate the inside of the car, but even in that dim, orangish glow, Eric could see that Arjula was furious with him for turning off the computer.

"Eric, what the fuck are you doing?" she asked.

"Trying to get your attention."

"If I wanted you to *get* my attention, as you put it, I wouldn't be sitting on my butt in this car so early in the morning."

"Ooo, oo, ooo . . . You sound like your mama," Eric laughed. He tried pulling her toward him for a kiss. "And I get along just fine with Miz Bernadette. Bernie, I call her."

Arjula slapped his hands. "I can get down and dirty too," she laughed. "So don't be talking about my mama. You know Bernadette

Whitcomb won't allow any signifying. And just cause you know how it's said, don't mean you know how it's done. If you tried that stuff around her, she'd rap your Dutch butt a good one. You think we forgot . . ."

"Oh-oh . . . I can hear this one coming. One morning in 1619, a Dutch frigate pulled onto the northeast coast . . ." he began.

" . . . with a load of thirty slaves on board," Arjula added.

"Such a piddling lot," he said.

"Saved your butt. You know, *your* mama would have a fit if she knew how far you'd gone from home."

"Hey, I wasn't on that ship. And if one of my ancestors was, it was under protest. Just doing their job . . ."

"I've heard that before."

Eric grinned at her. "Aww, Jula . . . Are you going to be mean to me? When I thought we were getting along so well too," he teased.

Arjula pretended to ignore his flirtation. She knew what was on his mind. Although the waiting line in a gas station was the one chance they had to be alone together without the interference of children, house, or job, she just hadn't quite decided whether or not she was interested. "Careful," she told him. "You're going to work those dimples overtime, Eric Van Ayns."

"It's for a good cause, Jula Van Ayns," he whispered.

"Arjula Whitcomb," she corrected him, but she gave up the pretense of objecting to his embrace—and almost hated herself for it. At the clinic, she was Dr. Arjula L. Whitcomb-Van Ayns. She could check the viscosity of cranial fluids, chromoprotein density, and linkage of synaptic connections. But here, inside the confines of the Lakrits 606, she could not resist her husband's chauvinism, the biological urge that possessed him when he decided she was indeed "his woman." As he lowered the seats, Arjula allowed herself to go soft, an attitude she did not dare assume at the clinic. In the politics of her profession, there was no room for sexuality. The idea of gender had taken on almost homophobic proportions. Bodies were scanned but they were not loved. Bodies were cured but they were not caressed. At home, it was sometimes all too easy to fall back on sex, to leave the clinic behind her, and engage in an act so simple, so absolutely self-indulgent and satisfying that, for the moment, all that business about the Project's experiments was reduced to trivia.

Arjula pushed the button to slide the tinted daylight shields over the windows, not caring that, like the car she'd spotted three lanes away, the slight movement of the Lakrits' chassis might draw attention to their lovemaking. Before the shield clicked into place, she caught a glimpse of the jet trail of an westbound intercontinental flight, then the sky, with its mottled stratus, disappeared from view. For the moment, she could forget about the mess of society, Marion X, and workers pulled off the construction site on Clearwater Mountain. Whatever she needed to do or say about Willow was stored. At that point, she and Eric became just another couple taking advantage of a bit of privacy while they waited in a lineup of cars. Eric wasn't going anywhere, and for the moment, neither was she.

She kissed the fringe of hair where his implants were taking hold, the lean bridge of his nose, his dimples, and the sweep of heavy lashes covering his gray eyes. And as they struggled to find a comfortable position, as she inhaled the sweet-almond smell of his skin turning warm to her touch, Arjula remembered her mother's stories of the 1950s when there were lovers' lanes, and enough gas to drive lovers to those deserted spots along a country road, or high on a bluff with a view and the night sky full of stars. Recalling the murky sky above the Lakrits' plexiglass roof, Arjula told herself, *"We've got no lane and a lousy view. But if I can believe Momma this car's no better than what they had back then."* She and Eric struggled with arms and legs that persisted in scraping against every button and knob inside the cramped space of the car. Once the front seats were lowered, they'd had to squeeze themselves between the dash panel and back seats in order to stretch out full length. Even so, Eric's legs were a bit too long, and Arjula's head ended up stuffed against the cushion rest in a rear corner of the car. But in that position, the plexiglass curve in the roof offered her a reflection of the two of them. One glance, and she was laughing before she could stop it. From that angle, they looked like a pile of laundry, or extra arms and legs worming free of some robotics experiment. From that angle, they looked like anything but lovers.

Eric fell back against the seat. "Don't mind me," he said. "Just keep on telling those jokes."

Arjula closed her eyes against the vision of arms and legs wriggling in every direction. "It's not you," she told him. "I'm not laughing now, am I?" She kicked off her shoes and pulled herself on top of him. With her bare foot, she managed to open the glove box, and using that as a shelf, she balanced one leg on the dash, the other in the glove box. "Am I laughing now?" she repeated.

Eric said, "Un-un," but he winked as she leaned over and kissed him.

Only later, after Eric fell asleep could she detach herself from what her body demanded. Only after she lay spent under the car's plexiglass roof, did she remember what Willow had said to her.

> If you like men, why you got to pick some Woebegone gray boy? All they gone do is moan about the "good old days"

> and what they lost. They lost it, not us. Messed it up. There some fine brown ones out there, Miz Doctor-sister. Don't be falling for the Prez's talk about future eugenics. They still cutting along the same lines, know what I mean? White/black, that's the u-genes. Better switch on your command mode. Jack up that computer on TAK merge. You can place with a Brother.

Throughout her third visit, Willow had stared at the hologram on Arjula's desk. After the first time Arjula had seen the girl, she'd debated leaving the holo on her desk, but she could find no real reason to remove it. *"I'm only going to rearrange my life so much,"* she'd told herself. *"They can take the roof off this clinic and let the UVs blast everyone in it for all I care."* So she'd buzzed Willow into her office, and immediately, the girl had aimed her comments to the hologram.

> Now, I ain't gonna say a Woebegone's gotta be white. They come in all colors. [pause] But I guess you know that. [grins] You know what they do to us? You know how they come after us? So why you got to go to bed with one of 'em? You want to see my scars? I got keloids in places you ain't looked for yet. Even with a scanner. I passed the quotient high. Soon as they give me that test, I was outta there. Up on that mountain. They came for me early in the morning. Got me fore I could think about what was going down. Got me one morning when I was thinking bout going back to school. Now ain't that a reverb? No shit, I was really thinking bout school. Gave me a choice. Said I couldn't get no allotment less I was working the mountain. I outran 'em for two months, you know. They got my sister, Dru. And my brother, Todi. Both dead now. Soon as I turned fifteen, they was out there waiting for me.
>
> AVA: How old are you now? The Project doesn't take anyone who's under fifteen.
>
> MX: Yeah. Well, I'm fifteen and a half. Well, maybe three quarters. You forget time up there you know. You ever been on the mountain? Hey, up there, you hallucinate. That mountain's a pseudo-mother. Fie, fie, twe, twe, twe, the giant screams and up we ride . . . the rim of the world, Ma. [pause] You see everything from up there. Like a negative print. [pause—voice monitor records shift to AVA's range and modulation] You know, a camera can record in one-

eighteenth of a second what the human eye records in less than one-thirteenth of a second? [laughs—returns to normal tonal range] Cept we don't forget. Not up there. Totally Rad, huh?

Arjula was astonished at how quickly the girl's attitude could change. And not just her attitude, her whole mental picture, voice range, posture. The cranial function graph zigzagged throughout each interview, and Arjula couldn't decide if the girl had learned various patterns of malingering, or if she really was suffering from what seemed to be infecting the other Clearwater workers: melanoblasts accompanied by lapses in memory, the internal changes that left patients drug-dependent and unpredictable. She knew Willow's eyes glowed with that translucent patina artifical lenses assumed when they have been exposed to too much sun. Overexposure. That password was played across the research teams' microcorders like a euphemism for error. According to the chief of staff, the hospital unit had done sixteen corneal implants in a single afternoon. Eric had lens implants. And so did their daughter, Cassie. But Arjula had decided not to mention the Clearwater eye problems to Eric. He was touchy enough about his hair transplants. Why bring up the visual ones? Besides, his implants had nothing to do with the effects of UV flash on Clearwater patients, and if she had anything to say about it, neither would Cassie's. Fifteen. Babies.

Eric sat up and looked at her, his smile as smug as a cat's purring. "Hey, sweetie," he whispered. "Come back to me. Now, if I didn't know better, I'd say you were distracted."

"Pleased with ourselves, are we?" she laughed. She kissed the tip of his nose. If her profile was cut from the same mold as the Kishi statues of West Africa, as Eric was always telling her, then his was cast from a Roman coin. "Just because I've closed my eyes, doesn't mean I've left," she said. "As Willow would put it: Do I look vacuumed?"

"You may not look that way, but I sure feel that way," Eric grinned.

She gave him a playful push. "You know she means lobotomized . . . but in your case, I guess sex does leave you a little stupid."

Eric grunted, and stretched as much as the car would allow him. Arjula finished rearranging her clothes before clicking the computer onto the weather channel. The screen showed a satellite recording of a storm front buildup. From a distance, the night mist took on a life of its own. Billows of wet air roiled inside the neap and ebb of winds blowing off the Strait of Juan de Fuca where the Kuroshio Current, north of the coast, gave way to the Pacific Drift. There, several storm systems already raged out of control. With weather like this, the clinic was likely to be deluged with injured workers pushed beyond capacity. Arjula knew the Clearwater Project was fighting against a deadline set for them by ecological mismanagement of more than fifty years ago, but correcting the problem by wasting human resources was more than she could understand.

Arjula said, "You remember that kid they brought in about the same time Willow arrived? Buck, that double amputee?" Eric grunted sleepily. "Well, he's got the whole staff in an uproar. They put him in a hospice . . . community service, except there is no community to service anywhere near the clinic."

"Beats the ward," Eric said.

"True. And that kid's beating the odds. He's rigged a contraption on his bed so he can screw the brains out of any woman dumb enough to fall into the sack with him. He just swings by his hands and rams it in. They ought to call him Bull."

Eric laughed. "Good for him. I'm glad to see a man with ingenuity. Maybe I should look him up."

"Funny . . ." She shoved him, but she was still smiling. "You know, Buck wouldn't have to do that if they hadn't put him on the Clearwater in the first place. And now, Willow's all bent because two of her buddies are sniffing behind his tail."

Eric laughed again. "Without legs, tail's about all he's got."

"Now that's not funny, Eric. And with Willow, it's irrelevant. She's interested in the girls. A few weeks ago, I saw one of those girls loping across the compound with that kid tucked under her arm like a football. It was Neva. Being blind doesn't stop her one bit. Damn, they get strong up on that mountain."

Eric fell asleep chuckling over the image of a legless man tucked under the arm of a modern Amazon. He thought he'd said: "I'd sure like to see that," but what Arjula heard was a series of moans and snorts that signalled his sleep state. As she watched his eyelids pulse with REMs, she called up the records on her latest conference with the supervising physician and the rehab team.

> AVA: I can't see why we won't fund outpatient care for Marion X. She's recovered enough to function independently, and as long as she stays on her treatment schedule . . .
> RS: As Chief Medical Officer, I can not condone a program of that sort. She hasn't stablized on any of the tests and she is likely to cause trouble in the hospice . . .
> KLM: It can't be any more trouble than I already have. Last week I had four patients in the city on a trial visit. I had to bail three of them out.

BZ: Well, any shop keeper who would extend credit to a man with half his skull missing, and a man with no legs carried by a girl with pupils the size of melons, deserves whatever they can cheat him out of. They bought wedding rings, for Chris'sake! Three sets!
AVA: Marion X hasn't been involved in any of that. What's the problem here?
RS: The problem is the company she's been keeping these past few months. They renounce race, and worse yet, gender. Some have applied for genetic alterations. And those three, those . . . patients in the hospice, they all want to get married to each other. Three of them!
BZ: [laughs] For the sanctity of the state, they said. No doubt we'll pay for that, too.
AVA: I see. So we keep her confined until they are released. Great. Now we're a prison facility.
KLM: At least we keep her confined until Buck learns to hang onto his prosthetic device.
BZ: Yeah, those legs cost a mint. As much as a gallon of ground-crew fuel. But since the damn legs are polymar, it's all fuel anyway. We infect 'em, fix 'em, and kill 'em with the same stuff. Petroleum products. Economic, huh? [laughs]
AVA: Has it occurred to you that Buck gets more mileage out of being a double amputee than he would out of having a set of plastic legs? I don't care what color you paint them, they're still phony. Almost as phony as we are.
RS: Dr. Van Ayns, don't you think that's a bit harsh? We all just do our jobs as best we can.
@$$$ End Program: X-98-4-30 Clrwtr Unit @$$$

Inside the Lakrits 606, Arjula said to herself: *"Just doing our jobs."* She sighed and looked at her husband sleeping beside her. Then she lowered the daylight shields, and checked the horizon where trails of various air transports crisscrossed the sky like varicose veins.

Another mandate: Decrease daylight air travel to allow biotech organisms an unobstructed opportunity to regenerate ozone and increase the oxygen supply. Problem: Now the night sky was totally obstructed.

"Who needs a night sky anyway?" Arjula thought as she looked down the line of cars. *"Not a creature was stirring, not even a mouse,"* she added. Cars filled all of the service station's lanes, even those paths that edged the transportation roadway connecting suburb to suburb. The cars on the periphery were no doubt pirates, drivers who had exhausted their

rations in neighborhood stations and were forced to invade outlying areas. On the other side of the eastbound transportation tunnel, Arjula heard the high whine of a graffiti eater cleaning the wall of a week's worth of protests.

She and Eric saw the graffiti on their way to work, the bright flashes of paint applied, God knows how, on the hairpin curve of an inside wall, or midway an overpass girding six lanes of fast-moving traffic. Or worse, those lumps of clay sculpted into life-sized figures, weapons, flowers, whatever the sculptor thought worthy of attaching to a wall. Those could overwhelm any inscription tag—be it some artist's name, or a symbol as geometric as Marion's water sign. Usually Arjula hated lonely bits of graffiti, but some, she relished seeing. Before the graffiti eaters destroyed it, she'd almost grown accustomed to VOID SPACE in six-foot letters that consumed the entire Petra Tunnel. Her favorites were the messages that invoked responses. Those made her believe in the need for people to talk to people. Those were the ones she remembered, like the prophecies painted on the walls of the legislative buildings: IT AIN'T WORTH A DIME IF YOU AIN'T GOT THE TIME, to which someone had responded, I GOT THE TIME AND IT AIN'T WORTH DUCK SHIT, or MOVE BACK YOU'RE CROWDING ME. SIGNED: THE WALL, and below it, BLOW IT OUT YOUR BRICKS I DON'T MOVE TILL YOU FALL. And the most popular one of the year, the one that was making frequent appearances on the Peninsula Road near the Clearwater Project sites: THE PRESIDENT EATS COSMIC SOUP, to which someone had added, WHEN HE CAN FIND A NUCLEAR SPOON. Arjula would have liked to believe that bit of paint had been applied by a colleague, but no one she knew had enough guts to do it. Certainly they had quaked like the rest of the populace when they'd spotted the graffiti sculptures. Arjula had to admit the sculptures were scary. Conventional wall scribes amused her, but the sculptors were serious, and the authorities knew it.

It wasn't the birds, flowers, or even the weapons that set the authorities on edge. What raised their hackles were the lifesize replicas of people cast in biodegradable plastics, and treated with acid to speed up a decomposition process that would leave an indelible blueprint of the figure on a wall. The graffiti eaters could not remove the "ghosts" after the originals dissolved. Nothing seemed to be able to move them. She looked into the Lakrits' rearview mirror. Already, the clay figure of the screaming girl placed beside REVOLT AGAINST THE REVOLTING was beginning to fade into a chalky silhouette. Only the tag was visible. Arjula shuddered. She had only seen a few of the sculptures before decomposition, but always, the ones she'd seen were recognizable images of teenagers who had died while working on federal Projects, such as Clearwater. And like the sculpture on the service station wall, they had been cast with their mouths open in a perpetual scream. As Willow said, "You don't need to be able to read to get the message." Now, goon squads scoured the city for graffiti sculptors. "We sympathize with the families of those lost in our present efforts to regain ecological balance . . ." the latest address had begun. And the squads had stepped up their patrols.

> MX: When somebody dies, they cut them out of the line. It's the only sound we hear—the screaming. It's contagious. You shriek when the pain hits. It's like you been hit even if its down the line. And the whole lines goes like into orbit. You feel it building . . . Hot/cold. Like lightning. Like a whip crack and it finally snaps right where you are. Your lungs start to rip open and the only thing that keeps you in one piece is the screaming. The Woebegones drop back. They think it's gonna hit them. We chant: "Our safety is slightness, our pride is denial, our victory is ab-so-lute." Neva taught me that. [pause] And all the time, you breathe, try to hold on. [pause] Lord, I ain't had a period in two years. My insides hurt. But the doc up there, he says it's cause we're oversexed. The air is so thin up there, you know. And the light, it's like water. Bleeds all the color out. This stuff grows on your skin. Itches. Burns.
> AVA: Melanophore?
> MX: Yeah, on the palms of your hands, feet. Your tongue. I seen kids blast it off with laser. Takes them right out. Zzz . . . whippp . . . That's when the screaming starts.

Arjula leaned away from the thimble screen and tried to rest her eyes. When she rubbed them, she was surprised to feel moisture. "*Crying, are we?*" she thought. "*How can a good researcher give in to tears? Somebody's got to lay out those solar discs. Somebody's got to plant those trees.*" Still, it was a useless argument to try to equate one human life in the present time with thousands of lives in the future. Especially when only one type of human seemed to be expendable. It was too easy to use black kids from housing units and welfare rolls. And with the research casuality rate, it wouldn't be long before kids outside of public housing areas, pubbies like her children, Cassie and Famein, would be targeted. As always, the argument brought her back to the melanin studies.

> CLINICIAN'S NOTES—FINAL REPORT: Neva Williams
> Returned to Clearwater eight days after release from hospice. All vital signs normal. Corneal and optic nerve patterns

stable. Decrease of melanoblasts. Some fluctuations of EEG stimuli right hemisphere, but below exceptional quotients. Readiness for reclassification: plus.
X-98-5-22 Clrwtr Unit @$$$
ADDENDUM: casuality while entering laccolith chamber below wave-cut platform. Apparent seizure pattern during circumflex operation. Patient would not release laser unit before download. Body not recovered. Terminate File.
X-98-5-24 Clrwtr Unit @$$$

Arjula signalled overwrite and typed in: *Ref. to: Arnold,* and waited for the access modem to load the file. She held her breath. At this point, she was almost willing to give anything to turn away from the screen, to avoid reading the report of another failure. What had Willow said? "When somebody dies, screaming is contagious."

CLINICIAN'S NOTES—FINAL REPORT: Bruce Arnold
Equipped with mobile unit, and reassigned Graffiti Removal/Sanitation eight days after release from hospice. Vital signs within stable range, extremely low dopa count despite high-range melanin traces. Melanoma increasing. Maintain low contact, close supervision. Prognosis uncertain.
X-98-5-22 Clrwtr Unit @$$$
ADDENDUM: suspected of defacing lower wall along Peninsula. Road. Slammed mobile unit into wall, full bore against so-called "sculpture graffiti." Suggested explanation: uncertain prognosis supports initial questions of suitability of this patient for Eco-balance Project. Terminate File.
X-98-5-24 Clrwtr Unit @$$$

There was something all too convenient about research results with equations making black folks the ones genetically more suited for the most dangerous tasks of saving the planet—a few good souls sacrificed for the good of all. Arjula thought: *"Sounds like one of those religious theories where hypocrites divide up heaven by color. The ultimate solution."* She programmed in the research quotient. That's what she always found herself doing when she reached this stage of reviewing a case. Each time, she hoped she'd find a glitch in the formulae.

MX: [tears finally under control] You see that? [points to window: Two mallards are mating as best they can while being harassed by an arctic loon.] That's what you up to. Fucking

with somebody when they minding their own business.
AVA: You don't think this is my business?
MX: Give me one good reason why I should. What the hell was Neva to you?
AVA: I have kids . . . [pause] It's all about saving this planet. Right now, it's the only one we have.
MX: [laughs] Go back to output #1, Miz Doctor-sister. It's all about your kids. Your little pansies. That's why you're here. That's why I'm here. That's why Buck and Neva died. [pause] You got close-circuit to the bedrooms too, Doctor-sister? You watch us at night, then go home and try it with your Woebegone?
AVA: That's not true.
MX: Yeah? Well, tell 'em up on that mountain. They had us on CC morning to night. Always looking for something up under your clothes. Talking bout scraping samples. I gave 'em samples alright. I humped every beaver patch they sent near me. Guess that's why they left me hanging when my cam disc flared. SLAM . . . Stuck me in that crevice like a sliver. I musta been there for hours. If Neva had been there . . . Shit, I'm gonna miss her . . .
AVA: Didn't you scream? With the flare, I mean?
MX: [points to window] Look at those fucking birds. Fighting over the same piece of tail. [leans over desk] What do you think, Miz Doctor-sister? You think I screamed? [pause. Looks at hologram] Mas'suh . . . Mas'suh . . .
AVA: Have you ever had a boyfriend?
MX: [laughs] Doc, what do I need with some boyfriend? I'm looking for the same thing they looking for. A girlfriend. And there ain't been no girls up on that mountain for years. Up there, you don't need to hear no man say: I love you. Up there you know who you are and where you are. [pause] Your daughter got a boyfriend?
AVA: [hesitates] Yes.
MX: Pity. A waste.

Arjula patched in value compatibility, and the screen blinked purple, red, green, until finally, the chemical breakdown of cellular structure appeared: a normal chromoprotein pattern—the cell growth spread evenly over the structure—then the abnormal growth pattern. That stuff churned like Brewer's yeast. She plugged in the tests for Dru, Todi, and Marion X. "Yeast," she muttered as she scanned the first two. She repeated the procedure, over and over, until finally, she flagged a flow break on Marion's graph. "The right quadrant," she mumbled, and magnified that section. At first it was there, then gone. Arjula hoped she wasn't just seeing things. She remembered how her mother had spent one whole summer plaguing the family with talk of a poltergeist. She took a deep breath, and told herself she hadn't turned into her mother either. She hoped it wasn't a ghost dance appearing on the screen, a computer virus like fading graffiti sculptures etched in concrete, like the one of Neva, with its three waves, the water sound echoing Mar-i-on.

In the end, the procedure wasn't as difficult as she'd expected. A little imagination and import of entry level values isolated the Golgi function and accelerated the chromosomal activity. She wondered how she'd ever missed that little blip, that change in parameters she'd always warned Eric to look for. But there it was—a single sickle cell dancing right at the edge of her vision. She moved the image on the screen to fast forward, and it responded as if it were being hit by a strobe light. One by one, she cross-sectioned the tests for melanin count, adding the additional parameter. Now all she needed to do was clean up the files. She began by reconstructing the events. She couldn't reverse the process, but maybe, with isolation, she could have Willow declared unfit for the Clearwater. That is, if Willow would agree.

Minutes later, almost sweating, Arjula muttered an oath and slumped back against the seat. The movement woke Eric, and he came to life sneezing. "It's the night air," Arjula told him.

Eric shook his head. "Un-un. It's that fake pine shit. Nuke it. Either we got real trees or nothing."

She turned off the cleaning system. "We're in a good mood, eh?"

Eric grunted. "God, the dreams I had." He took a sip of bottled water and grimaced. "Even this tastes like computer printout. Don't we have anything that's real?"

"Sure." Eric followed the sweep of Arjula's gesture across the windshield.

The sky was shredded by exhaust, but if they looked closely, they could detect the first faint rays of light at the outermost edges. The decrease in air traffic was another sure sign of morning. A few people had ventured out of their cars, and face-masks in place, were walking between the lanes. Somewhere on the line, an entertainment module was tuned so high, it caused Arjula's thimble screen to lose its vertical control. Under that stress, Willow's cellular function graphs began to look like test patterns.

"You've been playing with this all night?" Eric asked. Arjula nodded. "I had dreams about things that moved like that. Ebullient orange and round. Eggs. Except they kept disintegrating."

"You want me to analyze that?"

He laughed, a short blip of a laugh that matched the interference hiccoughs on the computer screen. "Analysis is my job, remember?"

"So what do you think it means?" she asked him.

Eric shrugged. He was watching the computer screen, scrolling now, lifting one eyebrow when the insert line indicated a matrix change. "I don't know what it means. Job-related, I guess. What would it mean if you dream about broken eggs?"

"Depends on whether you're Humpty-Dumpty," Arjula laughed.

"You putting this egg back together?" he asked her. He had run the program back to the beginning of the sequence, and was catching up with the final stages of Arjula's alterations.

Arjula pretended she wasn't watching him. "What do you think the weather's going to do today?"

He examined a cross-section of cellular decomposition and shook his head. "You asking me or telling me?"

"Sure. Modern science can predict weather with the mathematical progression of the Brahma system as well as it can with a vaporization grid. How many times have you been faked out by some erroneous report of fair weather when in fact brume was gathering at the north end of the shore? You understand, of course, that weather is a system of relationships and for most men, that is the determiner of their perceptions of space."

"And if these equations don't work, we can get caught as easily too," Eric said. "Ten years in maximum security." He came to the end of the program and leaned back in the seat. "Shit, Arjula. It seems almost too easy."

"What else am I going to do?"

Eric frowned. "You mean, what are WE going to do? I'm in this too, you know. Do I have to keep saying it?" She smiled. "So, how much time do I have to change the route pattern on this one?" he asked. She remained silent. "Arjula, I'm in systems analyses, not magic. At least let me know how many people I'm moving and when."

"What's a VTS capacity?" she laughed—a little too loudly until he noticed someone walking toward the car. The man tried peering through the windshield. Eric quickly pulled her across the seat and kissed her, maybe a bit longer than he needed in order to create a diversion.

"No matter what those theorists have to say, you are emotionally deprived," she told him when the stranger had passed. But she was laughing when she said it.

"Depraved," he grinned. "Now tell me about this one. I can't figure out the chromoprotein discount. You saying, she's not black enough? Or did you track a new immune deficiency?"

She sobered up. "Nope. If anything, she's got more than enough of her share of melanin. And no sign of ARC. What we've got is one cell gone beserk in a pattern of genetic cells. Somewhere in the last century, we didn't bother to clean up that little hereditary characteristic. She's got sickle cell. She's a carrier. Maybe it's like they say at the clinic: We can use the same thing to cure 'em or kill 'em. This time, I'll be damned if I'm not saving one."

"You always do, don't you?" Eric grinned. "Correction: We do."

"I don't think this time we'll save just one, Eric. Cassie's birthday is less than a month away."

He was silent for a moment, watching the screen take a file-path to a general program of hybrids, natural pollination, and controlled eugenics. The two of them idly scanned the information as the computer ran through the rudimentary functions of genetic research. Arjula thought about the problems. With Willow already half sick, and likely to grow worse, it would take some convincing to get her to travel peacefully with the four of them. She would hate the notion of even being around Eric, his whiteness marking him a Woebegone and not to be trusted. Not that the girl trusted anyone, but trying to keep her in line along with Cassie and Famein was going to be a chore. "A reverb," as Willow would say. And then there was Cassie, full of questions, and eager to get on with life. There was no mistaking the girl as Arjula's daughter, with generous portions of her grandmother, Bernadette Whitcomb, thrown in for good measure.

Eric interrupted her thoughts. "That's it for us, you know. Out of the Project altogether. Why pick this one as the last one? What about all the others?"

"I can't save them all. As it is, we only get one or two out every year, and in a month, Cassie will be fifteen. I can't stop them from testing her."

"They need you at that Project, Jula."

"My child needs me, too."

He nodded and looked up at the sky. "We could move to one of the colonies."

"No. Not me," she told him. "I don't want to be running around in a rubber suit sucking oxygen straws for the rest of my life."

"You know, they do take them off of support systems."

"Yeah. I've been reading Willow's account of that."

"OK. No space, no Clearwater. How's about the Ocean Six Project?"

"They tell me my people followed the North Star off the tip of the Drinking Gourd straight into Canada." She looked up at the sky. In the east, the sun was beginning to filter through the smog layer, and the horizon glowed with the burnished copper light of morning. But the western sky was still muddy and dark, that starless cosmic soup graffiti artists offered the president. "We've got no more gourds to follow through this darkness, Eric. We're fresh out."

He started to respond, then they both fell silent as they heard the muted hum of the hovercraft. The station lights blinked on and flickered a bright sequence of green, yellow, and red. Drivers responded by revving their motors in readiness for a drink of precious gas. Eric turned off the thimble screen, and reached for the door release. "We'll find some place," he told her. "Forget about that Drinking Gourd and the clinic and all that systems crap. I love you, buffle head. We'll find some place." Then he kissed her and left.

"Yes, I know," she told him, but to herself, she said, *"We're no more than lemmings sniffing the air for some traces of the sea."* She listened to the hydraulics wheeze shut. The station lights changed from red to green, and the view screen above the pumps spelled out the amount of petrol available for the morning rush. Eric gunned the Solenoid 500. As he rolled into place behind the first cars, Arjula whispered, "Watch the lights. Watch the lights. They tell you where to go, even if it is misleading." Then she punched the Lakrits into gear.

The Simple Language of Drones

"WHAT A MAN SEES and can't understand will drive him mad," Boucher told the nightwatchman.

"Ain't nothing left to understand, keeper. The very day they started building those drones, they took all the understanding out of everything. I'm just saying, *we* got to survive."

The man paused and glared at Boucher, who was squatting on his haunches about twenty feet in front of the fire. In the light of the fire, Boucher's face mask was more mirror than window, and that same light made the dusky oilskin of his workman's suit seem as dull green as rain-soaked leaves. The nightwatchman narrowed his eyes and tried to gaze beyond the fire's death sweet smoke to the cascade of the Clearwater Mountains on the other side of the valley.

They had been burning bodies for days. The pyres dotted the landscape like bonfires, and the air was fetid with the smell of scorched flesh. Teams of men searched the ruins for the dead. The men on burial detail did not talk much to each other. They had come to know one another only by occupation. No one claimed homes or families. There was no trace of belonging by age or race. Now they were all bound together by one task—collecting the dead. The nightwatchman and the zookeeper stood apart from the others. Only by following the plume of smoke could they even find a hint of the horizon.

"*We* got to live," the nightwatchman added. "And we best keep a close eye on what *they're* doing."

Boucher nodded. The southern edge of the sky was streaked with layers of pink and azure where smoke funnels of several other fires billowed into the air. Boucher stood, then walked up the rise where he could get a clearer view. There wasn't much to see. A moonscape ending in a strip of land that dipped toward the southern boundaries of Kalava Park and beyond it, low-hanging mist that roiled toward the Strait of Juan de Fuca and beyond to the sea. What had not been charred or disintegrated was covered with a fine layer of dust that seemed to obliterate any details.

The crew had started in the southeast end of the city and worked north and west toward the sea. Each day they had stacked sixty to a hundred corpses, torched the pile, and moved to the next quadrant. The area was a natural weather inversion, caught between the Clearwater Mountains to the south, and the wintry brume pulling the land seaward and north. The burn-off had left the area covered in slick gray dust, and the land seemed to be marblelized into layers of chalky rubble where there had been city blocks. Last week, the houses near the park had been clothed in a sense of smugness left from the days when they were part of a nineteenth-century carriage trade neighborhood. Last week, those houses had been another of those political nightmares that had not been solved by moving its occupants into the city built in the bowels of the Clearwater Mountains under an artificial sky. Now, they were just so many upturned stones, abandoned like Roman ruins.

"A week?" Boucher mumbled. "I've been away a week?" He held his hand across his eyes like a cap's visor, and squinted through the dust. Then, so the movement would not be wasted, he lowered his face mask and hawked a wad of spit onto the ground. Somewhere in that movement, Boucher decided he'd tended the fire long enough and that burn site wasn't big enough to need two men. He was already starting to move away when the nightwatchman spoke again.

"That park'll be socked in by morning," the man said. "Looks kinda green from here but most of the trees burnt right down to the nubbin. Besides, ain't no way you can keep them animals from breathing this stuff. All of 'em dead." He wiped his forehead, then rubbed his fingers and watched a haze of fine dust drift away.

Boucher muttered, "Un-un. Not all of 'em. There wasn't much time, but something's bound to be breathing out there." Once again, he squinted toward the horizon that was quiet now but still ominous, and once again, he listened for sounds of animals. Had he failed them?

He had been the only keeper able to handle Lan-ling. It had moved him up in the hierarchy—second in command, the only black trainer in the zoo—and all because of Lan-ling. *"It ain't the first time we been thrown together and called beasts,"* he'd thought the day he'd walked into her cage. Then he'd said her name, softly, "Lan-ling," and wondered why some fool thought it better to give her a Chinese name just because she came from China. At first, the zoo had tried using Chinese keepers too. Then white ones. In the end, only Boucher had been accepted. The irony of black-and-white with black had not escaped him. At the time, he'd looked at Lan-ling and thought, *"I hope it won't come to a choice between me and you cause ain't many folks gonna care bout losing one black zookeeper."*

Now there wasn't anyone left to care or anything left to care about. All of it was gone, the whole area flattened from the desert, east of the Clearwater, to the rain forest ribbed by the sea. Everything wiped out in a firefall of drones. Drones! And no one to stop them.

On the day of the attack, Boucher had managed to open the three interlocking doors to the storage tunnel under the cages after the first shock wave. When he'd returned to the surface, the second series of eruptions had thrown him clear of the entrance and he'd been unable to reach the access corridor between the animal pens. He had tried scrambling to his feet, but the groundswell tossed him backward as easily as it tossed the trees toppling to earth all around him. The third quake rumbled only seconds ahead of the sonic boom, but in that interval, Boucher had heard Lan-ling's bleat of anguish and somewhere near the mouth of the storage tunnel, her mate's answering cry. He had awakened to the stench of death left in the wake of drones. They had swept in from the coast, then—following a circular pattern—had come in wave after wave until the firefall. Boucher had regained consciousness in a first-aid camp in a section of the new city, three miles underground and thirty miles south of Kalava Park—stark, clean, and for Boucher, more frightening than the any of the animal cages at Kalava. Only after he'd joined the aid corps did Boucher know how lucky he had been.

The teams worked methodically, moving across a landscape that finally accepted all of them for what they were—desperately alive and trying to stay that way. The tedious work of burning bodies dismissed all the inventions and equations. In the rubble, all of them—white and nonwhite, national and immigrant, computer banker and transit worker—all of them were lumpy shapes scuttling away from the stench of funeral pyres. Squad leaders moved quickly from one area to the next, marking entries in their microcorder logs as if looking for some exacting formula for life and death: one section of the city times so many residents equals X number of bodies per crew. Fires marked an irregular path behind them, and the men wished they could move even faster. But this section, more densely populated than the outer regions, had been heavily hit and the going was slow.

"How long before we reach the park?" Boucher asked. He couldn't remember the man's name. There had been four or five changes in shifts, men dropping out because they were injured or because they simply had no stomach for the task. This was the watchman's first day on detail. It was easy for Boucher to catalogue a man according to his job—nightwatchman, computer jockey, or like him, zookeeper. But jobs no longer mattered on burn detail. *"We all go when the wagon comes,"* Boucher thought. Except there were no more wagons. Just drones. He looked up at the sky again.

"How many more hours before we reach the park?" he repeated.

The nightwatchman had tilted back his head and was treating his smoke-raw eyes with an ophthalmic. When he handed over the tube, Boucher began to laugh.

"What's your problem, zookeeper?" the man snarled.

"Your face," Boucher chuckled. "I just saw your face."

The watchman snorted and turned his back to Boucher.

"Hey, no offense," Boucher added, "but I just never imagined you with a handlebar mustache." He tried to control his laughter. "I . . . I don't know why that's so funny, nightwatchman, but . . . but damn if you don't look like something out of a history book. Like some damn politician off some old history video. Lordy, Lordy," Boucher sputtered. "I been burning corpses with a senate man!"

The man spit into the dust. "You won't think I'm so blasted funny if I save your butt from whatever's been howling out there." He paused. "Well, what the hell . . . Maybe if I saw your face, I'd have me a laugh too."

"Maybe," Boucher said. "IF you saw it. But right now, all I want to see is that ridge of trees near the park. There's a . . ."

The man interrupted. "Now don't get thin-skinned on me, keeper. You had a good laugh, so fair's fair."

"FAIR! What's fair out here? A thirty-percent kill? That's what the chairman said. Thirty percent. Is that fair? Maybe they don't pull your number. Maybe you get lost in the paperwork. Maybe you just didn't fall in that thirty percent for this war. Fair? Fair? Not on this earth. Ain't nothing fair on this earth." He paused. The wind shifted for a moment and the thick smoke clouded his mask, then dissipated. Boucher sighed. "OK. You're right, man. Maybe we ought to take a good look at each other." He removed his mask and leaned toward the man. "You take yourself a good look, nightwatchman, you hear?"

Boucher's face was bisected by a line just below his eyes where his face mask kept the dust off his skin. The upper part of his face was coated in a powdery gray film while the lower half, where Boucher had perspired under his mask, was dark, as shiny black as onyx. But what caught the nightwatchman's attention was a scar that ran from Boucher's left ear to his chin, a thick keloid like a trail marking an angle through both his upper and lower lips, and giving him the appearance of a pariah, a black satyr, or some hoodoo dancer trapped forever inside the split halves of fleshy mask.

"Before you ask, consider the fact I probably got this beauty from whatever we been listening to for the last hour." Boucher put the tube of optic lubricant to his eyes.

The watchman sucked air through his teeth. "Jesus!"

Boucher grunted. "Don't be calling Him. He ain't gonna help us now, nightwatchman. He done turned His back on this earth, so we best get to moving." Boucher blinked his eyes to clear them of the ophthalmic solution and said, "Watchman, I'm gonna ask you one more time: Pull out that televiewer and tell me how long you figure fore we reach the park."

"That's low land down there," the man muttered. "We got about five square miles between us and the slope. You figure it."

Boucher pulled his mask in place. "Why do you think I asked you to do it? I figure by daybreak tomorrow."

"Whoa!" the man yelled. "Ain't nobody travelling all night. We gonna make camp and rest the night. I ain't crazy. Besides, ain't nothing moving out there I want to see at night."

Boucher laughed. "Thought your job was nightwatchman?"

"That don't make me crazy," the watchman snorted. "I watch. I don't go looking for trouble. You so all-fired interested in what troubles left in that park, you should've stayed there."

Boucher stared at the dark green shadows encasing Kalava Park. He was about to comment when he thought he saw movement near the gate. Not anything definite, just a reflection of light, like a sunspot near the rim of the park suggesting movement.

What drew Boucher's attention was the flicker of trees crashing to earth, and clinging to one of them, Lan-ling. She had tried to climb a cedar, but its fire-weakened trunk had snapped and it had fallen, taking Lan-ling and several other trees with it. She was near the tide pools where crocodiles had dozed on the day the sky suddenly had turned burgundy and pelted the ground with burning cinders. Now the dead reptiles were barely covered in the sluggish brown current. They lay like rotting wood, and the smell was overpowering, even to Lan-ling. She paused, her bulk propped against an uprooted tree as she stared morosely across the tide pool to the tangle of grillwork and broken fountains that had once housed over a hundred birds. She dreamed of tender young bamboo shoots, then shook herself free of the image. She had gleaned those from the area surrounding the aviary days ago. Now she was forced to forage for roots, gentians, and pikas. She lowered her massive head toward her chest, and began a melancholy wail that lasted so long, Boucher feared she'd never stop.

"What in Jesus' name was that?" the nightwatchman asked.

Boucher shook his head. "It came from Kalava," he answered. "I don't know . . ."

"Christ almighty, we already seen what them big cats can do to a body what's already dead. Think of what they can do to us!"

"What you worried bout the animals for? Bet is, your death's gonna come from the sky." Both men looked up. "Besides, that wasn't a cat," Boucher continued.

He didn't say he'd already seen the droppings of puma and tiger. Although there had not been total darkness since the firefall, Boucher knew the cats would not travel again until early morning. Even then, they were in little danger. The cats would pick off anyone who was helpless or freshly dead before they'd try fighting a man who wanted to stay alive. Still, Boucher frowned as the bleating grew loud again. At this distance, with the baffle created by the dust and wind, he could not be sure what sound the wind carried from the park.

Lan-ling's keening seemed to rattle the empty cages. In the compound next to hers, she could see Ling Chou's still form. Her mate had never been thought of as clever, but even Lan-ling knew he had been asleep too long. Confused, she slowly approached him and leaned down, filling her nostrils with his familiar scent. He was too quiet. Everyone was too quiet. First she'd left the cub in the corner of her own pen, and now Ling Chou. With one swift backswing, she knocked him aside, then reversed her movement, slicing the air near his ear. Still he made no sound. Lan-ling hunkered down beside him, and angrily chattered her teeth. Her eyes, masked in their tear-shaped patches of black fur, seemed more sorrowful than ever. She beat her breast and rocked to the rhythms of her own wailing.

Lan-ling's cry of "hu-hu-hu" made the nightwatchman shudder. "You hear that, keeper? Enough to cause a grown man to cry. Sounds like a whole herd of them."

Boucher laughed. "Kalava couldn't hold a herd of anything."

The nightwatchman grunted. "What about elephants? The ones that redheaded kid said he saw over near the west end?"

Boucher's jaw tightened. "Four! Four elephants! They killed four frightened, stupid elephants." He spit in disgust.

"He said they was wild! And big! Too big. That kid said they thundered like . . . like DRONES. Like drones with legs! They had to shoot them. Never should've had them in the city nohow. You folks should've . . ."

"Should've WHAT!" Boucher yelled. "Started all THIS?" He made a sweeping gesture toward the ruins they had yet to cover.

"Well, ain't my fault," the man grumbled. "Was bound to happen. You should've figured out some way to keep them animals from running loose. You shouldn'ta brought them here in the first place."

"You plugged in the wrong code, nightwatchman. I ain't the one brought them over here chained in the belly of a ship. I ain't the one thought they was exotic and cute."

"Don't make sense having all them cages. I can't understand it."

Boucher heard him and didn't hear him. That was easy enough after he moved upwind and closed himself away from the nightwatchman. Easier still by pulling the hood of his coat over his head.

Shuddering, the nightwatchman also turned up his cowl. "You know, zookeeper, ain't nothing left to understand," he muttered. "Everything's dead."

Boucher peered over his shoulder. In that light, set against the slow-burning fire, the watchman looked like a seal, his body curled like a comma inside the thick hide of the waterproof parka. The man's square set jaw and wrenlike eyes were his only discernible features. Boucher tried to remember what the man's face looked like without his mask. He shook his head. In this world, any man's face was forgettable, and the nightwatchman had more or less the same profile as the other men in the squad. It was only by body shape, Boucher's angular frame and the watchman's low-slung barrel shape, that the men were able to identify each other. Or by sound, Boucher thought as he once again heard a plaintive cry from the direction of Kalava Park.

"Don't seem right that they got to suffer for what we done," the nightwatchman said.

Boucher banked the fire even higher and tried not to imagine what had happened in Kalava during the last week. Already he'd seen the bloodied remains of pronghorn, lemur, and eland. Once he'd seen four snakeskins lying side by side as if the owners had left them there to dry. But he could only imagine the fighting, smaller animals trampled or fed upon by those more agile and fearless. The mournful sound reached him again. It can't go on much longer, he thought.

But for more than an hour, Lan-ling's keening filled the silence of the compound. After ignoring its body for nearly a week, she had brought the cub into Ling Chou's pen. For a while, she caressed and nuzzled its fur, ululating as if her sound would give it life, or at best, awaken Ling Chou. Finally, when she could no longer ignore her empty stomach, she placed the bundle of fur in the corner and moved toward the entrance, stopping only once to grunt as she looked back to the silence of Ling Chou's pen. In the compound, the light through the viewing window seemed to break and shatter, distorting the reflection of the sky so that the layers of color spread in disjointed patterns across the floor, but the glass allowed Lan-ling to view her reflection. Despite the matted clumps of mud and twigs clinging to patches of fur, she still resembled an overgrown toy: button-bright eyes inside a harlequin's mask, muzzle like a puckish nose, and swatches of black and white fur so artfully placed, they seemed attached by a puppeteer. That playful pose came not just from her face, but also her movements. Seated, she took on a quizzical look, her head tilted like a child about to ask some improbable question. But the movement did not end in a somersault or clownish tilt of her head. This time, she did not fold and unfold as she had done for Sunday crowds. This time, Lan-ling questioned the air, her tongue flicking across her snout, her eyes bright inside their mask. Then she ran to the window and slapped it. A tinkling echo resounded across the compound as bits of the middle layer of glass cascaded between the spiderwebbed outer layers. She watched the sparkling shower, and when it was quiet again, lumbered to the entrance.

The yard was littered with broken pieces of bamboo clum, hunks of rubber, plastic, and whatever else she had deposited after her daily forages. Stench filled the causeway between the compound and aviary. Lan-ling sniffed and immediately knew it was not the smell of the apes. Over the years, she had grown accustomed to the scent of their droppings, and when the walls had collapsed and the great steel doors had buckled under the heat of that first attack of drones, the primates had lost no time fleeing their prison. That smell was Shamba's, and the odor of the great bull elephant's rotting carcass renewed her keening.

"Jesus, there's that sound again," the nightwatchman moaned.

Ahead of them, Boucher could see a team gouging a pit for their next fire. A jet tram whizzed along the skyline near the city's epicenter, then turned back toward the Clearwater. Boucher could feel night air, although the wind was not cold yet, but the fuzzy light of afternoon had given way to the muted shades of early evening. He could barely see the ridge separating the park from the row of brownstones facing it.

"Give me the televiewer," he told the man.

"Infrared won't work in this light," the man muttered, but all the same, he handed the lens case to Boucher. "Even if you see something, what you gonna do about it, keeper?"

Boucher didn't answer. He adjusted the exposure switch and set up the view screen. The nightwatchman uncovered the receiver and when Boucher had the lens set for distance, they both hunched over the small screen waiting for the camera image to appear.

"Never did like this gear," the man said. "Never did like none of it.

Start with a little something like this and you end up with satellite nations and a whole bunch of fire-spitting drones raining shit down on you."

The camera's eye clicked off its measure of distance until it focused on the setting Boucher had estimated. The picture appeared, a blood-red negative print of Kalava's landscape. Then Boucher saw her. Lan-ling crossed the verge of the elephant rocks, turned her head south for a moment, then vanished from view.

"What the hell was that?" the nightwatchman shouted.

"One, just one," Boucher muttered. "Where is the other one?"

"Answer me, keeper! What was that?"

Boucher curled his lip away from the scar and said, "Panda!"

It was an innocent enough word, a storybook word, but to the watchman, his eyes still stinging from the dust and fine ash of funeral pyres, Boucher's way of spitting out the word robbed it of all innocence.

As Boucher aligned the view lens, he recalled the rainy day when he'd introduced Ling Chou to Lan-ling. He'd been cocky enough to think he knew their moods. He had watched them for months, clocking Lan-ling's tantrums and Ling Chou's fickleness. But all of it had been done with bars separating them from each other, and each of them from him. Boucher had been sure he'd timed it right, but in the end, he had been the one to receive the brunt of Lan-ling's anger. Yet after that, after she had marked him the way a child marks a favorite toy, Boucher was the only keeper she allowed near her. "The love of my life," he'd called her. And always, he'd thought to himself: *"You're gonna be the death of me."* Now he was out to kill her, to put her down before she died of starvation in a world where most living things would probably starve within a few years, the way he saw it.

"What poet was it said: 'Man kills the thing he loves'?" Boucher muttered as he slammed the lens case shut. "I'm going back," he told the nightwatchman.

The man pointed south where the helix marked the boundaries of the city beneath the mountains. "There?" the watchman asked.

Boucher shook his head. "No, there," he said, and walked away from the man, toward the park where he'd caught a glimpse of Lan-ling moving in the underbrush.

She moved quickly, always upwind. When she stopped, it was to climb the charred trunk of a tree in search of sweet green branches, or pull away the top layer of mossy underbrush that had somehow escaped the fire. Those scant offerings did little to quell the hunger she felt, but the sound of wind moving the trappings in empty cages urged her forward. That same wind still carried the smell of fires to the south, and on the other side of the ravine, the frantic barking of dogs. Lan-ling checked her directions. Even with the noise of the pack dampened by the hollows of the crevasse, the dogs seemed about to envelop her. She clicked her teeth in a chittering of warning.

Boucher could hear the dogs quarrelling. As soon as the sky began to lose its color, they had started their interminable yelping. He knew the noise would increase as the night sky took shape. The dogs had not yet found a leader for the night and their howls were still sporadic. Boucher gripped the oxygen mouthpiece between his teeth, and head down, set off in the direction of Kalava. Once he'd pulled clear of the squad, he forced himself not to think about the destruction he was passing, but he could not close out the noises. As Boucher sorted out the sounds of dogs, wind, and crackling fires, he heard the soft crunch of footsteps behind him.

He turned a corner and flattened himself against a ragged section of wall. He was almost relieved to be forced to stop. Already he was beginning to perspire, and his arms and legs, encased in the waterproof coveralls, felt metal-heavy and thick. Standing still would allow him to slow down his breathing, stop the lightheadedness he was beginning to feel. As the footsteps approached, Boucher concentrated on easing the tightness in his muscles until his fingers felt loose. He'd learned to do this when he worked with the cats. No matter how many times he'd fed them, he never took any chances. He'd wait until their yellow eyes found him, until both he and the cats knew they were trapped. Boucher's hands were on the man's throat before he could yell, but when he saw who it was, Boucher released his grip.

The nightwatchman rubbed his throat and stared at Boucher. "If you trying to scare the piss out of me, you done it," he said.

Boucher grunted, then remembered he hadn't removed his mouthpiece. "Man, what do you want?" he asked after he'd ejected the stoma.

"I'm going with you," the man said.

"Why?"

The nightwatchman shrugged. "You've got your job, keeper. I've got mine. If you ain't got nobody to verify you, they won't let you back in the city. Don't know what you carrying."

"Don't worry, nightwatchman. I ain't out to catch no disease." Boucher shoved the stoma between his teeth, adjusted the gauze mask, and turned away from the man.

"You still got to register!" the man yelled. "Might as well let me come along. The squad's camped for the night anyway. Replacements won't be here till morning." He secured his backpack and fell into step behind Boucher. For a while, they moved without speaking, then Boucher stopped and stared at the man.

The watchman was breathing hard. Boucher pointed to his mouthpiece, but the man shook his head. "That stuff makes me sick," he told Boucher. "But if we rest now and again . . ."

Boucher shook his head and walked away.

The watchman spoke between gulps of breath. "Can't keep me from following. Besides, I got the gear you need."

Boucher stopped and pulled his mouthpiece. "Suit yourself. But I'm going to make it to Kalava before morning. So you keep up or forget it."

The man swung his pack to the ground. "We best see if we going in the right direction," he said weakly. "Left the lens on the setting you had . . . Take a look-see . . . OK?"

But Boucher had started walking again. The nightwatchman had no choice but to follow him.

If they had checked the televiewer, they would have seen Lan-ling hunched at the edge of the ravine. The gorge had been freshly cut by tremors from the shock waves. Lan-ling could smell the damp mold of newly exposed earth, and if her eyesight had been more accurate, she would have seen how it sliced though Kalava's wrought-iron outer fence and curved north, leaving a wide raw cut that ran for miles through what had been the rain forest. That esker formed a barrier, trapping those who could not escape the park and giving comfort to those who were confined north of it. Lan-ling covered her eyes with her front paws, then rolled over the edge of the steep slope like a great furry ball. Only when she reached the bottom of the ravine did she uncoil, shaking herself.

For almost an hour, she slowly zigzagged her way across the floor of the gorge, eating the fragments of tree roots caught in the layers of soil along the sides of the ravine, and drinking the stagnant water trapped in the deeper pockets of the gully. She saw a pika, and in her hunger snatched the rabbit from a shadowy outcropping and crunched it in her jaws. It wasn't bamboo but it filled a small part of her stomach. Having found one, she decided to wait for another to appear. The ravine was a natural buffer against the wind and dust, so Lan-ling pushed her rump against the bank and sat there. With her head tilted back and one paw carelessly thrown over her eyes, she looked like a stuffed doll tossed in the gully by an absentminded child.

Boucher had also decided to rest. The hour's trek had taken its toll, and even with the oxygen assist, Boucher could feel the muscles in his arms and legs beginning to cramp. He squatted on a mound of debris and waited for the nightwatchman to join him. It was growing colder and in another few miles, they would be in the lowlands. Boucher could hear the dogs circling and barking. He estimated the number of packs and the size of each one. Whenever the rhythms of the dog pack changed tones, shifting from frantic yapping to a low baying, Boucher knew the animals had cornered their prey.

"There's at least one dog pack between us and the park, so we'll have to circle farther north," Boucher said as the watchman crumpled to the ground beside him. He propped the man upright, but the watchman kept heaving, dry rasping sounds as his lungs pulled for air that wasn't there. "Put your head down between your knees, watchman. You keep gulping like that and you'll pass out."

Boucher eased the pack away from the man's shoulders. He waited for a few minutes. The watchman's breathing didn't improve, so Boucher forced him to accept the oxygen mouthpiece. Seconds later, the heave turned liquid and Boucher had to pull the gauze mask away from his face.

"Nightwatchman, you either learn to use that oxygen or I'll leave you here. The squad's more than an hour away and you'll be on your own. Do you understand?" The man nodded. "And don't wait until you're hyperventilating to stick that damn stoma in your mouth." The nightwatchman nodded again, then pushed the stoma between his teeth. Boucher readjusted the headband on the man's gauze mask. "Now why don't we see what's out there?" Boucher added. The watchman grunted and set up the televiewer. After he'd caught his breath, he said, "Look here. That line there, keeper. Where the trees end."

Boucher peered into the viewfinder and spotted the raw slash of earth on the view screen's blood-red image. "An esker. Looks new. We'll just have to hope it's not too deep. We've got enough rope, so we should be able make it across." He began packing the equipment.

"You ain't going anyhow, are you?" the watchman asked. "We don't know how deep that cut really is."

Boucher tossed the polyethylene sacking. "Here, take this. I've had it with you, man. You can pitch camp here if you want. You got enough rations to last the night and the wind won't be too harsh behind that knoll over there. Like you said: I got my job. I'll take a sounding on that gorge when I get there. If I can't get in, nothing can get out."

"If you get in, it's gonna grab the other half of your face."

Boucher laughed. "Hey, I got this scar cause I trusted a female. She is big and beautiful and she's got sad black eyes. A little bit of me. A little bit of you. Black and white, black and white. Know what I mean?" he laughed. "But her nails are deadly, so take care, nightwatchman. She's mad as hell and she's on the loose."

The watchman quickly gathered up the tent sacking and tied it onto his backpack. But instead of making camp, he followed Boucher, all the while cursing the wind, the dust, the drones, the sky that wouldn't get dark and as many of the eighteen satellite nations as he could remember.

They kept moving the rest of that night, the men in one direction, Lan-ling in another.

In morning light still streaked with the purple afterglow of drone fire, Lan-ling began her climb out of the compound. Moisture and loose rock made the walls of the ravine slippery, but when she stood on her hind legs, she could reach the spiked ribs of broken fence jutting from the gorge. Boosting herself, she lunged for the fence, but the earth gave way and she slid backward, taking mud, rocks, and a long section of fence with her. For several moments, she sat there. Then shaking her head, she lunged for the mud wall again. This time, she used the fence as a ladder and clutching each rung, crawled up the steep slope hand over hand like a mountain climber. Once on the other side, she emitted a satisfied "heh-heh-heh," dropped on all fours and slid into the shadows of the rubble bordering the Kalava Park.

The area facing the park had not only suffered bad politics, but it also had endured a combination of bad weather and animal smells. In the winter, the bitter air carried the animal's restless wailings, hootings, and bleatings right up to the houses where the noises echoed and bounced back into the shrubbery of the park. In the summer, the heat hovered around the edges of the park like a barrier. The neighborhood had been equally divided into those who hated Kalava and believed no living thing should be caged, and those who loved it and therefore, claimed they loved animals too. Young children were either allowed to enter the park whenever they chose, or expressly forbidden to even pass through its gates. Boucher had been harangued by more than one parent whose child had been caught wandering through Kalava.

Now Lan-ling sauntered leisurely past the shells of the first few houses, the thick pads of her feet muffling the sound of her passing. She stopped every now and then to leave a scent mark or check the movement of the frenzied dog pack. The odor of dogs had grown heavier, but Lan-ling also smelled the faint sweet-sour scent of keepers. Perhaps that is why she chose the house, the scent of humans causing her large head to tilt to one side as if her questioning look might prompt a keeper to appear in the doorway. After carefully picking her way through the rubble, she entered the kitchen, and there, using her sixth claw, she developed a clumsy but effective way of opening containers of food. She found she liked dried peas rather than pasta, preferred dog biscuits to saltines. She was languidly searching the rest of the house, when she caught a movement that startled her. At first she thought she saw Ling Chou, but when she moved, it moved too. Lan-ling cocked her head and watched it follow suit: its round white face decorated with black ears, nose, and the eyes masked in teardrop patches. She clicked her teeth, but the thing would not leave. She moved forward, sniffed, then hooted at the reflection that mimicked her. That's when she heard the baby's cry.

Almost as soon as it started, the thin wail squeaked into a mewing "eh-eh-eh." Lan-ling stopped—nose up, nostrils quivering. At first she could not track the sound. The wind deceived her, bringing the noise closer, then wiping it away. She listened as the cry grew loud, then vanished as if she had not heard it at all. The baying dog pack was the only clear sound. Lan-ling leaned against the wall, and in that move, found herself clawing air as the wall gave way and sent her crashing to a stairwell below. Coughing and choking, she tried to heave herself upright again, but her weight was too great for the weakened staircase and she was trapped, her hind legs caught in a splintered step midway the stairs.

The boy had heard her roaming around the house. He had tried to quiet his sister, but the baby was hungry and frightened, and no amount of shushing would silence her weeping. That day, she had eaten nothing he'd given her. He had scrambled up to the ground twice, but no matter what he offered, she would not eat. So he'd cradled the baby in his spidery-thin arms and tried to remember what his mother would have done. In this, his six-year-old memory failed him. Then he'd heard Lan-ling on the floor above, and suddenly, the wall gave way and she was in the cellar.

Layers of dust swirled away from the stairs so that for a moment, the room seemed to be sinking into the ground. The boy tucked his head down, and wrapped the blanket around himself and the baby. Lan-ling roared, her noise drowning both the baby's cries and the yelping dogs. In a fit of anger and panic, she pulled herself loose and thunderously plummeted to the floor. It wasn't long before the air cleared, but to the three of them trapped in that cellar, it seemed to take hours for the dust to settle. The boy peeked out from the blanket just as Lan-ling turned her head toward them. When the child began to whimper, its lonely cries made her move toward them.

Perhaps Lan-ling would never have reached for the baby if the dogs had not caught her scent, but as she hesitated, sniffing the smell of boy and child, the stronger, acrid odors of the dog pack reached her nostrils. Then she heard the entire pack snapping and growling as it raced past the house. Looking up through the hole she'd made in the floor, she saw a lone hunter, a massive dog, its gargoyle's head filled with teeth. The boy cried out and clutched the baby tighter. When the child screamed, the dog's snarls grew wilder. Lan-ling stood on her hind legs and clattered her teeth, challenging the dog closer. For a few seconds, the two of them faced each other, then the dog leapt. With a single stroke, Lan-ling slammed the animal against the wall. The howls were heard by all within earshot. Several members of the pack stopped, but the lead dogs had caught scent of easier game west of Kalava where the primates had fled, and the urgency of an easy kill sent them racing in that direction. Lan-ling did not move until their howls had faded. Then she sat, staring at the boy and child, the quietness settling around her.

"Keeper, you got a woman or you by yourself?" the nightwatchman sputtered.

Boucher had not slackened his pace since they'd maneuvered past the dog pack. The man repeated his question. Boucher grunted and continued his slow descent into the ravine.

"Those dogs are too quiet. Can you hear them, keeper?"

"Hold the rope tight!" Boucher yelled. "Man, if I get a face full of mud, I'll bust your head." Boucher's feet touched the bottom and he leaned against the mud bank, panting like a runner who'd just finished a ten-mile lap. His lungs had begun to ache, pinpricks of pain spreading as cooler, cleaner air in the ravine replaced the dust-filled air of the ground above him. Boucher huddled into an embryonic position, his knees drawn up, his head buried under his arms.

"Keeper? Keeper, where are you?" the man asked. "Answer me."

Boucher groaned and forced himself to sit up. Finally the pain eased. The man called to him again and again, his voice hoarse and crackly as a macaw's. "Come on down, nightwatchman. There's a shelf about ten feet below you. Let the rope guide you. Another fifteen feet and you're at the bottom."

"I can't see, keeper."

"Neither can I. Throw down the backpacks. I'll set a flare."

He heard the nightwatchman grumbling, then the packs hit the ground, and as the man lowered himself over the edge of the ravine, loose rock and mud tumbled into the gorge. Boucher grabbed one of the packs and set up the flare. The violet-pink light elongated his shadow against the walls of the hollow. He had already begun to climb the other side when the man reached the bottom.

"Pull the rope down behind you," Boucher told him, smiling when he saw the oxygen mouthpiece clutched in the man's teeth. "Soon as you get tired of sucking up that oxygen, I'll throw the rope down. Send up the packs first, then you come up."

The man nodded and Boucher gathered up the slack end of the rope. When Boucher reached the top, he was immediately aware of the silence. The sound of the dogs and wind, even the distant sounds of men setting camps and fixing the position of the next squad, had seemed louder when he'd entered the gorge, but here the world was quiet. The watchman's harsh breathing was grating, but once the gauze mask was in place, Boucher shrugged and signalled the man to follow him.

"You never answered my question, keeper."

"What question?"

"Do you have a woman?"

Boucher walked away. Now that they were in the park, his steps were as loose and easy as a prize-fighter's, but the nightwatchman stumbled, his eyes darting from side to side as if he expected rhinos, leopards or hooded vultures to swoop out of the shadows at any moment. The silence, the absence of life that, in the park, seemed more unwordly than all of the ravaged houses in the city, left the man unsettled. He kept asking questions, probing Boucher like a journalist at a press conference. The questions overlapped each other, and soon Boucher realized that any answer would serve to fill the uneasiness the nightwatchman felt.

"Had a woman," Boucher told him. "She couldn't stand this place. Said she wouldn't stay around nothing that could twist around and lick its own butt. Wouldn't come out here even on Sundays. She didn't like it. None of it." Boucher pointed to the cloister of empty corrals and pens. "I don't know what she hated most, the animals, the cages or the keepers. Wanted to move into one of those ocean cities. So I let her. Not me. I don't take to water. That place can tie you up worse than the mountain city."

"Look who's talking," the watchman said. "This place looks like a prison." He sniffed the air. "Some kind of dung-hole prison."

"It ain't so bad," Boucher said. "We took good care of them."

"Yeah, I see that. Sit in your cage and let everybody watch you eat, shit, screw . . . all the time pointing and saying: 'Ain't that cute!'" The man narrowed his eyes even more. "I don't figure you, keeper. I seen black guys laying solar whorls or running transports. You know, jobs most white folks won't take. But this? Never figured Afro folks like you to do this kinda work."

"Nightwatchman, you talking color? You know better than that. What would the council say? We're past all that. This is New Age Time. Right? Just ask the satellite neighbors out there. Color ain't got nothing to do with it. Look around." Boucher opened his arms as if to take in the world from sea to mountains. "A world full of communes. Old ones, new ones. Got them under the sea and in the sky. Got you coming and going, so watch your mouth, nightwatchman, or I'll leave you here to rot," he laughed. "And by the smell of things, you gonna have lots of company, man."

Boucher's laughter made the nightwatchman jump. "How much farther, keeper?" His voice broke as fear rose in his throat.

Leave him alone and he'll panic, Boucher thought. He decided to circle the area in order to give himself the advantage of overlooking the paddock from the bracken behind the dens. But when they reached the aviary, Boucher felt his patience squeeze into a thin line as he looked at the floor littered with the feathers of birds who had not escaped. He wheeled around and confronted the man.

"Nightwatchman, why did you follow me if you're so damn scared of this place?"

"They said nobody should go off alone. You remember, back at the city . . . at the aid station. They said . . ."

"THEY? They *who*?"

The man shuffled his feet as if he hadn't decided to move to the left or the right. "Well, what am I supposed to do? Let you go off and get yourself killed? They said . . ."

Boucher stuck out his arm to stop the watchman's talk. "When I was little," Boucher said, "I had this set of blocks, the kind you hook together so they look like bricks. I'd build a house, then tear it down. Build a bridge, then slam it with my fists. Spent hours building and rebuilding. Taking things apart and putting them back together. Didn't matter that nobody talked to me. Stayed by myself. Building . . . tearing down . . . What for? What did I do that for?"

The nightwatchman shrugged. "No telling. I never did that. Not me. Ran around with some toughs. Had a band. Useta eat them keyboards. Brrmm-gunng . . . POW! Tear up the drum discs too. Turned out many a dance, and nobody ever messed with us. We was the baddest bunch of white guys in Port City. Baddest for miles. Everywhere they'd go, I'd go."

"Where did you go?"

The man hesitated. "Round," he said finally. "Just around."

Boucher shook his head and stalked off. "Come on. When we finish here, we can get back to the squad. We'll torch this whole mess and . . ." He stopped and motioned the watchman to be quiet.

There was no need to do that. The man had already seen Lan-ling. She was standing in the cul-de-sac behind the compound, her bulk blocking nearly all of the available light behind her. She was on all fours, crouched and ready to jump, her back humped and her eyes black dots in patches of even blacker fur. Boucher was tense, but he did not speak. He nodded to the space behind Lan-ling, and the watchman followed his gaze. The boy and child were huddled on the floor. The baby's eyes were still but the boy's eyes were bright with fear.

The man hissed. "Jesus . . ." and Boucher said, "Don't move, nightwatchman. Just don't move."

"A bear! Christ, must be three, four hundred pounds!"

"Easy, nightwatchman. This ain't your ordinary bear. This is your panda bear." He began to croon, his voice intoning a singsong rhythm. He could see Lan-ling following their conversation with her eyes, waiting for a change in pitch, a shift that signalled danger. He thought of the scar on his face and willed himself not to move. "This is Lan-ling. Right, princess? Where is your baby, princess? And where's Ling Chou? Where's the old man, the panda man?" Boucher watched light break and shatter inside those doleful eyes.

The nightwatchman trembled—first hot, then cold, as if his blood had congealed. He gripped the straps of his backpack. "You talking to that thing, keeper? You gonna stand there and talk . . ."

Boucher kept his voice low. "Pay no attention to the man, princess. The man does not know you're not supposed to yell when you look at a panda. The man does not know you don't much like white folks. The man does not know how fast you can move. If the man knew that, he'd keep his big mouth shut. Wouldn't he, princess?"

Lan-ling pulled back her lips, grimacing and clicking her teeth as she sniffed the air. Then, in a slow, rolling movement, her teeth clattering like a tailor's shears, she backed her rump against the wall. The boy's eyes were wide, and although he was not crying, he whimpered, a soft sucking in of air that sounded like a lamb's bleating. He began to unfold, and when he was half standing, half kneeling, he grabbed Lan-ling's furry neck and climbed onto her back, clinging there like a wraith.

"You just gonna stand there, keeper?"

Boucher was about to speak when Lan-ling turned and dashed into the adjacent corridor. She was loping at full stride, and by the time Boucher yelled, "Get the baby!" Lan-ling was already past the exit gate of the cage area, her melancholy "hu-hu-hu" trailing behind her. Boucher was standing on the ridge of the elephant rocks when the nightwatchman caught up with him. The man had wrapped the baby in a winding sheet of tent sacking. When he saw Boucher's questioning stare, he said, "It's alive. Just barely. Where's the boy?"

Boucher gestured toward the outer regions of Kalava. They could hear Lan-ling crashing through the underbrush. "She's heading toward the ravine," he said.

"You let her go! You let that stinking animal . . ."

"She's not going anywhere. The dogs will drive her back here."

"How can you be sure, keeper? You gonna offer her a new cage?"

Boucher sighed. "She's got nowhere else to go."

"But the kid . . ." Suddenly, he could not shape sounds into words.

Boucher unhooked his backpack and pulled out the torch. As it burst into flames, he took one last look toward the ravine, then turned in the direction of Shamba's cave. "We'll find him. And maybe he'll learn to forget all of this. Right now, that boy's more afraid of us than some panda."

The nightwatchman waited until Boucher was about to enter the cave. "Keeper," he yelled, "they'll find out. What are we going to put on the report?"

"They *who?* What report?" Boucher wiped his brow with one hand, leaving dust streaked across his forehead. When he held up the torch to check the flame, it sputtered and hissed, but the tip was red, brighter than the dull glow that now was beginning to spread across the eastern portion of the sky like a bloody paw print. "You got a job to do, nightwatchman, so do it before *they* decide to come and finish the job they started last week."

Startled, the man turned and looked in the direction of Boucher's gaze as if he expected to see a sky full of drones. The empty sky angered him. "What's your name, keeper?" he snapped.

Boucher had already started to walk into the cave, but he stopped and without looking around, answered, "Why, nightwatchman? I don't know yours." Boucher waited, but when the man remained silent, he laughed and said, "Boucher. My name is Boucher, nightwatchman."

"That's a good name, keeper." The man grunted, and cradling the sick baby, sat on the rocks to wait for Boucher to finish.

When the thick, fetid smoke from the elephant's burning carcass began to billow from the mouth of the cave, the nightwatchman rocked the child, cursing the wind, the dust, the sky that wouldn't get dark, the women he'd known and the jobs he'd lost.

The Way Station

Its name is a secret road, the one which few people know, which not all people are aware of, which few people go along. It is good, fine; a good place, a fine place. It is where one is harmed, a place of harm. It is known as a safe place; it is a difficult place, a dangerous place. One is frightened. It is a place of fear.

"Origins and Namings—
Aztec Definitions"

IT IS MORNING OR EVENING. No one knows or cares, but the day, to be exact, is notched on the calendar in a code fit for any language. The air is filled with the acrid odor of power from the machinery in the asteroid's central core. Those machines feed into transporters throbbing to life on the launching pods. The pods are some distance from the commons. Outside the commons, light slips through violet prisms and changes from red to blue, but inside, there are people who would rather see with artificial light. They land here after too many hours in tight compartments, and all the while, they count the days until journey's end, or swap theories about the origins of galaxies. Standing or sprawling, they fill the room with sound, as if their noise can drown out the memory of the silence of deep space. Occasionally, for diversion, one or two approach a guard in search of some bit of information, and guards, true to their timeless image, remain mealy-mouthed and stoic. They claim no knowledge of schedules or numbers of transporters and promises of comfort. Once this exchange is completed, the guard's window slams shut and everyone is left fondling useless tickets, or watching the fortunate ones whose transport departure time has been called. Some leave. Others stay.

Here, there is just the waiting. The constant stretching and cramping, the need to go on. And they do go. Eventually they go, leaving behind a phosphorescent trail as they slip into deep space where only radar will know of their presence when their ship cuts the arc of a tracker beam. And those left behind watch the sky until the vapors fade, then hurry back to their pocket of noise.

Some will go to their living quarters on the other side of the commons where rings of cylinders rise up from a delta of brightly hued travertine, shale, and slate like ancient coliseums worn rough by history. But this place has no history. These rows of dull gray cocoons were never meant to be permanent, and yet, because they are here, they are needed. Behind a line of Colombine ice needles, tide pools reek of chlorine, and fingers of color, streaked against rock, reach for the next star world. Sometimes those who stay to themselves are found on these lonely paths. At the edge of the delta, Lashia is hurrying.

She is returning from the fields beyond the delta where the asteroid's internal sun has warmed the rocks until nothing grows, not even moss pinks or lichen. Lashia moves quickly. Her steps are light and surefooted. She crosses the molten underbrush, leaving pockets of steam in her wake. She does not turn back to see the sod curling into place moments after her footprints are clouded in mist. She places her weight on the ball of each foot, and intuitively rolls into the next footstep. She does not alter her pace until she reaches the midline, the false horizon where the heat of the reverse tundra dissipates against a shelf of snowy coral. Once she has begun to descend into the delta, she is almost lost in the colorful profusion of vegetation. She is a stocky woman her complexion holding the colors of two deserts—the Navajo sands of her father's desert, and the parched Sahara, where centuries ago her mother's people were captured as slaves. Her body is dark and muscular, almost exaggerated, like the thick-limbed women in a Gauguin painting, like a Senufu statue, a wrestler or weightlifter. The silk fabric of her crimson chiton blends into a sea of red and pink blossoms. When she pauses to examine the colors, the asteroid's Day-glo light casts her in negative print until the undertones of reds, yellows, browns, making up her dark complexion seem to be highlighted as single hues. Against the glow of her skin, the color patterns of the plants growing near her feet are repeated in the triple braid of aggry beads crossing over her shoulders and under her breasts like a harness.

Lashia walks through a stand of whistling pickerel plants swaying at the ends of their long branches. She is as anxious to leave the delta with its sour vegetation as she is to leave the way station and the seedy travellers whose grumblings fill the commons. But she remembers the monotony of the voyage, of sleeping long hours in the ship's bunkers, the cabins stacked row after row in circles of six like inverted egg cups. The sterile cylinders where those on the starboard side sleep facing forward, while those on port side are stowed facing aft. Like stacks of computer chips or radon amphsoles. Like cords of wood, boxcars of market cattle or slave cargoes. And the smells, the rancid odor of alien scents mingling in the ship's still air. No matter what the conveyance, every journey is filled with the odors of those who are going somewhere or coming from some place, and the constant movement of travelling making each leg of the trip more depressing than the next. She shakes her head and thinks of work she must do. How, when she leaves, this place will become an illusion, an interesting afterimage trapped in her memory. The place is filled with guards, ticket-takers, and ground crews. And then there are the old men and women, the wanderers made old before their time, their bags and backpacks filled with useless debris, as if they have taken a straight road from city streets to the lonely paths of this asteroid. Lashia has seen them sleeping in whatever cubbyhole or corner the place offers, bringing a bit of the earth with them into the nightmare of this space station.

Thinking of the vagrant's voices reminds her of Bess. Lashia does not like travelling with an urban colony woman so full of herself she never listens. Travelling would have been better with a backcountry Slav or a silent Maori—yet the choice had not been hers, and once assigned to a trip, there was no question but to go. Today she and Bess will compare notes, hopefully agreeing on a single code that will be useful in the months of research still ahead. And today, Bess would no doubt press for a new name. For months, on the first leg of their journey, Bess has complained about her name. "Too plain," she has whined. Lashia has offered a multitude of choices, but none fit for public use. *"I should give her Primigenia,"* Lashia thinks, chuckling over the notion that Bess would not recognize the name of a Pompeian whore.

She is still laughing to herself as she nears the first row of hutches. There, she is pulled to an abrupt stop by a post guard's challenge. "HALT!" At first she cannot see him. After the light of the delta's bright colors, the gray monochrome of the compound blurs all images—even the wall, its surface covered with graffiti. Some are simple pleas of those afraid of what the next trip might bring: STATION 3YZ CARRIES THE FEVER! and I RISE TO FALL HERE? Some are just idle thoughts scrawled on any innkeeper's wall: BEAUTY LIVES! and ORI FUNG EATS IT OFTEN! And then there are others, like the one outside the commons: FIRST GAF GUNS THEN SIAMESE CATS!—frightening scrawls that represent some madman's threat. Still the graffiti is more visible than the guard.

Only by blinking her eyes twice can Lashia detect the gray cloth of the guard's uniform near the archway. He is standing at the end of the corridor that links the living quarters to the commons. He seems almost glued to the gray curves of a colonnade, and stands smartly, as erect as the column behind him. His body and the post cut the convex silhouettes of the nearest hutch into equal components. Lashia blinks once, twice, but from this distance, she is not sure what is living tissue and what is stone. *"Breathe,"* she thinks. *"In my country, the dead are white and walk backward,"* she thinks. *"Breathe. Show me you're alive and human."*

She wills him to step foward, and he does, repeating his challenge. "HALT!"

Now he is more discernible, but still she does not speak. In that light, all she can see is a red scar around his lips, the tissue so misshappen, the red seems almost black with shadows. The shock of it locks her in silence. It stands out against the roughness of his skin like a rosette or a wound. It is a pattern of single strokes protruding around the edges of his mouth, and more menancing than a weapon. Lashia raises her hand to her own mouth and immediately regrets the gesture. The guard's smile is almost imperceptible. She turns her emotions inward, her expression blank. She spreads her fingers as if to trace the angle of her cheek. She knows that to anger a guard, even over so small a slight as his knowing smile, would only make her time at the way station more uncomfortable. She knows making encounters uncomfortable is the way it has always been with guards.

"Your name," he says. It is both statement and question.

Lashia frames her answer in a clear, even voice. "I am Lashia Msichana Molenka." She hesitates, wanting to add: I'm North American, African by nature, and interstellar by preference. But that is the nonsense of a schoolgirl. Lashia knows this guard sees nothing but her color. Instead, she says, "I am on official pass." Even so, she feels her face flush a deeper shade of brown.

The guard raises his gloved hand. This gesture tells her she could have called herself Martian. "I have only your word for this," he tells her. His voice indicates he has seen too many travellers pass by him.

Again, Lashia holds the moment in check. Slowly she retrieves her papers from the pocket beneath her bandolier of aggry beads. "I have reserved living quarters in this section," she adds.

He returns the papers after a cursory glance. "You have been moved," he tells her. But he thinks to himself: *"Molenka! I will remember that name. Another one on her first journey,"* he tells himself.

Lashia's throat tightens. There has been no hint of explanation in the guard's voice, and although he could not possibly know that she has been handpicked for this project, she resents his preemptive tone. Perhaps if she were a man, or if she were taller, or . . . She reminds herself that she has forgotten more than he has yet to learn. She inhales deeply. "Moved? By whose orders? Why am I moved? I am not a soldier to be moved here and there."

"There's nothing wrong with being a soldier," the guard snorts.

"I want to know why I have been moved," Lashia repeats.

When he sneers, the whole of the red shape stands out against his skin, a hemisphere alive against the dead expanse of the rest of his face. "I don't have to answer you," he snarls. He waits but Lashia does not move. "I have not been given orders to answer those questions." Lashia holds him in her stare. He nods toward the area behind him. "You must get your things. This area is restricted to emergency rescue personnel."

Lashia frowns. "Rescue? Will the transporters be delayed? I'm scheduled to leave in less than fifteen hours! And my companion? Has she . . ."

"She has already been told. I know nothing of schedules. You are the last to go." He snaps his right fist against the ocellus emblem crested on his left shoulder, then returns to his niche between the archway's columns. Two clipped steps backward, and like a chameleon, he assumes the forms of the stones around him.

Lashia frowns again, embarrassed to have been pressured by a man, irritated by the inefficiency of the station. But she can not allow herself to be angered by a mere guard. After the months of signing endless papers and the painfully precise sessions of training, the tawdriness of this place is magnified by the boredom she remembers from the first leg of her trip. Space was supposed to be romantic, pure, enlightening. Not this. And after this, three more months in deep space. She shakes her head. Suddenly, she feels someone staring at her. A movement a short distance away. A woman draped in a dull green haik, the cowl pulled low over her eyes. Lashia turns to her right. The guard is no longer there although she has not heard him leave. She turns back. Now the woman is closer, moving silently.

"Who are you?" Lashia calls. "Why are you following me? I have no valuables. See. Nothing. Go to the commons. They have money."

The words tumble out. The figure stops. A hand pulls the cowl away from the face. The woman is pale, much lighter than Lashia's own dark sandalwood skintone. Lashia sees the woman's eyes, glossy and bright as the mirror stones in the fields behind the delta. The woman's hand is poised like a claw, and though the fingers are firm and strong, the skin is speckled with brown liver spots and the wrist bone is thrust outward, so pronounced it seems to be the stump of a mutated finger. In the crook of the arm, she holds a bag, oily with stains. *"It is this place,"* Lashia thinks. *"This place with its plastic rocks, ugly guards, and bag ladies. This place without wind where sound does not travel. Where light comes from everywhere. Where light surrounds you but there is no wind."*

"What do you want?" Lashia asks. The woman's face moves toward a smile. Centered on her left cheek is a large brown mole from which three strands of hair, thin as spidery limbs, waver against her sallow skin. Lashia cannot determine whether she is young or old. The woman moves closer, and Lashia can hear the rasp of air being sucked into her throat. The woman tilts her head, brings her shoulder forward to extend her arm. The heavy cloth of the haik rustles and the smell is vinegary, sour. The angle of her head, or perhaps the way she allows her feet to fall like anvils upon the sandstone path, causes Lashia to rush past her. Lashia turns back only once. The woman stands in the same spot, her arm extended, waiting.

Once Lashia is out of sight, the guard reappears. He moves into place as quickly and silently as he had disappeared. The old woman turns, her movement made deceptively fluid by her rippling cloak.

"You!" the guard snaps. "I want you to catch the next transport out of here."

The woman drops her hand and pulls herself into the shadowy depths of her cloak. "For the love of life, we move," she mutters.

"No more craziness, woman. You have been here too long. This is a place of waiting. You must leave." The guard leans forward until his face is inches away from the woman's face. "Go!" he shouts. "Go now before I tell them you have been living here." He forms the words carefully, spits them out as if he believes the woman to be deaf.

"Who are you to say you have never seen what others see?" she asks.

The guard laughs. "I've heard too many of your riddles, woman. Save them for strangers."

"They have come," the woman smiles. "I have seen them. The ship, there." She points toward the landing area. "They have come in the sky fish."

"Eh, what do you say? You have seen them? No one was to go . . ."

"They come in threes," the woman mutters. "In sixes and sevens."

"You best not let anyone hear you say that, woman."

"They will bring good . . ."

"They look like fish if you ask me. Like eels. Sliding all over . . ."

"They have power . . ."

"Well, I'll give you that. With muscles like that, I could . . ."

"One body into the other. One body turning. They are here, like stars to lead the way. They will take us with them."

The guard slaps his hands together. The sound clatters like thunder in the recesses of the corridor. "Not *me!* Not Muong Nong. They can't take *me* anywhere. Even the captain is not so curious as to have them around for long. And that big one, the leader . . . slippery! Slippery as fish oil. All those muscles . . . But he won't talk, that one won't."

"It is his right to choose. He is first man. Man of hunter. There are those who know that. They know if only they will see," the woman smirks.

"I know this," the guard exclaims. "You are going to be the first one on the next transporter. I will see to it."

For a moment, the woman stares at the red scar around the guard's mouth. Then she smiles, nods, and curtsies. "We all go when it is time." Smiling, she walks toward the corridor.

The guard makes no move to stop her. He strokes his lip scars and mumbles, "It's past your time, old woman. I've had enough of your trouble."

Still grumbling, Muong Nong enters the next ring of hutches and moves along the corridor checking the contact pads on the locks of each hutch. He shakes his head and mutters, but paces his progress with the sure, easy rhythms of a man who has done this chore for years. Checking the hutches is a simple task. He thinks of how a wreck always means trouble. He remembers an earlier wreck, a first contact made long before this way station had been built. Made when civilians just dreamed of space. When that girl, the one with the beads wrapped too tightly around her chest, had not even thought of leaving home.

"Molenka," the guard snorts. "These young ones come and go. And all of them thinking they own the universe."

But on that first contact, he had been young too. It happened near the end of his first duty. It was a year of new planets and stellar orbits. There were no limits and fewer rules. And until they docked the wrecked ship off the end of the home-base satellite, there had been no need for rules. Then suddenly the galaxy, awesome and frightening, had collected itself into one mass of flesh. He had not been afraid. "Just careful," he mutters. "I was just careful." He had been at ease even when the soldiers balked at handling the ship's survivors. "It was all that power," he says. "All those muscles and the eyes cutting right through you. Oh yes. Made the soldiers stand up and take notice just like the rest of us had to do."

And later, the stories had spread faster than anyone cared to remember, until finally any mention of that first rescue brought fear. He pauses and stares through the archway of the corridor where brain, rose, and soft coral-root form nests of colors near the outer walls of the compound. He is trying to remember the name of that first ship.

"Something to do with gold," he whispers. "Aura, or aeral . . . No, auriferous. Yes. Auriferous. The bearers of gold." He grunts. "Bearers of trouble . . . Pilobolean trouble."

And now, another rescue. Another ship and soldiers no wiser. "More stories," he mutters as he reaches the checkpoint between the storage compartments and the living quarters. Muong Nong's shadow is elongated as if it were evening, but there are no hours here. Time is counted by the pulsing sonars of landing beams. Those who sleep set time by the hours they have always kept. Others never sleep in this place. Lashia opens her eyes. Although she has secured the door to her hutch, she does not feel safe. Her pulse throbs to an ache against her temples. She feels tired, drawn, and frazzled as she has not been since her exams. A signal from the message panel gains her attention. It is Bess.

"No," Lashia explains. "Nothing is wrong. I've just returned from a walk, that's all. The fields . . . No, not too far. I'm just a little breathless, that's all."

For once, Lashia really does not hear Bess' grating tone. She is counting her pulse, willing it to follow a calmer pattern. It is not easy. It is almost as if she has had no training, but finally, she pulls away and answers Bess.

"Yes, yes. They told me this area has been sealed off. I will leave as soon as I get my things packed."

Lashia gathers herself in an air of patience as Bess begins to weave her usual conversation, shifting from subject to subject like a guinea hen following a string of seeds. Suddenly the room seems warm and Bess' voice foggy and somewhat out of snyc. Lashia closes her eyes, then opens them, startled. She looks around her. Everything seems the same, but somehow it is all different. She is sure that the blue coverlet on the lounge has always been torn and that she herself left the right corner folded away from the cushion. She remembers seeing the pale pink light recessed in one corner of the room, its rays counteracting the bluish shadows of this asteroid's natural light. And the ceiling. Surely that was always cracked and spiderwebbed with soot. Yet at that moment, with her eyes closed, with a finger of cold air pressed against the nape of her neck, she feels as if everything is being altered.

"They wouldn't let us wait," Bess continues. Then she quickly falls into her rapid-fire chatter. "They told us to leave right away. And here

I'd already started the translations. I hope you have thought about coding. My head is swimming with all that book stuff about burins, runes, and glottals. But we have to remember that some of the students have been on the Project site for six months already, and if we aren't careful, there won't be any engravings left to translate. We'll be up to our ears in old tablets before you know it . . . Oh listen, what do you think of Emerald for a name? It has much more class, don't you think? I've always . . ."

Lashia shifts away from the sound of that voice. She feels uneasy. Someone is watching her. "Bess, I'll call you as soon as I've moved . . . Yes, I promise . . . Yes, I'll be careful. I'll meet you at the transporter."

Lashia breaks the transmission. She rubs the back of her neck. It is warm to the touch, but when she removes her hand, cold again. She looks at the door. Perhaps there. Perhaps she is being watched from the doorway. She moves quickly. At the entrance, she is framed in rose-blue light. The corridor is empty. Quiet. She thinks of the woman in the green haik, but there is no trace of her pungent odors. She thinks of the guard, his mouth framed in florid incisions. But nothing moves in the corridor. She leans forward, bending as if she is carrying a weight. She steps back into the room and carefully locks the door. She is very tired. She barely places her head upon the cushion when her eyes close.

The air is thick and sweet as honey. Palmyra shades the floor of the basin. Lashia dreams herself sitting on a carpet of orchids, their petals radiant in the flannel light. She is hungry. Before her, there is fruit. It is just beyond her reach. She is beginning to breathe heavily when she hears a voice. It buzzes. It sings. It is more than one voice. It is one voice moving into another voice, the tones deep and overlapping, the words textured like fragments of cloth, like music.

. . . you . . . . here . . . . beyond . . . . your face like . . . . words . . . . . . I must find . . . . . command . . . . a point . . . . darkness . . . . come . . . . a hand . . . . my mouth feels . . . . I want . . . . alone . . . . now to me . . . . dreams enter dreams

Lashia sits bolt upright. She forces herself to focus on some object, something familiar and safe. Her eyes follow the path of irregular gouges along the wall, the scrapes and marks of carrying cases and awkward packs. She traces the circular shape of the room, first the dusty floor, then the upper section where the wall curves into the shallow dome of the ceiling. She wills herself to be completely awake, and only then does she become aware of the soreness across her chest and back where the aggry beads have pressed into her skin. She does not remember ever having fallen asleep without removing the harness of beads. In fact, she has always been a chronic insomniac, a condition that allowed her to study for her exams long after the other students had fallen asleep at their desks. More than once she has heard the joke, "Anyone who lives with the western woman must learn to sleep standing up."

She is distracted by the message signal. Again it is Bess. "I have only just begun to gather up my things," Lashia protests. "I could move faster it you wouldn't call every five minutes . . . What do you mean, two hours ago? I only just closed my eyes . . ."

Lashia releases the door and when it slides back, she is startled to find the light grown duller. Though there has been no perceptible change in color, the shadows are much thinner and the balustrades seem to curve away from the hub of the compound. "I must have slept longer than I thought," she tells Bess. She raises her hand to rub the soreness from her neck. Her fingers carry the scent of citrine orchids, plants that flower only in the outermost regions of the planet. Lashia has never ventured that far, and never outside of the asteroid's false sky.

She says, "Yes, Bess. Yes, you're right. I'll start immediately." Anything to end the transmission. She listens to Bess' final warning, then turns to the door fully intending to close it and begin packing. But there, flush in the doorway, is the bag woman in the green cloak. The woman ruffles the folds of her cloak, then backs away. She has a citrine orchid in her hand.

"Where did you get that?" Lashia demands. The woman retreats faster. Lashia softens her tone. "I would like to have some myself," Lashia croons. "Where did you find that?"

The woman points and Lashia, following the path of her bony finger, sees the blossoms scattered in a trail between her hutch and the adjacent one. Even in the dirt and litter of the pathway, they seem to emit a silvery brillance. *"I could not have missed seeing them earlier,"* Lashia thinks. "But where can I find more?" she asks the woman.

"They grow many lis from here," the woman answers. "Beyond the soft world. No one goes there."

"Then how did these get here?"

Lashia waits. The woman narrows her eyes, then begins to gather the flowers. "They grow a hundred li away," she mutters. A dozen petals drop into her bag. "They grow near the mint green land." Clusters of orchid petals disappear into her bag. "No one has gone there."

"Listen, old woman, someone has been there!" Lashia shouts. "These flowers didn't arrive by themselves!"

The woman lets a handful of blossoms fall back to the ground. She scratches her head, and Lashia can see that her scalp is infected with bugs and lice, the only animal forms thriving on the asteroid, and those brought by transporter passengers. As her cloak flutters, the air is latticed with the winey odors of the woman's body mingled with the heavy musk of flowers. "They grow in the likeness of good," the woman tells Lashia. She smiles, not at Lashia, but beyond her. "It is man love. They grow for man love."

Lashia shudders. She begins to wish she had never asked anything of the woman. When she'd left the desert for the Academy, her mother had warned, "Never listen to priests and beggars. They are both mad." Lashia turns back toward her hutch.

"You have already been touched by them," the woman calls before Lashia closes the door. "They came only hours ago. They came on the crippled ship. They are here and you are with them. Now you must . . ."

Lashia steps forward, but the woman has rushed into the next corridor. Lashia follows, and though she walks fast, the woman stays just beyond her reach. In the maze of circular passageways, she almost loses her, but the acrid scent is unmistakable. Lashia calls to her, but the woman does not answer. She even seems to move faster. Once when Lashia turns left, something pulls her to the right where she catches a glimpse of the green haik moving toward the commons. And again, when she rounds the bend before the last passageway to the commons, something tries to stop her. It is too late. The guard steps out of the shadows and demands her papers.

Although Lashia hears something behind her, she does not turn. With luck, she can catch the woman before she enters the commons. Lashia thrusts her papers toward the guard. But he is looking over his shoulder and into the corridor leading back to her hutch.

"More than muscle," Muong Nong whispers.

"I don't have much time," Lashia pleads. "Here. Examine my papers." She tries not to stare at the red stain circling his mouth.

The guard pushes the papers away. He still has not looked directly at her. "You know you can't leave the area," he says. "Go back with the others." He nods toward the passage behind her.

Lashia turns. The corridor is empty. "What others?"

Finally, the guard looks at her. "So," he grunts. "Molenka." The red scar is pulled into a sneer. "I told you to leave. Well, have it your own way."

This time, Lashia does not cringe. "Just why should I leave? And don't tell me it's restricted. Why is it restricted?"

The guard shakes his head. "How do you expect me to know? Do you think that any guard around here makes decisions? All I know is what they tell me . . . AND what I see. I looked at that wreck docked over the landing area and I saw what was going on." He snickers. "Even YOU should know that. Don't they teach that in school?"

Lashia deliberately puts an edge on her words. "Now you listen. I want some answers. Just tell me what has happened, guard. This place is only strategic, not military. So there are no secrets. Even YOU know that."

For a moment, the guard is silent. Then he shrugs. "We received a call to close off this end of the compound. A while later, the patrol brings in this flagship. A big orange gasser. Pilobolean. Only seen one other one like it. Not of this world or time," he smiles. "Not with all that moving and turning . . . Now we got orders to shroud the ramp from the landing dock to here. Even seal off this end of the commons. Said nobody was to go in. Move anyone bunked here, they said. Especially students." He sneers again.

"Follow the rules," Lashia thinks. *"Always follow the rules."* "I'll get my things," she tells the guard. "It will only take . . ."

"NO!"

"What?"

"You've been here too long. You'll have to wait for clearance."

"But I haven't done anything!"

"You'll have to wait."

The guard leans forward, pushing without pushing until Lashia takes one step, then two, and finally, turns and walks resolutely back toward her hutch. The light is changing again, bluish shadows are merging into darker hues as the planet leans into its half-night. For a moment, Lashia lets the guard's piercing stare feed her anger. She follows the winding path back to her quarters, but she moves only because she has no choice. Somehow she has moved from observer to participant. She wants to say that she has dreamed all this. That this barren place with its delta full of crisp colors growing in a garbage fill, with its rest stop of shabby travellers, has all been conjured up to ease the stress of exams. She wants to feel as she did when she listened to the stories her mother told of how the cities died, and textbook stories of continents before the volcanic chain shifted and the Sahara consumed all but its tip. She wants to feel that this is a dream that happened years before, and she can move in and out of the dream unscathed. But dreams, like visions, allow the secrets of one moment to be flashed to the next. In the path in front of the hutch, she sees the Pilobolean.

He is, at first, all shadows, then light and light into shadows. He is what the woman in the haik calls: man coiled into man. His limbs swim together, then flow apart, his skin like oil and clouds and velvet. He is a warrior, but not a warrior at all. He is father, brother, the man she dreams when loneliness demands her attention. He is all arms, legs, mouth. Colors break pale dark into tan and peach, brown into bronze. Stretching and bending. He is sponge or horse or the sea frothing. He is a reflection Lashia knows too well, like her own hand turning now, thumb bent toward palm, fingers following thumb until the hand is no more than a cup, waiting. He is what she can say without sound, and a voice singing into voice.

.... I of rain .... I dancer .... lion helmet ..... I of mist .... need .... circle once ..... now .... for you ...... I ...... Wulfen .... we .... to say .... I of sorrow .... come ...... this cave .... soon

Lashia runs. Only when she is inside the hutch, only when the door is latched and she has covered her ears with her hands can she silence the words. Still, her breath comes in ragged gulps. She slides to the floor, her knees drawn up and her head tilted back against the door. From this angle, she can see herself in the shiny metal surface of her valise. The face is still the same. It is a little too long, but comfortable. And the hair, brown-black and kinky, frames the face with its wide full lips, the nose spaced almost too far from the eyes and mouth. Yet this reflection is what she knows. What she has just seen is not real. Still she smells the scent of flesh, and the warmth of shapes changing, and how she has thrown herself into the rhythms of a dance as if the only place she'd ever been was the ceremonial ring of some African village. All of this has taken away her knowledge, the special papers and training. To be so vulnerable angers her. But finally, she closes her eyes and sleeps.

Muong Nong makes one final check of the outer hutches of the compound. He is almost ready to settle his watch. Today he has earned his keep and looks forward to the time in a room alive with only his smells. Already he sees himself burrowed in the warmth of his hutch. Soon, he reminds himself. For now, the thought is enough, and he is happy to know that for even such a small pleasure, he needs only to rely on himself. Nong has learned to live like a soldier, although the state never saw fit to make him a soldier. But most important, he lives without the comfort of lasting friendships. This place only offers other guards, and passengers who arrive smelly and ill-tempered, and leave no worse or no better for the visit. Then there are those who do not leave. He thinks of the girl with the bandolier of beads, and the woman in the green cloak. Having thought of the bag woman, he sees her standing in the grimy frost-light of the next archway as if he has conjured up her presence.

One step—and he is shadowed by a gray column. The woman does not move. Two—and he shifts his weight so that he is directly behind the woman. The musty folds of the green haik remain motionless. She is leaning forward, expectant. Nong inhales and steps away from the column, his arm already extended so that he might grasp a handful of her tattered cloak. It is only when his line of vision is parallel to hers that he sees what has held the woman captive. Wulfen is bathed in iridescent light, the whole of his form tinted neon as if his movement generates its own brillance.

Muong Nong whispers, "Pilobolean," and feels his mouth opening and closing as if he suddenly has grown dumb as a fish or a frog. Only by bringing his fist against the ocellus symbol shouldered on the left side of his jacket can he break the gill-like movements. He clears his throat and aims for the deep authority of a soldier's voice. "Stand aside," he commands.

The old woman turns and glares at him. Wulfen glides to the center of the corridor.

"Stand aside," Nong repeats.

"Let him pass," the woman hisses. The hairs growing from the mole on her cheek quiver like antennae. "His rules are not of our world."

Muong Nong's mouth tightens and the tattoo garnishing his lips is flushed with color. "And what do you know about rules, woman? He is to stand aside. That is my rule." Nong shifts his weight slightly, deliberately keeping some distance between himself and Wulfen.

And yet he is curious. He wonders what star has twice thrown him in the path of a Pilobolean. He watches Wulfen's writhing mass as if he were watching the code center's printout on the galactic location of transporters. He is certain Wulfen is following some system, some built-in mechanism that controls his amoebalike changes. Nong has heard that Piloboleans are an assemblage of bodies, a grouping of forms into one mass. He tries counting the number of individual beings. The shapes are in continuous motion, muscular limbs swimming together and splitting apart until they seem to flow in and out of sensual entanglements. But Nong is always aware that what he sees holds a distinctly human sensibility, and that it is always, without a doubt, masculine. Nong begins to examine his own virility.

He pulls himself up tall and arrow-straight. "You were told to remain in the restricted area!" he shouts at Wulfen. "We can't have you floating around scaring everyone." He gestures toward the woman.

"He is what we are and what we will be," the woman murmurs. Her eyes are glazed with reverence. Again Nong extends his hand to grab the woman's cloak. "And you return to the commons," he demands. Perhaps he would have said something else, but before he can utter the words, Wulfen moves closer. Shapes and colors shift as he slides across the hallway. The guard fights to maintain his balance.

. . . . I am . . . . for only . . . . when she needs . . . . to want

Nong holds up his hand as if he is pushing against a door or signalling all movement to cease. He sees color. He feels the heat of color. He is bathed in color, and for one moment believes that without the old woman, he would be lost in a chroma of color. And just as suddenly, he is released from all thoughts of color.

. . . . . . she who knows . . . . I dream . . . . . will find soon . . . . . . this

Nong smells the air. It is summer and there is rain. His face is awash in the sweetness of flowers. And then it grows cold and there is wind and ice. And there is the Yurt, his mother and the smell of soup ladled from pot to bowl and his father moving closer, the branding iron blazing in his hand.

. . . . new earth cloud sky . . . . I will bring . . . . what she can hold . . .

Muong Nong moans and although the sound grates his throat, he is not sure the voice is his. "Stop," he whispers.

"Let him speak," the woman cries. "His fingers hold the wind. He knows the mouth of the cave holds the sun."

"Quiet!" Nong yells. "No more voices. No more gibberish. I'll call the commander, I will. Now get back to the area."

When the guard steps backward, moving away yet circling, Wulfen seems to fold into himself. His movements are plainer, simpler, more to be gazed at than probed. Nong watches and feels a surge of his own strength.

"I don't want you roaming all over the compound," he tells Wulfen. "I suppose I could get some release time for you. Just enough so's you won't feel penned in . . ." Nong pauses.

Wulfen is humming, a low moaning sound. It is words played over the sound of words. It is lyra, the oud, and the melody of verbs. It is spirituals, psalms, madrigals, and cantos. The old woman begins to sway to its rhythms. The air cooks with the smell of her clothes.

. . . . I have lived . . . . in the body . . . . . to need . . . . to know . . . the heart . . . she of lion . . . . . she who is . . . . . . dark as first woman . . . . . . dark as mountain . . . . . . the path of fire . . . . . come to know me . . . . . as one . . . sees a dream

Muong Nong cannot be sure if Wulfen repeats the words once or twice. He is trying to form a question. He is looking for one question out of the many questions he wants to ask Wulfen. But suddenly, there is only the old woman.

The columns are there. The corridor still curves in its circular pattern around the center of the compound. The arch still throws heavy shadows across the end of the passageway. The floor is still littered with strips of packing fabric, flail wrappers, and shards of containers while YOK WISHES DEATH TO STATION K IV is still carved into the balustrade leading to the next level. But Nong does not remember seeing Wulfen leave. Nong rubs his eyes to clear his vision. He tries to imagine Wulfen's form, but there is only the reddish-blue light sieving through the network of columns.

The woman laughs. "His fingers hold the wind," she says. Her laughter is the sound of stones rubbing against stones or the blue-white light of primal storms.

The guard tries gathering spit inside the dry walls of his mouth. "And you hold a space on the next transporter," he grunts as he walks away. He strokes the scars around his mouth and wonders why he saw his father. And he wonders about the Pilobolean's father, or indeed, if the Pilobolean can be thought of as fathered. Yet Muong Nong cannot be sure of what he has really seen.

Nothing is as it seems at first glance. Beyond the ridge of Colombines, soft stones take the shapes of teardrops, discs, saifs of crystals, batons of wood or bone. And Lashia, sitting alone in her hutch, cannot say what she has seen until she has a word for it. At the Academy, she was taught to believe everything is an illusion. That when it dies or crumbles, it does not leave a space. It is simply replaced by something else. The asteroid is a world of illusions. There are no flowers. No sun. Illusions all.

Inside the hutch, Lashia begins to unhook the harness of aggrys. A braid snaps loose and beads roll to the floor. As she bends to retrieve them, moisture falls onto her hand. She watches, astonished.

She remembers her mother's African myths, those her father has echoed: "Before the desert became larger than the sea those who cried were sent to live in the smallest rooms of the women's quarters. They were made to do the hardest work and were never allowed to hear the stories of the lion keepers who own windows into the dark world."

Lashia brushes the moisture from her cheeks and goes to the door. The corridor is empty. She walks a few feet in either direction. Nothing. She stops before an archway that faces away from the commons and toward the delta. She can see the glimmer of mirror stones. Like fire opals, the air seems to gather light. Shadows are maroon silhouettes flickering against a purple backdrop. Debris from the compound floats in the shallow breeze that always seems to cling to the ground. Otherwise, it is still, minty quiet as the shaded area under the paperbark tree behind her mother's kitchen.

"He says the true artist knows him," a voice behind her announces.

Lashia turns, startled. It is the woman in the green haik. The woman's skin is gritty and her smell even more acrid. Lashia backs away.

"He says a stone that has lost its color tempts the artist. He says the true artist arranges. The true artist adorns. Only the artist without vision works at random."

"Get away from me," Lashia cries.

The woman holds out her bag. Grins. "Do you have anything for my bag? There is always some use for anything you have."

Lashia tries to move around her, but the woman suddenly spreads the folds of her tattered cloak like wings. Lashia moves closer to the hutches. Her fingers, gliding over words carved into the wall from ground to eye level, send her no messages she can understand. Then space. She has moved beyond the wall, and where there should be a door, there is emptiness. Without turning, she knows the Pilobolean is behind her. It is not just the old woman's cottonmouth smile but the scent. A mixture of damp, moldy walls and musk and too many flowers, too many citrine orchids until the air is thickly scented like patchouli. The woman drops her arms. Lashia waits. She is not waiting for the woman to allow her to pass—that permission has already been given. She is waiting for the Pilobolean to summon her. And when he does, his voice a blur of sweetness and sadness and joy, the woman nods, then shuffles down the corridor.

What Lashia will remember later is how the Pilobolean seemed to adjust to the size of the hutch. When she had seen him earlier, he had appeared to be larger than life, but here in her room, he is no bigger or smaller than any other man she has known. Yet he is not a man. He is man heightened and intensified, both good and evil. He is man multiplied, forms changing rhythmically, hypnotically. He is what she romanticizes. The heat of flesh gathering into flesh, the muscles pulling like glue, like quicksilver or the whipcord of transparent metal. He is hips and thighs, worshipping, commanding. He is the sweet cold air touching her, his arms bent, his shoulders curled forward like a woman's. But he is thief and cossack. He is poet and dancer. His smell pulled from the anther and pollen sac, the stamen of flowers sweeter than orchids or plumeria, sweeter than earth damp with spring rain. He moves form into form, unexpectedly with a puzzled glance or a leer, shifting as quickly as any man might shift moods or personae. Shifting with no apparent sense of contradiction. An actor altering postures and roles, and each body singing to the other in harmony, words without words without time.

And now she will remember he has said his name is Wulfen.

Later she awakens in her hutch. She is on the lounge. A pile of aggry beads is nested on the floor beside her outstretched hand. Slowly, she unhooks the remaining braids. Her fingers are thick and clumsy. She is placing the beads on the table when the message signal beeps.

"Lashia, is that you? I've been calling for the last two hours. Where have you been?"

Somehow she manages to respond, but as Bess offers a detailed account of why the area has been restricted and how Wulfen and those like him are shadows of other worlds, Lashia only half listens. She is not yet here in this room. Not yet. Not all of her. What is here is listless and tired. This part of her does not know danger. This part cannot see beyond the pulsating light of the launching pods. Lashia does not need to hear that on Wulfen's planet, words are like mirrors, like music, and those like Wulfen use their bodies to announce themselves in shapes like road signs, like arrows pointing the way. She does not need to hear that women are warned against them, against the smell of their skin, the pollen of flowers strewn along a path. What Bess does not know is that each of those postures begs for attention. And that is what Lashia does not dare remember.

"That guard, the one who is posted in your quadrant. You know, the one with the awful red scar." Lashia hears Bess' audible shudder. "I think he's called Nong. He told me they've changed the schedules. Because of the wreck. He says they're going to keep this post on low runs until Pilobolus sends a repair ship. All of the outgoing ships will leave in the next few hours."

"My ancestors believed in the lion keepers," Lashia interrupts. "They were evil and powerful. They were the tallest and the strongest."

"Lashia, do you understand? I *have* to leave. Otherwise, I'll be in quarantine . . ."

"My father said they could read the stars."

"Lashia, what are you talking about? What lions? You've never seen a lion in your life, except in video or hologram."

"My mother said the lion keepers could turn themselves into beasts," Lashia continues. "They feared no one. Believed in no one but themselves."

"Oh Lashia, don't talk crazy. I'm not going because I want to. I have no choice. There's no need to have both of us stranded here. And Nong says that the quarantine will be lifted . . ."

"A woman chosen by the lion keepers was given an honored place in the council. She was thought to be the most beautiful, the most . . ."

"Lashia, stop it! I don't know what you're talking about and I don't want to know. Listen to me."

Lashia trembles, but this time not from fear. She has been afraid, but now, with the shadows of ancient stories moving like trace elements through her memories of Wulfen, she forgets her fear. Now Lashia fights her way from dream to dream.

"Before the desert turned to sea," her mother had said, "Africa was the home of the lion keepers. They knew water bird and falcon, and how to measure the rain. They knew earth and stone," her father said.

"Lashia, you must listen to me. You must," Bess repeats. "As soon as I can, I'll let them know where you are. They'll send for you. They have to. You're one of their best students. I'm not just going to leave you here and forget you. It will be alright, Lashia. Everything is going to be alright."

Lashia begins to sway. "He is light," she says. The music is louder now, more beautiful than ever. "He speaks to me. Just to me! And he is full of laughter. Wulfen . . ."

"Oh joyous heavens! Talk about the desert. Talk about the Sahara. But not this. You didn't come all this way just to be thought of as a woman! And he's an alien! Wake up, Lashia."

"He is more man than any man," Lashia whispers. She feels the words building almost before she can say them.

"Lashia, that Pilobolean is a savage! Forget him. Think about your research. There's nothing greater than finding the key to worlds of thought. Think about that, Lashia. Think of the work we have to do. Important work. And it's there if only we can get out of this filthy place. Do you know . . . someone stole my favorite boots? There are thieves here, and the sooner we leave, the better . . . Listen, they're starting to load now. Lashia, not to worry. I'll have everything all ready for you. You'll be away from here in no time. Stay in your quarters. And stay away from that Pilobolean!"

As Bess breaks the transmission, Lashia whispers, "Yes." And again, "Yes." She watches her hand on the transmitter as if it holds the life of a living thing of which she has no part. Lashia sees fingertips, nails, knuckles, veins. And how skin changes.

"*I am trembling* she thought, and she yearns for the safety of theorems and coded material. She pulls the report disks from her case and arranges them on the table in piles, one for each subject.

"Boustrophedon," she recites. "A method of writing in which lines run alternately from right to left and left to right, or conversely left to right and right to left in a winding course." She lets the words soothe her.

In the labyrinth of the following days, with only the darkness of half-night, Lashia spends her waking hours reviewing her data as a measure of time. Yet the time belongs to the dancing hours, those shadowy spaces when she is pulled toward Wulfen. Soon, she sees in him not just one face, but many faces. In one breath, Wulfen is as clever as a thief, his eyes hooded under thick lashes. In the next, he is innocence, so naive she needs only to open her arms as the first act of mothering. He is her first love leaning into manhood, and her father's father aging into wisdom. And the postures change patterns, ebony to beige, and the words quickening. Soon, she learns his words.

........here........we dream........a darkness that is..... ours.........the sea........dreams........you of lion........to know..........I............only.....give you.....to need...... no one......but you......to need......and see......what no one knows

In this passing of dreams, she becomes a prisoner of his time. She is neither in her room nor outside of it. The hutch is a well or a cave of sparkling limestone. "In the myths of Africa, the spirit of lion keepers travelled like sand," her mother had said.

In Wulfen she sees the sand, crags, and rivers. He is caves and secret roads. Lashia stands before the cave. She tries to gather her memories of Bess. She wants to remember what women speak of at night. She wants to remember how dreams were formed before she came to live in the narrow space of the hutch. But each time she leans out to gather what it is she knows, Wulfen calls. And each time, the calls are soft and satisfying and she is drawn by musk and walls that move like flesh. Soon she learns to awake only for waiting. Soon she learns to move with the rhythm of dreams within dreams.

Early in the fourth cycle of days, Muong Nong, finally tells her the quarantine has been lifted. "You are scheduled for an early departure," he says.

The strain of the quarantine leaves a thread of hoarseness in his voice. From the checkpoint at the outer level of the compound, he can see the transporters, their noses cloaked in mist as their outshells expand against the burst of fuel. He can also see the Pilobolean ship, its girth wider than two earth ships, and if he can believe what he has heard, its fuel banks regenerating by themselves.

"We want to clear everyone from here as soon as possible," he tells Lashia. "We need as much space on the landing area as we can get."

Lashia ends the transmission. She knows Wulfen is ready to leave. She selects a fresh chiton from her valise. It is yellow, its color heavy as mustard. Under its folds, her skin is tinted dark as desert twilight. She replaces the aggry harness and dusts her face with powder. As an afterthought, she rubs lychee oil into her hands until they are burnished with light. When she has finished, she knows she has done all she can.

Lashia comes to a low place along the wall of the outer circle. She sits on the railing, her hands resting lightly on her knees. She does not see Muong Nong watching her from the archway at the end of the corridor. And the guard does not see the woman in the green haik. From a distance, Lashia is a bright swatch of yellow accented by a thick cloud of hair and the aggry bandolier. Then Wulfen moves into the space between Lashia and the others.

He calls to her in the night cries of Arabian black horses. He calls as the wind would climb into songs, into water. She smells the sheen of his skin and the strength of it. "I have been waiting for you," Lashia says.

Wulfen extends a hand. Fingers touch her lips. His arms move as one arm. . . . . it is you . . . . I have lived to know . . . .

She smiles to his singing. "Once," she begins, "we had the desert. Now my people have no place to go."

Again he touches and limbs move into one, and the smell is safe, usual and familiar. Thick as hemp turned to rope, and steam to boiling. His voice, tenor and bass, gathers echoes in a single tone, and she hears him say, *one to love.* And the words build.

. . . . . you who know me . . . . see as I . . . . . it is for us to go now . . . . .

Lashia paces her breathing. At the edge of her hearing, the guard calls and the bag woman chants some unknown song. There is nothing more. No voices to aid her. No sign that is absolute. Only her pulse, her body wanting so much it does not know.

"But I know nothing of other places, of worlds," she whispers, and in saying it, she is afraid. She steps from fear to the laughter of childhood and back again to woman. She watches Wulfen his muscles rending and bearing down. Ankles, wrists, chest under a ribbon of muscles, under the oil of thighs and echoes of breathing.

"I am Lashia," she says. "That is all I know."

Lashia, Wulfen repeats. His voice is clear as a kiss to welcome home a traveller, and Lashia holds her breath as if she is sailing into the wind. Gently, he pulls her to her feet. Beside him, she seems more fragile than when she began the waiting. She smiles into his eyes and leans against his broad chest, into his warmth. Lashia sees one man, and the end of waiting. Muong Nong sees Wulfen shifting forms, each form leaning closer and closer to the next until Nong believes Wulfen has absorbed all light. The guard shouts a warning. Lashia trembles at the sound, but Wulfen warms her hands with his breath. Then he turns, circles of light facing the guard.

. . . . . together . . . . . we would know . . . . . this time . . . . what . . . . . . she has known

Nestled against him, Lashia hears him say, *I will go when she goes,* and she smiles.

Again Wulfen speaks. . . . . . you . . . . . . must see . . . . . as I . . . . . . of flesh . . . . . . and she . . . . . to see . . . . and say . . . . . what we see . . . . . .

And again, Lashia hears him say, *We will leave when time brings us to leave.*

The woman in the green haik moves closer. Muong Nong worries the scars around his mouth. "Molenka!" he calls. "The transporter will not wait."

Nong hears Wulfen reply, ... this I . . . . . . will need . . . . . . when she knows . . . . . . as I have known . . . .

And Lashia hears Wulfen say, *We no longer have to dream.*

They are moving away from the compound. Lashia is pleased to see that Wulfen's stride is sure and lithe as a hunter's. They move in unison, her right side to his left side in a step of singular motion. When he feels her watching him, his hand traces the line of her cheek. In her memory she has painted him standing motionless against a sand-sky. When they reach the landing dock, he releases the hatch cover and pulls forward on the hinge. The strength in his shoulders moves through his arms and to his fingers. She believes his skin is bronze and glistens in the amber-blue light. When he has finished the task, he takes her hand and leads her to the open maw of the ship. Lashia turns once. Her face is dark, smooth and soft as if she were asleep.

On the knoll behind the landing area, Muong Nong watches the Pilobolean. From time to time, Nong cannot see the girl, but always, he sees Wulfen. That glimmering mixture of animal and man punctuates the launch site. Wulfen moves with an almost detached pulsing, changing from shape to form, swaying hypnotically, breathing satiny light one moment only to shift and reassemble in a haze of light a second later. Muong Nong does not try to count the number of forms. In the haste of departure, Wulfen folds and unfolds faster than ever, his mass appearing as fluid as a lake full of tiny silver fish, or gorged and unsettling as lava flowing toward the sea. And Nong begins to believe that sight is pleasing. He feels himself grow warm as each shape moves into a new phase, each one full of its own beauty.

"It is this place," he thinks. *"This place of rocks that hold the scent of both naphtha and rose. This place of blue sapphire flowers and fingers of coral glowing like ghosts. This place with its spongy paths and filthy way station set in a circle of hills red as the devil's necklace. A place too lonely even for sleep."*

"Maiden into slave and slave to fortune," the bag woman whispers.

The guard shakes his head. "She will go mad in less than a cycle of moons," he snorts. "He changes shapes as quickly as some men lie."

The haik quivers. "She will see what she must see. What women have always seen. Something to love." The woman sighs. "With your first love, that is enough," she adds, then shakes the folds from her green cloak.

Nong blanches under a musty smell that is foul as dragon's breath. He is dreaming of home. There it is spring. The flumes are washed with water. The cuesta is alive with flowers. The forests are thick with ancient shadows of leopards and deer. And the men who have been soldiers move back to the mountains where colors are neither divided nor lost. Muong Nong pulls himself away from the memory and heads back to his post along the outer ring.

"He should have taken you," he mutters as he passes the woman.

"I am not for him," she laughs. "I am only for you, like stones and wind." She opens her bag and frowns, then searches the horizon for the next ship. The light changes.

Matchmaker, Matchmaker

CASSIE'S HAIR was cut like a whisper and barely covered her scalp. Her knee-high boots extended the length of her slender legs, and the Tuareg shawl she'd draped around her driver's jacket merely confused the old men who turned to watch her pass. She had no sooner stepped into the metallic light of the entry-level vestibule when one leaned forward and in a hoarse voice, wet with the rattles of age, called to her: "Hey girl." Cassie pretended not to notice the men. On her routes, she had seen groups like this in terminal buildings of every city—old men who had been transit workers or veterans of the last war or those who simply loved the notion of travel, but now were confined to watching others come and go while they basked in the fake solar light of an atrium preserve. There were six of them sitting on the benches in front of the Kalava Station atrium. Two at the end of the bench were dressed in old-style Army uniforms, fatigue greens the military hadn't used for over a decade. Those two concentrated on a fast-shuffle card game, but the other four chewed on random subjects like goats put out to pasture. It was one of those four who had yelled at Cassie.

The culprit was at the periphery of her vision, but Cassie could see his buddies were egging him on. They were the type who made daily visits to the terminal, and after years of watching women walk away from them, they had fixed notions of what they were willing to accept as female. Cassie did not fit those notions. Not that she knew, nor would have cared to know exactly what those old men were whispering. As she walked down the aluminum sweep of the hallway, past the benches where the men squandered a great deal of their remaining days, she had only one thought on her mind: She was late, and her lateness would limit the amount of time she'd have to relax before her next client. Fran would already be in the lounge, ready to chide her for being late, although Fran had never been known for her punctuality. But more importantly, Willow would also be waiting, her electric chair locked against a table, her agenda set, her mind impatient to get on with the day. Cassie wasn't quite sure she was ready to deal with another one of Willow's lectures, and she certainly wasn't willing to be the brunt of a discussion of how time was running out for everyone. She pressed the button on her watch, but almost before the sequence appeared, one of the old men yelled: "Hey what time it is?"

She looked at him and shook her head. It was the same old man who had called to her before. She recognized him by his dark skin, creased and more leathery than the man-made fabric she was wearing. He was grinning, so she extended the movement of her hand from her watch into some gesture that might have passed for a greeting—partly out of deference to his age, and partly to acknowledge that his color, like hers, set him apart from those around him. But even as she wiggled her fingers in his direction, her inner voice told her to ignore him. *You'll never get rid of him,* the voice said, and as if to confirm her suspicions, the old man shouted: "Hey, com'here. I got some talk for you."

Cassie walked a bit faster. Not that the old men could tell the difference. From the way she walked, they would not have known she was hurrying. She timed her stride, using the muscles of her hip and leg to extend the width of her next step. Her shoulders turned into each footfall so that her body moved in a coordinated measure of shoulder, torso, and leg. With this pace, she could have walked for hours, if she were allowed hours of walking time. She was not. In fact, as a licensed driver, Cassie rarely walked, and when she did, like today, she had to make the most of it. So she walked in a way that loosened all of her muscles, the echoes of her boots spilling into triangular patterns of sound—floor to wall and then to bench, where the old men's bodies blunted the reverberations of acrylic tiles and metal wall panels. Cassie moved past the men, her head held high, her footsteps propelling her forward in long lithe movements like those of a soldier or a pole vaulter. And the old men shook their heads and muttered about the decay of the young generation.

These old men had seen their share of generations. They had lived through births, deaths, the country's wars, the surprise of a new century. Now life had left them with the leisure time of occupying a hallway bench outside the transportation terminal's atrium. There, they watched people rush back and forth to vehicles they had only dreamed about as young men. In those days of watching, they saw travellers, like Cassie, who could make a trip from from one continent to another, indeed one space station to another, in as much time as it took them to remember the names for all the modes of travel. Watching filled the time of their days, and travellers, like Cassie, occupied their minds for comfortable stretches of that time. While she was in view, several of the men would consider the earth tones of clay, sky, and feather painted onto Cassie's loosely woven shawl, or the glimmer of her light brown scalp showing through the dark smudges she passed off as hair. Fewer still would recall the leathery gleam of her polymar boots and jacket emblazoned with the insignia of an independent driver, her long fingers clustered with rings, or her eyes, bright with the relief of indoor light after so many hours of driving across the midland states. But most would enjoy the conspiracy of watching that allowed them to exchange comments about Cassie or any other hapless passerby. And when she reached the bend in the corridor, they would let Cassie's image disappear from their minds as easily as if that turn in the hallway had led her into deep space or another dimension. But all of them would follow the pattern old men had followed for millennia: As she walked away, they would look at Cassie's hips swaying and try to remember how it was to feel a woman's body next to theirs.

It was just as well they could not let Cassie know what they were thinking. In her world, she gave little time to any man who examined a woman in terms of how well she fit some imagined form. And unlike those old men, she was well aware of how a body's shape could be altered, how liposuction or diapliation or molecular surgery could bend the body into new configurations. Cassie knew how to operate the many components of a complicated transportation unit, and for her, the body was a muscular unit that could be tended with the same detachment as any machine. Fifty years earlier, she would have been labelled athletic. Twenty-five years earlier, that label would have changed to naturalist. But in her world, the line between the natural and the artifical was a mere convenience marked by survival and degrees of efficiency. No, it would not have been a compliment for the old men to suggest that it was simply a pleasure to watch the youthfulness of her body. "Sometimes you have to download all that efficiency crap," Fran would say. And Willow, who years ago had run out of patience with sex, would add, "What are you going to do when you're sixty? Look back at nothing?"

Cassie may have had a vague second of wondering what those old men were thinking, but she stuck to her primary objective of placing one foot firmly in front of the other, and high-stepping to the terminal lounge. As she covered the distance of the entry-level hallway, she barely acknowledged the sight of the atrium—its dingy palm fronds leaking color onto plaster-cast statues, set there to represent the new century's celebration of natural life. Three dwarf deer and the handful of birds managing to survive in the terminal's preserve drooped from the mid-day heat of solar lamps turned too high for a northwestern climate. Cassie remembered her parent's description of early atriums planted throughout the city—"so dense with vegetation, leaves rustled like running water, and flocks of birds mated and squabbled all the time," her father had told her. Cassie moved faster, urged not only by her lateness, but by the desultory sight of animals too drowsy to move out of the direct rays of the solar lamps. As a result, she was almost overpowered by the aquarium's green darkness when she turned the corner at the end of the corridor.

The sea pool marked the shaded area leading into the lounge, and unlike the vestibule entry, where the old men were soaking up the atrium's artifical sunlight, the shadowed hallway was slightly damp and rank with the odors of salt water oxidizing on the retaining walls. Cassie could see a few bottom fish scouting the depths of the aquarium, but she was not close enough to the wall to view the upper levels of sea life. Not that she needed to. There were thirty or forty such atrium-sea pool preserves in the city, and down the coast, near the space portal, nearly twice as many. More than once, she had picked up a client who wanted to tour a city's preserve. When she was first licensed, those tours were a respite from the hard driving of open road. Later, they became an excuse to park at the landing ramp and stay inside her vehicle while her clients marvelled at how nature could be incorporated into commune living. Now, all she recognized was the integrated stench of chemical solvents and algae. That, and the absence of sound.

"Silence. That's the way it is up there," one of her clients had told her when she picked him up at the launch base. "It's so damn quiet that sometimes all you can monitor is your own sweat building. Then you start to hallucinate and think it's some kind of ship coming after you." As soon as the car had left the launch site, that client had ordered Cassie to take him to the nearest public place—"anything with human noise," he'd said. She'd taken him to Kalava. In less than an hour, he was ready to go home to Ocean Six. "My ears hurt," he'd told her. When he'd left, the silence was deafening.

Now, she pushed her way into the lounge through three sets of automatic doors, and walked smack into the noise that had made her client's ears ring. After that silver tube of a hallway, with its ooze of mold and old men dozing on the benches, the mass of bodies crammed into the main room of lounge made her stop for a moment. She was always surprised when she entered those places where throngs of people crammed into such a small space, as if, somehow, the planet had shrunk into one room. On this visit, she slammed into a knot of bathers heading toward the steam rooms. A few steps farther led her into the middle of another group bound for an inter-city shuttle about to leave one of the eight loading platforms. A tour guide counted bodies while a cart, heavy with luggage, squeezed the group out of position for the next lift. The guide's job was not made any easier by people yelling at each other, or stepping out of line to talk with friends waiting for another outbound shuttle. Cassie elbowed her way through the group and into the main chamber of the lounge.

There, it was impossible to tell who was doing what to whom, or going where and how. On the viewscreen, a dot matrix printout flowed red with the usual schedule of arrivals and departures of various craft, while the intercom continuously corrected those announcements. The computerized voice intoned destinations in an asexual whine that garbled the messages every time. Travellers cringed as they tried to unscramble the noise. Tour guides hurried groups to loading ramps at either end of the room. Land cars waited at the docks. Cassie saw a few cars bearing the insignia of the same dispatch office she used, but this was her R-and-R time, so she plunged toward the escalator, and headed for an upper level. Looking back at the horde clamoring for space aboard transporters, she could understand the government's ban of private cars, and the restriction on the number of licensed vehicles used in any form of travel.

"But Francine, I can't understand why everybody has to be on the move all the time," she said. "It's like go-go-go before the cosmos catches up with us."

"It's a living," Fran laughed.

They were sitting in a juice bar on the upper level of the lounge. For Cassie, the room's only saving grace was the comfort of its seats. Like most drivers, the molded curves of transporter seats had left her with lower back problems, and she welcomed a chair built for comfort rather than efficiency. But the room had its drawbacks also. On one side, it was bracketed by a nursery, with the squeals of young children sliding into a multi-colored cloud of small plastic balls occasionally overriding the soundproof glass wall that separated the bar from the nursery. The wall allowed mothers to observe their children in the act of "safe swimming," as it was called. Cassie had yet to realize her dream of watching one of the little brats disappear forever into Ping Pong heaven, or remain suspended against the ceiling of an adjacent room that had been designed to keep them weightless. When she grew tired of joyous toddlers, she could turn in the opposite direction and watch their older siblings tune out the world. In that room, sixty or so pubbies were slouched in transporter chairs, receivers in place as they subjected their fourteen and fifteen year old brains to the concentrated stimuli of cathode lights. The room was pitch dark, except for a big screen above their heads, where the flicker of light rays changed as the pubbies thought-provoked low input beams into simulated attack patterns, their eyes riveted on this neon light show.

Cassie sighed. "And there it is, folks. Pubescent training for space wars. But at least it's quiet up here. Where's Willow?"

"In the W.C.," Fran nodded. "They've plugged a new delf tube into her gut. This one's mega-duty. It's got her in the W.C. every few hours."

Cassie grinned. "Hey, it spared me a lecture on being late."

"That is provided I keep MY mouth shut," Fran said. "Look, go easy on Willow. She and Elise just had a fight. Willow's really having a rough time with this round of treatment."

"Yeah, she always is," Cassie muttered.

Then she swiveled her chair toward the view windows. The entire upper level of the lounge was designed to revolve on a 360 degree orbit. When Cassie turned to the window, the orbit was just moving past the sector where the new proton generators had been built. It was no coincidence that the generators had been erected on the clinic site of the old Clearwater Eco-balance Project. Tearing down the Project's clinic facilities and building a new power source on the site was the government's attempt to erase the Clearwater fiasco. But Willow was a product of that fiasco, and there was no way to erase Willow.

"I didn't mean that the way it sounded," Cassie said. She unwrapped her shawl and began loosening the multitude of zippers on her uniform jacket. "I just warp-out sometimes."

"You get warp-out? Nooo . . . Don't tell me. Not my little sister," Willow said as her electric chair hummed into position at the end of the table.

Her raspy laughter drew the attention of several lounge patrons, and when Cassie stood up to greet her, those who had tried to follow decorum by not looking at Willow and her chair turned to stare at Cassie, who had discarded her uniform jacket and left her six foot frame covered only by a second-skin undergarment of shiny latex. When Cassie leaned over to kiss her sister, her tall, muscular figure, so perfectly shaped she could have been sculpted out of the red-brown clay of Tuscany, made Willow's stick-thin body seem unmistakably pathetic. From the waist up, Willow was as wiry as her name indicated, and with the light sparkling against the pale green corneal implants, her eyes, in contrast to the darkness of her skin, seemed as bright as moon-fire. That look gave strength to her friends, and put her enemies on guard, but that look only held true from the waist up. From the waist down, she was dependent on the by-products of the very technological systems that set the fire in her eyes: her modular chair, the blood transfer units, the colonic apertures, and the hours of clinical treatments. After more than a decade of medical attention, Willow carried the scars of the Clearwater Eco-balance Project, and it did not take much to trigger her most recent treatise against genetic experimentation. Cassie always stepped lightly around the subject, but Willow did not make it easy for her.

"So . . . how's the taxi service? You ferry any late-great scientists we should know about?"

"A simple hello would suffice," Cassie laughed.

"I said hello," Fran offered.

Willow grunted. "You'd say hello to a penguin if it appeared."

"Only if he were pushing your chair, sweetie. I draw the line somewhere. Speaking of drawing the line, where're our drinks?"

"I cancelled them," Willow said. Her expression was deadpan, and at first, Francine wasn't sure she hadn't done just that. Then Willow added. "I don't think this is a bar. I think they're running some kind of twenty-first century beauty contest back there. All those pusses are leaning into the comp panel like the light discs can measure their bustlines." She pointed a skinny finger toward the service cubicle as if she were about to zap a waitress. "Twelve years old and they can't punch in a drink order."

"They're sixteen, and probably it's not their fault," Cassie said. "Maybe the system's just down. Hang onto your remote, Willow. They'll be here."

"I knew more than all of them put together when I was sixteen."

Fran laughed. "When you were sixteen, you knew more than everybody, put together or not."

They all laughed. Cassie reached over and patted Fran's shoulder. "Get her, Fran. Don't worry about that chair. It can't be more than a hundred or so volts."

"Un-un, sister dear. Mega-volts," Willow giggled. "Mama made sure I got the best."

"That's our mama. Looking out for her own." Cassie had pulled off her boots, and was scratching the soles of her feet against the bottom rung of the table.

Willow caught the motion, and frowned. "Getting naked, are we? Putting on a little show for the people, princess?"

Cassie stuck out her tongue. "Doesn't that chair have an orbital pattern I can set for your skinny ass? Willow-in-space. Has a nice ring to it."

"DRINKS . . ." Fran announced, as they were interrupted by a waitress. They were quiet as the glasses were set in place and Willow counted out the correct number of tokens to pay the waitress.

Cassie took that opportunity to begin massaging her feet. The pressure of the rung against the instep of her feet pulled all the tension from her body. She could imagine herself at home with Willow and Famein, their younger brother—the three of them waiting at the table for her mother to serve them tall thin glasses of her special drinks, usually made more palatable by the color than the taste. Cassie smiled to herself. It was so convenient to think of three of them, but actually, only she and Famein were related. Willow had been adopted at the age of sixteen. She had come to live with them after Cassie's mother had treated her for injuries sustained while working on the Clearwater Project—"hard labor in the laser fields," as Willow put it. But now it seemed Willow had always been with them, a snappy little voice whipping Cassie and Famein out of childhood and into the minefields of adulthood. "Well . . . puss-puss, look at the little pubbie," Willow had sneered when she'd met Cassie. They'd fought for the first six months, and later, that uneasy peace had ripened into friendship. Willow never gave an inch on her appraisal of Cassie's privileged life, and Cassie never allowed Willow to use her physical limitations as leverage in their battles. In some ways, this had bonded them closer than many blood relatives were bound to families.

But as Willow had said the day Cassie brought Francine home from school with her, "Sometimes you get sisters where you can find them."

The three women silently toasted each other, then savored the first swallow of their drinks. Willow had ordered Cassie's usual thick red drink, so deeply colored it made natural beets look pale by comparison but, as Cassie swore, was potent enough to hype her adrenaline and leave her road-ready. For herself, Willow had ordered an equally thick green, gooey mess full of protein supplements, while Francine had a frothy cream something laced with calcium and iron. When Willow questioned her concoction, Fran shrugged. "Who knows? Maybe Gil and I made a baby by mistake. This girl's got to be prepared."

"If I believed in something other than the Great-oneness, I'd say: Lord help us. You're not seriously considering adding another life to this dreadful misfortune we're in, are you? Look around you. Do we need any more?"

Obediently, Fran and Cassie looked. Obviously, the departure time for a few transporters had been called. The population in the room had shifted to afternoon arrivals. Their faces held the jumpy expressions of travellers trying to track their body clocks. A group of official types—"captains of industry," Willow liked to call them—were occupying one of the booths. They had plugged their equipment into the lounge's main computer terminals, and were readying themselves for an impromptu meeting. At another table, a woman was engrossed in cross-checking data, her fingers moving across a keyboard like blackbirds pecking for bait in a small patch of ground. In the booth next to her, a pale man of uncertain ethnicity spoke directly into a microcorder. He was so involved in this task, he did not notice the old man leaning over the edge of the booth, watching him. But Cassie recognized the man as the one who had spoken to her when she'd entered the building. Usually, the guards chased the bench warmers back to the corridors, but this one seemed to have evaded detection. It wasn't that he was harming anyone, but his obvious wealth of leisure time was likely to set people on edge. Cassie, aware of how little R-and-R time she was allowed, began to grow nervous watching him. Her mother had said: "Time is like the sea—always moving vast and restless." Cassie was forever at the restless end and on her way to somewhere. It was difficult for her to remember idle time, time to do nothing, time to play as the children were playing in the nursery, or space out like the pubbies in the video room.

"I don't know if I can imagine myself being a mother," Fran said. "But it could happen with me and Gil, you know."

"Oh, not the *L* word! Not LOVE!" Willow sneered. "What fantasy!"

"OK," Fran said. "I'm having an out-of-body experience. OK with you, Willow? Make you feel better?"

"Speaking of fantasy, how's Elise?" Cassie asked.

Willow laughed. "She's fine. And don't get me wrong. I'm not condemning fantasy. Each of us must have fantasies. Even I . . ." Fran rolled her eyes and hooted. "Go ahead," Willow continued. "Laugh. But you know I speak the truth. I'm talking about the difference between instinctive and learned acts. By allowing your fantasies full rein, you do what you've learned. With that man . . ." She fiddled with the buttons on her modular panel as if she were going to push back from the table, then she added, "Well, you act it out, that's all."

Fern held up her glass and saluted. "Sex, the final frontier!"

But Cassie wiped red foam from her mouth and said, "Hush Fran. You too, Willow. Remember: We're not all anti-anti-male."

Willow rolled her eyes. "Really? Aren't we all bedeviled by the same moon, a luminescent force drawing us to our deaths? We are all half-wives, clocked and checked by the same cursed cycle of events, and male or female, we are strapped by the tides of this moon."

"I told you," Fran whispered. "She's been fighting with Elise."

Willow ignored her, and gestured toward the viewing windows. "A poem: Behold the moon on a summer's night. It swaddles us in after-birth, and dancing in its eerie light, we scream and feed the fire. We . . ."

"Too much medication," Francine added.

"So . . . How's the research coming?" Cassie interrupted.

Willow grinned. "Not bad. I've got a couple of Woebe's on the run. Got their white butts trembling. With luck, I'll get this shit licked before I die."

"You're not going to die," Fran laughed. "You're too evil."

Willow pretended to growl. "So Fran, how's the hubby?"

Fran arched one eyebrow. "You're asking about Gil?"

"Yeah . . . And I didn't choke on it either," she added when she saw Cassie and Fran exchange looks. "Hey, I didn't marry the man-child. Although it is beyond me why you would want to marry someone who is playing around in the same sandbox your father played in. Job-wise, that is. Weather! What could be more Pavolian? I guess that comes from having your plumbing hang outside. That's the problem with men. Makes them worry about performance. Gil has a one-track mind. Every night, he lays you across that track and screws you silly."

"As long as I'm the only woman on that track," Fran said, "just pull in your probe, Miz Talking Head. And my father was a damn good weatherman. He spotted the Clearwater effect before anyone else."

Cassie shook her head. "Willow, you amaze me. You can go from moon cycles to weather to Gil and sex without dropping one megabyte."

Willow grunted. "Speaking of sex, dear sister, you getting any? Who's beating down your door? Are you still turning them away because they're not quite right? You know what's wrong with that business you spout about people-of-colour . . ." Willow began.

"Oops, here comes another jump," Cassie laughed.

"And it calls for another drink," Fran said, and signalled the order.

"For your information, it's all connected," Willow told them. "The idea of cosmic order is pre-Babylonian, even discounting the unification of world science, it's still a matter of chance. Weather is a matter of chance, but Gil is still caught up in stimulus-response. Positively medieval. Think of how simple our lives would be if we depended on such preliterate ideas as: Thunder makes it rain, or trees make the wind blow? A one-track mind thinking somebody is going to make something happen to you. That's why the world wasn't ready to cope with 'people-of-colour' when this century turned up. Take it into account, Cassie. Look at all the books written back when about how things were going to be now. We'd invent this and this would happen. We'd invent that and that would happen. The future would be pristine and white like Orwell's world. Something was supposed to happen to all people-of-color by the last day of 1999. Otherwise, would I be in this chair?" She held up her hands to salute with a "Voilà," and almost upset the incoming tray of drinks.

Cassie waited until the new drinks were set in place, then pointed to the window. "Fran, does anything look different to you out there?"

Fran shook her head. "Un-un. Looks like the same old burnt-off piece of ground to me. Little patches of stubbly trees trying to take hold. The ocean. A couple of proton generators setting out there on the mudflats. A new road between here and Clearwater, but otherwise, half the town here and half the town gone. Looks the same to me."

"I thought so, but damn if it didn't seem like we'd hit a Möbius somewhere between Babylon and 1999. I've got to stop looking out of a window when Willow flags that chair into high gear."

Willow smiled. "The window is always there, Cassie, my sweet. It is solid glass, albeit composed of tiny molecules in constant motion giving us the illusion of solid matter."

Cassie reached over and pinched her. As she yelped, Cassie laughed. "She's right. All that illusion shit is solid matter."

"Why do I put up with you?" Willow groaned.

"Cause we're all you've got," Cassie winked. "So, you and Gil are going to try for a baby, huh?" she asked Fran.

Fran nearly choked on her drink. "Whoa . . . Slow down. Who's talking baby? I said: maybe. Maybe! Get it? I know it sounds the same but keep your hands in your lap. This girl isn't leaning into anybody's nursery yet."

"One of us has to, and you're the only one married."

Willow cleared her throat. "Excuse me. Have we overlooked an important clue here? I was out of that race from day one, and that was before I ever knew about lesbian births. Now thanks to the government's sweet little experiments, even that alternative doesn't matter. So what is this one-of-us crap? From where I'm sitting, strapped in I might add, looks like it's up to you two."

Fran leaned forward. "You know, I had this dream. In the dream, Gil and I did have a baby, but we also had this big dog. Kind of a like an old man of a dog . . . Wait, before you jump on me, Willow, it could have been an old woman of a dog, OK? I don't know how to describe it. But what happened was we left the baby and the dog in the room, and when we came back, we couldn't find the baby. The dog was sitting there grinning at us. Then I noticed the dog was sitting on top of the baby. The baby was perfectly naked . . . Yeah! Perfect. Except it had this blue belt tied around it. And the dog was all furry and covering up the baby so the thing couldn't breathe. When I yelled at the dog, it moved back and looked down at the baby as if it didn't know it had been sitting on top of it. What do you think?"

Cassie looked at the metallic sensory band circling Willow's chair, and shrugged. "I don't know. What do you think, Willow?"

Willow grinned. "Beats me."

"You two are full of it," Fran said, and went back to her drink.

"Now there you go with two again," Willow protested. "I told you to count me out. We just need to get this one paired up." She nodded toward Cassie. "Look, I've got this new thing the lab developed . . ."

Both Fran and Cassie groaned.

"No, no. It's great," Willow said. She pulled her microcorder from its pocket, and hooked it up to something that looked an oblong box with a panel opening at the top. When she peeled back the panel, a sticky residue, like soft Velcro, clung to both sides. Willow smiled. "Cassie, this will give you a perfect match of genetic type. I just need a specimen."

Cassie frowned. "Excuse me? I beg your pardon?"

"That does it," Fran laughed. "She's gone totally nova. She wants you to pee in the panel."

Willow said, "I can do without the derision, Francine. This is a simple scientific experiment. Cassie, give me some skin. Just let me scratch a little dermal tissue. The panel runs a bio compute for your mate. Totally scientific."

"Oh, like the scratch-and-sniff litmus for allergies," Fran said.

"More like a litmus for black-enough," Cassie snapped. "You can nuke that box, Miz Matchmaker. It's chance meeting or nothing. Like weather. Get it?" She began pulling on her boots.

She had one leg in the air, the boot halfway up her calf, when she felt a slight movement on the seat next to her. A sharp nudge at her elbow tipped her drink, causing some of the ruby red liquid to splatter. Fran and Willow both gave startled intakes of breath as Cassie grabbed the glass before it fell. Then Cassie turned. The old man was about three inches away from her.

"Hi," he said. His face was small, heavily wrinkled around the corners of his eyes and mouth. His mustache was wispy and frail, a pencil line of hair under his nose, but most of the creases around his mouth were hidden by the stubbles of a gray beard. Even without his wrinkled skin, just the presence of facial hair marked him as a throwback to another generation. His eyes, once brown and now rummy gray with cataracts, attested to the fact that he had not attempted corneal implants, and confirmed the generational difference.

"What-cha-want?" he asked.

Cassie sighed. "Nothing." She swirled her drink, mixing the foam with the liquid.

"I said: Wha-cha-want?" he repeated. When he signalled the waitress, Cassie could see his knuckles were oversized and as gnarled as tree bark. "See those men over there?" he asked. "They my friends." He squinted at the corporate types sitting at the window booths. When the old man waved at them, they did not wave back. "Yeah, they my friends," he added. "Years ago, I could relate to them, but now they cut me off. Think they too busy for an old man. Hey—Bert, Bertie!" The businessmen whispered to each other, but never acknowledged the old man's greeting.

"Maybe I can get a sample from our friend here," Willow laughed.

Cassie glared at her. "Don't you dare."

"I get you anything you want," the old man said. "Just ask. I get it."

Willow put her gadget on the table. "Let me try it, Cassie. It won't hurt."

"Put that away," Fran snapped. When she grabbed the box, she inadvertently touched the test panel. It was only a slight touch, but she drew back her hand as if she had been stung. "That hurts. Like getting stuck on a cactus."

But apparently, the contact carried directly to Willow's microcorder. As the input signal beeped, she said, "It's a take," and watched the computations appear on the screen.

"That one of them fancy phones?" the old man asked.

Willow halted the printout, and showed him the instrument. The old man touched it, then jerked his hand the way Francine had.

He was sucking the pain from his finger when Cassie asked him, "Don't you have something to do?"

"I do whatever you do," the man said. "Where you going? You over up there?"

He gestured toward the window. The sky had gone from a stone gray flatness to clouds as hopeful as pillows. Cassie did not know if the old man meant over, as in the booth with the businessmen, or up, as in the sky where the exhaust trail of a transporter was still visible. "Look. See that little tail? They waving from the sky. They got life on Mars?" the old man asked. "You been on Mars? Why they go up there if they got no people? All the ships always going and coming everywhichway. Like Johnny-jump-up-here-I-go. Like somebody throwed them up in the air. Green lights flashing. Like all the stars gone wild. I got to ask: You think Johnny-jump-up throwed down stardust so we know he still there?" The old man gave a squishy giggle—part air, part spit. "Say: twinkle twinkle winkle star . . ." he sang.

Fran and Willow started laughing, but Cassie shoved her way to the end of the seat. "I've got to go," she snapped, and began pulling on her jacket.

Willow checked her computations. "Not a bad match," she said.

"However, Fran's chart skews a bit more than the one on our friend here. Your turn, Cassie."

"Forget it," she muttered.

"The sky and stars, they too far away," the old man said. "They been swallowed. The sky is a great big church whirling right off in space. You seen it?" he asked Cassie.

Cassie stopped mid-zipper. "Look. Why are you picking on me?"

He was going to answer, but the waitress arrived with his order, a watery drink, pale colored like the skin of an oyster. A tube of lemon extract was on the plate beside it. Cassie curled her lip at the sight of the glass. Fran said, "Yum-yum," then winked at Willow.

The old man pulled a pile of payment tokens from his pocket. "Count 'em," he said to the waitress, "but don't cheat me."

The waitress looked at Cassie and Cassie turned away. "Count 'em, and take what you need," he added, then took a loud slurp of the drink. The waitress picked up some tokens and shuffled away, shaking her head.

Cassie was remembering her route schedule when she felt another sharp nudge. Sighing slightly, she turned to face the old man again.

"You married?" he asked.

"Right question," Willow said. "This is working out better than I'd imagined."

"You'll pay for this," Cassie told her.

"You married?" the old man repeated. "You cute. I like to talk to women."

That was obvious, but Cassie said nothing. She reached for her drink. It was weaker now, more foamy. Just as the glass reached her mouth, he nudged her again. Cassie sighed more deeply this time. "You two could help me," she told Fran and Willow. They merely grinned.

"You sure you don't want anything?" the man asked.

"No," she said.

He was persistent. "You got kids?"

"Whamo! He's sure full of the right questions," Willow laughed.

"What is this?" Cassie snapped. "A get-Cassie virus infecting everybody? If I wanted to be married, I'd plant myself in some commune and pretend I couldn't breathe without help. Maybe I could find me somebody like Gil."

"Whoa . . . Do I look like that's what I did?" Fran protested. "Do I look like I'm helpless? You better check your data banks, sweetie."

Willow waved away her protests. "We're not talking about you, Francine. We talking about Cassie. Now you say you're straight, Cassie, but you keep letting these men get away from you, girl. Check the ratio.

Three in the last five years. And you let that woman from Ocean Six take the last one. Come on . . . give me a dermal specimen."

Cassie shook her head. "I just have to go on losing them, Willow. Sometimes all you can do is fatten the frog so the snake can have a nicer meal."

"I get you something to eat," the old man said.

The three of them turned, startled to find him still sitting there. As Fran and Willow finished their drinks, Cassie deliberately thought of the exact route she'd take to get to her next client. She was halfway there when she noticed the old man duck his head beneath the shadow of his arm. Quickly, he removed his teeth and put them in a napkin. She hid her quick smile behind the sleeve of her jacket as she hooked the side zipper to her waistband. He nudged her again.

"Squeeze my lemon," he grinned.

Cassie looked at him. He smiled and wrinkled his nose. Even his eyes held laughter. Cassie had no idea of how to tell an old man she didn't want to squeeze his lemon, so she shrugged and picked up the citrus tube. Carefully, she let the juice dribble into his drink. "There," she said.

Fran and Willow applauded. The old man looked pleased. "I asked if you had kids."

Cassie finished her ruby red in one long, determined sip. "And I told you: NO!" she shouted. Her obvious anger startled Fran and Willow.

"You don't have to get so smart," the old man said. He eyed her as he gummed the end of the citrus tube.

With his head cocked to one side, he reminded Cassie of her own father—just a little tired but still working with a sense of humor. That humor walked a thin line between hurt and anger. Over the years, she'd watched her mother channel anger into her work. Finding an outlet had been more difficult for her father, especially after he'd been injured in the riots that followed the war. These days, he could not talk about the difference between whites and blacks without making a wry joke. These days, he was liable to keep some insignificant injury hidden for weeks until even he had trouble pinpointing the cause. At those times, her father could almost convince her that the world had grown past its old battles with race. Almost. "Open your eyes," her mother would say. "That stuff didn't die just because it's a new century, a new day. We're still dealing with the same old wrecks called humans." As the old man's gnarled hands reached for his wallet, Cassie remembered she had not called home in over a month.

He held out his wallet. "I got kids, you know. I was alright when I was young. You want to see my kids?"

Fran said, "Yes," and Willow added, "Sure. I'd love to."

It took him a while to get to the pictures. They were sealed in plastic like old-fashioned ID cards, the plastic scratched and slightly yellowed. Those worn pieces of paper were his identity, his family. He squinted at each of them before putting them on the table. His face was close to Cassie's, but she didn't turn away from the sour smell of lemon on his breath.

"This is my youngest, Benjamin," he said. "I call him Ben, but when he turned eighteen, he said call him Benjamin. He's in the military. Up there in the sky, they tell me." The face of a young boy, five or six years old, smiled at them from the yellowed print.

"That's Eddie. He's a devil. Smart as a whip," the old man said.

They nodded at Eddie's picture.

"And this is my girl." As his grin spread, he didn't try to hide his bare gums. "She's ready to go into high school in this here picture. She was so smart, they put her to work on the Projects."

Cassie handed Willow the picture of an eighth grade girl. Willow shook her head. That face could have belonged to any one of the thousands who worked the Clearwater. Cassie cross-checked the district pin, the gold locket hanging around her neck, the chipped front tooth and pressed hair done up in pigtails. Maybe she'd seen other pictures like this among the ones her mother had studied at the clinic. She wondered what her mother would say, how she'd react to her only daughter, the girl who'd left home vowing never to return, but was now, sitting in a dingy terminal lounge looking dreamy eyed at a faded picture held by an old toothless man. Then laughing at the kind of joke her father might have made, she wondered what her mother would have to say about her daughter squeezing an old man's lemon in public.

"I can't stay here forever standing between you and daddy," she had screamed at her mother. "I can't stay here proving you saved kids like Willow for a reason. There's more to me than that. I'm not just the good side of whatever went wrong with Willow. You can't keep trying to make me into something I'm not."

"Whatever you are is right here," her mother had said.

The old man interrupted her thoughts. "They cute, huh?"

"Just look at their father," Willow grinned. "They had a good start. See, this is what I mean about hanging in there."

"Quite a family," Fran added.

Cassie smiled. "I've got to go now," she said and checked her watch.

"What time it is?" the old man asked.

Cassie told him, but she was thinking of the client she'd picked up at the launch site, the one with tender ears and heart. "Time stands still out there," Cassie's client had complained. "It's quiet and it doesn't move.

Dawn is no more than dusk. Days are the same without weather. Down here, we put tags on life—a golden age, the faded past, the dark ages, a velvet night, a bright future, light years, pretty soon. Time in assorted colors. But up there, it's all the same. Never changes. We still try to make time, try to jam 4000 years into a matter of hours. The sky is littered with our wrecks."

She double-wrapped the Tuareg shawl around her jacket and stood up. "See you later, Fran. You too, Willow." She leaned over and kissed her sister. "Tell the folks I'll call them real soon. And give my love to Elise."

Willow patted her hand. "Come by and see us. Elise doesn't bite. I've trained her."

"Come back and see me again," the old man said. "I get lonesome sometimes. Even with all these fine ladies around here." He smiled at Fran and Willow.

"Yeah," Willow added. "And bring some dermal slides. I'll have this scanner set for a perfect match next time I see you."

Cassie waved and kept walking.

"Don't take but a little time," the old man called out.

"Yeah, I know," Cassie said.

"And say hello to that guy from Ocean Six if you see him," Fran giggled. The others giggled along with her.

Cassie answered without breaking her stride. "Say hello yourself. I'm not speaking to that space-jockey."

Their laughter trickled out the door and followed her into her vehicle, where it settled into the seat beside her. Or was it their laughter she saw trailing a red streak across the horizon where the sun was racing toward Japan, New Guinea, Australia . . . ending another day there as it promised the beginning of a new one here?

ABOUT THE AUTHOR

COLLEEN J. McELROY is a professor of English and Creative Writing at the University of Washington, in Seattle, Washington. Winner of the Before Columbus American Book Award, McElroy has published a textbook on speech and language development, six books of poetry, and two collections of short stories. She also writes for stage, screen, and television, and has received many awards, such as a National Endowment for the Arts, and a Fulbright Fellowship.